PANDEMIC

Pandemic

How Deadly Will It Get

Dieter Gartelmann

Rev. date: 02/10/2022

To order additional copies of this book, contact:
Xlibris
AU TFN: 1 800 844 927 (Toll Free inside Australia)
AU Local: 0283 108 187 (+61 2 8310 8187 from outside Australia)
www.Xlibris.com.au
Orders@Xlibris.com.au
824094

CONTENTS

Dedication vii
Inspiration ix
Preface... xi
Acknowledgements...xiii
Prologue.. xv

PART 1: THE TRUMP PRESIDENCY

Chapter 1 1
Chapter 2 18
Chapter 3 41
Chapter 4 55
Chapter 5 74
Chapter 6 96
Chapter 7 114
Chapter 8 136
Chapter 9 149
Chapter 10 161
Chapter 11 170
Chapter 12 187
Chapter 13 208
Chapter 14 226
Chapter 15 246
Chapter 16 262

Chapter 17 280
Chapter 18 297
Chapter 19 313
Chapter 20 328
Chapter 21 347
Chapter 22 375
Chapter 23 394
Chapter 24 413
Chapter 25 430

Epilogue 449
Appendix 453
People in the Story Part II 457
Demonstrators 459
Footnote References 463

DEDICATION

To my Children, in age order: Timothy, David, Sally, and Felicity Gartelmann. You keep me wanting to be a better man. You were glorious children, and now you are magnificent adults.

INSPIRATION

For my readers

'This is the true joy in life, being used for a purpose recognised by yourself as a mighty one. Being a force of nature instead of a feverish, selfish little clod of ailments and grievances, complaining that the world will not devote itself to making you happy. I am of the opinion that my life belongs to the whole community, and as long as I live, it is my privilege to do for it what I can. I want to be thoroughly used up when I die, for the harder I work, the more I live. I rejoice in life for its own sake. Life is no brief candle to me. It is a sort of splendid torch which I have got hold of for the moment, and I want to make it burn as brightly as possible before handing it on to future generations.'

George Bernard Shaw

PREFACE

I started this book when I became furious about the way America was handling the pandemic. I had worked in America on two occasions, and was so impressed with the good in America. I wanted America to be strong, but it was getting devastated by a pandemic because of politics. And the world needs America to be strong to balance other superpowers flexing their muscles.

I started daily plots of deaths and infections for the US, UK, France, Germany and later South Africa. Cases in China were hardly rising whilst the rest of the world treated the pandemic with disdain and then paid the price. The exceptions were Asian countries that had learned from the SARS pandemic ten years earlier.

Then I imagined standing at the funeral of my daughter if she had died from COVID-19. It sent shivers down my spine, and I just started writing. That made COVID-19 real: how it affects people. Covid-19 had hardly started in Australia. Statistics don't make a story, but how families are affected do. I subscribed to the Washington Post, CNN and The Guardian and saved all news items in a research directory to access them any time I needed them. Only much later did I find new references to the link between the WHO and China.

I started Part Two after the inauguration. The shackles were off, and so was I to invent the story. I gave the new President all the powers he ever would have wanted to save his country.

The book deals with a vastly more infectious strain from February on. How would that be handled today, and how would mass protests be controlled? I had a field day inventing solutions. The baddies became very bad, the good guys extraordinary, building the core of a new America.

Don't look for existing reality. The existing reality of US politics has not solved massive problems like automatic rifles in the last three decades. A new approach might work. Fanciful but this is fiction, so just enjoy the story.

In April 2021 the virus's mutations had only just started in Britain and South Africa. My choice in the book for a much more deadly strain had been deliberate. Mutations could always make a much more deadly beast. What could governments do then?

The whole world is fighting two new dangers now. Just as countries had removed restrictions and opened borders, a new mutation, Omicron, is scaring governments to shut borders again. All at the same time as those who oppose vaccination become a threat to their fellowmen. This is a people pandemic. Global social media had empowered all those who prefer conspiracy stories to science, and new civil disorders exploded in anger at mandated vaccination and lockdowns.

There is no US in the US, only the Me, me and Me.

For all readers of a paper copy please feel free to visit my website to open the references.

I would love to hear from readers. This is my second book, and I would love to know how it is received. Contacts:

E: gartelbooks@gmail.com and www.gartelbooks.com

ACKNOWLEDGEMENTS

My first thank you goes to Tony Adams, my agent from Xlibris publishing. He was my teacher and mentor. He helped me transition to someone with a real understanding of a pandemic and the publishing process. I was still green behind the ears.

My second thank you goes to my sister Christel Russell who was my quality assessor. She was like that parent on the sidelines of a kids' soccer match screaming her head off when sonny kicked a goal. Not only a cheer squad, though, she also provided needed advice.

My next thank you to Pamela Howard. She assessed the chapters and made many corrections, and I'd hate to count them.

For this third edition, I found Olivia Veronese, a university student studying biological sciences with a strong science analytical background. Initially, I wanted a quality assessor, but she started editing and was so good that she became my first real editor. Choosing her was easy – her strong interest in biological science and the pandemic in the US made her a perfect fit.

When the book gets near publication, others will be acknowledged: the production team, the designers, the marketing assistant and probably more. Thank you all, the production team.

Prologue

History

Argus E was an indigenous man who lived on South Andaman Island most of the time. His real name was Eashan Acharya. His father had been a doctor in Port Blair, so Argus was forced to have an education. He wanted to be a scientist and had spent his university days in Chennai and obtained a Master of Science majoring in natural sciences. He now lived on Tarmugli Island just west of South Andaman Island.

He occasionally travelled to North Sentinel and other small isolated islands. His wife was from North Sentinel Island. She could not travel there as often as she liked because the tribes were so afraid of viruses that had wiped out half or more of the population generations earlier.

Argus used his short name when talking to himself. He had a satellite device to keep up with world events. He was in constant contact with the Indian authorities under whose supervision they lived. The Andaman Islands became part of the Republic of India in 1950. It was declared a union territory of the nation in 1956. He was asked to be their defacto health advisor for the Andaman Islands and surrounds.

July, 2020

It was easy for Argus to monitor the US pandemic. He had an office in Port Blair on South Andaman Island with access to the University of Chennai supercomputer. It had an Artificial Intelligence (AI) package that could take in streaming data from the whole of the US internet traffic and the Library of Congress, the nation's oldest federal cultural institution.

He could drill up or down to get the feel of what was happening. More importantly, he could go back in time to see what happened six months ago.

When the pandemic broke out, he discussed this with his elders. They wanted to know how dangerous it was for them. It was disastrously destructive, so the Indian Union authorities contracted him to monitor and report back weekly.

'Argus' was the computer language on his father's Honeywell computers at University when studying medicine, and he had loved that language, so his son was named in its' honour. Argus had added an E for his real Indian name, Eashan. Just in case others had the same name.

He used his AI system to absorb the history of America accurately in the blink of an eye. He could play the past back from 300 years ago to the present time. Dispassionately, of course.

He was analysing the American experience. He had been instructed to switch himself to dispassionate mode to observe without judgement in his weekly reports.

He played the history back from 300 years ago to the present time and summarised it. Slaves, often badly treated, and then in the 1860s, there was a war. The north wanted to wipe out slavery: not purely for humanitarian reasons. No. The north felt disadvantaged by the free labour the south enjoyed.

And discriminations went on and on. Oh dear! Then progress brought education to the blacks. When they took the jobs the white people thought were theirs, resentments manifested in brutal attacks against them. Argus wondered what would happen if the injustices were to be reversed. But that was just his passionate justice persona speaking, and it was the reason why they had told him to switch to dispassionate mode during his observations. He summed up the current American experience: Too divided politically to solve any problems, let alone the pandemic.

The way the pandemic affected countries differed vastly. The virus that had spread from China across the world was particularly affecting the US. People were unaware that they were infected until about a week later. They were infecting everyone around them in the meantime. Then Argus noticed that President Trump took no measures to stop or reduce the spread. People feared for their lives after the pandemic ran out of control. All this whilst the Presidential elections attracted Trump supporters in the tens if not hundreds of thousands and spreading the virus. They had obviously forgotten the lessons from the Spanish Flu that devastated countries starting in 1918.

He did not know the future yet. Nobody did. But what would happen if the virus mutated into more infectious and deadly strains and then again into even more seriously deadly ones? All Argus knew was that he had to report on what happened and hope to avert a catastrophe at home.

Argus observed how families in the US reacted to that. He would have been thoroughly pissed off with the election rallies and wondered how the families would react. He noted that some wives often left home for two weeks to protect their children if the husband had gone to a rally to avoid getting infected by the returning husbands.

Argus then noticed a new phenomenon. Some state governors tried to stem the infection rate with lockdowns, but the Trump supporters organised mass protests against the lockdowns, spreading the virus even more. He was supposed to be a dispassionate observer but wished the police would eliminate them in the blink of an eye.

How would this pan out?. In his view, it all seemed to depend on who would win the Presidential election. It was clear that if Trump won, then the pandemic could wipe out half the US population.

As time went on, he noticed that a bigger fear manifested itself. What if the virus mutated into a much more virulent and deadly strain to race across America? No cure for those infected and dead in under a week? What stresses would that add to the two warring sides, and would it result in civil war?

He planned to send thoughts about the mood of what was happening to those who were desperate to know. Yes. That was his job. Monitor them and occasionally send a message to those he was monitoring, like a prayer for them.

He had never disclosed that he had followed his father's footsteps in the Alpha Dynamics meditation training. It was almost natural for him to go into deep meditative states to visualise medical issues with remote patients. Argus had pictured his future wife that way, and notably, where to find her.

When he had to monitor the US experience, he decided to find two reporters, one from a newspaper that was not pro-Trump, the other that was, and followed the trails of their connections to get himself a group of people from each side of politics to start his monitoring. This way, he could get names and even email addresses to contact them. But before he did, he used his Alpha Dynamics skills to visualise them. He did this to satisfy himself that they were people he could work with.

Part I

The Trump Presidency

CHAPTER 1

Part I – the Trump Era is history as experienced by American families during the pandemic. How they respond is frequently a function of how they met – hopefully through common beliefs that will sustain them when the going gets tough. Some were lucky in that their belief systems matched even if their decisions to join were often hasty. Some found out later that they did not share many beliefs but made a go of it as best they could.

History is the study of people, actions, decisions, interactions and behaviours. People grow up, meet, and like each other. Sometimes it's a good match, and sometimes there are regrets, but the families have too much at stake and make it work.

July 2020

Argus E., the Andamanese scientist, thought monitoring the whole of the USA would be just too much. It would be better to find some families best able to contribute to an understanding of the population. What better choice than to start with two reporters: one Democrat leaning, the other Republican. He also decided to follow trails to their acquaintances to form the basis of friendship for a balanced debate. That went well when he started with the Washington Post reporter Dorothy Thompson. As his focus would be so much on her, he decided he might as well find out everything he could about her, leading to her close circle.

Aha, he thought, great idea. He had already noticed the anti-blacks bias from the Trump camp, so having people of colour in her group was great. So Dorothy was a perfect first choice, and the trail of her close friends begun with her husband, Michael, a lecturer in public health. Yeah, beauty, just what he needed, a lecturer in public health, which led to Michael's close work friend Michelle Anderson, same job. That sorted out Argus's main interest in the whole exercise of public health.

As a bonus, Michelle's husband James was a Psychologist, just what he needed. And as they were all on the East Coast, he looked for West Coast friends and found one of Dorothy's early school friends Sue Anne, now married to John Orthallo in Oregon, a carpenter/builder who just happened to have built Max and Dominique's house.

He felt that long trail of Democrat-minded people was almost incestuous, so he looked for people from the opposite side and started with Daryll Braithwaite, a St. Joseph News-Press reporter in Missouri.

That paper was only the second from six to endorse Donald Trump, writing that the GOP candidate "represents something different for a broad swath of America that is serious about wanting a less intrusive government. Then robust economic recovery and leadership that protects our interests around the world was mentioned". Argus wondered how others would view that last bit after invoking the massive China tariffs on US goods that had followed. Braithwaite had a suitable list of fervent Republican supporters. That led to Gus Teehan, Blew Ohrtman, Jason Pennewell and Mitch Upton, and Braithwaite had been at the military academy with General Christopher Paul Roberts (retired), Dallas, Texas, and Colonel George Jeffry Edwards, (retired), Ohio.

Argus wondered if he should have more people. Stop right there. Enough, four families and two prominent Republicans. Well, he thought, that is one big shopping list of characters to follow. But it defined his scope of research.

He went back in history to see how the family members had met and what they were like now; how aligned they were in their thinking now. He collected more history for those he thought would have more impact on the unfolding story.

2000

Democrat Family origins

Sue Anne Orthallo, nee Donaldson, went to College in Baltimore and met Dorothy Thompson, nee Richards. They had been picked on by 'white trash' in school, making their lives there a misery. Being smarter, brighter, better looking, having more friends, and eventually being picked as school captains levelled the score. *Rub it in, baby*, they thought and grinned. And there is nothing quite like combining to beat bullies for making best friends forever. They had a name for it too. BFF, or BFFE, which they pronounced as 'Biffe.'

They studied, played and partied together and shared holidays at Sandy Point Park, Maryland. Being a pair of friends made it easy to party without risk and come home to their dormitory and giggle about the boys they met.

Sue Anne was one lucky girl. She had grown up in a harmonious family and had always felt loved. Her father had been a teacher too and taught her to read before she started school. She was the eldest of four in the family and adored having a younger brother and two sisters. She loved it when they suddenly saw the light of something that she was reading to them, and they were off into a new universe where everything was exciting. So she was destined to be a teacher and later studied for teacher training.

Towards the end of Sue Anne's training, she wondered where she should teach. To solve the problem, she organised a week-long party with Dorothy, again at Sandy Point Park.

*   *   *

John Orthallo in Oregon had finished his apprenticeship of four years, and he was ready to hit the road for work. Real work. Not as an apprentice. A fully-fledged carpenter/builder. His family had lived in Oregon for three generations, and their name may have originated from the Italian name Othello. John certainly had the dark Italian colouring. He grew up in a loving family.

His father was a cabinet maker passionate about working with wood, and what better place than Oregon, the home of the redwoods. The father was a singer, had a deep bass voice and broke into arias at the drop of a hat. His mother was a cook, and Sunday dinners included many family members and neighbours. A happy family.

His friend Nat had also finished his apprenticeship, and who knew where they would finish up later on? Nat had grandparents East in Sandy Point Park, Maryland. Great fishing. They decided on a real road trip. Over the Rockies, Salt Lake City, Pawnee National Grasslands, Omaha, Des Moines, Chicago, Cleveland, Pittsburgh and then Baltimore, all places they had heard of and never visited. However the mood took them, two thousand seven hundred miles, six or seven days, or longer if any girls held them up. Nat's grandparents were both surprised and delighted when they arrived and installed them together in the two-storey guest house that overlooked a park.

The next morning John and Nat woke to the sound of girls squealing with delight. When they got out of bed and looked down, they saw two lovelies rolling about in the grass chasing their chickens, hysterical with laughter. John looked at Nat; Nat looked at John. Two minds at work, one conclusion. Those girls needed help. For sure. Out they went into the park, serious faces plastered on and asked: 'Can we help you?'

'Oh, how lovely. Knights in shining armour. Can you catch those chickens without killing them?' came the giggling response from Sue Anne. John was enthralled with this blonde one. He did not want to mess this one up with uncalled-for hilarity. He read the field, understood what he needed to do to get brownie points, and said:

'See the corner of this field over there on your left? I'm John, and this is Nat. We'll hide in the grass there, and you girls ease off a bit and then gently walk them to us. We'll make chicken noises and grab them when they're close. Is it OK if we hold them by their legs, upside down?' Long story short, chickens were caught, and so were the girls. Sue looked at this marvellously wicked but smiling bearded man and wanted him. But devious as always, she asked:

'Where are you boys from and do they need school teachers there?' It was easy to imagine the dynamics, but they all agreed that it would be great if she came back with the boys – such a long trip and Nat could sleep in the backseat. That is, unless Dorothy wanted to come back with them to keep Sue Anne safe.

Sue Anne loved Portland and the redwood trees she could see nearby. She was enchanted by John's family. Her own family was close but mostly concerned with everyone getting an education whilst John's family was an unabashed love affair which embraced the whole neighbourhood. She was soon part of the family and even joined in with the singing that John's father was famous for, adding her contralto voice to his deep bass.

*   *   *

Dorothy came with them, had her holiday, went back to Baltimore, and started her PhD in History. Some people would be terrified; what subject to choose, would it be enough to get the Doctorate she would need to reach her desired position as a lecturer? Well, there is no writer's block when you choose a subject dear to your heart. She followed the advice: 'Love what you do, and it will love you right back.'

She had been horrified by TV reports of all the wars lately, especially in Syria and Myanmar. Dorothy had tried to put herself into the shoes of victims and later into the shoes of the reporters. How do they cope with all the gory details and stay safe with bombs going off all over the place? And there it was, the PhD subject, which she devoured like a starving animal. She had grown up in a family with black roots, so she understood danger and repression. Her grandparents had been educated; her grandmother a history teacher and her grandfather a doctor. Education was their mantra, and despite racism and white oppression, they missed all that discrimination because of their excellent jobs and standing in the community. They were happy families and raised confident children who grew up in their footsteps.

Dorothy needed to travel and visit the wartime reporting zones, a gruesome task. Still, it was necessary for authentic reporting, and she started her PhD on wartime reporting and the effect of war on public health.

They were all intelligent people, both socially and academically. They would need that to navigate the upcoming chaos.

Michael Thompson's parents had black roots and had suffered ill health because of industrial pollution. He came from a happy family that dealt with the injustices around them without anger but with a determination that their son would escape that vicious cycle. He went to university on a football scholarship studying public health. He saw the film 'Erin Brockovich' starring Julia Roberts, a film about a coverup of industrial pollution with devastating health effects. That did it for him. He wanted the widest possible audience for his concerns about public health, and three classes of over 200 university students each week sounded like a good fit. He became a lecturer after completing his PhD.

He sat there in the Public Health Conference, listening to two presentations before lunch. When he subsequently returned, the auditorium was almost completely packed. *The speaker must be famous*, he thought, and he settled in. Then Dorothy Richards walked in. Was his heart beating? Yes, but racing was a better description. Black background and drop-dead gorgeous. He was used to attracting women. He was a rockstar footballer, six-foot-two, and sleek as a seal. Then she started talking, and his genuine interest picked up, going off the charts when she was fielding questions from the floor; she handled it with wit, charm and the occasional snort and putdown when needed to deflect sexual innuendo. What a package. He sat in his chair for a while and then noticed she was walking towards him.

'Coming?' she asked. She had seen him whilst she was talking, especially his interest when she was fielding questions. Did he like smart women?. They must have recognised the event when the earth shifted for both of them.

Later their families would wonder what precocious intelligence their kids would inherit, but they never needed to worry that there was no love between them. It was so visible. Their love showed itself in Dorothy's coquettish teasing of Michael to get more affection, and Michael's attempts to be a he-man, picking her up to swing his squealing woman around.

*　　*　　*

Michelle Walter's family background was mixed-race too; Hispanic and African American and both their parents were lawyers supporting suppressed blacks.

Even though most of their clients could not pay much, the family enjoyed great respect in their community, and many people came to visit. Many clients became friends too, helping to make a happy household. Michelle's younger years were full of love and laughter. Naturally, as her parents had been oppressed, she followed in their footsteps to help others. Help and health were foremost for all her parent's clients. Her studies at university took in public health, and she found she needed a PhD to advance to the top.

A scholarship and three years later, she was Doctor Michelle. Sparkling intelligence fuelled by success meant she could only ever marry someone of equal character. She was previously married to Christopher Hernandez. She left him after suffering abuse and took custody of her daughter, Deborah, a bright spark with inherited great looks.

She used to holiday in St Marys City on the Chesapeake Bay, where she met James Anderson. She was fascinated by his reasoned approach to everything, and he was a dish. His family had been piss poor and insisted on education so he could advance. They swamped him with love and affection and gently pushed him to achieve the grades needed to go to university. He didn't like the idea; no, he loved it. His father had an IQ of 155 when tested once but did not have the education to get a good job. James wanted a PhD so that he would never face that discrimination. The Army offered free university tuition and pay whilst studying Psychology, one way of avoiding war but helping returned soldiers. He went on holiday in St Marys City on Chesapeake, and when he saw Michelle, he forgot what he came for, and when she smiled at him in response to his raised eyebrows, he was lost. Or found, whichever. They worked well together. His mum had been worried he would never marry. He had been adamant he could only ever live with someone of great intelligence. They understood. They were thrilled when James introduced Michelle and her daughter Deborah.

They had wanted him to have a suitable partner but had never imagined the happiness that shone out of both their eyes. They were just like chipmunks chasing each other round the yard, but so much noisier. The parents were not quite jealous of what their kids had. Not quite.

*   *   *

Max Sanderson was running a wine shop in Santa Rosa when, near closing time, in walked tall, curly headed Dominique. She was one gorgeous woman. The sight of her brought out a dazzling smile in Max that wrapped itself around Dominique, who responded by telling him that she had intended to go home and cook some pasta and watch a movie. Max's smile expanded at the possible invitation and cautiously explored it.

'I have a bottle of red that is to die for, but I can't drink it by myself. Would you help me out? I could bring two bottles and some steak I had been marinating for tonight,' he said.

Her response was, 'as long as you don't tell your friends that I came to buy a bottle of wine but finished up taking you home instead.'

Max did not answer that one. And instead, asked, 'How many kids do you want to have?'

Dominique was thrilled and scared of that question and replied, 'I always thought I'd have one of each, and if you don't want any, I had better go home alone.'

The answer must have been satisfactory because he went home with her.

One day Max commented on how many people wanted to invite them to dinner. Dominique replied that she had told all the neighbourhood that her name was Dom, short for Dominatrix, and they were all so curious to find out more, so kept inviting them.

*   *   *

Terry Balzarini lived in Baltimore with his wife, Lorraine. He came from an Italian family with a medical background. Terry was a serious man who loved discussing things, not arguing, but honest discussions, like researching other people's knowledge. Terry did medical training specialising in Virology. He had worked a stint in Africa during the Ebola outbreak, which taught him social distancing. Then one day, he saw the honey-skinned Viking girl strutting her stuff at a medical research seminar. Bang! Bang! That was the noise of his heart beating. A first experience for him.

Lorraine came from Swedish stock. Her father was a philosopher teaching history in Baltimore. She loved science; it was clear, the way people often were not. People argued, science did not. She studied medical research at Washington State University and was committed to finding cures. Then she saw Terry at the conference. A tall, dark, handsome and trim man with mysterious sadness. She had to fix it.

They became a team, a medical research team. Would they be needed?

Terry and his wife Lorraine often discuss escaping the looming chaos. They are scientists and understand viruses. They live and breathe virus behaviour and how to combat and avoid it. They understand the implications of rapid spread, panic, and misinformation that comes with viral outbreaks.

Yes, they were serious people but occasionally Terry became a bad boy. One morning Lorraine was complaining of a sore back as she started to get dressed. Terry had a fix. A scientific fix, as he showed her the soft leather straps he had attached to the wall, just over five feet up.

He said, 'Lorraine you need to stand on your hands, I will attach these to your ankles, and then when you let go you will get a marvellous stretch of your back.'

She did, he attached the straps and told her, 'Now, let go of supporting yourself.' She let go, and moaned in pleasure at the stretch. Terry had this evil look as he said:

'I will just get the neighbours and show them how to fix a bad back.' Lorraine screamed at him.

'Don't you dare, my skirt is round my ears not my ankles!' Terry heard a satisfactory terror in her voice but went to talk to the neighbours. Terry came back inside, alone, and told her that he was miming and only talking to himself, as he would never

ever embarrass her. Because he loved her. 'I'll get you for that' were Lorraine's words.

*   *   *

Republican Family origins

Daryll Braithwaite came from a wealthy family. They ran a road construction company in St Joseph, about 55 miles north of Kansas City. Easy money and the government work always paid. Their smarts lay in their ability to gauge the opposition and occasionally let them win a contract. It looked better that way, but they competed with low ball bids so that the opposition never became strong. Street smarts made money, so they were Republicans. And incidentally, St Joseph was the home of the Pony Express and Jesse James, the famous train and bank robber. James did not make his father proud. James's father had been a preacher, and Daryll's father had always been proud to be associated with the place that had this notoriety. His father was not a bank robber, but he did sort of rob the hand that fed him. The motto was charge like a wounded bull if he could, but back off occasionally to look like the good guy.

Darryl had wanted to be a writer rather than a street brawler like his father and spent his early years writing short stories for the St Joseph News-Mess from a young age. He was offered a reporter/journalist rookie job and quickly progressed. He was not a physical street brawer but had inherited that attitude from his father, brawling with words. The editor loved it. He loved that the kid took the fight to all who belittled property and business owners. Darryl did it the smart way, though, making his poor victims look funny to take the sting out of the article.

*   *   *

Blew Ohrtman and his wife Petal live in Columbus, Ohio, close to two of the great lakes. It's a good and primarily flat country close to other major cities, an industrial heartland with a large black and white population. Columbus is a lovely city. Ohio seemed to have five political alignments, with double the national average for violence. Columbus is not in the ten most dangerous cities in this state, so it's pretty good by comparison.

Blew grew up in a family of big strong men who worked jobs that required a fair bit of rough treatment to be handed out. His grandfather had been a debt collector whose mantra was 'pay up or get beat up.' His father was an overseer in a factory, and he had to be tough. The wives in those families knew their place. There was often laughter at home, sometimes at the expense of black people. Mostly, in fact.

Blew played football at college. It was a tough sport, but he liked to be tough too. That became tougher as he got older and played in higher leagues where some massive black guys busted him up. He admired their strength as much as he hated them.

The city supports high tech and advanced manufacturing, and that is the work that Blew Ohrtman does. His wife Petal is a nurse and often tends to people who have been violently attacked. To say that she hates guns is an understatement.

Theirs is a complex family. They're so opposite it might work because of that. His environment is increasingly threatened by a black population that is becoming more highly skilled.

He fell in love with Petal whilst on holiday in a Mexico seaside resort. He was attracted to her vivaciousness and lithe, athletic looks whilst she was attracted to his maleness and life of the party playboy attitude. The dichotomy is that when it's too late, he discovers she has black in her origins. It does not help that he had not met her parents until after the wedding as their jobs did not allow them time off for a long trip to Mexico. They were both Lecturers, one in History the other in Philosophy, at the University of Indianapolis. Blew did not like feeling inferior to his wife's family and education but knew he was. A powder keg that does not blow up… Yet.

Adding to the family dynamics is their son Fred, an easy-going Democrat without a hateful bone in his body and unable to understand his father. And there is their daughter Summer, who is a nurse, solemn and taking after her mother. Blew knows he's the odd man out, so he stays out of trouble at home. Their philosophies differ as much as those of Republicans and Democrats. One could say that they are a microcosm of those differences, and their arguments are only limited thanks to Blew's awareness of his disparity from the family's political views.

Petal's parents often wondered how those two got on in private and wished that they could be a fly on the wall. It's a good thing they weren't. Their marriage was punctuated by moans of pleasure and lengthy silences as both tried to keep out of each other's way on politics and philosophy. But they produced two great children and Blew became a good father who loved nothing better than to have his kids crawl all over him.

*   *   *

Mitch Upton is an oilman and a Republican through and through. A Democrat presidency would kill off oil exploration, his career, and his wealth. So he is a Republican and wealthy. He is not just an oil man; he is the dynasty of oilmen for three generations. You could say he had a leg up being part of such a prominent family. When it was time to choose a wife, he knew that she would have to fit in with his family, a euphemism for monied background. Old Money. Superior education and university provided the necessary opportunities.

Mitch was a tall, handsome young man who played football at university. He was noticed, and then some. He had access to the best of everything and played the field for a long time. Then he met Danielle when he was thirty-five. Danielle had all the social skills and attributes he wanted in a wife: young, beautiful, playful, sophisticated, and her parents owned a bank in Houston. What is not to love in that package? So they married, had a son and daughter, partied and had grand holidays. But Mitch was the boss. He had moulded her thinking to a great extent, so it was a harmonious household.

One day, when Danielle disagreed with him, the argument was so unexpected from his previously docile wife that he became angry. The angrier he got, so did she. To calm down, he went to his study muttering curses, but when he got there, he burst out laughing. It had been so refreshing being himself, and his previously somewhat bland marriage could develop into something great. He went back to see Danielle and grinned.

'Darling that was wonderful. So liberating. Please, from now on, challenge me any time you like and it will make for a much more satisfying marriage. Full of passion and both of us being ourselves. Without fear of retribution. You on?' he asked.

'Yes, shithead' she giggled, and collapsed on the floor in laughter that would not stop.

*   *   *

Gus Teehan was a rancher from Tennessee, and ranchers were Republicans. He came from 3 generations of ranchers, the earliest one a cattle thief. Defend your ground or die was their motto. He loved the outdoors and camping in the wilderness, where he met

Mary Rose Gawler, a horse breeder and stout Republican. Her soft nature attracted him; he knew that she needed to be in his life if he wanted any joy at all. He could be summed up as 'I can't do joy.' It was a strong animal attraction from both sides, from him for her soft joyful nature, and from her for his typical cowboy slow smile and scorn. An early pregnancy decided the issue of marrying him.

*   *   *

Nathan Luke Walker was from Chattanooga, Tennessee. He was Totally Trump. A particular source of disagreement was over Chattanooga's black population, which Nathan described as 'the Undesirables.' Nathan carried Armalite rifles, had three magazines, and looked friendly but is deadly with enemies. Chattanooga is internationally known for the 1941 hit song "Chattanooga Choo Choo" by Glenn Miller and his orchestra. It's cool music. It is also home to the first and largest National Military Park, Chattanooga and Chickamauga Military Park. For climbers, Chattanooga is a mecca. There is more rock within a 25-mile radius of the Scenic City than Boulder, Colorado. The military and rock climbing had combined to forge Nathan Walker into one tough hombre. His family had always been military, and that and the rock climbing that moulded the family for generations.

From an early age Nathan had learned that when you follow one particular football team, you stick with it through thick and thin. He called it Character. So, when it came to politics, he had already learned that you never ever listen to those who disagree with you.

*   *   *

Jason Pennewell was a white policeman, and white police officers were Republicans. Simple. To get away from his stressful job, he went to the great outdoors and adventure courses, where he met Lilly, a budding school teacher. She wore those straps that went between her legs to support her on a rope. For him, they were the sexiest thing he'd seen on legs, emphasising the triangle there. Had to have her. It's a good enough reason to be together.

*   *   *

Argus heaved a sigh of relief. His list was pretty long, but he was sure he could base his observations on those characters.

CHAPTER 2

Late August 2020

Argus E hit paydirt when he picked up conversations by people intent on solving the pandemic problem, and he started monitoring the Orthallo and Thompson families. They had known each other for twenty or more years. Following the trails from the reporter Dorothy Thompson gave him a great choice of people to monitor.

*   *   *

In Oregon, Sue Anne Orthallo asked her husband, John, "Darling, how did it get to this state? No social distancing and now a massive increase in infections. Everyone knows the rules. But Trump supporters ignore it, and we are up shit creek with infections". And John said, "Honey, I work with carpenters, and they all want to work. They are Trump supporters, and they hope he will help them. And he should; it's a national emergency."

Sue looked at John with big wide-open eyes and asked, "Oh honey, do you really believe that?" John sniggers:

"Come on, girl, you know what I mean. I'm not interested in arguing with them about anything. So, shall we see how it really all started instead, or shall we be cross with one another all night then? Go and get your iPad and start a search, like, 'Where did COVID-19 originate? 'And then let's look at the search results. What comes up?"

"There are lots of results, and the earliest one is published Jan 21 2020 'Novel Coronavirus (2019-nCoV).'[1] says Sue Anne, "Let's look. It says:"

> On December 31 2019, the WHO (World Health Organisation) China Country Office was informed of cases of pneumonia unknown aetiology (unknown cause) detected in Wuhan City, Hubei Province of China.

"Well, that's a mouthful and means nothing to me", mutters Sue Anne, and they discuss it and replace the statement with:

> On December 31 2019, the World Health Organisation in China reported the first cases of a new virus.

"And then a whole lot more. I shudder at how they wrote those articles. I would not dare to present such mumbo jumbo to my students. Let's find out what other countries did."

"Ah," said Sue. "Here is one. Taiwan. This report is dated June 25, 2020, named 'Taiwan Responding Successfully to COVID-19.'[2]

But look at what it says":

- Taiwan's fight against COVID-19 was an immediate response with stringent coordination of state and private actors.
- Taiwan got ahead of the outbreak with early testing, treatment, and protocols. Their experience during the 2002

---

[1]   20 Novel Coronavirus (2019-nCoV)

[2]   Taiwan Responding Successfully to COVID-19

SARS pandemic had prepared the Government, and the public, to be willing to follow government instructions.

Sue added, "Note they were more willing to follow government instructions. We don't even know how to spell that, and if we did, Trump would overrule us. We need new policies if we want to live, and I want Trump barbequed if he stands in the way."

John is impressed; "My word, you are wound up", and Sue adds, "You should be too. This is dangerous."

Sue Anne had one more search result dated March 27, 2020, from Italy's Response to Coronavirus.[3] "They should have hit it hard at the start and suffered because they didn't."

"The Trump response is the worst; You gotta work and stop testing. No testing equals no cases," uttered Sue Anne.

John decided it would be better to look at having their findings published. He said, "Honey, let's contact the Thompsons we met at your school reunion. Dorothy is a journalist with the Washington Post now, and he is a lecturer in Public Health. They may be just what the doctor ordered. We could drive ourselves nuts talking about this shit and achieve nothing but a heart attack. Should we call them?"

Sue thought they should work out what they wanted to say first.

"John, let's write down what we want to say, then send it in an email, and tell them we will call later to discuss it."

After many corrections, this is what they had, ready to send:

Dear Dorothy and Michael,

It's a good thing we have kept in touch all these years, but now we have an urgent mission and

---

3   Lessons from Italy's Response to Coronavirus

will call to talk to you about it. We are looking for someone with access to a great newspaper to publish some facts about the pandemic. And after arguing about this, we researched some stuff but found the stories too outrageous. It needs to be dealt with appropriately.

I hope you can write a series of articles, say the weekend edition, where people have time to read detailed reports.

Michael, you are a lecturer in Public Health. Would you be able to project COVID-19 cases and deaths if a new wave of infections starts, with Trump urging to test less to get the numbers down? People really ought to see the danger they face. And Dorothy, could you write about the deceit practised by Trump? It's so infuriating that the truth needs to be out there.

We will call you in the afternoon.

John and Sue Anne Orthallo

"Ready to send?" asked John. "Ready, set, go", echoed Sue as she hit the send button.

Fifteen minutes later, the phone rang, and their daughter Lindsey raced to answer it. She was expecting a call to a birthday party and answered, "Lindsey here, did you call about the birthday party? No? goodbye then," and she hung up. The phone rang again, and she answered: "Who is it?" John took the phone from her. "John Orthallo here," and he heard Dorothy Thompson's voice. "Oh Dorothy, how good of you to call. That was my daughter answering earlier, and she's desperate to be invited to that party. Did you call about the email we sent?"

Dorothy's reply was playful, "There are coincidences, but not that many. Yes, and we discussed the problem with Michelle Anderson and her husband James in Washington just recently. She is a lecturer in Public Health like Michael. We have forwarded your email to them, and we will try to set up a conference call later tonight when the kids are in bed or glued to the TV."

"Well, that got off to a good start, or out of control," said Sue, "and I don't want to be in charge anyway, do you, John?" His response was: "I think you just want your name in the paper every week without doing the work.".

Later that afternoon, they received an email from James and Michelle Anderson, who introduced themselves. They had made it easy by attaching their resumes. Impressive, and now they knew a bit about them.

The phone rang, and Lindsey wanted to answer. But John took the phone and said, "John Orthallo." There was a gush of enthusiasm during which James and Michelle Anderson introduced themselves.

They discussed how to go about this.

Everyone had a different idea. Not a good start. John brought his building persona to bear, the one that sorted things out on site.

"How about this: Michael and Michelle feed Dorothy selected subject articles for the first week then leave her alone and look for articles for the following week, whilst James works on the psychology showing how dangerous the Trump approach is, and on the psychology of new proposals from Dorothy. Keep a document of anything new for the next week's open slather. All happy with that?" asked John. They were.

Dorothy later consumed about 25 reports on the subject, comparing the US response of other countries, finishing with an outline of next week's piece: cases and death projections.

John and Sue were discussing this and wondered what articles Dorothy would use and quote. Sue was angry and wanted blood. John wanted an education, something the people could understand. That was the brief. "Honey, I just love it when you go off the rails. Warrior Princess and all that stuff. You will make sure the article bites, I know, and I'm sure James Anderson will make sure the draft gets under the psychology of all readers. Both sides need to be effectively engaged to drive policy change."

They received the first draft from Dorothy, and John printed copies for each of them.

"So, let's see what she said.

Well, we can see what she said. Let's move to the second item, but better still, let's just look at the executive summary first. It says":

- The first recorded case was reported on November 17 2019
- BBC News Reports on December 30 2019, show how a cover-up happened.
- How Taiwan, Hong Kong, Singapore, and Japan excelled.
- How the US handled it – woeful and spiteful.
- Next week – how it will get much worse.

"And guess what? It hooks me. As a Democrat, I want to see how well they will slaughter the Trump approach, and as a Trump supporter, I want to see how many lies they told," says John.

Sue concurs. "It's a great start."

They settle down, all tension gone. They had made a start. More importantly, they were engaged meaningfully with experts with access to a news distribution paper to enlighten the US citizens. And they had a process to continue this work every week, satisfying their need to help in the process.

*   *   *

Argus thought they took a long time for their research that he could do in the blink of an eye with his AI machine. But they aimed to get it published in a quality newspaper as TV was just ten-second grab fests that no one could learn from. And he could not publish in the Washington Post. Hang on, he thought, there's an idea. Maybe I can send articles to Dorothy Thompson, and the readers will go nuts trying to work out where his Argus name came from. Good idea.

Argus E was still monitoring. He had found some other families also making decisions about the pandemic: one in the east, a virologist and one in the west, without a bachelor's degree in sight. He was very interested in them and their ideas.

*   *   *

Max Sanderson, 36, is married to Dominique, 33, and lived in Santa Rosa, north of San Francisco, with Johan, 9, and Emily, 12. They met when she was buying wine but took him home instead. They have a wilderness hideout in Bothe-Napa Valley State Park. Their son Johan is a dreamer, and daughter Emily likes playing mummy to younger children. Not Trump supporters.

Max and Dominique discussed going off-grid, away from danger. They called their daughter Emily and their son Johan into the lounge for a family conference.

Max started with, "Guess what? We are considering going camping for six months. Just our family, and we need to make sure you understand why."

"Can I invite my friend Jackson to come with us?" asked Johan, and his father tells them what it's all about. He starts with: "Johan, did you see that violent protest in Michigan on TV last night, and would you like to be part of that?"

"Too bloody scary for me, Dad. What was it all about?" asked Johan, and father Max tried to see how he could explain it all.

"When was the last time you fought with a boy at school?" asked Max.

"Last week. Bud Holshausen pushed me, and I pushed back, and he hit me, and I hit him. Everyone was cheering, wanting us to continue, and when we had enough, they didn't want us to stop," said Johan.

Max replied, "Well, son, and Emily too, that's the mob mentality. It's dangerous. They completely lose track of what it's all about, and they just want violence. There are election rallies for the President, and they run around without masks on and make everyone else sick with the virus. The Democrats, the other side in this coming election, are angry because they may have to stop work or even lose their jobs because of those Trump supporters. Or get sick and die. So there will be fights about that too.

And it will get a lot worse as the number of daily virus cases increase. And there is the danger the virus could mutate, which means it develops a new strain. Viruses want to live, fight dirty to multiply, and the only way to let you see the danger we are in is for you two to watch a movie with us. It's called 'Train to Busan', a horror movie about a virus that makes people eat each other for it to stay alive. It's pretty horrible, but remember it's not real. But the way people behave to stay safe is real, and we are facing the same problem, whether the virus mutates or not. Shall we watch it now?" asks Max.

They settled down to watch the movie, and after a while, Johan got scared. "It's a movie, son, just watch how people behave to stay safe," said Max. Then Max had to reassure both of them several times and asked them to concentrate on how people behaved. When the movie had finished, Max got them all a drink and asked Emily, "Who was the hero you liked best, Ems?"

She replied, "That's easy. The little girl. She was trying to help old ladies and gave them something. When her father told her she should only look out for herself, the girl said, "That's why Mum is not living with you anymore," then added, "We have to stay safe, but there is no reason not to help someone else. The pregnant lady was so scared at the end when they went through the tunnel, and the girl was just as scared but sang that song she had practised for her father. That was what saved them from being shot in the end, as the soldiers at the other end of the tunnel had orders to shoot if the soldiers could not see if the two were infected or not. I loved her," finished Emily.

"That is pretty smart of you, Ems. You picked up all the good and bad she had to deal with. Now you, Johan, tell me about another hero, or two or three."

"Dad, the big guy stood there holding back the biters to allow his pregnant wife to escape. He sacrificed himself. So did the man at the end when he had locked the two girls into the moving train drivers' cabin because he got infected himself when he fought the train driver," said Johan, and his dad replied, "Son, I'm so proud of you too. You worked it all out. So now, let's have a look at the people who were biting. Were they bad?" asked Max and both kids said they were bad but could not help it because of the virus, but no one could help them, and they had to be left to their own devices and die.

Max continued: "Now I will tell you what I'm afraid of; the virus getting a lot worse, hospitals closing, no doctors or nurses, bodies in the streets giving off virus-infected air, infecting anyone who picks them up, and the stupidity of Trump supporters protesting against lockdowns to slow the virus. A lockdown is the only thing that will get rid of it. Americans have become so obsessed with their own views that they are the only important ones on earth, and anyone else can jump in the lake," finished Max. Johan added, "Yep, they can all get fucked," and Emily wanted a dollar in the swear jar, but Dad said this is one time when that phrase was appropriate.

"And when the election is over, both sides may want to claim victory, and if Trump supporters do not like the result, they will roam the streets and shoot people, or just threaten them, so after the election, we will go bush. And if Trump pulls a swiftie as he did in 2016 and as Bush did in 2000, the Democrats will start shooting Republicans and judges if they overturn the election results in court. It's called civil war, but there is nothing civil about it.

And now comes the good part. You get to write down what you need to take. It's like a wish list for Christmas. Mum and I will make a list of adult stuff, like chainsaws to make log cabins, solar panels for light and refrigerator, a satellite phone so we can see what is happening, rifles and ammunition to keep away baddies."

Max asked. "Just some last questions. Could you save a person who had been bitten in the movie? And how long did it take for almost everyone to be infected?"

"You could not save anyone, and if need be, you had to shoot them," said Johan, and Emily thought that the infection started and that then it was like wildfire, all infected at once.

They settled down to make their lists. Max wondered whether other families were planning to escape, or were they all just hoping for the best, taking the Trump line: 'It's only the flu.' *Well, good luck with that*, he thought.

There is an urgent knock on the door, and the bell is ringing, and Max answers it. It was Lilian, their eight-year-old neighbour's girl; she was distraught.

"Can you please help? My dad is very sick, and my mum is too now, and I don't know how to help them," she wailed. Max asked her, "Lilian, have you touched your dad or your mum today?" She had, but she was not sick. Max called Dominique and asked her to bring sanitiser, gloves, a mask and a blanket to wrap her up. When he had everything, he explained to Lilian, "Honey, there is a nasty virus, and I will put on protective gear and wrap you in this blanket in case you are infected. Then I will spray your hands with this disinfectant, and then I will sprinkle this face washer, and you need to wipe your face but with your eyes closed, or they will sting.

Then I will put on my hazmat helmet and walk with you to your home and talk to your mum, and if she agrees you can stay with us, but you must wear this mask, OK? You understand why don't you?" Lillian nodded her head. She looked frightened now. So did Max's kids, Johan, 9, and Emily, 12. This was terrible and frightening. Worse than watching a movie.

Max told Johan and Emily to stay home, and he went next door and entered after an OK. Brett was lying on a couch, wrapped up, coughing and wheezing. He looked a mess. Mary Rose was a bit better, but not much. So Max asked her if Brett had been to a rally in the past week. He had.

Max took charge. "I will call an ambulance for you two. Do you want Lilian to stay with you or with us? We can keep her isolated, but if she gets sick, she needs to go to hospital." and Mary Rose chose to keep Lilian with them as they had touched her a lot. Max had some kind words for Lilian and went home.

"A total fuckup in that house. Trump rally, and they are all infected. I'm going to have a shower and wipe down with disinfectant, so don't touch me till after that."

*   *   *

Argus wanted to see that movie himself now and streamed it from Netflix. Holy shit, he thought, That is an impressive interpretation of a Pandemic. It didn't have to be those biters in that movie; it could just be a more virulent and deadly form of the current pandemic. Must keep an eye out for new mutations, he thought.

Argus switched his concentration to a new resident, a Virologist. This was his main interest after all. A bit like changing TV channels, he thought, pleased with what he saw now.

*   *   *

In late August Terry and his wife Lorraine are at home in Baltimore discussing escaping the looming chaos. They are scientists and understand viruses. They live and breathe virus behaviour and how to combat and avoid it.

"Lorraine, list the things people have to do to keep safe, please," says Terry.

"Easy," replies Lorraine, "You know it yourself. Social distancing, masks, and hand and surface sanitisation. Child's play." Terry asks, "So why aren't we doing that?" Lorraine says, "You know the answer. It's that egomaniac Trump who belittles all those who oppose his view of the world, and his view is that he must be seen to attract 150,000 to his election rallies. I'd like to say 'The Dumb Prick', that OK with you, or do you need me to be more vicious in my description of our own Nero?" She asks.

"You did remarkably well without swearing, seeing that you missed out on one bad word back there. I saw it forming on your lips, you know," said Terry, grinning. "I'm going to call him 'President Motherfucker' if that is not too rude for you." Lorraine responded, and Terry added, "Not rude enough. He is so stupid. I heard somewhere that important national security briefings and notices get thrown in the trash, unread. National Security staff work all night analysing the thousands of Reports that come in overnight, whittle that down to priorities, take the techno language out of it so a pre-schooler can understand it, and what does he do? He flicks them in the trash and wants a verbal. I wonder if he can actually read. Imagine if there is a war and he throws away the intelligence".

"You're kidding, right?" asks Lorraine. "And if that is the case, God help us if China or Russia choose to attack; the president doesn't read any intelligence and stays unaware."

So let's discuss what we should do, what is the trigger point for action, and where would we go?"

Lorraine starts. "If deaths hit 1,900 a day, then hospitals won't cope. That's only a bit more than now. Nor will doctors and nurses cope. Why they put themselves in harm's way for those infected fuckwits is beyond me. The other trigger is 200,000 daily infections. At that rate, the testing can't keep up with millions of infected people running around unknowingly infecting millions more."

Terry adds one proviso: "When that limit is reached, three days in a row of those case numbers or violence would be better. And ain't it grand, the kids are downstairs and can't complain about us swearing. So liberating. But there is one other proviso: Violence. When mobs start mass protests that police try to stop, there will be trouble, initially from looting and burning offices and shops and then shootings. These pricks are running around with ArmaLite rifles, for God's sake, and if we get that happening twice, we leave."

"OK, Boss," says Lorraine, "we've set the parameters. Time for a smooth red." And she wonders: *are there actually people like that, and is the rest of the country like that? It would it explain why America has the highest infection and death rate in the world? Is it just stupid politics or something else?*

*   *   *

Back in Ohio, Sue Anne Orthallo wondered what the next bit of news would bring. *There must be so many families trying to decide what to do. So many families split along the political divide.* She was happy that she and John were not fighting like so many families would be.

Sue Anne received a call from Dorothy Thompson again. Dorothy asked Sue Anne, "Hey pardner, did you see that article on how Singapore handles the pandemic?" Sue Anne replied, "Yep, I did. And isn't it disgusting that we sneer at those countries, call them by disrespectful names like 'Chinks', and they beat us at the response by a factor of at least twenty times better if not a hundred times? What shall we write about then? I mean you, and you can quote me as a 'well-connected source.' Which I am, as I am well connected to you, haha. And what your article should aim at is not so much shaming us but urging us to be better than Taiwan. Something that gets people to want to be better."

"That's a great point, Sue Anne; rubbing the readers' faces into how stupid they are won't get the required response. And I will add the lessons from Italy as well. Had you read that? This is what it said:

> Much had been written about the practices and policies used in countries like China, South Korea, Singapore, and Taiwan to stifle the pandemic. Unfortunately, throughout much of Europe and the United States, it is already too late to contain COVID-19 in its infancy, and policymakers are struggling to keep up with the spreading pandemic.

> "And the April article on the First-wave COVID-19 transmissibility and severity in China[4] as well. That article quoted China's infections on March 18, 2020, which was still high despite massive public health interventions that showed the cumulative case count exponentially as a function of relaxation duration."

Sue Anne picked on the lifting the restrictions having an exponentially disastrous effect and suggested that Dorothy's next article should hammer that point home. "Make people feel good about being sensible, a small cost now to avoid a much bigger one later. Show them the cost Italy paid as well." She suggested to Dorothy to also check with John Anderson in Washington. Then they chatted about how things were going, and they signed off.

---

[4]   First-wave COVID-19 transmissibility and severity in China

Sue Anne wondered where it would all end. She knew that many republican families had divided loyalties – the men going to Trump for rallies and wives against rallies. They had children to protect. How many were sharpening kitchen knives to defend their patch? There would not be much love left in so many families. Love could not possibly survive with such a large divide, and without that, would wives be ready to kill to protect children from infected fathers?

Whilst she knew she would never have to attack John, she wondered what it would be like if he came home from a rally, which would not happen, of course, and wanted to hug his kids. She decided not to go there; just too gruesome.

*   *   *

Argus -E decided to download the latest Washington Post articles by Dorothy Thompson, enjoyed those, and looked at TV programs he could stream. Bingo, got one that showed her in full flight for a press briefing. She was a lovely and lively woman. He chuckled at the thought of finding other programs that would show the other characters he had decided to follow. Dorothy had just nailed it with her piece on Trump's irresponsible electioneering that was causing COVID-19 cases to go off the chart. He was gleefully waiting on a reaction to that and told himself that he could always email her and ask for photos of the people he was following and google them if they had a social media presence.

Argus emailed an invitation to Dorothy Thompson at the Post.

Dear Ms Dorothy Thompson, Washington Post

Please allow me to introduce myself. My name is Eashan Acharya, MSc. I am contacting you from Port Blair, in the

Andaman Islands. The Indian Government has contracted me to monitor the USA's pandemic to better support health advice for my people here. I have followed your press releases with great interest and admiration. From the responses to your pieces, I have started to monitor the activities of those you hold in high regard, and I use that to form my own microcosm of happenings and the mood in Washington and all over the US.

I am better known in India by my pet name, Argus E. I would occasionally like to post you some findings and questions. One of the first questions is to ask you to copy me items you receive from new sources, especially any from republican individuals, as I am short on those. Not much around. Are they lying low?.

With best regards

Argus – E, India Times, Port Blair, Andaman Island South

*   *   *

A channel change for Argus – like Breaking News on TV, and he was intrigued. He decided he needed to get to know his Republican contacts. He already knew that This mob would be a mixed bag, from impressive to nasty. Mainly because many of them would be Trump supporters and the enemies of the democrats he had already studied.

Mitch is an oilman in Houston, Texas, and a democrat presidency would kill off oil exploration, career, and wealth. So he is a Republican and wealthy.

Mitch's wife Dannielle asked him what he thought of that Republican Senator urging his troops to attend rallies. Trump had booked an auditorium for 40,000 people. "How do they conduct social distancing in a place like that?" asked Dannielle, and Mitch replied, "They can't. But what is important to them is to get the atmosphere pumping, with shouting and braying people adoring the President."

Dannielle asks him if he will go, and Mitch replies, "Don't be stupid, woman. I pay the republicans money, so they do it, and I don't have to risk getting infected. What would happen to my important job if I had to go to hospital for weeks on end? No, I contribute not with being here but with money. It's the way of the world."

Dannielle felt stupid not to have thought of that. She was more worried about seeming stupid to her husband than people getting sick. She is not a Trump supporter, but she knows her financial wellbeing depends on having a Republican President. The Democrats would stop oil exploration, and Mitch's job would be gone. And her lifestyle, of course.

"Look at this shit from Singapore.[5] where they shut everything down," said Mitch. "In March, they had 266 cases and no deaths. A miracle? I bet you they had no income either. We can't afford that," he concluded.

And for the nth time in their life together, his wife Danielle disagreed with him. She had learned to be herself, and how he loved to have a good fight.

"Don't be a smart arse. We can't afford for this virus to go viral either, and then no one goes to work; just not allowed to, as the others don't want to be infected," she replied, holding her breath, afraid as she had seldom contradicted him before.

For a good reason. He could be deadly when crossed. "If that is your attitude, then I will cancel your weekly allowance," was Mitch's response, and she had expected worse, so she rammed it home.

---

[5]   Why Singapore's coronavirus response worked

"That's OK Honey, I will move in with my parents, and you can have your ever so important dinner for business associates tomorrow without me. I don't care what you tell them, but you threaten me, and from now on, I will always respond appropriately." It was her first major confrontation with him, and she was going to confront him from now on. Yep, she was going to be a force to be reckoned with.

The issue remained unresolved. They both stayed quiet. Mitch was wondering how many other families had the same split thinking. The men knew they had to work, and the wives knew they had to protect the children, even if grown up by now. But he wasn't going to stir the pot at work and ask the other executives there. 'Quietly, quietly' was his mantra.

*   *   *

Darryl Braithwaite from the St. Joseph News-Press was in Trump heaven. He had just listed Trump's ten biggest achievements. Darryl's earlier hero was Jesse James, a courageous outlaw with slave owner roots and the family battling skirmishes started by Union militia and Confederate raiders. Braithwaite saw Trump as a modern-day Jesse James as Trump was pushing back against China's trade imbalance with the US. No other country had been prepared to call a spade a spade. Braithwaite posted the following bulletin.

> Every morning I wake up smiling. Why? Because we have a president who puts America first, and he has bloodied the nose of those cheating Chinks by imposing tariffs on imports from them. Why did he do that? Easy. Anyone could see the trade imbalance. They sold to us but did not buy from

us. That needs to stop. They steal our jobs with their imports. Blind Freddie can see that.

Please send your replies to Daryll Braithwaite at the St Joseph News-Press

Braithwaite loved the positive feedback, and it came in a rush

Dear St Joseph News-Press (attn. Mr Braithwaite)

I read your article with such pleasure. It's a smack in the eye for all those Democrats with university degrees that seem to be unable to see the trees for the woods. The Chinese steal our patented designs, dump their cheap aluminium on our shore, and destroy our factory jobs. So Trump smacked them in the eye with tariffs. Good man, Trump.

Jason Pennewell, Pittsburgh, PEN

Braithwaite loved that one and was pouring himself a drink when another response came in. It was from Mitch Upton, an oil Executive.

Dear St Joseph News-Press (attn. Mr Braithwaite)

My name is Mitch Upton, a Republican from Houston. I am an oilman, and our business needs to understand the world finance mechanics as a significant part of our business. The following point may be of interest to you. Donald Trump started a trade cold war [6] with China, and he has lost that one, I'm afraid. Two things define a

---

[6]   The U.S.-China Trade War Has Become a Cold War

https://carnegieendowment.org/2021/09/16/u.s.-china-trade-war-has-become-cold-war-pub-85352 trade imbalance: our product costs and whether China likes our products. And all of that is driven by the soaring U.S. federal budget deficits, which have little to do with China. And after starting this trade war, our trade balance is worse than ever, in line with the worsening US deficit.

Mr Braithwaite, I endorse your enthusiasm, but your paper would benefit from access to facts, and I suggest an economist organisation like the Carnegie Institute.

Mitch Upton, Republican, Houston.

Braithwaite decided to start one of his most senior investigators on this, and if Upton were wrong, he would publish Upton's response and his own research. No point in looking stupid, was there?

*   *   *

Dorothy was in her office when her assistant walked in with a note and said, "A little girl, about nine, just walked in and said it was urgent to see you."

The note was handwritten.

Please help me. My granny shot my dad, and My mum is at work. You need to call the ambulance and police. My name is Natalie Burrows.

Dorothy asked for the girl to be brought to her now, sat her down and asked her assistant to bring a hot chocolate, not too hot.

'Hello Natalie, that is so brave of you to come here. First we need to call an ambulance, then the police. What is your address please, so I can tell them, Natalie?'

Natalie was sobbing. 'Oh yes, it's 1005 12th St, NW, just a few hundred yards away, Third floor.' Dorothy called an ambulance and directed them to the third-floor address, then called Colonel Mathew Wade of the Capitol police to send someone there immediately and come to her office afterwards to talk to Natalie.

Then she wanted to hear Natalie's story, just as the warm hot chocolate arrived, putting the first smile she had seen on Natalie's face. Food. The problem solver.

'My mum is a nurse and had to go to work, and Dad had been to a Trump rally and came back pretty drunk. Mum did not want him to touch me. She wanted to make sure I did not get infected. Her Mum, my Granny, had been told to have her gun ready; to threaten Dad to stay away from me. He always wanted to cuddle me. When she knew that Granny understood, Mum left for work.' and Natalie paused for a bit.

'So what happened next?' asked Dorothy, and Natalie burst into tears.

'My dad woke up and came to the kitchen and saw me. Granny told him to stay away from me as he might be infected. Dad screamed abuse at her and called her a stupid fucking bitch, so he turned on her and told her to leave the house, or he would beat her up. Granny whipped out her gun and screamed at him. 'One step closer, and I shoot.' Then Natalie paused and burst into tears again. Dorothy looked for a distraction and asked Natalie to come and sit on her lap and play with those steel balls on strings. That did the trick, and the sobs stopped, so Dorothy probed, 'And what did your Granny do then?' That started the crying again.

'Granny's gun wobbled, and then there was a very loud bang, and my dad fell to the ground. I was so scared. I thought he might get up and strangle Granny, but he didn't. He moaned and held a hand to his chest, and blood was oozing out between his fingers. Granny is terrified. I don't want my dad to die, but I don't want Granny to go to jail either. What can we do?' she asked and Dorothy cuddled her on her lap and whispered 'I'm going to make it all better, with your dad getting better and granny not in any trouble. How's that?'

Then Dorothy told her that Granny would not go to jail as she acted in self-defence and to protect you as well, and your dad may be OK when doctors have patched him up. It wasn't a shotgun, was it?' asked Dorothy. It wasn't. It would have killed him.

The phone rang, and commander Wade said he was coming to interview Natalie. He liked kids. A good excuse to do some nice work instead of having to clear up messes, he thought.

When Wade arrived, Dorothy sat Natalie on her lap, hugged her and briefly told Commander Wade about Natalie's situation. The Commander was a switched-on man and realised there was nothing more to the story. So he just asked Natalie 'Honey, is that all there is to say? Just nod your head.

'That will do for tonight. If you remember anything else come and see Dorothy tomorrow and she can call me then, OK?

Do you want to go back to your granny now? I can give you a lift. All you have to do is tell me if you want the police sirens on or not.'

Natalie smiled at the thought of the lights and sirens blaring as she arrived at home.

'Oh yes, please! But not too loud because I don't want to scare granny.'

CHAPTER 3

Late October 2020

Argus is there in his office, monitoring the events and terrible mood, and he wishes he had not. People were scared of the worsening pandemic, potential violence, and civil war as Trump ratchets up the possibility of a stolen election if postal voting with its supposed massive fraud is allowed. Argus noticed that every man and his dog has an opinion about the election debates and thinks *This should be interesting.*

Argus reminds himself that he will follow many different people today.

The election debates were seen as good or bad, depending on your politics. Even now, before the election, Trump hammered home the point that the election was being stolen. The culprits were postal voters, of course, and the unspoken word was 'Blacks.'

The first debate had Trump supporters ecstatic; their man talking over Biden so much that Biden could not get a word in. The infections went up sharply after more election rallies in between debates, all pulling massive crowds.

More and more people were flocking to their hero President Trump, braying like cattle, shouting 'Make America Great Again!', and disregarding all advice from Dr Anthony Fauci, the nation's senior infectious diseases expert. They all knew better, of course; they listened to Trump. The country is so divided.

*   *   *

Terry Balzarini and his wife Lorraine live in Baltimore, and they are Democrats. They can't believe Trump's utter stupidity and selfishness, urging voters to the last hurrah rally in the many tens of thousands, infecting the whole of the United States.

'What will happen?' asks Terry, and Lorraine answers:

'Simple. Shit will happen. In a nutshell':

'Increased threats of actual violence, like the threats to kidnap the Michigan governor; Trump is inciting violence against postal voting as he knows he is going to lose, Trump supporters will run amok and shoot people in the streets, thousands will die every day. They don't care. It's all about Me, Me, Me.'

Lorraine had snapped her fingers for each item.

'How do you like that?' she asked, and Terry was impressed.

'It's so much easier to see when you explain it like that. It's so easy to get the message lost in all the noise out there. We are facing a perfect storm of disasters. Some people seem to think it's OK if oldies die. Less of a burden on society, but a large proportion of sick people will actually be health care workers, and if carers and doctors leave in disgust, the hospitals will be full of dead bodies; too infected for anyone to enter.'

He continued. 'We need to make a plan for escaping into the wilderness. A proper preparation. Maybe an all-terrain vehicle that can carry a good load of stuff that we need to build a warm log hut. Let's be ready to escape and leave if Trump loses the election and violence starts.'

Lorraine wonders if he is overreacting. 'Do you really think it will get to that? This is America, not some third world country.'

Terry's reply stumps her. 'This is no longer the America you grew up in. Violence in third world countries arose because of social injustices. Rich versus poor, and protestors get locked up; or shot. It's not an equal playing field there. And now we are the same, but our violence will be based on utter hate. Blacks vs. whites, no universal health care insurance if Trump has his way, he is egging on white supremacists and has the police in his pocket as he lifted their funding.'

'So what do you suggest then?' asks Lorraine, and Terry proposes they draw up a list of everything they need to stay in their wilderness hideout for six months away from everyone.

Then he adds, 'You and I are a team, cemented in love, common interests and beliefs. We would never recover if one of us got killed; we would just have one lonely, sad person not wanting to live. So let's fix that and be ready if Trump loses the election. And maybe as well if he won, as the virus would explode all over the US in that case. Or shall we migrate to somewhere; do you like Tahiti? If we can get there.'

They settled down, made lists, laughed, decided to add many books to their bucket list, and settled down with a cuddle and a good glass of red.

*   *   *

Mitch Upton is discussing the first Presidential debate[7] with his wife Danielle, reviewing what the Washington Post said about it.

'OK clever wife of mine, who do you think won the first debate?' asks Mitch.

---

[7] First Trump-Biden meeting marked by constant interruptions by Trump

'Easy', answers Danielle, 'The one who was speaking 90 per cent of the time, and that is Trump. Biden had to revert to bad language telling him to "Shut Up, Man", but he couldn't stop him. Some people will love him for riding rough shot over Biden, but I loathe that man'

Mitch is puzzled by his wife's response. 'I'm a Trump supporter, but I wish someone would teach him some manners. If that had happened in our boardroom, we would have called security and had him thrown out, even the chairman. I can't see how he would win over the general population with that performance, and the GOP must be cringing. Didn't they prepare him for that event?'

Danielle remembers how incredulous she was when she watched the first debate. She had wondered how angry Biden would have been at the intolerant rudeness of the man, and the insipid performance of Walker, the Fox moderator, who was too scared to mute Trump when the time was up for Trump's reply.

Then she responds with, 'Now that I think about it, I want to kick him in the balls, or chop them off, even better. I loathe that man and the Republican Party too. I spew when I read the 'Peter Baker and Maggie Haberman' article in the New York Times. He expects his new Supreme Court judge nominee Amy Coney Barrett to settle any disputes that may arise over mail-in ballots in the November election.[8]. Conservative should not mean cheating and make it look as if the other side cheated and robbed. We need to stand for our good conservative values, or we become irrelevant.'

Mitch's response is:

---

[8] Trump Selects Amy Coney Barrett to Fill Ginsburg's Seat on the Supreme

'I'm impressed. You said what the GOP should say, even if I want them to win. But everyone in the party is afraid to speak out, or they get their head chopped off.'

There was contemplative silence. Then Mitch added, 'Today's Republicans need to have the courage of Christians in the old days. State your belief, and you get thrown to the lions, as for real. They knew what a lion would do. Tear you to bits. Extreme pain, and then you die. Any Republican who rails against Trump gets the shove, and you don't get re-elected. End of income and status.' Then there was more contemplative silence as Danielle considered what it would take to go into the Lion's den. *Just not possible.*

*   *   *

Argus is impressed. Republicans can be good people, and being Republican does not mean they are necessarily Trump supporters. He is much happier with good people on both sides of politics and will follow what the Uptons are up to with great interest.

*   *   *

Dorothy Thompson had called Sue Anne Orthallo in Oregon. They were best friends since college and used each other as sounding boards when needed.

'Sue, I've found a monster of a problem the Democrats will face. Wanna hear?' asked Dorothy.

'Well, that is obviously why you called, so spill the beans,' replied Sue Anne.

'I will read out some stuff I've dug up in an article. It says: "Nancy Pelosi begins mustering Democrats for possible House decision".'

And that may be the worm in the woodpile. It's truly horrible.'

Dorothy continues, 'They can try to get the State Electoral College officials to declare for Trump on December 15, but those officers will never be employed again and may experience a bit of discomfort, like lead poisoning. So, self-preservation should stop that despite any attempts by Trump to sway them. But the real bugger is the Constitution. On January 6 next year, the house votes to approve the submitted state results. Have a guess who votes?' she asks, and Sue Anne thinks the answer is all the electoral college officials, e.g. twenty in Pennsylvania.

'That would be wonderful, but Congress had amended the Constitution in 1876 so that every state's delegation gets a single vote if there is not a clear winner. The Republicans have 26 states, Democrats 23, and each representative is legally allowed to vote for Trump or Biden. It's a joke. What should we do?'

Sue Anne had been thinking about the laws that govern this election. 'Dorothy, I have been thinking about all the lawyers and all the people who would want to sue Donald Trump. I have been looking at this sort of stuff with my students. One of them said, "If you look at all the laws before or after the one being used against you, then all you need to do is find another law from earlier on or afterwards that could invalidate the law they are trying to use against you".'

Dorothy is thrilled and says: 'I think I can find a hundred lawyers who would love to find the solution to that problem, and take Trump down, where he belongs. That's it, leave it to me. And you know what? I needed a smart thinking solution, don't fiddle with the law, but use it. Haha. We'll chat later then.'

*　　　*　　　*

James Anderson was also discussing the same article he had read with his wife, Michelle, about the speaker, Ms Pelosi, who began mustering Democrats for a possible House decision. James says, 'This is so ridiculous. Trump can overturn the election decision on January 6 when Congress has to vote on the election result. Legally,' shouted James, giving in to his anger at all this legal bullshit.

Michelle cut in with, 'Darling, they could not possibly do that and expect to live.' James helped her read the article and added:

'If the Democrats want to challenge the decision in the Supreme Court, there is nothing the judges could do about it, even if they wanted to. We are stuffed. It's legal. And it's probably the reason why Trump would say he won and why he would leave gracefully if he had lost the election legally. We need Dot Thompson to research this and find out how such a decision could be overturned.' They called Dorothy, and when it went to voicemail, they sent her an email.

James was pleased with his efforts but doubted it would succeed. He did not want it to go to yet another court case. The country was getting too used to ignoring the truth if they could bury it in court, which made the court responsible, not the people who brought the case in the first place. The Republicans wanting to overturn the election results were the ones that needed to get punished. He wondered what other families were plotting.

*   *   *

Meanwhile, in Ohio, discussions erupt about the reporting of the storming of the Michigan Capitol. Blew Ohrtman read the article about men accused in a plot on the Michigan governor and blew a fuse. He was irate and shouted at his wife Petal.

'Did you see that drivel? They accuse the armed protesters who rallied at the Michigan Capitol of being in plots to kidnap the Governor, storm the Capitol and start a "civil war"! For God's sake, they only protested against Governor Whitmer's coronavirus lockdown. And worse, they now claim that the rallies were organised by conservative groups and were egged on by President Donald Trump himself. What an insult. Fake news.'

Petal smiled and simply remarked that the Democrats had failed in a gun ban in the building even after they reported being threatened by rifle-carrying protesters who had entered the State House. No one should enter a public building carrying rifles. But she simply said: 'If they kidnap Whitmer, or if there is a kidnap plot for her, I want Trump arrested for inciting murder.'

'You're not on my side, are you?' he asked, and her reply was simple:

'Never been on your side ever since Trump stole the last election.'

Blew wants to know, 'How did he steal the election? You can't just take an election and take it home and alter the results.'

Petal thought this would be good for his enlightenment. 'Go and ask your son Fred. He can explain it better than me. You steal by cheating with lawyers. A Trump specialty.'

Later on, Blew contemplated the debates and complained to Petal. He was not impressed but angry. 'Did you see how that bitch Kristen Welker, the NBC News correspondent, controlled that? She did not allow President Trump to shine, and how she allowed Biden, that prick, to speak when Trump wanted to say something? Disgusting.'

Petal had a different view that annoyed him even more when she said: 'I do like Kristen Welker, a smart, no-nonsense woman.

They both had been allotted five minutes for each question, and because Trump is so incoherent, he forgot what points he needed to make, and then it was too late, and she muted him. She was just so much better than Chris Wallace from Fox. That man was just not willing to stand up to Trump. I would have loved to be a fly on the wall when he watched this show to see how it should be done. She showed Trump who is boss here, and he didn't like it. No one ever stands up to him, or they get sacked.'

Then Petal continues with, 'That man would sack God if he could get away with it. Even the last question where Welker asked what he would say to people if elected, Trump just promoted himself, the stupid prick, whilst Biden told a story America could believe in. Later on when you've cooled down we could have a dummy debate and see what it's like when you have five minutes and did not finish because you were too incoherent.'

Blew was irate. 'Are you saying I'm incoherent? That it?'

Her response was, 'Not normally, but when you talk about Trump you can't get your message across in half an hour or we would both be on the same side.' That shut him up.

They stopped talking. There was no point in it; just more aggression.

*   *   *.

At home in Oregon, Sue Anne Orthallo told John about a COVID-safe lesson at school. She told him about a demonstration to help kids better understand how the virus spread.

'This is what happened. We had invited a health care worker, Lilly, to turn up in protective gear at school. Kids got all goggle-eyed and wanted to know what's going to happen. Then Lilly showed them how the virus spreads.'

'OK', Lilly told the kids. 'I have water in this spray bottle, to which I have added some tea tree oil. Quite safe.' She demonstrated that by licking the water and oil, and then added: 'I'm now going to spray that Coke bottle on that table with this mixture, then turn the lights out and shine my special torch on it.' She sprayed the bottle, turned the lights out. Gasps were heard as the kids could now see green and red patches with the torch shining on the bottle; they were not visible before, and the lights turned back on. Lilly then told two kids to touch the Coke bottle, rub their hands on the table, then rub their noses. She then asked five kids to rub their hands on the table where the first two had rubbed their hands, turned lights out and shone her torch on those kids, and you could see red and green patches on their faces and hands.

Sue Anne addressed John, 'Those kids understand social distancing far better now than all the stupid Trump suckers.' She had more to say: 'I don't believe in God anymore. The church tells us that God created all men equal. But it didn't tell us that many had no brains, so instead of understanding what is said, and maybe taking it in with a grain of salt, all they can do is repeat what Trump tells them.'

*   *   *

Rudy Giuliani had called one of his donors, Mitch Upton in Houston, to raise more money for the upcoming court cases. He wanted to have SCOTUS, the Supreme Court of The United States, turn those *'illegal'* votes from the swing states to Trump, and he had to start the conversation.

'Mitch, you have no idea how much money those lawyers want, just to persuade the Supreme Court of the real intention of the written words, and once they've done it, they have a precedent for using again and again, but we need your help now. How much can you spare, please?'

Mitch replied, 'Well, I'm not happy with your approach. Why don't you find something concrete that will work instead of twenty to thirty court cases that you lost all over the place? Why don't you do your homework instead of running off like blue-arsed flies hoping someone will listen to you. No more money until you demonstrate some logic; right now it's just a waste of time and resources.'

Giuliani had one last plea for him. 'There is a report in The Conversation on how the Congress decision could see Trump win.[9] That is our last resort, though, and we need to try to overturn the election earlier. Much earlier. And I will note your point about testing an approach first before we take it to court. On that note, are you willing to donate now?'

'OK, I will send a cheque for $5,000 in the mail today. Goodbye,' came Mitch's response. Giuliani had wanted more, much more, but he knew it was truly goodbye.

Mitch Upton was still stewing about that phone call when his wife Danielle had a visitor, their neighbour Julianne Klimmer. Julianne was a healthcare worker in the nearby hospital. Julianne and Danielle were friends, and they often had morning tea together. This day being a Saturday, Mitch was home too. He had heard a lot about Julianne over the months and was interested in meeting his wife's friend. Mitch started by asking her: 'how are you today, Julianne?'

Her response was, 'Well, you don't want to know.' and as is so often the case, that was like a red flag to a bull.

---

[9] How the Congress decision could see Trump Win

'Of course I want to know. You are amongst friends here, so spill the beans,' replied Mitch.

'I'm so tired I could cry. I could literally burst into tears. Don't get me worked up, or I will tell you why,' Julianne says.

Mitch, being the polite southern gentleman he was, decides she needs to unload herself and says, 'Well, you are amongst friends here now, so just unload, woman.' Well, an order is an order, right? *You asked for it,* Julianne thought. took a dep breath and let loose.

'To start with, we all work six days a week, 16, 8, 16, 8, 16, 8-hour days in a week,' and after she paused, she said, 'But that's not the worst. It's the emotional drain,' as she caught her breath again, noticing the confusion on Mitch's face. 'Have you ever tried to drown a baby and see the terror on their faces when they can't breathe? Of course not. You don't look like someone who goes around drowning babies. Now imagine a normally healthy 45-year-old drowning in a bath with a pleading look on his face as he asks for help. Got it?' she asks.

Mitch remembers when he was a kid, and his father had asked him to drown a litter of kittens. 'Holy shit, woman, you are not drowning patients in that hospital of yours, or are you?'

Julianne replies, 'No, Mitch, but I watched my good friend and co-worker Wendy die this morning. She could not breathe, and why not, you ask? She contracted COVID-19 from a patient a week ago.' Julianne took a deep breath and let loose.

'My friend died because some motherfucker idiot Trump supporter went to one of those rallies and got infected. He's well now, and my friend is dead. You have no idea how we all loathe Trump supporters, and the next one to come in will be sent home without treatment, and if anyone complains, then all our hospital staff and I will retire. Permanently.

'Why should we die for those stupid idiots and don't look at me like that for swearing? This is a disgrace, and if Trump shows up in our hospital, I will personally plunge a needle of HIV into his arm and notify the world so no one will ever have sex with him again.

'Do you have any idea how angry we all are and how much energy it takes to still look after patients to our best ability despite their gobsmacking stupidity?!' And with that, she stormed out of the house, thinking she was no longer welcome there.

Danielle looked at Mitch and saw that no explanations were needed. They had never bothered to find out what happened in those hospitals and how patients drowned from fluids in their lungs. Mitch had been held underwater when he was playing with his elder brother and remembered the terror. He told Danielle about it and said, 'That's why I don't want to go to rallies.' Danielle replied, 'That's why I don't want anyone to go to rallies.'

*   *   *

Argus-E contacted *Darryl Braithwaite* from the St. Joseph News-Press after reading his article saying that China did not buy American goods. Argus was not a finance expert but knew that he only bought what he wanted to buy. Always. So he sent Darryl this email:

> St. Joseph News, Attn. Darryl Braithwaite
>
> Dear Mr Braithwaite, my name is Argus-E, MSc, and I live in Port Blair, Andaman Island, Bay of Bengal. I report on the pandemic in the US to the Indian government to advise on public health

for our islanders, whom a virus could wipe out. I just read your bulletin that mentions the trade imbalance, implying it was China's fault.

Whilst I approve of enthusiasm for all people, I think the media and reporters have a responsibility. Over here, we call it truth in reporting. I wonder how you concluded that the trade balance was China's fault. I would agree that China may be manipulating its currency, making their products cheaper for us to buy, but I want you to think of any time this year where you went into a shop and bought something just because it was from another country. Maybe the Chinese do not like the products the US wants to sell them because they already make those themselves. Even possibly with stolen patents, I acknowledge.

I look forward to your response.

Argus-E, MSc., Port Blair, Andaman Island, Bay of Bengal.

He was looking forward to the response; it should be interesting.

CHAPTER 4

December 6

Argus had been following the fast and furious email exchanges between Sue Anne Orthallo and Dorothy Thompson about the attempt by Trump to use the Constitution to overturn the election on January 6. The plan was to use a lesser-known amendment made in 1871. That amendment allowed a single state senator to cast the vote to Biden or Trump, which had been introduced to solve a deadlock situation if a clear winner was not established. And it just so happened that the republicans had 26 states vs. 23 for the democrats.

*   *   *

Dorothy Thompson always posted her articles using her name unless there was a security issue when she wrote as Rebecca Sanders. She wrote this new article using Sanders name. She wrote about Trump's attempt to skew the run-off Senate election towards the Republicans.[10] Her article said:

Rebecca sanders Reporting

---

[10]   Trump Continues Attacks On Election Results At Georgia Senate Runoff Rally

Steve Fowler writes that Trump is urging people to vote in the January 5 Senate run-off election after previous intentions of boycotting them. Trump reminded voters that they needed this to stop Biden.

That was a fairly accurate assessment of the situation and correct process for Trump, then he messes it up with his usual trashy denunciation of the election, and I quote Fowler's words now:

> 'If I lose, I'd be a very gracious loser.' Trump said.
> 'If I lost, I would say, I lost', and I'd go to Florida, and I'd take it easy, and I'd go around, and I'd say, 'I did a good job. But you can't ever accept when they steal and rig and rob.'

The first part of that paragraph made Trump look far more worldly than he had ever seemed, but then he spoiled it. Assuming that there were, say, 160 million voters, it appears that 80 million Trump supporters were happy to accept that the election was stolen. Without any evidence at all. To me, that is a bit like getting a speeding fine in the mail that just said you were clocked doing 85 mph in a school zone. The penalty is $2400 and you pay up even though you don't have a car.

I'm inviting readers to write in if they saw fraud. Not if you heard someone talk about it, but if you saw it personally. But please, if you want your reply published, you need to state your name and your city residence.

*   *   *

Jason Pennewell from Pittsburgh saw this item and decided to write that very day. He wasn't stupid, but he was a Trump supporter. Therefore liable to make mistakes in his enthusiasm to defend his hero. He knew the vote counts for Pennsylvania for both parties in 2020 and also for 2016. He had smelt a rat; Biden had so many more votes, almost 200,000 more in 2020 than in 2016. Where did they come from then? They came from people double voting. That's how. That's it. Easy. He was writing to the Washington Post; to set the record straight:

> Dear Washington Post and Ms Sanders
>
> You implied President Trump had no evidence of voter fraud to make his claims. Well, I have news for you. The Democrat vote in Pennsylvania was 200,000 votes more this year than in 2016, despite no increase in population. That has to be proof that many Democrats voted twice, first by mail and then again in person. Please do your homework next time before besmirching President Trump.
>
> Jason Pennewell, Pittsburgh PN

The responses to that bit of enlightenment were quick to arrive, first from many Republicans congratulating Mr Pennewell and admonishing the Washington Post, but then one reply caught Dorothy's eye. It was from a prominent Republican. She decided to print his entry:

> Dear Ms Sanders, congratulations on your excellent reporting.
>
> I find it refreshing that people urge you to do your research before publishing your opinion pieces. That allows me to suggest the same caution on your readers, even if it is amusing when they fail to apply the same principles to their own opinion pieces. To save you having to reply to all the

letters you would have received, you may wish to print this response:

A two-minute Google search shows that past elections had about a 59 per cent voter turnout, whereas the 2020 election had a 73.7 per cent turnout. Hello, is anyone listening? Were there more voters now? Before you besmirch the integrity of a well-respected journalist, it behoves you to do your own homework.

Colonel George Jeffry Edwards retired, Ohio.

Dorothy grinned with glee. A smack in the face for Republican opinions that did not pass the pub test.

December 8 2020

Dorothy reports for the Washington Post using her pen name. She cites reports from the BBC that describe the propensity for violence fuelled by President Trump himself, as well as by Trump and his team. They were not just querying the election results but claiming widespread fraud. *Will somebody please sue him for defamation?* she thought. This had led to Republican officials wanting to scrutinise the voting machines in an attempt to prove fraud. Of course, they would then damage the voting machines, hoping to render the result void. Democrat officials were seeking police protection to prevent the GOP officials from entering the state-building.

The republicans delivered the request with language that threatened violence, and by men carrying rifles. *Would the police actually make the problem go away, or would they make it worse.* Her thoughts were *I want police who shoot intruders rather than pal up with them.*

*Dorothy r*eports that this was now the second recount of all votes, done manually, which had nothing to do with voting machines anymore. She found a new post and read:

> Trump campaign spokesman Tim Murtaugh said his team was trying to make sure 'that all legal votes are counted, and all illegal votes are not.'

> But if their team of lawyers were allowed to handle voting papers, it would be so easy to put a mark on them and thus make those papers void and then declare the whole lot void. Despite his own team and US Attorney General William Barr stating the Justice Department had found no trace of any fraud.

Well, thought Dorothy, *Is this evidence of the stupidity of the Trump teams or what?* And she remembered one of the first lessons in politics: if you want to win you really need to give up on integrity and lie through your teeth. All you need to do is shout louder than the opposition.

> Dorothy Thompson reporting

> When Cybersecurity and Infrastructure chief Chris Krebs contradicted Trump's baseless fraud claims on a massive scale, he was sacked.[11] Most agencies had reported that this was the most secure election in American election history, and demonic Trump dishes up unsubstantiated fraud charges. No evidence at all, whilst the rest of the world watches and chokes, laughing at the

---

[11]   US cybersecurity chief fired for contradicting Trump.

absolute stupidity of the American system that allows such vaudeville behaviour.

On Tuesday the state's voting systems implementation manager, Mr Sterling, rebuked his fellow Republicans, including the President. Sterling had reported that a 20-year-old contractor for Dominion Voting Systems had received death threats and the worker's family was also being harassed.

Dorothy concluded her report repeating warnings that someone would get hurt, and that President Trump chose not to disown threats of violence. *Is he actively advocating it? It looks like it.* Many Republicans are worried about the future of the GOP if they don't stand up to Trump, but so far, few have broken ranks; risky business. They know Trump had already asked for the names of those who did.[12]

The next day Dorothy concentrated on Donald Trump's attempts to overturn the election. She wrote:

Dorothy Thompson reporting

Donald Trump has not learned that you can't beat back the waves by waving a red flag, but he has raised many red flags to infuriate the Democrats and delight the Republicans. He's going to screw everyone with his new Supreme court numbers and had issued a statement.[13].

You, the American people, it's time you started to understand what democracy means, and

---

[12] Just 27 of 249 Republicans in Congress willing to say Trump lost, survey finds

[13] President Donald Trump has tweeted that he will be 'intervening' in the presidential election.

whether you want one. Would you rather live under a dictatorship where all your rights are stripped away? That is what Donald Trump is doing. He just dresses it up as a minor legal issue to stop cheating. Idi Amin would have been more honest than Donald Trump. He only tortured his opposition. You think I'm upset? No, I'm absolutely furious, and you should be too.

Then there is the proposed attack on the result of four swing states.[14] The Texas Attorney General Ken Paxton announced that Texas had filed a lawsuit against the four lost states of Georgia, Michigan, Pennsylvania and Wisconsin at the US Supreme Court. He called changes those states had made amid the pandemic to postal vote procedures unlawful.

They were ordered to stave off COVID infections, you intolerant buggers, as you all know.

The conceit of Paxton publicly showing he would throw democracy under the bus and ask the courts to prostitute themselves. Someone, please, give Paxton a nice dose of COVID-19, and see how he likes that.

Dorothy Thompson, Washington Post

Dorothy asked her readers to write in and comment on any fears for the violence they had experienced personally, whether they thought that Trump promoted it or whether he had invited violence from the Republicans. She wanted people to remember

---

[14] A long-shot lawsuit against Georgia, Michigan, Pennsylvania and Wisconsin in a latest legal effort intended to reverse Biden's victory

that Georgia will also hold two run-off elections on January 5, determining who controls the Senate. How will voters react to a Democrat win if that were to happen? Will there be another dozen court cases to overturn such a result as well?

The responses to the Washington Post were almost instantaneous, split evenly between hate and love letters for her articles.

General Christopher Paul Roberts, retired, is a stout Republican in Dallas, Texas. He resides on his spectacular ranch, living in splendour in a southern mansion suitable for a retired general. He had served his country. He was a leader of men, and his definition of a leader was someone whom people followed, especially in battle. He could not stand armchair officers who avoided standing in the line of fire but expected others to do so. He was proud of his achievements that others honoured. He was a gentleman, and he had a big dose of disdain for those who were not.

The General read Dorothy Thompson's invitation to comment. This was serious stuff, and he organised his table to support his response. A whiskey decanter was nearby, a sparkling clean crystal glass at the ready, and an ice bucket with a few cubes in it. He pressed fresh tobacco into his pipe, lit it, and had a first draw of the sweet aroma. He was ready.

He was ready because he had spent half an hour making a mental copy of the letter he would write. There were two subjects, one the Trump attempts to use legal means to steal the election, the other, Trump's attempt to corrupt the integrity of Republican officials. He decided that an attack on Trump's attempt to corrupt the result using his court majority should start his reply. A stinging rebuke to someone who had never stood in the line of fire. His well thought out response was committed to paper:

Dear Washington Post

I am writing in regard to your journalist Dorothy Thompson's invitation to respond to her article.

First, I congratulate Ms Thompson on an excellent piece of work where she uses valid quotes to attack the destruction wrought by President Trump and his yes men to subvert the legally won election. I look forward to similar articles should they be needed if the Supreme Court, in their undoubted wisdom, decides to allow a superbly run election count to be overturned and make a mockery of our democratic principles.

Secondly, I use this opportunity to urge all Republicans to act with honour and integrity; remember the oaths you made when first inducted. They were sacred oaths to serve the country, for the best of the country and not for a Commander-in-Chief who is such in title only. He has not served, led men into battle, nor demonstrated any personal traits that should allow him to lead this country again. Just the opposite, and he should certainly not be able to pardon himself for all the gross acts of dishonesty he has committed.

Thirdly, I fear for our country. It is being torn into pro and anti-Trump camps, many protesting and attending these rallies carrying military-style rifles. Leave your rifles at home locked up. They aren't meant for use in crowds. Most of you have no idea of the damage they can do. It's not a pig shoot, folks. Stay home if you need to carry a rifle. I have served in wars and carried wounded soldiers to safety; badly damaged bodies.

Lastly, I address the military leadership. If asked to step in, do so for the country, not for a dishonourable President. If this civil disorder continues, I fear you will be asked to solve it. If you do, please save your souls by only doing the right thing.

General Christopher Paul Roberts (retired), Republican, Dallas, Texas.

*   *   *

Argus E was delighted. At last, a Republican he could admire. So much better now that there was a demonstration of the difference between Republican civilians and Republican politicians. He was a nerdy type by nature, but he discovered he could become passionate about the events. Seeing General Roberts's letter had returned him to a more peaceful state of mind. He now saw that being Republican did not always mean being a Trump supporter.

*   *   *

The following reply was from Mitch Upton in Houston, Texas. Mitch was a Republican, and like the previous reply from General Roberts, he was also a man of integrity, one who wished Trump would be swallowed up in a big hole and come out in China. He took issue with the report in which Ken Paxton, the Texas Attorney General, had announced that the state of Texas had filed a lawsuit against four of the swing states they had lost to try and overturn the election result. Mitch knew that the GOP had to rebuild using trusted values or be irrelevant and wiped from the map. He wondered again why stupidity and loyalty worked so well together to wreck a country. So he wrote:

Dear Ms Sanders, I applaud your article asking people to revert to values, integrity and honesty. So well supported by your references. There was your article on Ken Paxton, the Texas Attorney General, urging ludicrously dishonest behaviours to grasp at some last straws to betray his country. I would love Ken Paxton to answer and tell us how much he was paid for that, and secondly, if he can remember the oath he swore. Please contact the Post and tell us what it said and what he signed up for. It would be such a delight to hear back from Mr Paxton, and, my dear Ms Sanders, if he does not respond within three days, please find the oath and publish it under the heading: 'The Oath Ken Paxton signed up to and seemed to have forgotten.' I'm sure your readers will applaud.

Mitch Upton, Houston, Texas

*   *   *

Michelle Anderson, a Public Health lecturer, abhorred the Trump support for encouraging or even demanding mass gatherings before the election. She hates the Trump incitement to violence to overturn the election even more. She is no fool, and during her studies, had learned how to construct compelling arguments. She stood in front of a class of 220 students most days and knew how important it was to have a clear message.

Dear Ms Sanders, I applaud your article and love that it seeks to have people revert to values of integrity and honesty. I lecture over 200 students in Public Health daily. I honour their intelligence by treating them with respect, which is missing in this Trump attempt to cheat.

I admire that your article does not blame so much as urge people to revert to their integrity and remember the oaths they swore to. That is such a masterstroke. It leads me to the question of social distancing, as in not practised by Trump supporters, and worse, our President himself encourages his followers to disregard such measures. A small reminder: he would have sworn an oath to serve his country. I have watched inaugurations for the last three elections, and nowhere have I seen the oath of office include serving your re-election needs above the need for public health and safety.

Therefore, Trump is personally responsible for the health and economic aftermath of the pandemic, and I urge his supporters to remember what is good for them and the country.

Now this man repeats baseless claims of election fraud and sacks security chief Chris Krebs when that man bravely contradicted Trump. Chris Krebs would have signed on to a pledge to ensure and certify the security to ensure the electoral system could not have been hacked, subverted or used illegally. Working day and night whilst Trump plays golf. Notice the difference? Krebs's work was so solid that all overseas attacks from un-friendly agents were all stopped and bounced off. Good job, Mr Krebs, and you can stand tall.

Dr Michelle Anderson, lecturer in Public Health, Washington.

December 14, 2020

Dorothy Thompson reported as Rebecca Sanders that Trump had asked for names of Republicans who had responded to a Washington Post poll of Republican senators saying that Mr Biden had won[15], probably to dish out punishments or have them excommunicated or something. She reported on the James Crump report in the Independent on December 14, which stated that Donald Trump had wanted to get the names of the 27 Congressional Republicans who had acknowledged Joe Biden's victory. A survey by the Washington Post of all 249 Republicans showed most had not responded, but two said they wouldn't accept Mr Biden as the President no matter what.

Dorothy contacted her friends Sue Anne Orthallo in Oregon and Michelle Anderson in Washington to discuss the increasing likelihood of Trump attempting to usurp the house role in passing on the election results. She sent emails to both and asked if the next day at 8:30 pm EST would suit. Sue Anne agreed – she had a DVD for the kids to take to the dungeon. The next day the phone rang, and Sue Anne answered.

'Well, hello Dorothy, have you seen all those articles by Rebecca Sanders in the Post lately?' asked Sue Anne. Dorothy replied: 'If you tell anyone, I will steal your husband, Sue Anne. Rebecca Sanders is my nom de plume to keep me safe from idiots and bullets.' After the mandatory pleasantries, she outlined her Supreme Court challenge should it be needed.

---

[15]   Trump demands the names of Congressional Republicans who have acknowledged Biden's election victory

Dorothy continued: 'The most important news is that we have found a Constitutional judge who was passed over by Trump who installed Amy Coney Barrett instead. He would love nothing better than to defeat her if it came to a court case. The court should immediately dismiss the Trump move to claim victory, even if the Constitution allowed it. He is so fired up that he hopes it comes to this final showdown. He has researched thousands and thousands of pages and has come across twelve cases where the intention of the founders of the Constitution finished up winning the day in court. Now he can use those cases to defeat the words in the Constitution that allows a vote to be cast either way.'

'As he is a keen fisherman, he intends to play his victim like a trout, so he will start with the weakest case to give them a false sense of security, then ratchet it up. He has shown me the last case, and believe me; the hook is firmly planted to roll up the case.'

Sue Anne cuts in with, 'All the other Trump machinations will only ever amount to this day in court. I'd be delighted if many Republicans bow to Trump's wishes and prostitute themselves, ruining their future forever. But in the end, all that matters is the house vote; and if they allocate the win to Trump, the Supreme Court challenge by the Democrats will win the day. I guess a win at the last post would be far more satisfying than Donald Trump rolling over now.'

Then she engaged in her fantasy and told Dorothy,

'Imagine this. Trump walks in to the Supreme Court. He has that smug look on his face. He's gonna win and sock it to the Democrats. The press is watching his face and reports on his demeanour. Then they see anger when the Democrats remind the court of a previous case that would overturn Trump's defence that the senators could allocate a state to anyone they chose. At his stage he is angry, but that case was not strong enough to throw out the democrats' bid, and Trump smiles that look that said 'Told Ya.' This repeats five times until the lawyer for the Democrats brings out his secret weapon. The Democrats win the case and Trump sacks his lawyers with dramatic shouting. The democrats had taken a video of the last two minutes and played it back over and over again.'

Sue Anne was besides herself with laughter, and so was Dorothy

They reverted to friendship issues, kids, COVID-19. They were happy; they had done their job.

*   *   *

December 30 2020

Argus E had been searching for a virologist amid all these pandemic problems. Surely one would pop up and help save the world. He had used his Artificial Intelligence to find email links from Dorothy Thompson, and was delighted with the result. He used a voice command to thank AI. This weird world needed a good one to fix this mess.

*   *   *

Terry Balzarini was talking to his wife, Lorraine. They were in Baltimore and heard of the new virus strain[16], written in a report by Patty Nieberg and read:

> Jared Polis announced on Tuesday that the first reported US case of the COVID-19 variant seen in the United Kingdom was discovered in Colorado, adding urgency to vaccinating Americans. The variant was found in a man now

---

[16] 1st reported US case of COVID-19 variant found in Colorado

in isolation southeast of Denver in Elbert County. He had no travel history, so he picked it up locally, meaning others would be infected too.

Elbert County is a rural area of rolling plains at the far edge of the Denver metro area, including a portion of Interstate 70, the state's main East-West Highway.

'Oh dear,' exclaimed Terry, 'rural county but Interstate 70, a main east-west artery, with thousands of truck stops. A great way to spread the virus.' Lorraine corrects his interpretation. 'Honey, it's not the usual COVID-19 shit. It's a new strain from the UK that is much more infectious. 70 per cent more. And even though we have the vaccine now, God knows how long it will take to roll out.'

'The Republicans have held up the relief package for the vaccine rollout. Trump had been criticising the FDA to hurry up the vaccine approval, and then, when he had the opportunity to buy 200 million doses from Pfizer, he ordered just twenty million. I am so fed up with that man. Grandstanding with politics, "Hurry up with the vaccine", good news blogs for him, then he stuffs it up by not funding the massive logistics task of the actual vaccination rollout. No, that is spending money, and you know Republicans don't like that at all.'

Lorraine continues, 'Honey, forget all that. We need to make plans to leave. I hate mutations. I hate pandemics, and I hate violence. Have you been to Cameron County in Pennsylvania? Just east of Allegheny National Forest? There is nothing there except wilderness. Have you been there?' she asked.

'On a volunteering weekend and got lost, Yep. Great place. So let's work out the trigger point for leaving, plan for stuff to take and get our RV ready and packed. So good for off-road travel. will be cold, bloody cold, and a forest at least provides shelter from the wind. How comfortable do you want to be?' asked Terry.

Lorraine muffled an answer and then asked Terry the difference between a natural mutation and one engineered in a laboratory. Terry told her: 'In a natural environment, you only get a mutation if the changes to a virus's DNA amount to a single protein molecule, and the chances of that protein actually altering the virus's ability to infect people and replicate itself enough times to spread is very low. But in a laboratory, scientists can add a whole string of new molecules and if you are unlucky, it becomes deadly and far more infectious. They played with this in labs for bioweapon. Pretty out of control, the whole thing.'

Lorraine was ready. 'Look, honey, we could be in hiding for six months, and we don't want to be found, but we must be able to get in and out of that place, maybe once a month for supplies. We need to build a log cabin with a stove for heat, a pipe chimney and build it in a forest so no one can see our smoke trailing from the cabin. If we are in a forest, we won't get much sunlight to fire up a solar panel, but we could get one and use it to power up a battery it in a clearing away from our cabin. We can make a list later on but let's discuss this mutation problem first. I don't know anything about it, but you do. How does it work?'

Terry needed to keep it simple, as the biology stuff of virus interaction was very complex, but the principle was straightforward. 'Honey, it's like I told you a moment ago. When a large number of bodies infected with COVID-19 get close together, and a viral cell from one person touches viral cells from another many times, it is possible that their DNA loses or gains a protein receptor, and that changes how infectious and deadly it becomes. The new strain can then become more rampant. If the contact is more pronounced, it could make a bigger change or mutation. We don't know if existing vaccines could handle such a change. There is only one thing. Get out and stay out.' finished Terry.

So they made a list of things to take, modified it, took their RV to the shopping precinct and loaded it up.

*　　*　　*

December 31, 2020

Blew Ohrtman was talking to his wife Petal. He was packing to go to a Trump rally and was all fired up. This rally had two purposes, support overturning the election result and to drum up support for the January 5 run-off of the two Georgia senators. It was a long drive. He decided to go via Chattanooga, a bit longer but slightly faster. Also, he had a friend in Chattanooga. Sorted.

Blew nearly blew a gasket so many times in the last week. Those Democrats were crowing about winning. *Do I have news for you, boys?* He thought. Blew had seen mass demonstrations and people milling around with military-style rifles. If someone shot at him, then he would like nothing better than to mow down the enemy, stupid buggers, for walking around with rifles. He did not stop to think that most of them would be Republicans like himself.

Petal no longer cared. She had just one wish: don't come back disabled. She did not wish him dead, but at the same time, she did not want to be a minder for a paraplegic. Nor did she want him to come back at all. It had been so stressful having Blew run around with all that hate. She helped him pack his bags and begged him one more time to leave the rifles behind.

Blew left in the morning; stony silence from Petal. A long drive south he found Chattanooga and his buddy Wesley. It was such a relief to be amongst like-minded people - and they partied a bit, ribs on the BBQ, some beers and bourbon; life was good. The next day they left for Atlanta, a two-hour drive at most, and settled in to bully the opposition.

Later that night, Petal watched the news; she wasn't really watching but saw the Breaking News banner for 'Shootings in Atlanta.' *Stupid buggers, grow up*, she thought and turned the TV off.

Later she went to bed with the answering machine on, recording, and was just drifting off to sleep when she heard the machine answer, but she was too tired to get up. It could wait till morning.

In the morning, when she remembered that call last night, she went to the answering machine. There were seven messages. They all said the same thing:

'Please come to the Atlanta South police station and post 20,000 dollars bail for Blew Ohrtman or call this number.' *Well*, she thought, *that can wait a bit*, and she went out.

*   *   *

Argus noticed this. He grinned. He knew he was in for a bit of fun with this couple, even if it did not change his view on what he needed to report. This was just for himself. A reward for working so hard.

CHAPTER 5

Mood, January 2021

The 'Do or Die' moment had arrived, the countdown to the house vote, occupying every conversation in every household in the nation. Dorothy Thompson, as Rebecca Sanders, was writing daily articles, concentrating on the fight against bribing Republican house officers to give the swing states to Trump. Most Democrats were fearful of that outcome. They were not aware of the secret defence already planned, so they concentrated on how they could get away with a paramilitary attack to kill some Republican House officers who would cast the state votes. There was lots of talk, but people weren't quite ready to shoot anyone, but the conversation was dangerous.

*　　*　　*

Argus-E was observing this bunfight with great interest. He realised immediately that the outcome would determine the danger for his tribes. A Trump win would in his mind lead to vastly increasing infection numbers. And Trump's 'America First' attitude would probably also hurt trade with India. But he had some confidence that Dorothy Thompson's Supreme Court defence would win the day if it were needed. His mischievous side wished she would stop being so nice all the time, and he sent her an email inviting her to cut loose and be strong in her opinions. Tough and brutal if need be.

*   *   *

Dorothy, as Rebecca Sanders, summed up the mood in Washington when she wrote:

> This town lives and breathes tension. There are only two topics of conversation: the cold weather, and whether the Republican house officers selected to cast their state vote to Trump or Biden would follow party lines giving Trump victory. Or if they would preserve democracy and allow the votes to stand.
>
> This is a do-or-die moment, with the cinemas showing movies to reflect the atmosphere. They went over the top, showing Apocalypse, Deep Impact, Twister, and all the pandemic movies ever made including, 'Train to Busan.' They seem to be working from the principle: 'If they want horror, we'll give them what they want.'
>
> The talk at breakfast and dinner tables is about one thing only; across the nation, at bus stops, church and even funerals: will they persuade the Republican voting officers to pass a vote, or will they throw democracy to the wind and reinstate Trump? The only interruption to this talk is kids asking to go to McDonald's, watching TV or a DVD. The broad spectrum of the national conversation has been subsumed to this one topic and everything that went with it. Such as: who

has the guts to tell those officers what has to be done, are the officers scared, and what are they most afraid of? Being shot by a sniper rifle, being mobbed, being lynched? Or what they will say to their wives and friends?

Just so you know my thoughts. I normally report what happened and leave my opinion out of my articles. It's what good reporters do. But it's time to shake so many of you out your cocoon of self-satisfied beliefs. This is the slippery slope to dictatorship, and you, the people and the state officers will bear the blame for what would happen if this insidious attempt to destroy democracy is allowed to continue. You will be responsible, so get your act together, and advise your representatives of your stand on this matter. Not next year, now.

The outcome will have a dramatic effect on the pandemic. The Republicans will oppose lockdowns that could stop the spread but benefit the economy. Until they all died, maybe? This is despite the importation of the new, much more infectious strain from the UK, so infectious that daily new UK cases have doubled in a week. The Republicans think the vote is for the party, but in reality, it is a vote for the country to survive this new mutation and other possible ones to follow.

Rebecca Sanders, Washington Post

Dorothy wondered why she was even trying to educate people, meaning Republicans, of course, and she turned to Michael.

'Honey, I need a cuddle', said Dorothy.

'And why is that? Cuddles don't come cheap, you know,' teased Michael.

'I get so worked up trying to write articles that should affect how Republicans, or rather Trump supporters and Senators, treat the pandemic. My aim had been to educate people but it's having no effect. What should I do?'

Michael grinned a wicked smile as he thought of a wicked solution.

'Honey, you know that saying: "Doing the same thing over and over and expecting a different result is not a sign of intelligence"? But before you hit me, I'm not saying you are not intelligent, just that you need to do something different.'

'Like what? I'm still trying to get them to behave differently,' replied Dorothy.

Michael corrected her with, 'I think that if instead of trying to get them to see your point of view, you could try to show them how stupid their behaviour is.'

He continued, 'try this one: Congratulations to all Trump supporters. You are just wonderful. I had no idea that it would be so easy to get rid of democracy. You are so clever, saying that the election was stolen. You will go down in history as the first people to solve a massive social problem, now recorded in the Guinness Book of Records.'

Dorothy burst into laughter, or was she crying? Both. She was crying with happiness.

'I'm going to publish that under a new name, not the Sanders name, I need to preserve that stern admonisher of correct public behaviour. How about "Nicky Palinitski" or something not quite so like Sarah Palin,' and she howled with laughter again.

Dorothy dried her eyes and took a deep breath. *Time to go to bed* thought Dorothy as she called Michael.

'Darling, I need one of those cuddles that don't come cheap. I don't care what they cost. I do not want to think about anything except my own hero. Quick, before I lose my temper.'

January 3

Rebecca Sanders had, of course, invited readers to write in and comment, and in the meantime, decided to comment on Trump's call to Brad Raffensperger[17], Georgia's Secretary of State. Trump repeatedly urged Raffensperger to alter the outcome of the Presidential vote in the state. This was one big doozy she intended to do a job on after obtaining the transcript of the hour-long conversation. She started her commentary with:

The following is the EXACT transcript of Trump's words. Incoherent but the true words of Donald Trump, and my comments will follow it.

> **Trump**: and if we could just go over some of the numbers, I think it's pretty clear that we won. We won very substantially in Georgia. You even see it by rally size, frankly. We'd be getting 25-30,000 people a rally, and the competition would get less than 100 people. And it never made sense.
>
> But we have a number of things. We have at least 2 or 3 — anywhere from 250-300,000 ballots were dropped mysteriously into the rolls. Much of that had to do with Fulton County, which hasn't been checked. We think that if you check the signatures — a real check of the signatures

---

17   Here is the full transcript and audio of the call between Trump and Raffensperger

going back in Fulton County, you'll find at least a couple of hundred thousand of forged signatures of people who have been forged. We are quite sure that's going to happen.

Rebecca Sanders' comments: We have an egomaniac who boasts that he got 30,000 people to his rallies and thought that meant he won. The irresponsible idiot is playing havoc with public health. Biden had ASKED his supporters to stay home or come in cars to protect the country. The different approach taken by two leaders to address public health.

She prepared her bulletin addition:

> Then Trump claims that anywhere from 250-300,000 ballots were dropped mysteriously into the rolls. If they were mysteriously dropped in, then how does he know that they had been dropped in, and who did it? The Post should offer a million dollars to anyone who can provide absolute proof of that.
>
> What sort of dope are his advisers on? Certainly hallucinating, I'd say. The electoral officers had been so meticulous that Trump's own lawyers said there had been no reports of fraud. Maybe they should sue Trump for defamation of their integrity as soon as Trump has lost. Please send us your thoughts.
>
> Rebecca Sanders, Washington Post

The responses were coming fast and furious, and Rebecca published the first few before writing her own daily issue.

Nathan Walker's was the first one she picked:

Dear Washington Post, I must strongly object to your partisan approach to all this. Blind Freddy can see that Trump won. I went to the rallies, and it's like the hallelujah trail. The numbers, my God, compare that with the miserly 100 Biden got and people in cars not getting out to spread the message. Wimps. We don't want a wimp for President, no Sirree.

Then the 200,000 ballots that were secretly tossed in – who knows where they came from? Are you really that stupid to think we would not fight that? And on January 6, I am helping with a mass demonstration. I'm hoping we can get half a million outside the Capitol to hear us when they vote. Strength through numbers.

Nathan Luke Walker, Chattanooga, Tennessee

The next item she printed was from General Christopher Paul Roberts, a prominent Republican, who wrote:

Dear Ms Sanders,

I am a Republican and was distressed to read your article on Trump's attempt to sway Brad Raffensperger, Georgia's Secretary of State, to throw away decency and commit a crime. I remind all party officials that you made an oath when you received your commission. Remember that if you publicly state you no longer honour that oath, we will strip you of your commission.

I publicly support any investigations into irregularities, but they need witnesses who will swear to that or face ten years jail if found to be false.

General Roberts, Dallas, Texas.

The next day Dorothy had heard that the news of the Trump phone call to Georgia's Secretary of State had gone viral in Congress. She decided to write about one particularly nasty aspect of the call; the threatening nature to turn a state official who had already declared Georgia for Biden two weeks earlier. In the national interest, she decided to elaborate and quote directly from the transcript:

Dear readers, the following is an EXACT transcript from President Trump addressing Brad Raffensperger. They are not my words, so please excuse the clumsy language.

> 'Another tremendous number. We're going to have an accurate number over the next two days with certified accountants. But an accurate number — and that's people that went to vote, and they were told they can't vote because they've already been voted for. It's a very sad thing. They walked out complaining. But the number's large. We'll have it for you. But it's much more than the number of 11,779 that's — The current margin is only 11,779. Brad, I think you agree with that, right? That's something I think everyone — at least that's a number that everyone agrees on.'

Dear readers, it seems Trump has made statements using all sorts of numbers. First, it was 250-300,000 to make his claim of electoral fraud. I remind you all. The numbers don't matter. What matters is that a loser is trying to force elected officials to lie and commit fraud. Is he attempting to blackmail Raffensperger? Blackmail should lead to criminal charges and instant impeachment, and if it's not blackmail but just filthy politics, then I want readers to know that Trump could do the same to anyone else including you.

Rebecca Sanders, Washington Post

Dorothy next described the uproar in Congress, and how despite that, almost all Republicans vowed to do everything they could to secure a Trump victory. She quoted from a Washington Post article by Philip Rucker and Josh Dawsey[18]:

> A last-ditch effort by President Trump and his allies to overturn the election thrust Washington into chaos on Saturday as a growing coalition of Republican senators announced plans to prevent the vote count to be submitted for approval.
>
> That is all but certain to fail when Congress gathers in joint session on Wednesday to count electoral college votes previously certified by each state. Still, Trump continues to press Republican lawmakers to support his baseless claims of election fraud. He is calling on his supporters to fill the streets of the nation's capital on Wednesday in a mass protest of his defeat.'
>
> Now, my own opinion on the matter. Why? I have a job to do, and that is to ensure you, the American people, really understand the insidious nature of the Republican war machine trying to destroy democracy. They are like the Grim Reaper cutting a swathe though long held principles of democracy and throwing them to the winds.

---

[18]   A growing number of Trump loyalists in the Senate vow to challenge Biden's victory

Is this really any different than treason? Treason is cause for shooting without trial during war, and this is war. But, please, don't take the law into your hands. Just frighten the living daylights out of those who are considering such treason.

How enlightening is that? Rebecca wondered. She had a few more choice words to say, especially after getting a call from the White House Press Secretary asking to write positive news items about Donald Trump, but instead she went on to quote an article by Martin Chulov,[19] Middle East Correspondent for The Guardian:

Despite the pandemic, the business of government must go on, including National Security. It was a time of greater threat for attacks from adversaries wanting to take advantage of the weakness caused by an in-limbo administration and the pandemic.

Concerns have increased in Tehran over the past week - that the US President could authorise a strike against Iran. He has been itching to beat Iran for four long years and the Iranian government knew it.

On Thursday, the Iranian Foreign Minister, Mohammad Javad Zarif, accused Trump of constructing a pretext to attack as the clock winds down on his sole term in office. Zarif's remarks followed the presence of two US B-52 bombers in the region earlier this week, and an aircraft carrier redeployed to the Indian Ocean.

Rebecca commented and added context to her report.

---

[19] Iran fears Trump preparing attack in final weeks in office

The background to this is that Iran knew that Trump failed in his bid to win a Nobel Peace Prize for brokering a peace deal with North Korea. Iran had been a thorn in Trump's side for four long years, and knew he would love nothing better than to leave it in a pile of ashes.

What really matters here is that Trump could not give two hoots if he left the whole Middle East in flames, as long as he beats Iran. He wants a legacy.

It is truly dangerous that Biden is not invited to security briefings, and the Republicans should inform him regardless of Trump's wishes. Their jobs won't transfer to the new administration team, so even getting sacked is not a problem, probably more a badge of honour.

I reiterate that the fight is party vs. party, but the result determines how the pandemic is handled and how many lives are lost. It could be the lives of your father or mother, or even your son or daughter.

Rebecca Sanders, Washington Post

Dorothy took a deep breath. She had enough of trawling through over-the-top news items saying all the same things. Dorothy remembered the fun she had with Michael when she was distressed at not cutting through with her articles and wondered if General Roberts could be coaxed in to being funny, so she called him. After the usual pleasantries, she got to the point.

'General, I need your help. I have just posted an article about Trump's refusal to include Biden in security briefings, and my article is ever so predictable, saying all the right things. I need to lampoon the whole idea that the new President should be informed. I want to do it under a different name. What would you suggest?'

'How about something really ridiculous. You could write that Donald Trump had suggested that we send Biden to Iran to get briefed by the Iranians, and that whilst he sat it, he should tell them how many nukes we have. Then we can sit back and wait for furious responses from the White House denying any such suggestions.'

'General, if I'm not careful I'll wet myself, and so will half of America. You must have learned the art of being stupid in school, or did it develop when you were married?' asked Dorothy.

'It happened when I was married to my first wife,' he replied, and they both broke out in laughter.

Rebecca, focused and serious once more, revisited the uproar in Congress, where almost all Republicans manoeuvred to secure a Trump victory. *Well, good luck with that*, she thought and decided that the bigger picture was that the whole democratic process wasn't just whittled down. It was thrown away and erased from Republican consciousness. She quoted from CNN's Gregory Krieg[20]:

> The scattershot efforts to overturn President-elect Joe Biden's election victory are coalescing into a movement led by top Republicans determined to exploit a manufactured crisis for broader political gains.

---

[20] Republican efforts to undermine Biden victory expose growing anti-democratic streak

Nearly a dozen more GOP senators, some soon to be sworn-in on Sunday, have now announced they will challenge Biden's Electoral College win over President Donald Trump next week. Their gambit is doomed to fail; they have acknowledged as much in its immediate objective, but likely to succeed only in fuelling the conspiracy theories making the rounds.

That is the end of Krieg's report and now I plead with the state senators. If you obstruct the will of the people, you may wonder at all those ArmaLite-carrying idiots who would have you in their sights. Be the leader that you were elected to be and stand up to Trump to save your souls and our country by preserving democracy.

Rebecca Sanders, Washington Post

Dorothy had enough of other people's articles or reports and decided to call her friends the Andersons in Washington and the Orthallos in Oregon. She connected to Michelle first. Michelle is as smart as they come. Her husband James is a Clinical Psychologist.

Michelle was the first to speak. 'I am so furious about Trump's call for mass protests. The insanity of it, now with this much more infectious strain making the rounds. I want that man castrated; take away his manhood if they can find it under all those rolls of fat. That might lose their fascination with their hero. Nothing else seems to work, least of all the truth. I bet you President Xi Jinping has guests every night where they see who can ridicule Trump the most. But that doesn't help you, does it?' ended Michelle.

Dorothy responded, 'What is Trump's most glaring fault we need to explore and expose?' Michelle being Michelle, public health lecturer first and foremost, snaps to attention.

'I've got it, Dorothy, an absolute doozy. Do you know what happens when you throw petrol on a fire? I know you do, but put it this way, and you see what I'm up to. Petrol multiplies the effect of the fire. There are three issues about Trump's response to COVID-19 that we should combine to make a massive blast.'

'One is the handling of the virus by America, ignoring the advice from the World Health Organisation. Another is Trump's attempts to convince the world the virus was manufactured in a lab in Wuhan, and the third is Trump's refusal to order a large quantity of the vaccines developed here.'

Dorothy wanted the dirt about the accusation the virus was manufactured in a laboratory, and Michelle had the details. She said:

'Dorothy, there are several reports, and I will mention them briefly, but remember it does not matter so much how it was created, but how we handled it. Trump is basing his statements on the report by The Guardian,[21]. They made unfounded claims based on a Chinese virologist[22], where she claimed she believed COVID-19 COULD have been "conveniently created" within a lab setting. Notice the emphasis on could. She did not have proof and offered her opinion on work done with the SARS virus, not COVID-19.

---

[21] Trump claims to have evidence coronavirus started in a Chinese lab but offers no details

[22] Chinese defector Dr Li-Meng Yan. She had published a report claiming COVID-19 was made in a lab

And then there is America's standing in the world now.[23] The Lowy Institute reported that what is most striking about the current moment is not that the United States failed the world at a critical time: what matters is that the world, by and large, did not even look to Washington as the crisis hit.'

'Wow, you know that stuff, but I guess it's your vocation, but still, so useful,' said Dorothy, 'I can create a report based on that which highlights the irresponsible approach to anything Trump has done, how he ignored the best advice, military and health. I will weave in a bit of the hasty withdrawal from Afghanistan into my story. As well as his bunfights with Iran, against all advice.'

Dorothy thanked Michelle and wrote her article on the 'Growing number of Trump loyalists in the Senate vow to challenge Biden's victory', this time concentrating on the call to mass demonstrations.

Dorothy wrote about the pandemic choice using her nom de plume, and then, quoting again from the article by Philip Rucker and Josh Dawsey in the Post:

> This is not just a choice between one President and another. Not just a fight between Republicans or Democrats. It's a choice of how the pandemic will be handled. This is a much more serious choice now that the UK strain, twice as infectious, has spread through the US. Donald Trump and the Republicans have always resisted lockdowns and resorted to violence and violent protest if it ever was imposed, whereas the Democrats want to stop the spread.

---

[23] The age in which American missionary moral language bolstered by economic and military dominance is now past.

You need to remember how Trump had criticised China for making the virus in a lab, blaming China for exporting the pandemic. This is from a man who has not acted to stop importing the virus from overseas and has not acted to stop its spread, instead prevented measures to stop it and blamed China for his problems.

To put this in perspective, after a few weeks of a cover-up by the Chinese communist party, they locked down 50 million people in the Wuhan area to stop the spread. For months. In the end, they had 3,000 deaths and 80,000 cases after one year. Hello, compare the mighty USA effort. Three thousand deaths DAILY one year later, and over 200,000 new cases a day, rapidly increasing.

With one quarter of China's population, the USA now has 21 million cases and 365,600 deaths, or 1000 times the cases and 500 times more deaths per million citizens. Ladies and gentlemen: that is the choice; pick someone who will not do this to you.

Trump continues to press Republican lawmakers to support his baseless claims of election fraud whilst calling on thousands of supporters to fill the streets of the nation's capital on Wednesday in mass protest of his defeat.

What is the purpose of that? This is Trump trying to make so much noise in the street outside the Capitol that senators would be reluctant to come out after the vote if Trump lost. Will the demonstrators be armed?

Then she added a new post:

> Trump has pressured Georgia Governor Brian Kemp on many fronts in December. Trump also asked the Governor to demand an audit of signatures on mail ballots, something Kemp has previously noted he has no power to do. Kemp had declined the President's request.
>
> How must Kemp feel with this new vote coming up and Trump getting his hordes of rifle-carrying supporters roaming the streets and threatening violence? The Georgia State Police Commissioner should declare mass rallies illegal. Additionally, carrying rifles in the street should be an offence with a $2000 on the spot fine.
>
> Commissioner Mark W. McDonough is the Chief Executive of the Department of Public Safety and holds the rank of Colonel in the Georgia State Patrol. The Commissioner needs to set up solid security. The police hate crowds carrying guns, let alone rifles that should only be allowed in war.
>
> But I would be happy to see 5,000 Trump supporters break the law at $2000 apiece and get fined. Even if they have no bullets in their magazines as far as I'm concerned. Ten million dollars into the strained police coffers. Mind you, the only way to enforce that is to have the death penalty for killing a police officer doing his duty.
>
> Rebecca Sanders, Washington Post

That's it for the day, thought Dorothy, and signed off.

January 4

Later that day, Dorothy read the article in The Guardian about weapons being prohibited[24] for the inauguration on January 20. Washington DC Mayoress Muriel Bowser had requested hundreds of National Guard members to help marshal protests expected around Joe Biden's inauguration. She wanted the same protection notices issued for Georgia for January 5 and 6.

She quoted The Guardian for the Washington DC protection now arranged for the capital for the congressional votes.

> The US capital has mobilised the National Guard ahead of planned protests by Donald Trump supporters in the lead-up to the congressional vote to affirm Joe Biden's election victory.
>
> Trump's supporters are planning to rally on Tuesday and Wednesday, seeking to bolster the President's unproven claims of widespread voter fraud.
>
> DC police have posted signs throughout downtown, warning that carrying any firearm is illegal. Acting Police Chief, Robert Contee, asked residents to alert authorities of anyone who might be armed. 'There are people intent on coming to our city armed,' Contee said on Monday.

Dorothy then added her own wishes for the protests, as follows:

> According to a US defence official, Bowser requested to have Guard members on the streets from Tuesday to Thursday to help with the

[24] Trump protesters were warned not to carry guns as Washington DC calls up National **Guard**

protests. The official said the additional forces would be used for traffic control and other assistance, but they will not be armed or wearing body armour. *How useful will that be?* There were strict arms control notices posted around the Capitol prohibiting any firearms between Monday, January 4 and Thursday, January 7.

Whilst the attempt to have the National Guard unarmed seemed to be aimed at avoiding violence, I urge the authorities to have a backup plan. Trump supporters have shown scant regard for the law in the past. It would be dangerous to have this volatile situation become a police issue.

Would you like to know how I feel about all of this? I'm irate. I'm irate that a reporter has to try to arrange security. It's the job of this government that is still too afraid to go against Trump. I hope the Capitol Police is listening. Are you willing to protect this state, or would you like to resign now?

Unless you issue a message of a real deterrent, there will be rifles and shooting. Please consider a notice that if firearms are carried, then the military would come and get you. These idiots must be made aware of the consequences.

Dorothy Thompson, Washington Post

Dorothy signed off and waited for the fallout from that notice, and it arrived later that day.

Nathan Walker wrote in with this message:

To the Post.

Who do you think you are to suggest that they send in the army if we carry firearms? It's my constitutional right to bear arms. It says so in the Constitution, in case you don't know. I have two handguns and a military-style rifle. If you think you can scare us, go ahead but don't bet your life on it. We are the ones protecting a legitimately won election that those Democrat bastards are stealing. We may even follow you home when you leave the Washington Post one day. Not meaning to scare you, of course.

Nathan Walker Chattanooga, TN

January 5 2021

General CP Roberts saw this article, and he decided to respond. Not to calm down this hothead alone, but all others like him. He wrote:

This letter is in reply to that by Mr Walker. I am a retired Army General. I have led men into battle and killed enemy soldiers whilst carrying our wounded soldiers back behind the lines. Killing is not a pleasure but sometimes a necessity. Keeping firearms out of mass protests is a necessity, and these days drones do a marvellous job of identifying people and the weapons they carry. If you or your friends are armed, you will be found and dealt with. And if you raise your rifles at the guards, you will be shot. It's a necessity.

General CP Roberts, retired, Dallas.

Dorothy sent this to press and decided it was time to watch what was happening in the Senate run-offs, which promised to be a two-week-long drawn-out affair if the Democrats won. All hell would break loose, with more triple recounts and quadruple lawsuits. In other words, par for the course.

Blew Ohrtman also replied. This is what he said:

Dear Post,

I think it's time you learned to appreciate President Trump the way I do. Just so you don't go all democratic on me, let me list his achievements:

He tackled China's trade imbalance. Those Chinks sell us their stuff and become strong and don't buy our goods, and we become weaker, and Trump makes America Great Again. I've listed these achievements nice and neat for you to see.

a. He cancelled that ridiculous Iran nuclear deal. It was full of loopholes; no certainty they would stick to their promise not to build the bomb.
b. He wanted to cancel that disastrous and expensive Obamacare plan; can't wait.
c. He's bringing our troops home. No one else has since the war in Afghanistan started.
d. He's making sure those greenies don't stop coal-fired power stations; cheapest electricity around.
e. He's curbed those nutcases at the Environmental Protection Agency. Those are our rivers; they don't belong to the EPA.
f. He stopped China dumping cheap aluminium in our country, putting our workers out of jobs.

So you had better remember what is good for America before you blast off at our best ever President.

Blew Ohrtman, Ohio

The following letter received was from a German politician acting on behalf of Angela Merkel, a Dr Hausmeister. He had been following the Trump Election defeat with glee and was hoping to improve relations with the US now. He had written:

Dear Ms Thompson,

I wish to congratulate you on your objective reporting. If we were ever to meet, I could offer you a blueprint for a better election process, but it would only echo your own thoughts, I imagine. Here in Germany, our processes were updated by the American Marshall Plan during your occupation after Hitler's defeat, and we are grateful for that, I can tell you.

It is a shame that a once-great nation has become the laughing stock of the world during President (not-elected) Trump's tenure. We look forward to massively improved relations with the US as undoubtedly do most other nations.

The only recollection I have of adoration by a large number of people for an unsuitable leader is unfortunately only from my own country, who shall remain nameless so that I don't inflame your partisan readers.

Dr Rudolph Hausmeister, Interior Minister, Berlin, Germany

The day ended with more letters, some pro-Trump, others anti-Trump. A Nation Divided.

CHAPTER 6

5 January

Argus E could monitor Dorothy Thompson's thoughts pretty well to know what was going on in the States. She wanted to thump Trump because of the need to get on with pandemic planning and public health. The daily conversation needed to change to the pandemic rather than always about Trump. There is also the question of prosecuting rioters, and fortunately, the FBI has been using their devices to record and identify the main culprits. To Argus's mind, the mob needs to know that they didn't get away with it. He hopes Dorothy will take up the issue.

*　　*　　*

Dorothy Thompson woke and decided she would witness events at the Capitol. A must, especially after believing that the security around the Capitol would be inadequate.

The day before, she had quoted The Guardian for the Washington DC protection - now arranged for the Capitol for the congressional votes, and read:

> The US Capitol has mobilised the National Guard ahead of planned protests by Donald

Trump supporters. Those supporters plan to rally on Tuesday and Wednesday, seeking to bolster the President's unproven widespread voter election fraud claims.

The Washington DC police have posted signs throughout downtown warning that carrying any sort of firearms is illegal. Contee said on Monday 'There are people intent on coming to our city armed.'

Then Dorothy prepared notes for a later article that read:

The news showed no signs of forceful protection. Several hundred National Guards would act as traffic wardens, and signs indicated that firearms were prohibited. Well, that's nice to know. I hope they can read. It looks like a paper tiger to me, but let's see what actually happens.

She also recorded her views for the protests in her journal, not for publication, as follows:

To me, that means the protesters can run amok.

There were strict arms control notices posted around the Capitol prohibiting any firearms between January 4 and 7. *Hallelujah, that will keep us safe, won't it? What good is that?* These idiots must be made aware of the consequences.

6 January

When Dorothy arrived at the Capitol, all her worst fears were confirmed. No one was wearing masks either, and she secretly hoped they would all gasp their last breaths during COVID-induced terror.

She thought the lack of security for the Capitol was criminal. Heads will roll. Well, they should. The marshals who were present seemed more intent on staying out of trouble than preventing entry to the perimeter.

Pro-Trump protesters stormed the U.S. Capitol[25] Wednesday breaking through several layers of police barriers. The Capitol was placed on lockdown and surrounding buildings were evacuated. There must have been over 50,000 supporters present.

When protesters breached the doors of the Capitol and swarmed in, Dorothy knew that everything had gone to shit. There was no security, the US Congress was stormed by fuckwits, and no one was there to stop it.

The Washington Post had already noted that Trump's critics have warned that his scorched-earth effort to invalidate the election outcome amounts to the first attempted coup d'état in U.S. history [26].

Time to go home and stay safe, she thought.

Dorothy went to work, where she had multiple media feeds to help her get the real story.

She got to her office in time to see the last Trump speech, where he incited supporters to march on the Capitol. Cause for impeachment, surely.

Trump needed to be removed from office this day for inciting a mob of 50,000 idiots not wearing masks, allowing the new UK strain of the virus to run rampant.

---

[25]   Protesters storm Capitol building, woman shot

[26]   With brazen assault on election, Trump prompts critics to warn of a coup

---

Daily cases in the UK had doubled from 30,000 in November to over 60,000 now and expect to top out near 85,000. That was whilst most of the UK was in lockdown, for Gods' sake.

She called her husband Michael, asking him, 'Michael darling, I need your help to kill off the remaining Trump presidency days. I want him in an asylum. Have you watched what's happening?' she asked.

'Honey, we are all working in the common room with the TV playing. We are gobsmacked. I saw your article yesterday where you were dubious about the security arrangements, and I thought you were over the top, but you weren't strong enough. Go and turn on the TV and watch the mob trashing the Congress building and walking out with Nancy Pelosi's lectern and some computers. For fucks sake, they contain confidential secrets. And the police stand by, staying out of trouble. End of career for them. How can I help?' he asked.

'Well, just to let you know, there will be a Post article by you know who tomorrow. Now I need advice on what would constitute incapacity to act so that I can get him removed. Out of office, his Facebook and Twitter accounts blocked. Because of the large number, like over 50,000, running around spreading the virus, and if just one of them carried the new UK or African strain, then we are in for a doomsday scenario.'

Dorothy continued: 'I need to know whom I need to talk to in order to get Trump impeached, and as an expert in National Health, you would know the effect of fifty thousand unmasked idiots close to each other spread the new super infectious strains of the virus.'

'Honey, you need to find a Constitutional lawyer to assist in the Trump impeachment question and concentrate on the pandemic,' advised Michael.

'OK, Thanks. I'll run with that. See you tonight,' said Dorothy as she called off.

Her first job was to contact General Christopher Paul Roberts. Her thinking was that there would be civil war if a Democrat proposed impeachment. It needed to be done by a Republican. So she called him.

'General, this is Dorothy Thompson, also writing as Rebecca Sanders. Is it a suitable time to talk with you now?' she asked. It was.

'My dear Ms Thompson, I have enjoyed your column and how you invite comments from both sides. Trump certainly looks like a candidate for the asylum today. I look forward to whatever you have in mind. I know it could be a doozy,' was his response.

'Well, General, I don't know your thoughts on this, and I hope you don't find it distasteful. I want to engineer a Trump impeachment and think the country would go up in flames if a Democrat initiated this. My reason is to stop a push by Trump for a 2024 election run and to stop him hindering the vaccine rollout. What's your thoughts on that?' she asked.

'You are one forward-looking schemer, my dear,' said the General. 'I had not thought of that before, but if he is around in 2024, then he will destroy the Republicans if they don't choose him. I will initiate this, but keep you informed. How would that work for you?'

'Great, then I can get on with my main aim about stopping the spread of the pandemic, Trump's legacy. My husband is a lecturer in Public Health, and he is terrified,' replied Dorothy.

'That is certainly best if I handle the work with the lawyers and leave the Washington Post squiggly clean,' suggested General Roberts, and they agreed to proceed along those lines.

7 January

The morning papers was saturated with news of the day before. All about the riots at the Capitol. The first item she saw was about the storming of the Capitol[27] It covered the violent protest, one woman shot, and Facebook had removed all Trump posts, and deleted and blocked his Facebook and Twitter accounts.

Every man and his dog was trying to outdo one another in describing the chaos, what should happen to the Capitol Police, what should happen to Trump, and to his supporters. There was nothing for her to add. It had all been repeated ad nauseum.

Time for a coffee.

*　　*　　*

General Roberts got back to Dorothy shortly after. The question of impeachment is a vexed one, and he called Dorothy to discuss it.

'Good morning Ms Thompson. Do you have time for the impeachment question now?' asked General Roberts. She did, and the General spoke.

'I spoke to many people about this. I also read this morning's article by the Post on the chaos in the Capitol,[28] and I have three options: impeachment, removal from office, and get him to resign, with the last being the quickest but unlikely. But let's look at the purpose. What is your number one priority?'

Dorothy replied with an answer that General Roberts was not expecting.

---

[27]　US Capitol secure after violent protest, occupation, bombs, shots

[28]　Chaos at the Capitol – Washington Post

She said, 'Number one is that he must not interfere with the necessary pandemic measures. There must be no delay in all the logistics of getting the vaccine into people's arms. All Trump ever did was saying "don't worry - go to work". This dangerous advice has to stop. Now.'

'My second priority is to see him held accountable for so many of his criminal actions. The third is that we want to make sure he does not rise again. What if he decided to run for the lower house. No one would ever get a word in. It would be like the first election debate.'

Then she lost it and shouted: 'There he will be, talking over everyone, even the speaker, who throws him out, so he fires the speaker, and when that doesn't work, he just enters the house and refuses to leave. I want him smite, combusted, and converted to carbon dioxide!'

General Roberts was impressed and said, 'What I like about your response is the fact that you are more interested in getting the country's health under control than pursuing a personal vendetta, and that last bit hits hard. Would you like to talk about the Pandemic now, and I can see if I can help with that as well?' Dorothy was ready.

'General, this new UK strain is a monster. I'll summarise it:

In the UK, cases were running at 15,000 daily in November,

they went to 32,000 daily infections with 500 deaths by Christmas,

and surged to 62,000 daily cases and 1,000 deaths by January 7.

'This UK strain is now here in the United States. That's four weeks to double from November to December, but only two weeks to double again from Christmas to now. And, the UK was in almost complete lockdown. How long will it take to double again? One week? Even less?'

Dorothy continued: 'What I need to know is how long it would take to race through the US so that I can warn our citizens. TV is a "Breaking News" type of ten-second gabfest that does not inform, but people need to read the papers to see what it all means. That's my job, to inform them. It's my mission to make sure everyone is aware of what is happening.'

The General replied, 'My dear, you remind me of Xena the Princess Warrior, the one in the TV series - going at it hammer and tongs. Why is this not covered by the media now?'

'They are all busy with Trump and stolen election stories. We need to change the conversation, and that won't happen if all the news is about Trump,' said Dorothy, and General Roberts suggested she call Terry Balzarini, a virologist. He would be able to help with the pandemic question.

Dorothy contacted Terry to help her understand mutations. Terry had left indefinitely to escape the chaos, but people still working in his lab were able to help Dorothy and sent her an extract from an article on the UK strain spreading in the US[29] now.

That lady had understood that Dorothy was not a virologist. Still, she needed to understand the basics for her audience, and she sent her an article, titled 'January 5 New Covid Strain Spreading Across US - What We Know.' It was fairly detailed and suitable for health care professionals who needed to understand the mechanics of the spread, and Dorothy extracted the essentials for her audience:

---

[29] New COVID Strain Spreading Across US - What We Know

Viruses such as Covid and SARS that encode their genome in RNA, a simpler version of DNA, tend to pick up mutations quickly as they are copied rapidly inside their hosts and prone to making errors.

There are 23 changes in the UK mutation, which seems to have made it 70 per cent more transmissible and therefore able to spread much faster.

Dorothy wonders: *Is it possible that you get this when many infected people are close together? If it is, then the protestors are up shit creek.*

Later that day, Dorothy called the Virology lab again and asked why the search for the initial source of the virus was so important.[30] She read the report, quite a few pages long, but what it boiled down to was this:

The Covid virus is just like an animal virus we would expect to see in wild bat populations. Similar viruses have jumped between non-human animals in the past, so I see no reason to speculate how it happened.

Dorothy thought, *this would be of interest to anyone who blames China for the pandemic, but the main interest for me is how we dealt with it.*

If they could prove this jump from a bat to another animal before human infection, that could explain how the virus made it from the Chinese province of Yunnan. Over there, scientists found its closest relative some time ago in Wuhan, in Hubei province, more than 1,000 miles away.

But a key question remains: What, and where, was the intermediary animal?

---

[30]   Why the search for the first origin of the coronavirus is a global concern

Dorothy condensed this from the previous reference for her audience as follows:

> Viruses have jumped from non-human animals to other animal species in the past, so this is possible for COVID-19 as well. To help with research, scientists need to know the intermediate animal that infected the first human. That would allow them to plan future defences. But Trump only wanted to prove that the virus was manufactured in a lab in China. For political purposes, of course.

8 January

Dorothy now had some material, but she was not ready to use it. She returned to the question of holding Trump accountable for the massive loss of life in the US. She called General Roberts again:

'Good afternoon, General, are you free to talk?' she asked.

He replied, 'Ms Thompson, what's on your mind? The Trump failure to manage the pandemic?'

Dorothy replied: 'Yes, General, Trump has failed to manage the pandemic, but he has also conditioned the nation to ignore it with sayings like, "Drink some of that disinfectant" or, "It's just the flu with some extras added on, less deadly than the Spanish flu". He also made it sound like that happened during World War Two and how it got fixed when America joined the fight in 1942, the ignorant ignoramus. It so happens the Spanish Flu happened in 1918, not World War Two. What scares me is whether a more infections strain could run through the world like that Spanish monster. It had 500 million infections and 50 million deaths. We need a protocol for future worse scenarios. But what I would like from you now is your opinion on how we can hold him responsible for all those deaths.'

General Roberts had also done his homework. He had seen that the FBI had been taking photos on their tablets. He gleefully told Dorothy:

'The FBI had put a name on so many protesters using their digital devices fitted with facial recognition software. Jail is awaiting. Some could lose their houses to pay fines that Trump won't pay, would that dampen the enthusiasm for more protests? This may be as effective as shutting down Trump, especially if you suggest in your paper that it is Trump's fault and he won't be paying them.'

'I'm looking forward now to the Supreme Court disallowing Trump from pardoning himself. Then I look forward to you writing the stories on those court cases, which will not have the financial support from his supporters to pay for lawyers. That is holding Trump accountable,' said the General.

They smiled at each other like the conspirators they were. On the phone they could hear the smiles in their voices. They called off, and Dorothy decided to collect material from the news items available for the next day. She had fixed everything that needed fixing now, and it was time to put the nail in the coffin.

The first read produced a bit of schadenfreude. Sidney Powell was being sued. *Hooray.* Attorney Sidney Powell spoke during a November 19 news conference with Rudolph W. Giuliani, the lawyer for President Trump, about lawsuits contesting the Presidential election results.

Dominion Voting Systems filed a defamation lawsuit against lawyer Sidney Powell, demanding more than $1.3 billion in damages[31] for the havoc it says Powell caused by spreading 'wild' and 'demonstrably false allegations, including that Dominion played a central role in a fantastical scheme to steal the 2020 election from President Trump.' *That should help accountability.*

Dorothy's next read was scary too. The Cabinet was fearful that Trump would initiate war with Iran.[32] Daniel Ellsberg had written:

> 'I fear he may incite something far more dangerous in the next few days: his long-desired war with Iran.'

Then she read that a B-52's nonstop round-trip from North Dakota had been directed to the Iranian coast, a provocation. In November, the President had to be dissuaded at the highest levels from leading an unprovoked attack on Iran nuclear facilities.

*　　*　　*

Argus E had picked up on the Ellsberg article too. If Trump attacked Iran and it got bad, would he nuke Tehran? The radiation fallout would hit the waters running off the Himalayas and poison the water for India and Bangladesh. Surely he wouldn't, would he? But if Iran had a bomb and were prepared to use it, retaliation would be immediate, and the world as he knew would cease to exist. Stock markets crash, finance dried up, fear running every decision, isolationist. God help us. He had better not mention it anywhere. It might give rise to copycat acts.

*　　*　　*

---

[31]　. Dominion sues pro-Trump lawyer Sidney Powell, seeking more than $1.3 billion

[32]　Donald Trump's parting gift to the world - It may be war with Iran

We need to stop this man now, thought Dorothy. Her next research article by Joanna Walters was right up her alley too:

> Alaska Senator Lisa Murkowsk[33] this afternoon asked for Donald Trump to be removed from the Presidency immediately. If the Republican party cannot separate itself from Trump, she isn't sure she has a future with the party.'

Great, it's a start; to stop him.

Dorothy's next read was from the Washington Post, which read,

> In the wake of Wednesday's siege, Capitol Police Chief Steven Sund planned to resign, and Congressional lawmakers vowed to investigate.

The last items of interest for Dorothy were the COVID-19 case increases in the UK between January 5 and 8, up nearly twelve per cent, but the death rate had increased almost 60 per cent. In three days. She knew she would have to watch this, and whilst a small sample could easily change this reading, the increase in deaths was still massive.

Dorothy decided to hold this material till the next day to see what else would unfold. Time to go home and have a glass of cold white wine, followed by a decent whiskey.

When Dorothy got home, her husband Michael was waiting for her.

'Hello honey, you look frazzled.'

Dorothy just grinned. 'I have a fear and I need to discuss it with you or I will not be able to sleep.'

---

[33] Republican Senator Lisa Murkowski calls on Trump to resign

'I read reports showing Trump's intense desire to attack Iran, on any provocation, and my fear is that it get out of control. It is hard to believe that they do not have one or two nuclear bombs. Use them and they would be wiped off the map but it would result in total destruction of so much. Their country, other countries, economies, instant lack of finance, isolationist tendencies, wealth destruction. Tell me your views of two things. First, do you think Iran has a bomb, and next, would the US retaliate with the nuclear option if Tehran used it first?'

'Oh, honey, I can make you go to sleep without answering all that. Or do you need to know the answers?' She did, and Michael told her:

'First, do they have the bomb? Not their own, but probably one bought from North Korea. For sure. Like an insurance policy against the USA Satan. Will they use it first? No. They may be portrayed as Islamist idiots, but they are not. They'd have to be pretty smart to now control not only their own population but also Iraq, Syria, and Lebanon. All despite the efforts of the mighty US. I don't like their regime, but you have to admit they have been super effective, which does not happen without smarts. They know the use of the nuclear option is immediate destruction of their country.'

'But now for the good news. Do you want me to put you to seep with my special skills or do you need to know my good news first?' asked Michael.

'You can use your special skills to your heart's content later, but give man, give.'

'The good news is that even if Trump decided to start an attack with conventional weapons today, it would take the armed forces two month minimum to plan a successful attack, and if he ordered a nuclear option to start a war, I absolutely doubt that the US Airforce would deliver a strike. So you've been worried for nothing. Shall we watch Apocalypse Now or a girly movie?'

The tension was gone. Time for a nice dinner, so they went out to a local place. An Iranian restaurant for good measure.

In the interest of delaying Michael's promises to send her to sleep, she decided to contact Argus E and sent him an email:

Dear Argus E,

I would like your help. As you seem to be a mystic able to intuit information from people a long way away, I would like you to use your skills to see the likelihood of Iran starting a nuclear or conventional war with the US. There have been many reports of Iran warning the US about provocations. Trump would jump at the chance to retaliate for any attacks from Iran. In his last twelve days in office, I want to use my newspaper to be able to warn officials against any attempts by Trump to stir the plot.

Dorothy Thompson, Washington Post

Argus E replied almost instantly.

Dear Ms Thompson

I'm so glad to receive your message. I have looked at this very same problem this week after seeing reports from the Iranian Foreign Minister. I see it this way: Iran is in a precarious position to keep its population reasonable happy. The regime does not understand that most people would love to see their administration swallow a nuclear poison pill and just go away. So it's all about propaganda and guess what? News Media outlets thrive on it and blow it up into a self-fulfilling prophecy. The media has a lot to answer for.

In Iran, you have hotheads that would like to start a war. Fortunately, your country does not have such hotheads, I believe. But the regime in Iran is pretty smart. They have manoeuvred to be controllers in Iraq, Syria and Lebanon against massive opposition from the US. And I believe that they know their country would be wiped out if they started a nuclear war and that they might shoot down a plane or enter into a naval attack just to prove they are willing to defend their country. A major war? No. Tell your newspapers to pull their heads in on war talk. It's not helpful.

Respectfully,

Argus E, Port Blair

*   *   *

Darryl Braithwaite had seen the Washington Post report about Trump's feud with Iran *That needs a reply*, he thought angrily.

Dear Ms Thompson, Washington Post

Your suggestion that Trump would love nothing better than leaving Iran in a pile of ashes is so disrespectful, as it is just referring to Trump. He has a title, and you know it's President Trump. Please maintain your standards by observing this.

You would also know we all wish for something but would not dream of carrying it out. I do as well, and it has to do with what I would love to do to those pesky Democrats.

I have also been in the military. I have absolutely no doubt that a nuclear attack can only happen when a military man presses a button to confirm the President's order to fire that weapon. And that man is trained. He is trained to not only obey orders but also orders he believes are correct. Any first attack by the US using nuclear arms would not succeed, especially in such a transition period.

Please use your influence to strengthen our armed forces and avoid further media drama. It is read overseas and can be a provocation. I'm sure you can do a good job on that. You have influence. Use it.

Regards,

Darryl Braithwaite, St Joseph News-Press, Missouri

Dorothy saw the reply from Braithwaite and considered it. She realised he was not the idiot she had perceived him to be and decided to thank him for his words. Maybe they could work together towards containing the pandemic.

Dear Mr Braithwaite

I am truly grateful for your reply to me. It is easy to slip into a non-respectful partisan mode when so much of our country is at loggerheads with the other side. Your message maybe just in time to salvage my reputation.

My aim as a reporter is to promote beating the pandemic in any way I can. Unfortunately, I believe that the action of mass protests with a much more infectious strain of COVID-19 looming is insanity. Unfortunately, ex-President Donald Trump seems to encourage those protests, and it is hurting the nation.

What would you rather have, Mr Braithwaite? A massive increase in infections that will require lockdowns or an absence of mass protests that would cause just that?

Maybe we should both work towards better public health.

Regards,

Dorothy Thompson, Washington Post

CHAPTER 7

January 9

Argus E was happy that no one had overturned the election, but what might happen now; could it be overturned in court? He noticed that the mood was one of anxiety by those who had stormed the Capitol. The other fears were about the last days of the presidency. By now, the protestors all knew that their police force, the FBI, had filmed most of the storming on their digital devices and used facial recognition to identify thousands of the protestors. And Argus also knew how a wounded animal would hit out. Whom would Trump strike out against next?

*   *   *

Dorothy Thompson sums up the main news articles for the day and the mood they invoke. She copied some notes from the new items:

- Protestors, some rabid, some angry with Trump, now fearful of being targeted by the FBI after the news they have taken photos during the riots.
- The FBI had used their facial recognition software to identify thousands of rioters.

- The COVID cases are rising steeply for LA residents, many planning to escape to the desert.

Dorothy was sitting at her desk, thinking about this day's article. There were a plethora of themes, and she decided to summarise those first. It's better if readers get a taste of what is to come. Get them interested. She wrote a draft of her next piece:

> Many of you would have woken and watched the morning news. Very little information and a lot of talking heads rehashing yesterday's news. And very little about the fast-rising Covid cases in Los Angeles. On TV, blah, blah, blah. All covered in seconds. Can you remember what they said? Of course you can; you're smart, right? But I hope to grasp your interest here today.
>
> The protestors were ecstatic. What a day when they ran amok and trashed the Capitol, including papers, computers and files, just waiting to be prosecuted? I mean, all they had done was to follow Donald Trump's request.

But the day had turned out to be dangerous, with their moments of fame shared on social media. A treasure trove of identifications of everyone who was there and what they were doing. *Thank you for that*, the FBI would think, *We need that to prosecute you.*

The other effect of sharing pictures of themselves on social media was that their interstate families could see their heroic role played out in public. But sometimes, it worked against them. One woman was seen crying after dejected Trump supporters left

Washington;[34] her son had texted her that he had now disowned her. One wonders at the number of supporters returning home with just a note on the table. One that said, 'I'm out of here. For good.' So many families were split along Trump and anti-Trump lines, causing deep divisions in families across the country.

One of the most surprising aspects of the day of the vote was the lack of security,[35] with people proudly walking out with Nancy Pelosi's lectern[36]. What was worse, it included stolen and possibly compromised computers with possible security breaches.[37] They had just set themselves up for a friendly FBI interview. A Floridian had been arrested on Friday on a federal warrant. The FBI had identified him on social media with help from local residents.

Many supporters were probably thinking how stupid to leave yourself identified for later prosecution. When they read the reports, conspiracy theories had a new lease of life. They were all in agreement that it was Antifa activists who fuelled the mob violence. No evidence, of course. *Well, you guys, there will be a knock on your door despite your beliefs.*

What a difference one day makes, thought Dorothy. And a top Democratic politician has called on mobile carriers to preserve social media content related to the incident. How would the Republicans look if they opposed that? They have to distance themselves from Trump now and tune in to the general population if they want to be re-elected in the future. Many Republicans had already denounced Trump, and it was easier to do so now.

34 Dejected Trump supporters leave Washington, create new theories for Capitol violence.

35 A Man pictured carrying away Pelosi's lectern, two others charged in Capitol riot

36 US Capitol rioters arrested as senator urges mobile and social media providers to keep data

37 Post-Riot, the Capitol Hill IT Staff Faces a Security Mess

Dorothy thought it must be a bitter pill to throw away four years of belief, but she was not sorry for them. They always had a choice.

The Democrat lawmakers were in much the same boat as the Democrat voters. They were gleeful at socking it to Trump, but had a specific aim: impeachment to stop him running again in 2024.

The remaining dangers were now limited. Many were anxious that Trump would try to serve the execution command for all coloured inmates on death row, many of whom never had a fair trial in the first place.[38] In one case, the man was so mentally disabled he should never have stood trial. But Trump hated blacks; they had cost him the election.

The other danger that he would start a war with Iran seemed unlikely now, but there was a chance that Iran might provoke an attack, something Trump was waiting for. One bloody nose before he exited the White House. He did not think of US casualties. He had never served in the Armed Forces and did not understand war. But there was less fear now that Joe Biden had talked to defence chiefs to prevent the US from initiating such an attack.

The plan for impeachment would need to be passed by the Senate. But that was unlikely to be passed now.

What was absent from the conversations was, *what would the new President do?* So far, all thinking had been rooted in one desire; to get rid of Trump. It was time to change that conversation and steer it towards the pandemic and the worsening infection rate.

*   *   *

---

[38]   Trump's rush to execute prisoners proves the death penalty is arbitrary

Dorothy had enough of her worries and visited her Washington neighbour Mary Lou who was delighted to see her.

'Well, hello, stranger, what kept you?' she asked.

'That four-letter word: *work*. And thinking of four-letter words, I've been using some lately. I've been running around in circles trying to get a new article together. There is so much information out there it's hard to see the woods for trees. Change of subject, please. How is Marcus?' asked Dorothy.

'I could kill him. I could swear so that a sailor would blush. The idiot went to the January protests and had a wow of a time and then got himself arrested. He wants me to post bail. I think I might send a text to say I've gone to Florida to get a tan and will be back in two weeks. He should know if he has contracted the virus by then. Cheaper than a hotel quarantine,' Mary Lou giggled.

*   *   *

Then it was back to work for Dorothy, and she hunted for news on the new UK strain found in the US.

Los Angeles was the top hot spot for COVID-19, where the new UK strain was circulating. Hospitals were full and at breaking point, as were the health care workers. Many families who had sufficient funds had decided to escape to the desert or wilderness. The good thing was that January was cold instead of hot. They would need electricity for air-conditioning in summer; lots of it, not generally found in the desert or wilderness.

Many families towed a caravan packed with everything they would need. Ski outfits, ski gloves, thermal underwear, a freezer with frozen foods; they could leave that outside. They were resourceful and added a cross-country bike to hang off the back of their caravan or their RV if they had one. Bikes to go shopping for small provisions and explore the area to find the best spot.

January 10

Dorothy reviewed the news items of the day again. She considered the news of fears of an Iran v. US confrontation[39] first; then the problem facing the Republicans[40] next, the likelihood of an impeachment, the 25th Amendment or Trump resignation, and the choices facing Republicans. Then the worsening pandemic last, even though it was a high priority for her. But her readers were not yet tuned in to that.

The Republican problems were almost inconsequential to her, but the Iran issue could be explosive now. If they tricked Trump into an attack, it would definitely be explosive in about two weeks when Iran would have material to make a bomb just as the new President starts. All this whilst America was in the grip of a pandemic.

So Dorothy made some notes on the US-Iran issue:

> Iran is two weeks away from being a nuclear-armed nation. Of course, conventional delivery by rocket is easily traced, and Iran would be wiped out in a first attack. Would Israel be tempted into a pre-emptive strike, knowing they would be the first target for the bomb or blackmail?

> And the delivery method by Iran? Maybe a cargo shipment via two or three independent countries; let's say a road oil tanker and inside that a bomb in a crate with 8 inches of lead shielding to prevent

---

[39] 'Dangerous time' - Tensions rise as nuclear foes Iran, Israel and the US face-off

[40] Trump's final days put the country at a dangerous crossroad

radiation detection. Delivered to New York, Baltimore, Los Angeles, San Francisco or all four.

Next subject, she thought. *That one is just too scary,* as she perused the news on Republicans stewing in the juice of their own making. She could see the conundrum they faced. She read the article by Mark Humphries,[41] an Australian writer for the Sydney Morning Herald, who could barely believe his eyes when, instead of discarding the electoral votes that didn't favour Donald Trump, the Vice-President actually performed his constitutional duty!

Trump will be disappointed if he is counting on an outpouring of support from his old colleagues on Capitol Hill to overturn the new law that asks media companies to retain the data from the riots. Whilst Vice President Pence is keeping the 25th Amendment on the table, Texas Rep. Kevin Brady rejected it, along with any move toward impeachment, and suggested, ridiculously, that doing so was no different from Trump's incitements. *Yes, well, tell me another one,* she thought. Would invoking the 25th Amendment provoke more civil unrest or make the place safer? It will only happen if Mike Pence brings on the 25th. Would he dare?

Next Dorothy was intrigued by the plethora of articles by The Jerry Springer Show and Fox News trying to shift the blame to secret leftists. *Hello, did you leave your brains behind?* They were claiming that Pence would prevent Trump from running again. If this could be invoked now, then the heat would go out of the debate. Her main aim was to hold him accountable and stop him from pardoning himself for all he had done. Or executing death warrants for something like 50 on death row, all blacks.

---

41   Pence refuses to renew Trump for another season.

Democracy is at risk, but it will sort itself out, she thought, mainly due to the self-interest of all involved. Their political futures were at stake.

She was ready for the main article. Infection comparisons between California, Texas and the UK.

Dorothy had plotted the infection cases by country, comparing the cases and deaths per million of population. She found that daily death rates in Texas were 40 per cent higher than in the UK, and Texas daily cases were 50% higher. This was at a time when the UK was in total lockdown, for God's sake.

Then she hit the UK News, 3 million cases and 80,000 deaths.[42] She read the article from Al Jazeera's Neave Barker. Barker had reported that people were treated in ambulances and car parks because hospitals were full.

She wondered how long it would take hospitals to reach capacity in the US, where social distancing was a word only used in a dictionary.

She shook her head. Shocking. Then she read an older article to see how long this had been the case and found one from 4 days ago.[43] A disaster. She read:

> England's previous nationwide lockdown ran for a month ending December 5. Johnson said it would not be reviewed for lifting until at least mid-February when announcing the new stay-at-home order. Cases exploded during lockdown, for god's sake. Probably because of the new strain.

---

[42] UK coronavirus cases top 3 million as death toll passes 80,000

[43] UK hospitals stagger as new virus variant takes a huge toll

It also reported by Siva Anandaciva, chief analyst of the King's Fund, that half of healthcare was delivered in ambulances.

Dorothy was furious that the whole of the US was ignoring the pandemic. All they could think about was Donald Trump. She decided she needed some dirt on the pathetic US efforts to contain this new pandemic. She decided to compare the US average in California and Texas.[44]

California Governor Gavin Newsom revealed his state budget proposal calls for using $15 billion of surging tax returns into economic relief.[45] That's peanuts; for a population of 40 million, that's just $375 per person. Not per day, week or month. In total.

Newsom must now navigate a coronavirus pandemic that has had an uneven impact on the state's economy. Nothing was mentioned about hospitals.

Dorothy found an undated report, 'California Takes Action to Combat COVID-19', but it only mentioned funding for increased hospital beds as early as mid-2020. Nothing new. Typical.

*   *   *

At this point, Argus E got impatient with Dorothy. He sent her an email to get on with an article to post rather than just think about it. But Dorothy did not look at incoming mails and continued on her merry way.

---

[44]   California governor's budget booms despite pandemic problems

[45]   California budget proposes $15 billion for economic relief.

Dorothy found a recent article from Texas.[46]

It boiled down to closing schools, cutting their funding, and nothing about the pandemic but keeping the budget in line.

- Limits to pandemic disaster declarations; meaning no more support
- Abbott's handling of the COVID-19 crisis to try to keep two legislative bushfires from merging. Nothing on the pandemic.
- Coming from Abbott's right, both chambers will push to restrict a governor's powers to order lockdowns.
- A proposed Constitutional amendment would require a governor to call a special session of the Legislature to re-introduce a proclamation or order;.
- That would make it impossible to get any support at all. The Bastards.

This lengthy article on the handling of the pandemic made zero mention of deaths, and the only mention that the infections were rising fast was that they were rising. *If you need to shut the place down because of the pandemic and don't offer support, please expect protests in the millions and escalating cases in the tens of millions, you idiots.*

No numbers. Republican bullshit with 40 per cent higher death rates per million population than California, Democrat-controlled, of course. *I will nail you. May you all die on the road as the hospitals will be full,* were Dorothy's thoughts, and she intended to write it like that soon.

Dorothy researched contact tracing, and she read an article from the Atlantic.[47] The start showed a shocker.

[46] Pandemic. Recession. Political strife - The Texas Legislature's toughest 2021 challenges

[47] The Most American COVID-19 Failure Yet

THE ATLANTIC

With her thin eyebrows arched high on her forehead, Robyn Openshaw urged her 212,000 fans to stand up to a new menace: contact tracing. Openshaw, a widely followed health blogger who goes by the name 'Green Smoothie Girl' on Facebook, had recently heard of a Bill in Congress that would provide $100 million to mobile health clinics to help monitor the spread of COVID-19. She advised against any contact tracing.

That bitch needs to be strung up, Dorothy thought.

Dorothy felt a niggling urge to report what she had so far, but this was just too ridiculous. 'Stand up to a new menace: contact tracing?' She usually refrained from swearing, but she called her friend Sue Anne Orthallo in Oregon to let off steam before she would explode, and when connected, she exclaimed:

'That motherfucking stupid bitch Robyn Openshaw, the Green Smoothie Girl, is urging followers not to sign up to contact tracing. If you need open-heart surgery, do you go to the postman? For God's sake, people are so fucking stupid I want to explode. I want her boiled in green smoothies. Help me calm down, please, or I will blow up!' said Dorothy, and Sue Anne told her that they both needed a double scotch. On the rocks, and see how they felt then.

Dorothy read out more from The Atlantic to Sue Anne:

In the United States, this whole process is failing, allowing infected people to continue roaming about town, infecting others and spreading COVID-19. There is no national contact-tracing program in the US. Contact tracers who work for the 40 local health departments in areas with the most coronavirus cases have reached just a fraction of the patients who were positive.

'It's literally too late to do contact tracing in Texas,' Dorothy said. She went on from the Atlantic with the clincher, and read:

That month, Texas had <u>15,000 new cases</u> on some days.

'How are you going to go back and find all those old contacts? You can't trace if everyone and their cousin have it!'

She was going to research one more item. How did they keep the infections down in Australia, even now that the more infectious UK strain had arrived there? It was like reading about an alternate universe. Immediate area lockdowns, contact tracing and urging people who had been in announced places on given dates and times to get tested that day. That same day. They snuffed it in its infancy, and it was all over before idiots could stage anti-lockdown protests. She had enough of reading about the infantile American system and prepared her daily article.

But first, she emailed Terry Balzarini, asking him to advise her on the likelihood of an evil mutation, one worse and more deadly than the UK strain. Terry replied within the hour and told her how he had some such experience in a laboratory. It was not likely to be reproduced outside a lab unless you got many infected people together without the required precautions. Dorothy was pleased with that but apprehensive, as cases were getting so out of control.

She was not yet satisfied that she had a knockout for the day and researched the latest news items. And bingo, there it was, an article on the need to reckon with Trump's lies.[48] It was lengthy,

---

[48]   The need to reckon with Trump's lies

over 1700 words, and it took a bit of effort to synthesize. So she copied items of interest to a worksheet and deleted stuff not needed. A small summary where possible:

- News organizations fact-checked Trump, called out his misleading claims and exaggerations, and catalogued the thousands of lies.
- Washington is still floundering.
- Like many other populist leaders, Trump has an us-versus-them mentality.
- Polling before the attack on the Capitol found that significant numbers of Republicans doubted the election results.
- The thorny question is what consequences the President should face.
- Conversely, some senior Republicans say honest accounting of what brought the country to this moment needs to occur. 'It all started with lies, and lies, and lies, and intolerance,' former Republican California Governor Arnold Schwarzenegger said.
- Surprisingly, many European officials decried the shutdown of Donald Trump's social media accounts.

Well, that was too much for her audience. She needed to cut it to 750 words. There was still something missing. It was a message that would have all Americans look for accountability, and she decided to start with a bit of history to show its importance.

*　　*　　*

Dorothy noticed how tired she was. *Unusual*, she though, *It's not late yet*. But she needed to refresh with something active, like a conversation, before continuing her article that she was determined would go out today. She called her husband at work.

'Michael, I need to feel your muscles. That bicep and six pack. What are you going to do about that? she asked. Michael was no slouch at winding her up, and told her, 'Darling, I should have warned you. I'm on speaker phone and have 200 students listening. Do continue.' and Dorothy squealed in embarrassment, but decided she wasn't going to be the victim here so she said, 'OK Class, I insist you ask him to morrow about all the gory details. Do I have you OK on that?' she asked. There was some silence, then Michael spoke, 'They all just left to give me some privacy but I will give them your request when they think it's safe to come back in.'

Michelle laughed. 'You were never on speaker phone, were you, sweetheart?' and Michael's mumble was enough for her. 'See you tonight. That's a threat. back to work for me now though.'

*   *   *

She was finally ready for her report:

Dorothy Thompson Reporting

Before you read this, please try to empty your head of all thoughts. Have a go. After a minute, notice how calm you are and how wired up you were before. Do you know or wonder why? Or should I ask, is it any wonder you were all stirred up after the events of the last three days? Do you want to continue to be so stirred up, and if not, what do you need to do to change that? You, the American people, are you so on-edge because you are trying to solve the election problem about impeachment?

To start this, think of Germany after the war. Six million skeletons in concentration camps.

Do you think Germany or the world would have been able to move on if the Nazis had not been held responsible? Would you have been happy for Hitler and the Nazis to live out the rest of their lives on a good pension? To be paid for by you?

Ask yourself the same question about Pol Pot, who was responsible for murdering three or more million people. Would you have wanted him to live in the luxury of a generous pension whilst the rest of the country is starving? Of course not. You are Americans. You should be proud of that, but with that comes a responsibility.

If you are not Blind Freddy, then you would have seen the talking heads on TV debate whether Trump should resign, whether Vice President Pence should invoke the 25th Amendment, or whether the Democrats should impeach him. Bla, bla, and more bla. Do you think this President should receive half a million-plus in benefits a year as an ex-President whilst his supporters are jailed for attempted insurrection?

The 25th Amendment would take him out of harm's way. But you may have to ask yourselves. Who is responsible? You, the voters, put him into office. You, the voters, were also responsible for putting Republican senators into office at the state and federal levels. So, are you now responsible for telling those officials what you want them to do? Well, I'm not asking you to write into the Post and tell me.

Do you think that inciting the riots (as some say) is Trump's only misdemeanour? If your answer is yes, then I ask you why America's handling of the pandemic is so much worse than almost any other country. Is it because President Trump acted responsibly, perhaps telling you to go to work because 'it's only the flu' and to just 'take an aspirin?' No, you, the American people, have already decided that at the election.

Getting back to responsibility now. A new administration will be in charge in two weeks. Their stated aim is to stop the pandemic. It will take a lot more than just starting the vaccine rollout in a month. The horse has bolted, and now much more infectious strains are making the rounds. Maybe 100,000 protestors without masks is not a good idea? You will pay for their actions when your job shuts down because of them spreading the virus.

Not meaning to scare you here, but if these stains were to mutate into something that kills in a week, then you need not know the answer as you would all be dead. Because America has been led to ignore social distancing. Almost by order of the president.

It's a good time to compare results in the UK and the USA now. On January 10, the UK had 50% fewer cases per million citizens than the USA.

This new strain is so much more infectious. The horse has already bolted, and our mob is running around like blue-arsed flies without masks. Our flag-waving heroes. Aljazeera reported that the UK people are being treated in ambulances and car parks outside the hospital because there's no room inside. We are still waiting for this strain to race through the US. And it will. How should that be handled?

The country has an obligation now. Move forward with the new advice, and work out what you want. But you don't really want to fork out another fifteen million in pay to a President who ruined your country.

And talking of ruins? Do you think the protests are over, or will they come back fully armed? What advice can you give your state and federal representatives RIGHT NOW about having security on standby? And will you be willing for them to confront armed protestors with rifles by calling in the military?

I don't know what you, my Americans, really want to know about this pandemic. If you are looking for good outcome then you need to take appropriate action. What you have not had to think about yet is the disaster scenario of a much more deadly virus that kills in days, and what would you be willing to do to avoid that?

Dorothy Thompson, Washington Post

Dorothy drove home. She was exhausted but relived, she had done her best. Then the traffic stalled. There seemed to be an accident, but suddenly she was surrounded by screaming protestors. Men were rocking her car. There were hundreds. This was scary. Some were approaching her with big poles and one man with a big hammer.

They kept at it for many minutes till she was fed up as well. She activated her bull horn, first to sound a police siren, and when they backed off, she took her microphone and announced at maximum volume:

'In ten seconds, I am going to accelerate and drive over anyone in my way. One, two, three: get out of the way! I am on an emergency mission and allowed to run over you, you idiots.'

They stopped rocking her car, but idiots stayed in front. She blew her horn and started accelerating. One man finished up on her bonnet, but she continued to gain speed, and he dropped off. *Teach the bastards to mess with me,* she thought. She had attended defensive training and shooting classes and knew what to do. She pulled over at home, raced in the door and broke down, sobbing.

Michael saw Dorothy staggering inside and met her as she entered the lounge. She was crying. She didn't cry that easy and he folded her into his arms and just help her till she quietened down. Not for long, though. She exploded into expletive laden swearing at some protestors.

'Hey baby. slow down. It's gonna be OK.'

Still in shock, Dorothy explained everything that had happened when she was surrounded by a hundred or so wild men rocking her car, one approaching her with a hammer, and how she had used her emergency sirens and loud hailer to get them to move. And then how she had accelerated through the crowd and hit a man who finished up on her bonnet.

Michael said 'Scotch or double?'

Her reply? 'Triple.'

A short while later the phone rang for her. It was Commander Wade from the Capitol Police.

He advised her, 'Dear Ms Thompson. I have someone who wants to lay a charge of attempted murder against you. You ran over him. Can you come into the station please?'

Wade was stunned by her response.

'No way, Commander, but I will lay charges against that man for obstructing a car with emergency lights and siren and jumping onto my car. And if he had any witnesses I want them all charged with attempting to assault me. A lone woman and a hundred wild protestors. Go and arrest them; then we will talk. You come here and I will show you my dash cam footage. I'm not going anywhere until you get all those motherfuckers off our roads.'

Wade sensed that she was upset and offered to come to her place. He was shown the dash cam footage and laughed out loud.

'No court would uphold their claim of attempted murder, but they would uphold claims by you of attempted assault.'

Wade left with a grin when he was thinking of arresting a few more, and have the tables turned on them.

*   *   *

Half an hour later, reports came in, and Dorothy read the first one.

Dear Ms Thompson.

You hit the nail on the head with that article. I work for the Army to help returned soldiers who have PTSD. Without lecturing you here, your psychology worked a charm.

Your article brilliantly uses history to prompt people to examine the effect if Trump is not held accountable for those riots and all the unnecessary deaths. If you need a new job, come and see me, and I will plug you into my associates.

James Anderson, Washington.

Dorothy had a good laugh at that. Her friends, incognito, and looked at the following article from General Roberts.

Dear Ms Thompson,

I doubt Trump supporters will want their hero to go without his 15 million lifetime expected pension. They may rightly object to comparing his misdemeanours (your words) with the actions of Hitler or Pol Pot. Don't be surprised if you get a bit of hate mail. But I think it's a great way to open discussions on what should happen next.

Good job.

General CP Roberts, retired, Houston.

Well, speak of the devil, thought Dorothy when she saw an entry from Nathan Walker. *Here comes trouble.*

Ms Thompson

You need to be careful not to incite violence with your provocative words. I don't know what you are trying to do, but comparing Donald Trump to Hitler is dangerous, and you know it. You don't know what you are dealing with when you attack his followers.

Sleep well on that advice.

Nathan Walker, Chattanooga, TN

* * *

Argus E had seen that email and thought that Dorothy could not possibly achieve anything by replying to Walker. *It would be better if I did*, Argus thought. *It might intrigue Walker too.* So he wrote:

Dear Mr Walker

Ms Thompson forwarded me your email regarding Trump supporters. She obviously should not reply to you, but I will. First, I must say, you do write a very concise letter. And I see that what she wrote could so easily be misconstrued. She suggested that leaders who had wrought havoc on their nations should not sit back in luxury if you read it carefully. Many Americans do not acknowledge that President Trump's actions have caused half a million deaths and over 30 million infections. Other countries have managed this pandemic about 100 to 1000 times better, and it did not destroy their economies in the process.

My name is Argus E from Fort Blair, Andamanese Islands, Bay of Bengal. I have a Master of Science degree from Delhi University, and I advise the Indian Government on the mood and actions in the US that may affect the health of our indigenous population, one that is very susceptible to viruses.

My aim in writing to you is to let you know that we are very interested in how this all pans out and advise cool heads on both sides. The less violence, the more likely that Donald Trump will be allowed to run again in 2024.

I am definitely interested in hearing your views and look forward to occasional return emails from you

Argus E, Fort Blair, Andaman Islands, Bay of Bengal

Last job for the day, thought Argus. *I think I did a good job with that email to Braithwaite.*

CHAPTER 8

Mood, January 12

Argus was in AI heaven. Because his AI was able to do all his work for him, Argus could hone in on the important thing this morning: the mood. One voice command, and here it was, all nicely presented. With special attention to what Dorothy Thompson and Darryl Braithwaite and their friends were up to

The atmosphere in Washington was fearful. How dangerous would those promised armed protesters be, and when would they start? Washington breathed fear and loathing, and it was the only conversation in town despite the upcoming inauguration.

Dorothy Thompson called Michelle Anderson, best friends for 20 years, and asked her, 'honey, are you awake?'

'Well, now I am. Actually I've been awake for hours, and I was going to call you without waking you. I was talking to Michael this morning, and we are packing to exit this city. Too dangerous. We are thinking of a simple stay, past Sandy Point Park, where we met. We started packing our caravan; we've had the list of what to take ready for months. My grandfather has a log cabin nearby, across the water and nearer Centreville, Maryland, a bit more isolated. The place is good for three families. We would love you to join us. What do you say?'

'Absolutely, when?' asked Dorothy, who wanted to leave that day.

Michelle told her, 'We are leaving in an hour and get there another hour later. It's eight now, so any time after 10:30, we will be there. If you're earlier you can have a coffee at Centreville.'

'You are taking a satellite phone, of course, aren't you?' continued Michelle. 'And what other essentials are you taking? I will send you our packing list. And maybe you can send us yours?'

Dorothy received the packing list and saw they had included three home-style solar panel batteries. Michelle had added a note that they could always charge them at a caravan place. Great idea, Dorothy would take some and an inverter too. Way to go. Then she saw they were taking two rifles with 2000 rounds of ammo and two handguns with 1000 rounds, and she called Michelle back immediately.

'Michelle, are the rifles for food hunting or killing people?' asked Dorothy.

Michelle's response was startling. 'Dorothy, don't go all squeamish on me. I never told you, but after being confronted by a gun-toting crazy, I went to a shooting range and had proper training, including those maze things where you come round a corner, and there is an attacker. Came in handy when I found a man pointing a rifle at my son Mark,' said Michelle. Dorothy asked her what she did then. Her response was just as startling, 'I whipped out my Glock and shot him between the eyes. No worries.'

Michelle touched on another subject. 'Dorothy, you've met my daughter Deborah. She's nineteen now, and as a precaution, we have put her on the pill. A bit early, but it's not for dating. I am petrified that those bearded hordes masquerading as America's new heroes could capture her. Not whilst I'm around, of course, that would not happen. It would be horrible enough for someone to capture her and have her raped. But at least she will know she won't become pregnant. I have given her a small kit to fit in her purse to take a semen smear for police later on,' finished Michelle.

'Oh my God, do you think that is possible? Oh no, my daughter, Karen, is also vulnerable. I'd die if something happened to her, or even to her brother Richard,' finished Dorothy. Then she added, 'We were tested for COVID a week ago, negative, and we had another test yesterday.'

Dorothy was now a bit worried, 'can I assume you won't be shooting me in my sleep or any other time?'

'Honey, if someone is pointing a handgun at you, held from the hip, you are safe at fifteen feet, and I'd kill him in a quarter of a second. People pointing guns at someone's head are dangerous and stupid. No harm done in eliminating them. They are a public health hazard. Have you ever been confronted by someone pointing a gun at you, Dorothy?' she asked.

'No, Michelle, I'm a novice at killing anything, so I had better join your mob for friendship and protection. We can make up stories for me to publish later on.'

Then Michelle added, 'As you know, James was in the Army, but even though he was training as a psychologist, he did do basic training and infantry exercises. He had to know the pressures people faced about killing a live human being. That was his value to the Army. Would you like to go to a shooting school with me to learn basics, including when not to shoot?' Then she added details to make Dorothy feel more secure that she had not just swapped one lot of madmen for another when she said:

'Honey, I have a special trick that allows me to hold my rifle from the hip, seemingly not aimed or at least harmless, as who can shoot that way accurately? That only happens in old Westerns. I have a mirror on my rifle that allows me to look down and effectively see through the sights whilst holding it firm at my hip. That allows me to negotiate with the man in front of me. If he tempts me, I will warn him that I will shoot at his toes but miss the first time. If he still threatens me, I look down and shoot two inches from his feet. They usually go away after that. Even if confronted by four or five armed men, they suddenly value their lives when they see magic shooting from the hip. If they point the rifle at me, I shoot to kill.'

'I need to know that you are comfortable with me killing in self-defence, as these idiots are serious about violence. Dead serious. I can't have you stay with us if you don't want to protect yourself.' Dorothy was suddenly grateful that Michelle had opened her eyes for her and offered real protection. Subdued, Dorothy considered the real danger they were in, probably for the first time. This was not TV. It was a blood-curdling reality.

Dorothy and Michelle were media savvy, and they had seen the FBI reports that there were plans to stage mass armed protests in all fifty capitals plus Washington. Mass protests without masks amid the new strain of the virus looking for people to infect, like a used-car salesman trying to clear the yard on December 31. The idiots were armed, and still encouraged by Trump. Dorothy mentioned a report from the FBI saying that they had traced at least 1500 social media incitements to violence. They would talk themselves into mass violence and glory in it. In the meantime, they did a fabulous job of infecting the whole country, and Michelle's thoughts were *If only I could barbeque those idiots.*

Dorothy agreed to meet tomorrow after taking Karen to a doctor for contraception, certain that leaving very soon was the best solution.

Dorothy also called Sue Anne Orthallo in Oregon to see if they wanted to join them. Sue Anne told her that they were friends with Max and Dominique Sanderson from San Francisco. They had an excellent hideaway east of Santa Rosa, 40 miles north of San Francisco, at the Napa-County Regional Park and decided to join them.

'Sorry Dorothy,' she said, 'I should have called you earlier, but we've been stuck for hours in COVID testing queues. They are so understaffed, but we wanted to be clean if we went camping. We call it going bush, in the wilderness.'

Dorothy kept listening to the radio as they drove to Centreville, Maryland. Her husband Michael was driving, so she had time to appreciate the scenery - but did not. The radio news was enough to make her boil. Trump was encouraging the protestors to help reverse the 'Steal.' *Civil War Two?* She thought. *Civil war means half the population gets hurt. Well, you're not getting me. Never. May you rot in hell if you come for me.*

*   *   *

Also on the East Coast, Blew Ohrtman was preparing not to escape, but to do battle. He had an overwhelming desire to shoot someone, a black man of course, who had helped to steal the election through the change in demographics. If the blacks had not had the vote, then Trump would have won. Ergo. All guilty by association, and his anger had been simmering ever since he found out years after his marriage that his wife Petal had black roots.

He had not met her parents at their wedding as it was all arranged too quickly for them to come, and they were people with a lot of responsibilities: both lecturers at university, and he had never studied. Another stone in his gut. The anger of someone who feels inferior and can only counter that through imagined violence towards that enemy. Like a perfect storm, he was ready to do damage.

Blew had seen the FBI reports and knew that he would not take any social media devices, no sirree. Let them catch everyone else but not him. He had no record and would be hard to trace. *The FBI can go fuck themselves,* he thought as he prepared. So he also deleted his Facebook account. *Nothing to see here, Fibs.*

He did not want to join the fight in his state as someone might recognise him. He would go to Springfield, the capital of Illinois. There would be plenty of action, and afterwards, he would write to the Post, that bitch Rebecca Sanders, use a false name, and show her what whites could do, *yes sirree.*

He decided to take his sniper rifle. He could hit a tennis ball at 200 yards and a football at 600 yards. If he saw Joe Slimy Biden, then he would use the rifle. If he saw the gutless Republican Senator who had voted against reversing the vote, yes, that man would be history. He knew Springfield and decided to target the Springfield Old State Capitol. The St. Nicholas apartments were just over 300 yards away, and it offered a view to the entrance from their east end. He could go to the top floor car park and shoot people from the northwest, and any security officers would be looking to the north if they heard a shot - and he'd be gone and away. *Clever,* he thought.

But. There is always a BUT. After he left, his wife Petal worried about his plans. As she walked past the entrance to the garage, she noticed the gun locker was open. One rifle, but the sniper rifle was gone. *Oh my God*, she thought. *I must stop him.*

Whilst she did not want him in trouble, if the FBI could find him before he could commit murder, then yes, he would be charged, but if he executed his dream, he would hang. No matter how smart he thought he was, she was sure that not one sniper killing in the last fifty years had been left unsolved.

Petal sent an email to the Springfield FBI offices with her fears and a recent photo of him.

*   *   *

In Dallas, Texas, Mitch Upton was deciding what he would do. He needed to protect Dannielle, his wife, and remembered the saying, 'The pen is mightier than the sword.' He realised he might be one of the few remaining Republicans with any sense. *Scary thought, that,* he contemplated. Mitch was an oilman, and the last thing he needed was someone making a grandiose gesture of blowing up an oil pipeline or storage tank. Holy mackerel, his job and wealth would be gone. He mapped out the priorities he needed to address.

- Somehow set up oil infrastructure protection with drone monitoring to find suspicious activity.
- Post notices – that unauthorised entry to facilities would be dealt with by armed guards – with an order to shoot if necessary.
- Find armed guard services; every man or woman he could find, and post them around the infrastructure, with fast off-road vehicles to quickly get to danger points.
- Get State attorneys to certify that protecting those facilities was important enough that the use of firearms was permitted to stop trespassers.

- Get his senior staff to organise all that within two days to be ready by January 17 and implemented by January 18.
- Write a letter to the Washington Post that would take the heat out of any planned action, at least in Texas and nearby states. That was a hard one but must be done.

Mitch pondered the impossible; to stop mob action when they were determined to riot. When the Shah was kicked out of Iran and Khomeini took over, he wanted the Shah returned, but the United States refused to negotiate, and 52 American hostages were held for 444 days.

He realised he needed to use history to provide a framework for messages that would work. These were the issues:

- He must prevent the oil infrastructure from being attacked or held to ransom.
- He must change the conversation from destruction to acceptance but make a point.
- He must give them something else. Maybe 100 or 200 people would be allowed into a Republican chamber to present their grievances.
- A psychological hook of some sort: Who gets shot if you bring a loaded rifle?

He wrote to Rebecca Sanders to publish this letter:

Dear Washington Post. Please publish this letter regarding the upcoming riots.

My name is Mitch Upton. I'm a stout Republican. I am also an oil executive, and I am writing to help you ensure that a protest stays calm and not armed.

Just so you know, blowing up a pipeline would incinerate babies, young mothers and maybe your father, and if you were doing just that, you must know you will be hunted, and that your life as you know it is over. I don't want that for you, and to keep the oil infrastructure safe, we have deployed over 3000 drones that can monitor the activity. Just to remove the temptation and to keep you safe.

I want you to have your say too. I'm a Republican, the same as you. I have organised to have a hall with seating for 200 to meet those selected by your groups. You will go through a metal detector, of course, and we will allow you some ninety-minute hearings; every two hours, from ten till four. You will have your say, and two of you will be granted a five-minute television interview on each occasion. Not only will you be heard, but seen on TV, able to express your concerns, and hopefully share what you learned on the day.

Good luck with peaceful protests. That is your right. It's in the Constitution.

Mitch Upton, Southern Oil, Houston, Texas.

Dorothy read all that again. She was thrilled. A letter that would appeal to most protestors. She added to the last line from Mitch Upton:

'Yes, your TV interviews will go national and be covered by all the social media outlets. You will be famous.' She smiled at the hook she had added. *They are just like a bunch of kids, but dangerous ones*, she thought.

Then she added her own thoughts under Rebecca Sanders' name:

Rebecca Sanders reporting:

I don't care so much how many buildings you set on fire. They are only buildings, but we will catch you. A ten-year jail sentence awaits, though. What matters to me is that your refusal to wear masks at large gatherings will kill my mother and father, and if you kill my children, I will come after you. In case you had not noticed, there is a pandemic running rampant; wakey wakey.

That was a good time to stop work. She submitted it and sat back. A double scotch. On the rocks. With help, she had succeeded in having a piece that would be positive for sure. It felt good, and she turned to Michael. She needed a hug to chase all her fears of the pandemic away for a while anyway.

*   *   *

Terry and his wife Lorraine had already left Baltimore. They had decided to hide out in the Rachel Carson Conservation Park west of Sunshine, Maryland. They had been there many times – out of the way, a small town nearby for supplies, plenty of fresh running water. They had taken their satellite phone, trail bikes and caravan, and lots of warm clothes that they could easily take once a month to Sunshine to wash. The caravan had a big gas bottle used for cooking and even hot showers; a luxury in summer, and necessary in the cold January winters.

Terry was a virologist whose biggest fear was that there would be a further mutation of the UK strain. He was not the premier world or US expert, only because the experts were people like him who were appointed to government positions. Then they became mouthpieces for the work done by people like himself, who stayed more up to date as they worked on the latest issues. He was not bitter. He just knew his value. He also knew that viruses ALWAYS mutated, and it was only a matter of time before they created a newer, deadlier monster.

Terry had experimented with SARS viruses ten years earlier. They were making a decent pool of viruses to use in experiments. He had tried to accelerate the growth potential by soaking them in a saline solution with different vegetable proteins; he used avocado proteins in one experiment and pea protein in the other. Seeing that the SARS virus had protein spikes that made them infectious, he thought they might become more able to replicate by adding a vegetable protein. Wrong, it killed them.

Terry discussed those experiments with Lorraine, a medical researcher who understood his work with ease when she asked him, 'Terry, why were you trying to grow the virus? Most people wanted to kill them.'

Terry told her: 'We had a new strain, and the COVID-19 virus is very similarly structured. You've seen pictures of those tube-like spikes all around the outside. Well, we had some mutations that were nastier than the original. They had small needle spikes extruding from those tube spikes. Double spikes and double trouble. Those needle spikes made it easier to pierce a body cell and then have the tube spike do its job of replicating itself in the body by attaching to the protein receptors.'

'I had wanted to continue research on killing the virus. It was fascinating that you could kill a virus so easily. It would not be a vaccine but a cure, and if we get any similar mutations, I will contact the defence laboratories and offer to come in for a few days and fix a cure, first easily tested in a lab. If that works, I can offer to get infected and be cured. Luckily, they show accurate pictures of viruses these days, and we can see them on our satellite devices. That work from ten years ago may become a lifesaver,' finished Terry.

*   *   *

John Orthallo and Max Sanderson had been friends for years; they had called each other many times, now to see if they should join for an escape to a wilderness. John was a carpenter who had built Sanderson's first house. Max had a great hideout east of Santa Rosa at the Napa-County Regional Park. He had visited the Park many times; very isolated yet not too far from Santa Rosa, if that is not a contradiction.

John asked Max, 'Maxie boy, are you OK with me bringing a rifle and handgun to protect my family?'

Max was pleased about the question, replying: 'John, I was going to ask the same thing. Dominique and I are both great shots with rifles and guns. My life is over if she or one of my kids get killed in the coming violence. But we should talk about defence when we are there and make sure we are never in one another's firing line.'

Max said, 'John, let's talk about when you want to come. You have a ten-hour drive, and it would be best if you come to our place first. You don't really want to set up camp in the wilderness at night. Stay at my place, and we can spend the next day making sure we have everything we need, and we will leave the following day. How does that sound?'

John thought it would be great to walk into a warm place and sleep in a comfy bed. He also realised they would need to prepare both families for the event, including protection. The rifles would not be used for hunting. The noise would attract undesirables. It was all decided, and they would leave early the following day and pack everything they needed to take right now.

The next day the Orthallos headed off, and an hour later, there was trouble. Someone had decided to set up a roadblock. Lumberjack types with bearded faces and handguns. They would never be able to outpace a chase; the caravan would stop that, too slow. When they came to the road stop, the mob wanted money.

'Four hundred dollars, and you get through,' they said. John was used to talking to building staff with their knickers in a knot and decided to defuse the situation.

'Boy, am I glad to see you folk! I don't know how far to the next gas station, and I'm running low on gas, but for four hundred dollars, I can do an EFTPOS transaction if you have a banking device. I'll show you my wallet. I have five dollars. I hope that will help you,' said John, and asked, 'What is the money for then. A charity project? Good on you, fellas; you should be recognised in the local news.'

They were waved through with a sneer. 'Yeah, man, charity. It starts at home,' and a mile along, Dominique started to breathe again. 'That was scary', she observed. You smooth-talking man. That's as smooth as Dominique Sanderson going to buy a bottle of wine and taking Max home instead', she chuckled. 'You, just as smooth. You see armed thugs, and you say: "am I pleased to see you". What would you have done if they got rough?' The answer scared her even more.

'I can kill three people in one second with my Glock. There were only two cars and four people. They would be roadkill.'

CHAPTER 9

Mood

Argus E is monitoring. It's his habit. He is tracking the mood, mood being so much easier to assess than the millions of events across the US. People are scared of the potential violence and civil war, as Trump supporters threaten to attack that day. There were more soldiers to protect the Capitol than there were in Afghanistan and Iraq combined. This is a nation at war with itself. One man has to change that, a daunting task.

January 20

The Inauguration Day had arrived. Dorothy Thompson had seen the President-in-Waiting's request that there should be no crowds and the presidential walk down Pennsylvania Avenue would be blocked to all traffic for security. She was furious with the people who had planned attacks, and she lamented that people could not be arrested before committing a crime. But, it was America, even if it didn't look like it anymore.

The televised walk down Pennsylvania Avenue would be a permanent historical event which left America devoid of celebrations because it had become too dangerous. Dorothy and her husband Michael were commenting on the difference between the two presidents. Michael said:

'One President who urges people to stay home and watch the event on TV, foregoing glory in favour of stopping the spread. The other besmirching him saying no one wanted the new President to win, and he was robbed anyway - that's why they stayed home. What is really sad is that tens of millions of people are watching this worldwide, and our stupidity is on display. So embarrassing.'

They both commented on the President and his Vice President walking down that Avenue. 'They are so brave. I guess they have to be, but they must wonder how many sniper rifles are aimed at them; all the way along that walk. Can you imagine the fear that some Trump supporter wants to have the last word? With a sniper? They must know this is possible, but they cannot give in to that fear and be respected by America. If they find anyone with a sniper in the vicinity, I want that man, or woman, barbequed in public, and have the screen split showing Trump playing golf at the same time,' came from Michael.

'Ewe, a bit bloodthirsty, but that mob was threatening all-out war. For real. Maybe they should all be converted to liquid fertilizer... I can't believe I said that,' giggled Dorothy. 'I better not put that in print. ' She contemplated that going out in print and the hate mail she would get. 'But why not you ask? Because I must be seen to be a responsible reporter, not one enraging the mob further.'

Dorothy continued, 'But they do need to be taught a lesson. The Army must respond appropriately this time. It was reported that the head of the Capitol Police held back with arrests on January 6 so as not to infuriate the mob. The Capitol Police must be furious. They discovered that some of their own men were part of the rioting mob[49], and now the Capitol Police Chief has resigned or been sacked. I do hope the Army starts shooting if there are any attacks. Even if they have to kill thousands; I want to feel safe in this town again, and I won't till they are all dead. I mean it.'

Michael raises an eyebrow. 'Who is the bloodthirsty one now?'

And she answers, 'I want the protestors to be scared of inciting an armed attack rather than the Army being scared they might invoke a riot. They've got it arse about.'

Her report for the Post was angelic by comparison:

Dorothy Thompson reporting:

The American people have been denied a celebration because of Trump supporters who said they would kill[50], but that is not the reason the President ordered that there should be no march this time. Can you imagine the accelerated virus spread from election rallies of forty thousand at a time, doubling the number of daily cases? What would a tightly packed crowd of maybe two million do? In his first inauguration, Obama had a huge crowd estimated to be 1.8 million, and it stretched many miles. Trump had maybe less than a third of that, despite his bragging that it was a beautiful number. Then his supporters had to resort to the fake news for the Presidential walk that 'Biden has no followers.'

By the standard definition, the ex-President was a great leader. One Army General once said, 'A

---

49   Off-duty police were part of the Capitol mob. Now police are turning in their own.

50   FBI report warned of 'war' at Capitol before the riot

leader is someone whom men follow,' and by that definition, Trump was the greatest leader of all time. But where did he lead? Over the cliff? Will he pay the penalties for all those arrested for the January 6 riots? No. Now Trump wants to libel a brave man who walks down the Avenue knowing there could be a rifle shot to cut short his victory. Imagine if it was you.

There must be a hundred million Americans who can't wait to sue Donald Trump for all of his defamatory of his utterances.

Donald Trump's attempts to steal the election that he claimed was stolen from him would leave him open to be sued for billions of dollars. That is not a Federal Supreme Court issue, so he can't use his appointed Supreme Court judges to help him. The next time you dishonour a soldier, as Trump had when he libelled Biden's son, remember: soldiers have long memories. And rifles that you failed to outlaw. Sleep well on that one.

And she posted it, taking a risk, using her own name.

The President's mail officer saw Dorothy's Post and brought it to his attention. '*Wow*' he thought, She has the pulse of the nation. I need her to advise me; if she will, that is and he phoned her.

'Ms Thompson, I would like you to be a confidential public affairs advisor. Can you come in?'

Her response was, 'Sure, Mr President. Anything I can do if it makes your day easier but stirs you into action would be wonderful. To make your day full on such a boring occasion,'

Dorothy chuckled before continuing, 'I have a list of what I could urge you to do in your spare time:

- Change the gun laws. Rifles were meant in 1882 for militias, who were the Army at the time, not the Trump extremist or terrorists of today.
- Change the Presidential election system to be a federal issue, not the gerrymander by the states that we have now.
- Muzzle some senators to stop the filibuster they will use legally to slow down your agenda.
- Muzzle, blackmail, or use diplomacy to get some new interpretations in the Supreme Court. I mean, diplomacy is often blackmailing. Arm twisting, maybe?
- I have read about someone who claims to have a foolproof electronic voting system. You could have a test and offer at first one million, then ten million to anyone able to break into it. When you advertise that and run a referendum, you'd get close to 90 per cent acceptance for elections conducted by electronic means.
- Anything off the record stays off the record.

   'Do we have a deal?'

'I thought I was the one making a deal here,' laughed the President. 'Don't let me down. I would love some inspiration on the filibuster issue right now if you like.'

Dorothy's immediate response was, 'The previous President didn't mind using illegal means if he could get away with it. My preferred option is to have a complete takeover by the Army: House, Senate and the Supreme Court. Can you do that under emergency measures?'

Because it was essential to solve all of those, the President told her: 'A marvellous idea, Ms Thompson. I will talk to my brand-new Attorney General, even if he has not yet been confirmed.

That filibuster problem. I need a solution that does not split the country further, but as you mentioned, diplomacy is akin to arm-twisting, and you can take this one home. A solution will be found. Arm-twisting is also called blackmail, which I can't use, but arm-twisting is a time-honoured means for diplomacy.'

'Oh, Mr President, are you telling me that you have used these means in the past?'

The President chuckles, 'Ms Thompson, it's a pleasure to do business with you. Shall we get to the next point then? I have noted your input so far with great pleasure.'

'Mr President. I think I now understand diplomacy in a way I never had before. It will come in handy when dealing with a wily fox like yourself. So tell me how you would manage an unruly Senate.' The President humours her with a glib answer.

'I walk into the Chamber smiling. Then announce: All Republican senators are sacked. I hold up a copy of the Constitution as if it gives me that power. Then I invite them to come into the discussion chamber to discover how they can be un-sacked.'

Dorothy is aghast. 'You wouldn't. Or would you?'

There was silence; then the President told Dorothy he would invite her to the Senate chamber when it would happen.

'Ms Thompson. You can bank the statement that when I say I will do something, I will. Fail once, and they walk all over me.'

After a moment of silence, Dorothy touches on the problem of getting the relief package through the house, and he responds.

'I had promised a bipartisan approach, so that is what I need to start with. Because the unemployment relief is about to expire, I will place an eviction moratorium on housing evictions until the package is passed. Then in one month, I will bulldoze it through the house.'

'In the meantime, Army will feed all the unemployed people, and for every one of the coming thirty days, there will be Washington Post reports of how the GOP want desperate people to die. Dirty tricks every day. Supported by human interest stories published by your reporters. How's that?' he asked.

'How do we get paid for that?' she asks, and he grins as he tells her.

'Circulation.' That brought their conversation to an end.

When Dorothy got off the phone, her husband Michael wanted to know how it went.

So she told him, 'I found out what diplomacy means. It means getting cooperation by any means whatever. But not in public, and face is maintained. I got a lesson in evasion too. I asked him a question, off the record. Do you know what he said? "Lovely. Now to the next point." So smooth I nearly missed it.'

Michael wanted to know what they had discussed. Dorothy thought of teasing him with 'Oh, this and that', but she was too excited and told him everything that was not confidential. Then she added, 'I'm under no illusion that he will do whatever it takes to get his agenda through and that he will manage the Supreme Court the same way. He is a man of steel.'

Dorothy called the President. After waiting a while to be connected she asked: 'Mr President, can you explain the filibuster that delays everything in the Senate, please?'

He was delighted. 'There are rules that have been put in place in the 1780s to allow the Senate to evaluate any Bills that come before them properly. It did not stipulate how this was to be done, and an easy way to delay the Bill these days and bore everyone to tears is for somebody to insist the Bill is read aloud, in full, in the Senate. These days they all have laptops and can read the Bills at home, even search for stuff. So unnecessary when a laptop would do a better job, and if they need it read aloud, then the computer can do that for you too.'

'What can you do to fix that?' asked Dorothy.

'I have been working on this since the election. I am prepared,' said the President and continued, 'I want you to sit in the gallery and witness this. You won't see it all. So on condition of absolute confidentiality, I will tell you now, but it must not come out. Ever. Do you remember I talked about diplomacy? It meant thuggery in private.'

'So why do you want to tell me now, then?' asks Dorothy.

'I may need to have news articles to counter other conflicting and outrageous reports. Some channels are so pro-Trump that they will do anything to discredit me. So, as you cannot disclose my method, you must discredit false reports with the full credibility that the Post represents. I know you can do it. Nor must Rebecca Sanders let the cat out of the bag. Do I have your word?' He did, and he proceeded to outline his diplomacy attack on the filibuster.

'I and Six soldiers with sidearms will enter the Senate, and I will announce that I need to talk to the Republican Senators in private, then pause to build tension, and only then add that the soldiers are there for the Senator's protection. Whilst I'm out with them, I expect a hush in the Chamber: everyone waiting for shots. Then the senators return, smiling. At the very next opportunity for delay, one Senator speaks up: 'The American people want this Bill dealt with now, and we work for those people. So, shall we get a move on then instead of all this delay, please?' The Republican Leader of the House will almost certainly ask: 'Have you lost your mind? You work for the Republican party, or have you forgotten?' The senators all smile, quite disarmingly, and one may say:

'I used to work for the Republican party, but the President has made me see that it is imperative to work for the American people during this pandemic. I urge you to do the same, Sir.'

The Republican Leader then splutters, chokes with rage and threatens expulsion from the party, and the response would be: 'Of course you may, Senator. You can urge expulsion at the next Senate election. That's the protocol. Until then, you will just have to put up with me.'

Dorothy is delighted, but asks, 'Mr President, how can you be sure what they say when they re-enter the chamber?' and she had that 'aha' smile when he told her 'They will be coached when I have them with me.'

'Aha, said Dorothy as they finished their conversation.

January 24

The President had invited Dorothy Thompson to the White House for coffee. She wants to know what he said to those six senators to turn them. 'Diplomacy, my dear,' was the answer.

'What sort of diplomacy then?' Dorothy questioned, and the President had this angelic smile as he responded:

'The brutal sort. In private. None will ever speak of it.'

Dorothy gets up to leave. 'I don't like you anymore,' she says with a grim face.

The President interrupts, 'Sit back down, please. Let me give you an insight into the sort of diplomacy I might have used, and I was willing to use any of them but might have used a different one. Try this for a fit:

'I will explain my need for cooperation, and when they resist, I list these scenarios.'

- I can remove your personal protection units. Then I have news reports of how you resisted unemployment benefits to twenty or more million Americans out of work because of you. Your wife will wonder how many snipers will want to take you out.
- I have dirt on all six of you or your family, and if published, you will never be re-elected. This includes child pornography, rape dating back fifteen years, and two cases of illegal money transfers to Iran.'

'Then I will tell them: 'I'm the nice guy here. The previous President besmirched my son Hunter as a druggie. I will ensure the military gets the full published story. He served in the Navy Reserves. He would have seen horrors you never had to, and required medication to help with the resulting nightmares.'

'And your ex-President besmirched him for political gain. Don't for one moment think I will not execute those threats. But I'm not threatening you, am I? All I'm doing is **allowing** you to see that America needs your cooperation until this pandemic is over. Do we have a deal?'

Then one Senator will speak up with these magic words: 'Mr President. I will be so proud to serve the American people instead of an outdated political motive. I can hold my head high, and my wife will be so proud of me. And my kids. Thank you, Sir.'

The President returned to his next pet project, guns, or more specifically, automatic rifles.

He spoke. 'Ms Thompson, I'm giving you advance notice that I will urge the Michigan Governor to see if she can pass a bill in her state to outlaw all automatic rifles and guns. She has the numbers. Then the Republicans, bless their pure hearts, will take that to the state Supreme Court, which would probably overturn the decision. That brings the Democrats into play, and the day that case is going to be heard in the Federal Supreme Court, I would love you to be in the gallery and report the day's events.'

'The same type of diplomacy?' asked Dorothy, and the president replied:

'Of course. Gentle persuasion between gentlemen, but with a guaranteed outcome.' Dorothy wants to know:

'How will that be implemented? I mean, you would have to take the guns away from them.'

He responds. 'I have had ten years to ponder this. You can take this statement to the bank, but not to the press just yet. Once the law is the law, the police will have the power to arrest those with a rifle, and the courts will LOVE to impose lengthy jail sentences.'

They hung up. It had been a good day for both of them. Can it be made to happen?

Before returning back to her hideout in Woodstream, Dorothy opened her laptop to see what mail had come in. One from Nathan Walker. *Oh dear,* she thought.

> Ms Sanders
>
> I know it was you in that car that nearly killed my mate on January ten or eleven. The car had a 'Post' logo on the door and a woman was driving. So it's you.
>
> Next time you try to kill someone on the road with your car, just be warned. I will be watching and if need be use my sniper to take out your tyres so that we can apprehend you, bitch.
>
> Nathan Walker, Tennessee

Oh good, thought Dorothy, *This can go straight to Commander Wade.*

Dear Commander Wade,

I have forwarded you Nathan Walker's email to me. You may wish to know of this implied threat. I had this nasty email from this man, and it might be a good idea if the Tennessee police kept an eye on him and his sniper.

Dorothy Thompson, The Washington Post

It had been a long and exciting day for Dorothy. When she got home she found Michael had cooked dinner. He had experimented cooking an Asian prawn dish only to discover they had no prawns at home. Dorothy's response? 'No prawns means no dinner, but I want this dinner. I have a tin of shrimp. I insist we eat your lovely meal as long as you promise me a good cuddle. That's not for me but to reward you for being so brave and cook for me. What a man.'

CHAPTER 10

January 24

Argus E noticed something was different. There were different strains of Covid-19 now, and it confused people. Everyone was still thinking of the old one, and the new threat was ignored by many, as they were unaware of it, at least till now. The mood in Washington was fearful. Something bad had happened to some Covid cases.

Instead of five days before feeling unwell, some cases now had a nasty red and itchy skin after just one day. Then they went downhill fast and were dead within a week. When this happened a few times, they tested bodies for COVID-19. Was it something else? Yes, it was a new strain. At first, it looked like the usual Covid virus under a microscope. Just one exception, though. It had a needle projecting from the tops of the column-like protein spikes. Pictures of this new phenomenon were circulated in papers and on social media. It would be called Covid-666 by Terry Balzarini.

* * *

Terry had gone fishing with his daughter Keeta. They were camped out in the Rachel Carson Conservation Park west of

Sunshine, Maryland. Keeta was a curious girl and wondered why a fish would go for a wriggling flashing bright lure made of metal. She was definitely Daddy's girl. They chatted quietly so that they wouldn't disturb the fish, a picture of harmony. When Terry saw that her line had wriggled, he nudged her with the words, 'Gently. Make sure he's taken the bait,' and she slowly reeled in the fish. It had a green body with silver undersides and a dark stripe. 'Largemouth Bass,' exclaimed Keeta, proud that she knew. Father is proud of her too. For all manner of reasons. He loved his daughter.

'Shall we go home and have it for lunch now?' asked Keeta with excitement, but Terry said, 'But first, a good fisherman needs to gut and scale the fish. Here, by the water.'

A bit later, whilst they were walking home, Terry noted a disturbance in the bushes. *Man or animal,* he wondered and marked the spot by drawing a line in the sand with his foot. He would come back later to investigate—armed, of course. No point in frightening Keeta now.

When they got home, Keeta wanted to cook the fish. Terry joined Lorraine, who had beckoned him over to look at her laptop, and showed him an email she had received from his work lab. Lorraine knew what it was about, and she did not like it. Not one bit.

Terry saw the virus pictures and noted the thin short spikes were protruding from the protein spike columns. *Oh no,* he thought, *I have to respond to that even if I don't want to.* When he looked at Lorraine, he saw the fear in her eyes and said: 'I will call and see if someone can pick me up by helicopter tomorrow. There is something I need to do here first,' and he explained that he had noticed a disturbance in the bushes.

'I need to check, take a camera with me, and some strings I can use to mark the spot, and I will take Batman with me; he has a good nose, and he will see if there was anyone there and where they came from. Do you want to come with me, then you know where they were, or if it was a deer? Whilst I'm gone, I need to know you keep Batman outside. He won't wander, and you make sure you have a loaded rifle ready above the door. You've done that before, and you're my Viking girl anyway. Just without the sword,' and Lorraine sniggered, 'I brought that too.'

Keeta was busy cooking her fish, and Terry and Loraine nonchalantly wandered off with, 'We'll be back in five.' When Terry found the spot, he let Batman off the leash. Batman was in chase heaven, found a track and gave just one whimper, hardly drawing any attention to himself. They followed the trail and saw car tyre tracks, and a short distance along, there was a gate. No lock. He had brought a heavy-duty padlock with him and locked the gate. If anyone came, they would need to make a fair bit of noise to open that, and Batman would hear and whine. Good dog.

Back at camp, he collected his family. 'Now listen good, you mob,' he joked, and Keeta and Jason took note. 'I have to go to the office and save the world. It shouldn't take more than three days. If there are any suspicious people around, or if Batman whimpers, Mum will call a number, and a chopper will arrive with a SWAT team in twenty minutes and get rid of them. All you have to do is stay close to Mum, and she's a good shot and has a SIG SAUER. And Sauer means sour, and if you shoot them with a Sig, they look pretty sour, so you should be OK.' The light tone was wasted on Lorraine, who knew this was serious.

Ten minutes later, a chopper turned up, and Terry hopped in. Big hugs first, and when he was gone, Lorraine explained that their father had accidentally killed a SARS virus ten years earlier that was the same appearance as the new one he had just seen on their satellite device. That would kill everyone on earth if he could not produce a cure, themselves included. 'No worries, Dad will save the world,' said their son Jason.

Half an hour later, Terry was in the defence virology lab looking at the virus, and lo and behold, the very same needle spikes. Maybe a bit shorter and thicker. Less likely to break off then, but potent at piercing a cell. He retrieved his old notes from ten years earlier and showed them around. The scientists looked startled. Yes, so similar, and they made a few virus copies to do tests on. They prepared saline solution batches with three strengths. One with 80 units salinity, one with 100, and one with 120, the same as those he had used in his earlier tests.

Then they prepared protein solutions, one batch from avocado, one from pea powder, and divided this into 75 units, 100 and 125 strength, similar to his earlier work. Then they had six protein solutions for three salinity solutions and eighteen scientists, ready with stopwatches waiting to see a drop of solution dropped onto a virus parasite. How long would it take to kill it, and would they be able to see it was dead? They asked Terry, 'How did you know it was killed earlier on?' and he joked:

'They fell over dead.' Then he corrected that. 'What I'm hoping for is that the protein spike will wriggle like a worm, drop off, and then the protein spike column will dissolve. The last time I did this, it took about three minutes. So don't miss it, and record the time. I will call Lorraine and see what strengths of saline and protein would be good or bad for injecting into a body. I should have asked her earlier.'

'Good timing,' said Lorraine. 'The SWAT team just rounded up a six-year-old boy from a neighbouring camp. He was so excited that he would tell his parents, so I told the SWAT team to go with him and explain. So all clear here. What's happening with your team?' she asked, and Terry told her they were ready to experiment with different saline and protein solution strengths.

'I want to know what is the best or least dangerous strength to inject into my body.'

'Saline does not matter whether you use 50, 100 or 200 units per mil, and protein is OK with 200, 400 and 600 units per mil. The only thing is the upper end may give you an erection, so don't do it with any women around,' she joked, and his reply was, 'Sorry, they are all ladies here,' as he grinned at the men.

The team was ready for the experiment. First up, they tried the 80 units of saline without any protein. No effect after twenty minutes. They tested the 75 units of protein without saline that had no impact after twenty minutes. Then they tried all protein solutions with the 80 units saline, and the viruses shrivelled up after five, four and three minutes respectively, and repeated this with the 100- and 120-units saline. The 100 units worked fastest, and the higher protein was the fastest of all. Next, they tried the 100 units saline with 125, 150 and 200-units protein. The 150 and 200-units protein produced the best results.

Terry called Lorraine. 'Any more SWAT teams turned up?' he asked jokingly. 'Oh yes, such lovely men,' said Lorraine. 'We actually had some armed men practising with sniper rifles, so you had better get home soon.' Terry could not hear laughter in her voice and asked her to put one of the SWAT team members on the phone. A man introduced himself:

'Frank here. Your wife said you want to talk to me,' and Terry asked him what had happened. 'Yep. Sniper weapons, arrested and taken away. Part of the rioting mob. We have their devices and checked their content. They had not disclosed where they were, nor had they invited any others to join them. We are clear of any present dangers. But what on earth do those fuckers think they are up to? They were handed into an Army unit nearby, safer than a police unit. Many of the police were Trump supporters, so this is better. They will be charged with an attempted murder charge. That'll sort them out for a while.'

Lorraine had told the men that Terry was in Baltimore to help find a cure for that new strain that kills in a day and that he would be back in two days if he lived through the trial cure. Also that they needed to stay, or he was coming home, and everyone dies. Then Terry told Lorraine to keep the SWAT mob happy, but not too happy.

The scientists all had a break, and then Terry allowed himself to be given saline with 100, 150 and 200 units of protein to make sure he did not react poorly to that.

The following day scientists and medical staff assembled to monitor all Terry's vitals as they gave him an injection with the new virus. They held their breath. Nothing happened for five hours. Nothing. Was the virus in his body or not? An hour later, the attached monitors started to sing and then scream. Full bore body reaction. He told the team to hurry up with the saline and protein, or he would be dead. They gave him 50 ml of saline intravenously with 150 units of protein. Nothing happened; the machines were all still screaming. Then the machines screamed louder, and a new blood sample showed happy little Covid viruses with protein needles. Damn.

Terry called Lorraine again. He quickly came to the point. 'Honey, the cure was administered ten minutes ago and should have cured all by now. It's not working in my bloodstream, and I need your help now to think of what is happening. I need assistance right now,' he moaned.

Lorraine got the picture. He was in trouble, and she was a trained medical researcher, used to fast thinking. 'Honey, I think the protein has coagulated in the blood and is now in lumps rather than a liquid. I take it you did not add blood in the tests. You need something that breaks the surface tension of the protein globules to get them back into liquid form to reach a large number of the parasites. We have used Gatorade for that in the past. It would take too long to get into your bloodstream by drinking. You need to add 100 ml Gatorade to a smaller amount of saline and inject it through your cannula immediately. I'll hang up now and call you back in five minutes.'

It took no more than a minute to administer the new Gatorade bomb, machines still screaming, with everyone present holding their breath. It wasn't just Terry's life at stake here; it was everyone in the US, including their own. Three minutes later, the screaming machines went a bit quieter but then roared back to show maximum distress.

Three minutes after that, the screams went into a whisper. Will it work this time?

Someone took Terry's blood sample and looked at it under the microscope. The needle-like protein spikes were wriggling, then falling off, then the whole parasite collapsed. His attached machines were still singing at him, but the scientists and medical staff were smiling. Five hours later, he was back to normal but exhausted from fear. That could have gone horribly wrong.

Terry called Lorraine. 'I will be coming home in an hour and will bring a few doses of cure with me,' he said. Lorraine said nothing. 'Honey, you still there?' asked Terry. Then her bawling came over the phone. She could not speak, so Terry told her. 'I take it you are relieved, or were you hoping to get rid of me?' he asked. A circuit breaker had been needed. 'You bastard,' she screamed at him. The whole lab was listening, grinning from ear to ear. Serve him right, scarring the living daylights out of them all. He should have run the initial tests with blood to see what happened to the protein solution. They envisaged his reunion with Lorraine, and most of them being male, it had to do with life-enhancing sex.

When Terry had returned home by Army helicopter, the kids raced out to meet him. Lorraine was standing in the doorway of their caravan, legs crossed at the ankles, a relaxed posture, and she trailed one finger over a breast. Lorraine made sure Terry saw that. She also made sure the SWAT members did not. They were heading to the helicopter for a return home.

The following day the news Terry and Lorraine got from the satellite device showed a disturbing number of dead bodies in the streets of Washington. Police in hazmat suits collected them, took face and body photos on their devices, and put them into body bags with handles to carry to a truck. Those body bags were never to be opened. The dead were trucked to mass graves and covered with lime. The virus, if it escaped from the bags, would die in the lime. They did not want groundwater polluted with this very deadly stuff.

Then came the worst part. Advice to parents if they, or one of their children, had these symptoms, and one plaque showed:

> If you are a mother and have children, and one with these symptoms, what do you do? The child will want a hug. If you do that, you will die and leave one child alone in the world. If both have the symptoms, do you want to die with them?
>
> The only comfort you can offer is running a warm bath, adding a lot of salt and getting your kid into that warm water to relieve the itch. We will have a cure for you in a day or two, but this is it for now.

If you call this number after tomorrow someone can come to you. We hope it's not too late.

Do not touch anyone or let your children do so. It is the most contagious virus we have ever experienced. Only people in hazmat suits should touch you.

If no one in your family has these symptoms now, go straight to a hardware store and get a hazmat suit for both parents. Then you can hug your child without fear for yourself, even if you are more worried about your kid.

It took the Army a week to procure trained people in hazmat suits to administer the cure, the required media coverage on what to do if you got red skin that itched like the devil, and how much time you had to get to a cure centre. Hundreds of health centres were set up in Washington, and a helpline to ask for someone to come to your place. The Army had requested Terry Balzarini what he wanted to call it. He had first noticed the needle spike when working at a lab in 666 Orlando St, so it was named Covid-666.

The Army was holding its breath. Would this outbreak be constrained to Washington, or will they have to chase a deadly spreading virus all over the States? Was it too late, or did they nip it?

CHAPTER 11

January 26

The mood in Washington has not changed: fearful. How bad would those promised armed protestors be? What could they do, and can they be stopped? What are they protesting about anyway?

The morning news showed police in hazmat suits collecting bodies in the streets. The number of cases had grown from 100 to 200 to 400, and the President had ordered a lockdown. Complete and utter, and some Trumpists wanted to exercise their constitutional right to go for a constitutional walk. Just for good measure, they also exercised their right to carry rifles. The Democrats thought it was their constitutional right to attack people who would infect them but had refrained so far.

The hospitals had been ordered not to admit people with the new symptoms but to send them to one of the hundred treatment sites in Washington. They had a cure, but bodies stayed infectious for three days. COVID-666 was rampant.

The news had been saturated with images of bodies being photographed and placed in body bags for family enquiries. Then they were taken by truck to mass graves. It looked gruesome to see forklifts picking up those bodies. So cold and impersonal.

*   *   *

Mitch and Danielle Upton's daughter Kathy had returned from Washington that morning. She was feeling off. By afternoon she had that red skin they had heard about, and she was starting to itch. She was miserable and asked her mum for advice. Danielle had read Rebecca Sanders' article about this new mutation and knew about COVID-666.

Mitch called the published helpline and was told to go to a treatment centre, but to call them first and arrange for a COVID-666 cure injection so that when he arrived with Kathy, they would be ready with a fix.

Mitch called Kathy, 'Hon, it's gonna be okay. Just grab your stuff and I'll get you all fixed up good and proper. Will you be happy if you go home all cured?' Kathy smiled, a wan smile; she did not feel good enough for more just yet.

Two hours later, when home again, Mitch asked Kathy how she felt now, and Kathy's answer was, 'You know me, daddy. I always feel great when I'm with you.'

He noted her playful nature now, such a relief, and decided that an acknowledgement was due. He talked to Danielle first.

'What do you think of this new Administration and army support? If we still had Trump, Kathy would be dead. This arrangement of information and action is just superb. I'm going to write to the Post for a public acknowledgement. Danielle told him she had read the earlier article by the virologist Terry Balzarini. He had noticed that the new strain, COVID-666, looked similar to a SARS virus that he had killed accidentally ten years earlier and that he had volunteered to test the new cure himself. This virus was so deadly; the whole USA could have been wiped out in a month if they had not been lucky to have someone find a cure. Mitch wrote to the Post:

Dear Ms Sanders

The people of the USA owe a big thank you to the Administration and Army. Their ever so prompt information dissemination regarding this new COVID-666 to all states will save lives. It just saved my daughter's life. That's the truth. I don't have to tell you how that feels.

But if you are free to disclose the virologist's contact details to us, I would like to thank him personally. What if he had not volunteered to be a guinea pig to save us? Gutsy, I'd say, and of his wife too, to support him. Scary. Gutsy that was.

But what is also astounding is the speed at which the Army has disseminated the information. The discovery happened in Baltimore, and two days later, we read about it in Texas with instructions for taking the cure in a health centre.

I had been a Trump supporter. He had never taken the pandemic seriously, and this new Administration has put procedures in place to get stuff done instantly. That is what those idiot protestors need to have rammed down their throats. I am not a Trump supporter anymore.

Mitch Upton, Republican, Houston.

*   *   *

General Roberts had a son. Had, as in past tense. His wife had died some years ago, and his son James Christopher was all that was left of his family. But no more. James had been on a cruise and got infected. Dead now because all those Trump supporters would not wear masks or practise safe distancing. He decided he needed to write to the Post.

Dear Ms Sanders,

I find it necessary to inform your readers how I feel about that mob's current and planned protests. I used to think they were Trump supporters. But now I think they are just rabble-rousers. Those unthinking geniuses are the same mob as those who got everyone infected with COVID-19 and killed my son. I repeat: they killed my son. I'd like to lay a charge of murder at your door and would like to know how you will feel when a summons is served on you. Since you killed my son, I have nothing left. I will be walking around with a gun and hope you quiver when you see me. I have served in battle. From the front, and I can shoot.

Mark my words. The Army will step in and take mass protestors out. Out of the picture. Snap your fingers, just like that. You don't matter. They are there to protect the rest of America, and you idiots don't give a shit, so they shouldn't either if they have to remove you. Legally. From my point of view, permanent removal would be great.

I don't think you lot have it in you to look at the nation's safety, and if you continue as you have been, it's my sincere hope that the Army will stage a coup to save the country. If you protest, it's my sincere hope that they round you up and take you to a desert camp surrounded by electric fences. One where you look after yourselves and seeing you have mingled freely with men carrying the new highly infectious strain of COVID, it won't be long before you all have it. No doctor would want to come to your help. That's my wish for you.

Please read this and feel superior if you have to, but know a day of reckoning is coming.

General Roberts, retired, Dallas.

*   *   *

Dorothy had read an article about the riots from a week ago. The news reported that some of the Capitol police had joined the rioters. She knew that the police had been almost 100 per cent supportive of Trump, who had restored their budgets and made their police forces great again. That is why the police seem to get away with murdering blacks and why their reactions to the "Black Lives Matter" were so brutal. The shame was that the commanders were whites, and the ones having to do their dirty work were mainly blacks. She read:

> During the chaos at the Capitol, overwhelmed police officers confronted and combated a frenzied sea of rioters who had transformed the seat of democracy into a battlefield. Now, police chiefs across the country are confronting the uncomfortable reality: members of their own ranks were among the mob that faced off against law enforcement officers. At least 13 off-duty law enforcement officials are suspected of taking part

in the riot. This tally could grow as investigators continue to pore over footage and records to identify participants.

Police leaders turn in their own to the FBI and have taken the striking step of reminding officers in their departments that criminal misconduct could push them off the force and behind bars.

What a mess. It would take ages for the police force to wean itself off that sort of political obligation, but at least she knew she could trust the top order. Dorothy called Colonel Mathew Wade, a straight-talking man who despised the Trump mania that his union had been embroiled in for years. Dorothy hoped that Wade would get the police funding he needed from the new Administration, and she called him.

'Good morning Commander, this is Rebecca Sanders. I hope to have one minute of your time, please.'

He teased her and said, 'So you are not Dorothy Thompson today?'

She teased back, 'Oh Commander, but I will be later. My job commands me to be flexible, as you know.' He did. Only too well. Rebecca went on, 'Commander Wade; I just read the article of January 17 that showed many of your police force were acting with the rioters. I feel for a force that is so divided and for the Commander. I note that you are turning footage of rioters over to the FBI. I have a devious thought that might unite your force instead of turning them on each other, so hear me out.'

'I would like your teams to concentrate on following up the social media accounts of all identified rioters and see what they are up to. There are two reasons. The first is that you can identify people to look out for and where to look. They had come from all over the country, and they may be planning mayhem in Florida, Texas or Miami. Let them walk into your teams for an easy arrest. Your team will get a few brownie points.'

She continued, 'But this next one is a real doozy, and all credit will go to you. Suppose you had identified a trouble-maker from earlier footage. If the trouble-maker's social media account is now deleted, that tells me someone is smart, is planning something totally illegal, and does not want to be caught.'

'There may be a few of them planning an execution. Someone with a sniper rifle taking out a politician in front of your State Capitols. Put out an all-points bulletins notice of such people, driver's licence photo, and get their car registrations.'

Commander Wade was impressed but kept it light. 'My dear Ms Sanders, you have taken far more than a minute, and as punishment, you are ordered to come to my office to witness the preparation for such arrests. Do you need me to arrange a pick-up, or will you come willingly?' He asked.

Dorothy knew she had just been given a heads-up for a story to beat all others, and she also played along.

'Commander, I'm scared you will arrest me if I don't come willingly, so I will do that. I do not wish to have a police record,' she said in a seductive voice.

'Ms Sanders, I hope to see you today so that I can impress on you the importance of not disclosing our conversation. If you don't, then you need to be arrested.'

Commander Wade called Sergeants Andrew Kenworth and John McKenzie into his office, asked them to close the doors, and started with:

'For the moment, this discussion should not go to senior officers who are likely supporters of Trump and therefore of the rioters, so it's best not to mention this to Superintendent Wilcox for the moment. What you will do will make this police department proud in the eyes of the public, and it will not hurt your careers. Are you with me?' he asked. They sure were.

'I want you each to make a team of four or more and follow up on the identified trouble-makers,' said the Commander, and he continued: 'Their details are going to the FBI. But I want our team to have some extra kudos. So, if you were planning some big riot act, something that would get you a long prison sentence, would you advertise the fact or keep mum? Don't answer, not needed.'

'Where do most of them advertise their intent? Social media. So what would it mean, gentlemen, if someone, active a week ago, has suddenly deleted his social media account? And what would the biggest protest look like?' he asked. Sargent Kenworth was on the ball instantly.

'Assassinate a politician, preferably talking in front of the State Capitol, media presence invited.' He grinned; pretty sure he was on the ball.

'Exactly!' enthused Commander Wade. 'You have two tasks:'

'One is to trawl the social media accounts of all those identified miscreants and then record where they are or will to be. If social media accounts have been deleted, bring those cases to me at once.'

'The other job is to trawl for all mention of sniper rifles and bring that to me, whether it's been on social media or someone reporting to police that they had seen one.' Commander Wade then added:

'Seeing if their social media accounts have been closed will be faster than figuring out where they are now. Come back here at 3pm with everything you have. If an interstate operation is planned, we need to bring in the FBI, but if you want to, I will second you to them wherever trouble looks like brewing', and Wade sent them off on the hunt. *Nice of the rioters to make it so easy for us,* thought Commander Wade.

At 3pm, Commander Wade received Sergeants Andrew Kenworth and John McKenzie into his office. They were grinning. They looked like they had won the lottery.

Andrew went first. 'I think John should start. Smart move by him.' So John started:

'I volunteered to issue search notices about sniper rifles, put out a bulletin asking for info and ten minutes later, we had two hits.' John continued, 'One from the wife of a Blew Ohrtman in Columbus who had left home to go to Springfield, Ohio, with a sniper, and his wife did not want him hanged, and she notified the Springfield Illinois FBI. The other was Nathan Walker from Chattanooga, Tennessee.'

'I got someone in Columbus, Ohio, to check Blew Ohrtman's home address. His wife was just packing to leave, and she showed me the empty gun rack and the car rego number. It was a Chevy sedan.'

'Nathan Walker had also left home in Chattanooga, Tennessee, but we don't know where he is headed. Also, no social media account,' finished John.

Andrew added that he had sent Ohrtman's picture to the local Springfield, Illinois police to be distributed to all motels, noting that nothing was wrong, but his wife thought he was cheating. Don't react or mention anything, but contact John McKenzie in Washington DC at this number. There would probably be a reward.

*　　*　　*

Blew had a lovely drive to Springfield. Radio on, then CDs, a few stops, and ten hours later, at 6 pm, he arrived in Springfield, IL. Too cold to sleep in the car, he stopped at a run-down motel where he was unlikely to run into anyone he knew. He stuck on a false moustache before he checked in. Just in case anyone had circulated his picture. Then he went to a car yard and exchanged his Chevy for a less noticeable but newer car. With his face changed, the trail had gone dead. Time to find a bar, listen to some good music, have a few drinks and dinner, then a drive to his motel. He had picked his spot for tomorrow morning's assassination. There was a high-rise with rooftop parking just across the road that was a bit over 200 yards away from the Old State Capitol. The Alamo apartments at 115 N 5th St, Springfield, offered a clear view of the entrance of the Capitol.

Sargent Andrew Kenworth was fired up. Glory hunting? No, just the natural instinct of a policeman who had too many suspects slip through his guard and then commit murder. *What would someone intent on murder do?* Andrew flew to Springfield, rented a car, and drove to the Old State Capitol, just a few miles from the Abraham Lincoln Airport. He moved around looking for a place a few hundred yards away that offered a high rise with rooftop parking and a direct line of sight to the Capitol. The only ones that were not government buildings were the Alamo restaurant and the car park just north of it. Job one done. Job two was to look for a car yard where Ohrtman might have swapped cars, and coming from Ohio, and he would have gone through Champaign, either via route 71 or Mt Pulaski on Route 54.

179

Andrew decided to drive east along route 71 for ten miles. Change that, fifteen miles. Then he returned to check with all six car yards he had seen on the way. None had traded Ohrtman's car in the last few days. Then he drove northeast from the Capitol towards Mt Pulaski, also 15 miles. There were nine car yards along the way; a bit more work. The last one had bought Ohrtman's car and showed him the registration of the new vehicle Ohrtman bought. It still had four months' rego, so he would unlikely have gotten new plates. He now had a picture and plate details. Problem two was solved.

Andrew returned to the Capitol and drove around to find a place for dinner. What better place than The Alamo. He got a local paper and looked to see when there might be a speech in front of the Capitol. Found it on page seven, at eleven the following day by the incoming Democrat Senator. Problem three was solved. He relaxed. Nothing to do, but he nearly choked when Ohrtman walked in and ordered dinner six feet away. Ohrtman's nice fake moustache only helped to identify a problem. A perfect time to walk out. But he was going to get his car to follow Ohrtman to his motel. Then he could tail him the following day, with FBI support. He wanted him set up for a shot before arresting the bastard.

*   *   *

On the way to their hideout at the Napa-County Regional Park, John Orthallo and Max Sanderson had discussed deterrent methods and equipment they should get. They were going to a place with only one way in.

'If we get confronted by a mob that wants to get close, what do we do?' asked Max, and John told him of his skill in defusing situations, recalling his trip from Oregon.

He said, 'I can talk most people into standing down. But if they want to proceed to our camp, then we must set up some deterrents beforehand. I had ten hours driving to think of something after our scary experience just out of Oregon. There are two scenarios I thought of. The first is if they come during the day, say half a mile from our camp. A second place if they come at dusk or early evening, and I wondered what would scare them off. We don't want a gunfight with a hundred, do we now?'

Max is intrigued and wants to know what he has in mind. John told him:

'During the day, what would scare the living daylights out of them is a voice behind them, one that shouts, "Reach for a gun, and you're dead," and in the evening, what would do the trick is to be suddenly blinded by spotlights. From two or three sides.'

'We need some bullhorns rigged up to a mobile for daylight; I press a button, and one of us can call the bullhorn phones and say those magic words. When they are all stunned, I tell them, "This is a military site now, they found nuclear material here, and it's contaminated. So it's better if you guys go elsewhere. There's a nice place at Spanish Flat, on Lake Berryessa. Twenty-odd miles back the way you came."'

'We set up the spotlights for the evening, to operate from car batteries, again switched on by a mobile phone. We need spotlights covering a wide-angle, or several of them, and set them up as soon as we get there. And test them.' They rigged up the lights to shine on their stop point from 45-degree angles into their face. But it would still allow Sue Anne to see them clearly, and if anyone raised a gun, she would take him out. If the rioters arrived in the daytime, she would operate the phone to activate the bullhorn and be ready from a hundred yards to take out anyone raising a gun.

The next day John and Max parked their vans at the Napa-County Regional Park and settled in. It was dusk. The men were at the outside BBQ cooking some ribs, a beer in hand, radio playing music, all very relaxing.

The music was interrupted by an announcement:

> Police have stopped a large contingent of rioters at St. Helena, twenty-five miles east of Santa Rosa. There were a hundred people in about thirty trucks. The two policemen in their patrol car have called for assistance. Residents are urged to avoid this group and notify the police if they see them. They are a gun-toting mob yelling abuse.

'Oh shit,' said John and continued, 'We must get the wives to listen to that.' After a quick consultation, told the kids to stay in the vans with Dominique, the men deployed to their checkpoint, and Sue Anne to her shooting spot.

Half an hour later, a mob arrived. John Orthallo waved a small torch. The group stopped ten yards from him. They saw a man in what looked like a state guard uniform, one handgun in a holster. That's all they saw. John addressed them.

'Am I glad I found you lot? Before you get yourselves into a bit of bother. My name is Walker, a ranger. Not the one you see on TV, and I'm not as pretty either,' said John. There were chuckles all around, and John continued, 'My job is to make sure strangers don't get hurt and walk into this contaminated site. Someone was planning a dirty bomb, and it all went to shit, and this stuff is lying scattered around; it sets my Geiger off the charts. Get too close, and I can see you in the dark the next day.'

'So if you men want a good site that's easy to get to, I know of a place half an hour away, Spanish Flat, right on Lake Berryessa.

Great place. Up to you. But I'm not allowed to let you get past this point.'

They turned around. Relief all around. Then one idiot turned back, took his handgun and aimed it at John. Sue Anne raised her rifle, aimed, shot the man, activated the spotlights, then spoke on the bull horn, with a calm voice: 'Time to go, gents. It's not safe here, as you can see. Take your man with you.'

*   *   *

January 27

Sargent Andrew Kenworth had trailed Blew Ohrtman the night before and had contacted the FBI for help in the morning. He would have loved to keep them out of the picture, but they were happy to have him tag along. Well, he was the one who had seen Ohrtman the night before.

They were in position near Ohrtman's motel east of the Capitol by 8am, in separate cars facing west. Coffee holders in consoles, eyes peeled to the rear-view mirrors. They knew they had a long wait ahead. At 10:30am, they saw his car. Yes, it was; it roared past Andrew, who was closer to the motel, then braked and made a right turn. Andrew started his car and followed around that corner, but Ohrtman's car was gone. Ten seconds later, the FBI pulled up behind Andrew. Quick decisions were needed.

Andrew suggested, 'You guys know this town. Maybe if you trawl around between here, the Alamo and the high-rise car park until, say, five to eleven. The shooting won't start till eleven. So you go to one place, and I'll take the other, enter and park near the top. Wait till, say, three minutes to eleven, then find him all set up. To arrest him, he must have set up his rifle for a court to convict him, and he can't shoot from the car. He will be on the ground. Which place do you guys want to take?' asked Andrew. The Fibbers chose the car park, and Andrew got The Alamo.

Andrew went to his stakeout, waited till three minutes to eleven to start his car, then got stuck behind someone trying to reverse into a car park on a lower level. *Hurry up, for God's sake,* he thought. Then he heard a rifle shot. And a second one.

*   *   *

Gus Teehan and Jason Pennewell were settling in. Gus and Jason were both outdoor types, as were their wives, Mary Rose and Lilly. They had agreed to meet somewhere out of the way. Salt Lick, Kentucky, fit the bill. Route 60 between Salt Lick and Lakeview Heights might be the main road, but north of it was shut off from traffic by the winding Licking River, and hills cut off south of it. Halfway between those two places, they found the perfect spot. Fraley Road would take them to the base of the hills. Then a bit of off-road, and they were at the bottom. No one else around, no one to see them, and if they walked up a bit, they could see anyone coming from miles away.

Just as well they thought, They had heard of the potential violence at the State Capitols, and those mobs would roam around any time. Best to be out of the way of them.

They had both arrived in their motor homes, with all the creature comforts for a freezing winter. Gus had brought two large tarps as well and some foam mattresses. They laid those on top of the RVs with air gaps between them and then pulled the tarps over and tied them down, angled to get away from their motor home walls. If it snowed heavily, all they had to do was pull the tarps off, shake, and put them back. So much extra heat insulation. Easy as.

A few days later, Gus saw some people coming. Who were they, farmers or rioters? Gus called Jason to go with him, telling the ladies to prepare to shoot if trouble started. The two men strolled towards the oncoming mob, halted and introduced themselves.

'Morning all, long way from home on foot? Anyway, my name is Gus Teehan from Tennessee, and this is Jason Pennewell from Pennsylvania. We've been given the job of making a quantitative survey of birds, especially eagles, so I do hope you won't disturb us with shooting. Disturb the birds, I mean.'

'Well, no, we are not far from home; we're on foot, as you see? We are just making sure that there are none of those rioters around. My son got killed, and if we see any, it's short shrift,' said one of the men, and Jason asked them for a phone number.

'We have a satellite phone, and if we see any, I'd love to give you a call.'

'Men after my own heart,' said Gus, and they soon parted company, knowing that help could be on the way if needed.

*   *   *

A minute after 11 am, the FBI and Sargent Kenworth had heard the rifle shots, two in quick succession. That meant the first shot had missed. Both cars raced to the top in their different parking up-ramps.

Andrew Kenworth swung violently around the corner after corner, and then he saw Ohrtman's small yellow car come at him. His own was as big as a patrol car, and he accelerated and rammed Ohrtman, immediately calling the FBI. 'Got him on level six, come quickly. I need your help,' as he stepped out of his Oldsmobile, his Glock out, pointing at Ohrtman, whose yellow car was spuming steam. The motor had died, and Ohrtman was trying to get out. Andrew had rammed his door, which would not open. Ohrtman jumped out of the passenger door and down to the next level.

Andrew called the Fibbers again, 'He jumped down to level five and is probably trying to break into a car on level four or five.'

Nathan Walker had also turned up in Springfield, Tennessee. He had just finished a leisurely morning tea and was going back to his car. He'd left it on level three, he thought. Not there, so he walked up one level. Ah, there it was, his black SUV. Then a harassed man ran to it and tried to open the door. That man was distraught.

'This car yours?' the man asked, and Nathan had a stern look in his eye.

'Step away now, or you're dead,' he yelled.

Seconds later, the unmarked FBI car pulled up behind the black SUV, and two men leisurely strolled over. 'Any problems here?' They whipped out their shiny Smith and Wesson handguns. 'Hands up now, Mr Ohrtman,' snapping handcuffs on him.

Then they looked at the other man and asked him if he wanted to lay charges. He did, and they thanked him, snapped cuffs on him too and said, 'Nice to find you here, Mr Walker, and we have a warrant for your arrest.'

Ohrtman replied, 'If you want him can you let me go now please?'

'Sorry, Mr Ohrtman. We are arresting you on a murder charge. Correction, attempted murder,' just as Sargent Andrew Kenworth came running to them. Then he saw Nathan Walker as well. Was it Christmas?

Chapter 12

January 28

The first few days of the administration were marked by a dangerous new development and seemingly contradicting pandemic indications. There were accelerating infections from new strains from the UK and South Africa but reducing infections in the hotspot states. The President called a meeting of relevant advisors, and the new White House press secretary released the following statement:

> On Thursday, January 28, 2021, the President assembled his pandemic task force to plan the required response for the new highly infectious strains from the UK and Africa. Present were Dr Federico Ponti, his Infectious Disease expert, and other known advocates for stopping the virus spread, namely Jay Inslee from Washington, Gretchen Whitmer from Michigan, and Mike DeWine from Pittsburgh. Also invited and present was William Schuster, the new Deputy Attorney General, to offer lockdown advice. The meeting concluded an hour later when a press release was promised.

Dorothy Thompson received the promised press release and spent some time digesting it. Other news channels would also have received the same notice. Details could be reported as received, but the Post always offered the best opinion pieces, and she deliberated.

The release had the following dot points:

- The new strain spread is so vicious that the President orders martial law to get people off the streets in nominated hot spot states or cities for two weeks, starting the next morning, 29 January, 2021.
- The national guard will police the curfew. Anyone found on the street is to be arrested.
- TV and social media will advise people to leave notes for food delivery to their door.
- For medical help, they need to describe their health issues and their usual doctor, and an Army doctor or nurse will attend.
- You can open the windows for fresh air as long as you wear a mask. For claustrophobia, call the indicated helpline or visit the following website.
- If pregnant and going into labour, call the number below, and a midwife or doctor will be at your home within half an hour.
- Army guards will block travel between states or cities to these hotspots.
- We will release all details on social media and the pandemic website within the hour.

*   *   *

Jason Donovan, leader of the Bravehearts, had cultivated the smile of the kind assassin. Which is what he was. His mantra was: 'You can't do that to me and expect to live.' To get to the top of his 'DREAM' team, he had to lead, cajole, and occasionally kick ass. More importantly, he had to stay boss with all the protection that brought him. To stay boss, he needed to stage big successful protests. He was lucky to have a good second-in-command, Tim Highfields. Jason knew that the way to a happy leadership was to allow his second-in-command to be the next best thing to being in control and making major proposals.

That day on January 6, the election vote allocation day, had been a successful demonstration whilst also failing its objective to overthrow the vote.

Jason was talking with Tim Highfields about possible new demonstrations.

'We gotta stop those lockdowns. Those stupid buggers. They want to stop me from going to a bar and having a drink with my buddies. What would you do, Tim?'

'We need to be out in such large numbers that they can't arrest us all, and when bars and shops see the numbers, they will open up to make a buck. It has to be big enough to achieve that. The government loses credibility and stops lockdowns. Remember our creed. *"We come together to protect the country, defend it against the government."* 'Yep, doing the right stuff is hard.

*   *   *

Lockdowns had also been ordered in Pittsburgh, and Terry Copperfield of the Forcefield militia had called his Deputy Matt Davis to discuss the future, and he addressed Matt.

'Tell me, Matt, do you remember our pledge?'

Matt did, 'Not the words but the meaning is what I live for. I hate bloody sweating stinking blacks, and I hate that they take our jobs, our women even, and now to protect the blacks from the virus, they order a lockdown, and I lose money in my hair salon. We must take a stand. One with enough force to be effective,' finished Matt.

'And what else do you remember?' asked Terry.

'*That the US government is hurting the country or secretly planning to destroy it.* We need to overthrow that government. That's what,' answered Matt.

Terry brought him back to earth. 'We can't overthrow the government. All we can do is make them look bad, so they lose in four years. So what would make them look really bad? Think.'

Matt had already thought: 'The worst thing that can happen to the government is if the protest marches get out of control and the guards shoot a civilian. TV will be live, and if they capture that, all hell will break loose. So we need to make sure the guards shoot someone.

'Why?' asked Terry. and Matt explains 'If we shoot at them first, they will retaliate. Then the government will face a firestorm of protests in the House and on the streets. Protesters will come out armed after that. Chaos forever.'

*   *   *

Lt. Col. Freebody was a career officer with no blemishes on his record. There was a reason for that. He never took shortcuts when it came to morals; in his case, the morals needed to lead soldiers in battle. Soldiers are trained to shoot first and ask questions later. As the company leader, he needed to ensure his valuable soldiers did not lose the plot and shoot unarmed people. His job was to save the soldiers a fate of a Court Martial, destroying their career and costing the army resources.

He had previously been seconded to Syria for an officer interchange participating in Army meetings to manage crowds, with as many arrests as possible to get instigators off the streets. There, he had experienced what it was like to ask troops to confront angry and armed mobs of thousands of civilians. Halfway into his secondment, he attempted to transfer to Egypt. Syria had provided the unfortunate experience of being assigned to a murderous platoon. The Presidential Guards seemed to be paid by how many protestors they could shoot. It was a nightmare.

Then his transfer to Egypt was granted. What a difference when the Army does not pay lip service to the President against whom people protested. Egypt was one of the oldest civilizations, and the military behaved civilly. Funny that. They sat in their jeeps and on their tanks, yes, but instead of shooting protestors, they cheered them on whilst having a fag. He had queried a Lt. Colonel at one stage to ask what was going on, letting protests carry on despite orders from the President.

He was told, 'We have been trained that a soldier has obligations to protect the weak above the need to follow orders. Following illegal orders is a crime.'

Freebody had never forgotten that lesson, and his men loved him for it if there is such a thing as love in the Army. His subordinates Captain Braidwood, and Sergeants Bloodwood and Thomas had been trained to follow in his mould.

*   *   *

Dorothy Thompson wondered how people would respond to the President's press release. What was important? What was her role as a reporter? So she started her response:

Dear readers, the White House released a press report this morning that requires urgent action from millions of affected Americans tomorrow.

It is IMPERATIVE that you stop whatever you are doing and prepare yourself for this lockdown, with no exceptions from anyone. Go home, but do your last-minute shopping first, then prepare your shopping and medical needs list for later Army delivery. The pandemic social media and websites have details of what you can include in those shopping lists. If you are pregnant, please ensure your details are correct, especially if you are due shortly.

When you have done this, please ensure your partner has done the same. Make sure that the details for the whole family are correct.

It's no good complaining later. Notify all other family members and neighbours.

She looked over it briefly and sent it. There was no time to be lost.

Dorothy wondered how many people would ignore this curfew and decide to protest against this measure instead. Where would the National Guards take them if 15,000 turned up?

*   *   *

After leaving the President, Dr Federico Ponti, Jay Inslee, Gretchen Whitmer, and Mike DeWine settled down to work on the lockdown plan.

Dr Ponti offered, 'I am surprised the President accepted our prognosis of the D-xxxx variant. Just too infectious for words. If we get 5,000 cases one day, then 25,000 the next day, and 125,000 the day after. Drastic measures are needed, only for two weeks. What will likely happen now is that all family members of an infected person will get infected. So we must strongly warn them to observe social distancing in the home. Hopefully, mothers are not infected and must stay clear from her husband for four days and be able to look after the children.'

Gretchen Whitmer had lots of experience in trying to lock down a city and had survived multiple death threats as a result in the past. She suggested, 'We have a state population of just under ten million. You cannot staff a call centre for that number, let alone in Texas or California. We need a helpline that advises people on what website to go to and tell them to call triple zero for real emergencies. Issue heavy fines for trivial or nuisance calls. This is an emergency, and we have emergency powers.'

Gretchen continued, 'We need to notify the President immediately that the curfew does not apply to listed essential workers. Then we need to advise him just as urgently that we can only implement a voluntary stay-at-home order immediately. The full curfew must be delayed for two days to allow some immediate shopping, but mainly for our websites to be tested and running, and emergency centres to be staffed. The website needs to tell people everything they need to know, emergency links for health, pregnancy, and supplies. Tell people it's faster to use the links for emails. There will be no phone; It would be jammed and you will be on call waiting forever; extra people will staff the emergency centres on the links provided.'

Mike De Wine has his say. 'I agree. We need to advise the President that we cannot have this service up and running by tomorrow morning. We need to get the Department of Homeland involved to set up the website; they probably already have templates to work with after other earlier planning sessions.'

After the curfew discussions ended, the President asked William Schuster, the Deputy Attorney General, to stay back.

'William, this is why I called you back. If there is a mass insurrection, and tens of thousands turn out to march, what can we do? Police holding cells may hold twenty, but this would destroy any concept of enforcing the curfew. What can I do?'

William scratched his head but quickly had an answer. 'Mr President, if you make a threat and can't enforce it, you will never be able to enforce any orders in the future. The only suggestion is that you call in the Army and instruct them to prepare for massive civil disobedience that requires several camps to be created, each capable of housing, say, five thousand prisoners a piece. Let's call them temporary holding pens with facilities to cook their own meals. No phones or devices are allowed. It can be tent accommodation. Let them set up electric security fences outside. If you then publish what you have done with those arrested, you may get another protest and arrest them as well. After that, there won't be any street protests unless authorized. You only need to do this once.'

'Please discuss this with the AG and the Chief of Army and get back to me by this evening. And bring them along, please,' said the President.

Shortly afterwards, the President received a call from Mike Devine and told him to go ahead. 'Mr President, I'm calling for an urgent need to modify your press release. The three of us met and discussed the curfew. We advise these changes, Mr President

- The first is that you only have a voluntary stay-home order tomorrow so that people can buy last-minute needs. The next day you need to exclude essential workers, visits to a dentist or doctor.
- The second recommended change is that we need two days to create the necessary website to handle queries in each city. We also require that time to set up staffing for help centres.
- We may also have to rethink doctor visits by Army and instead have army pickups to take people to their doctor, and we may want Army to give hazmat suits to anyone they are to transport, and that would take two days to organize.
- Also, you do not want bus transport and may need the Army patrolling the streets to pick up people who need transportation to see a doctor.

We recommend you have a press release asking for voluntary stay-home orders for two days, and that you will issue details of exceptions and what to do later tomorrow, and avoid issuing conflicting instructions.'

The President thanked him with the words, 'Great work. Keep me informed,' and hung up. Almost immediately, the phone rang again. It was Dorothy Thompson who asked for a minute.

'Mr President, I was getting ready for my press release following yours, trying to advise my readers, and I realized you might need to consider some changes. Would you like to hear them, or shall I send you something in writing, Mr President?'

He replied, 'Thank you for calling, so go ahead.'

'Well, Mr President, you need to allow essential workers to go to work, and you need a nice simple solution for people visiting doctors. You don't really want infected people running around town, and you should consider the two-week period where doctors make house calls. In their cars, in their protective clothing, take an internet-enabled device along for patient history and email prescriptions to their pharmacy. You run a daily delivery service for pharmacies. For essential dentist bookings, give them a lift to the dentist but encourage them instead to take strong painkillers and see if they can wait for two weeks. Anyone going into labour should call an ambulance to take them to hospital.'

'Well, Ms Thompson, I think you are wasted as a reporter and should work for me. How well do you know that Rebecca Sanders, please? Do you think she might give me a call too sometime? She writes such wonderful, fascinating reports.'

'That is so kind. I'm sure she would like to know. How soon would you like to hear from her then?' asked Dorothy.

The President came back with, 'Right now would be good.'

Dorothy dropped her voice a bit and said, 'Good afternoon Mr President; how may I help you?'

The President chuckled and said, 'You just have, Ms Sanders. One and the same. But I won't tell anyone. But I could ask your boss if we could borrow you for a few weeks on 'Important Assignments' and see if he gives you a pay rise.'

'Mr President, that is so kind of you. But Dorothy wants to have a word now,' said Dorothy and continued, 'Rebecca Sanders needs to keep a totally independent profile to maintain her readership. Still, I, Dorothy, could afford to visit your offices and consult with your team. I would learn so much as well, and I would pass it on to Rebecca. We talk all the time.' She and the President both chuckled.

*   *   *

Terry Balzarini and his wife Lorraine were safe in a wilderness location but kept up with virus news via her satellite-enabled tablet. He was discussing the South African strain with Lorraine.

'Did you read about the B.1.351 strain, Lorraine?' he asked.

Lorraine replied with, 'Yep. Nasty one. So many mutations in the spike protein make it very dangerous. Further mutations could be a killer. This one is highly contagious already.'

Terry discusses that with Lorraine, and they decide to alert the public with precautions, calling Dorothy Thompson at the Washington Post. When Dorothy answers, Terry does the social thing and then quickly gets to the point.

'Dorothy, what do you know about the South African strain of COVID-19?'

Dorothy tells him, 'Not much, just that it's more infectious. You would know a lot more. So why don't you tell me why you called?'

Terry told her, 'The South African variant, known as B.1.351, has got scientists worried because of its unusually large number of mutations, especially in the spike protein, which the virus uses to attach to and infect human cells. It did not include one scary thing that worries me though. I want to discuss it with you so that you can alert the wider audience.'

'Geez, what is the scary thing, Terry? I hope I can help distribute the news effectively,' replied Dorothy.

Terry told her, 'The multiple mutations of the spike protein could mean future strains that are deadly and impossible to contain. We need people to get off the streets, and now. One new deadly strain nicknamed D-xxxx starts with a blue neck on day two, and people are dead on day three. It has not been named or identified by the WHO yet. Just so you get the picture of the danger, imagine two swordsmen training with a heavy sword. After two weeks, new muscles start to build. If one mutation gets together with a different mutation, then I'm terrified they will fight to get supremacy; and will make a much more potent form for themselves. We need everyone off the streets to trace all occurrences of the D-xxxx strain symptoms and isolate traced people. Unfortunately, contact tracing in the US does not work because people don't use their safe logins. You need to scare the living shit, I mean daylights, out of people to get them to cooperate to wipe this one out.'

Dorothy replied. 'I will contact the President, as I'm sure he would need to know and order people off the streets. I don't pretend to know how viruses mutate, but I will quote your example to him. Then I can report how the President has ordered this lockdown and why. Put some muscle behind it.'

Dorothy called the President again to update him. The President told her Dr Federico Ponti had already briefed him, and that was why he had ordered the lockdown in the first place. He thanked her and called off.

She updated her press release:

Rebecca Sanders reporting.

Dear readers, please take note. The proposed lockdown ordered by the President is not a joke. The new strain mutated from the South African virus is so dangerous that it needs your respect. Please follow the President's orders if you want to live till next week. I trust you not to disappoint me.

Well, she knew that the protestors would not heed her or the President's instructions. She hoped not too many would turn out to protest. As she knew about the proposed Army intention to lock them up in the desert and have it shown on TV, she was sure there may not be any more mass protests

January 30

Jason Donovan of the Braveheart Patriots in Washington calls his deputy Tim Highfields for a meeting.

'Tim, what do you think of this latest Presidential bullshit to have a total lockdown because of a new virus strain?[51]' Tim loves it when Jason gives him the responsibility for knocking the President.

'I think they need to show us more respect. I think we need to show him what he has to deal with here. We should have a quick test of resolve, and if that does not work, a bloody big demonstration. What can they do if a thousand of us turn up marching on the White House, arrest a thousand? You have to be kidding.'

Tim continued: 'I will send one of my soldiers out to buy cigarettes. I have someone in mind. A big bloke with a big laugh and an even bigger rifle. He is itching to be a hero. We'll send him to that shop at least a mile away – give the guards plenty of time to see and arrest him, if they are game.'

'Does he have a family?' asked Jason.

'No,' replied Tim. 'There is no one dependent on him. He's perfect in case things go wrong.'

'OK, Tim,' said Jason, 'but make it five of them as a team. A bit harder to take down, and we get more TV no matter what happens. We need exposure. Can we do it today, or do we need to wait till tomorrow?'

---

[51] 'That hurricane is coming' - expert warns the US to brace for virulent Covid strain.

Tim offered: 'Today is best. Less time for the national guard to get organized. Get set, and when ready, move out and text me so I can notify the media. It's still daylight, so it will make great TV when the street lights come on. Off you go.'

Thirty surveillance officers of the National Guards task force in Washington monitored phones from known militants when one of them called out, 'Found a message from Tim Highfields from the Braveheart Patriots.'

Someone else called out: 'They have decided to test the lockdown orders. Quick, someone, trace the call and see where he is and which way he is walking.'

They got the location. 'Those bastards are in Anacostia, of all places, hiding in plain sight amongst the military establishment. The phone's not moving. So, he is directing the moves, and they would be out on the street somewhere near Minnesota Avenue. Get some drones to fly over the area and pinpoint them and get back to me.'

*   *   *

Terry Copperfield was in Shadyside, Pittsburgh. He heard of the planned lockdown and wants to let the government know they are pissing in the wind with a claim of arresting protestors. How do you arrest two thousand or more protestors, eh? Terry calls his deputy Matt Davis and his next five lower deputies into the conference room.

'OK, beardy beasts, why have I called you here this minute?' he asks.

One smart-arse kicks in with, 'You want to make sure we don't shave. We gotta look like beasts.'

But the man next to him, Matt Davis, was a bit smarter. He wanted to retain Terry's respect, and started with: 'Pretty obvious you did not agree with that shitface President's lockdown proposal with threats of arrests. Methinks you've called us to show him he can't do that. You just can't arrest five thousand protestors, especially if we make sure the media is present to make them hesitate to use force. They will be neutered.'

'OK, youse all, how would you go about it so they don't know where we're going to protest, and so the media can see a force of five thousand marching down the Avenue with not a police guard in sight?' asks Terry Copperfield.

Matt Davis is his go-to man again. 'First, we use the dark web to organize five thousand warriors with rifles to converge on Lincoln/Bigelow Boulevard near the intersection of Herron Avenue. That would allow 2,500 people to march there from the northeast and another 2,500 from the southwest. Split both sides of Lincoln. Plenty of parking along the way, and we can organize some buses to take people from further out to a nearby street. One moment there is no protest; the next, there are thousands without being stopped,' said Matt.

One of Matt's offsiders suggests: 'We don't want the press there when we first arrive. We want them there when we are assembled. Only then let them notify the National Guard or whoever when we are there.' He continues, 'And we can notify two TV channels that we are planning a protest and to have drones ready on standby. We'll tell them where and when after we have assembled.'

Terry Copperfield is pleased with their progress. Also, if anything goes wrong, it was their idea. All he did was agree with them, but it was time to be boss again.

'OK guys, now come some details. How many days do you think it will take to plan all of this, organize people, what weapons to take and to get confirmation of who is coming?' asked Terry.

Discussions and arguments, and then Matt spoke: 'Let's use the YCSM channel, the You Can't See Me one.'

'To do that, we need to issue a social media alert with a hidden message that says, "You Can't See me doing this unless it's urgent". That alerts them where to look and how to get back to us. We want to allow all our members to be patriots, so let's say three days. For extra security, let's use a password to get in, 02F, for the date of the planned demonstration,' said Terry, and added:

'Use the YCSM channel to advise that they have to decide whether to bring weapons, what type and whether they are prepared to use them, or if only for show. It's their decision.'

*   *   *

The surveillance officer in the National Guards head office received the call he was waiting for. 'They are moving southwest towards the 7-Eleven store. Get a chopper to deploy twenty guardsmen just around the corner from there and say hello to those boys,' was the order.

Two minutes later, they switched to Fox News just as a story was breaking. Fox had a drone TV hook-up which saw the guard chopper set down, men deployed and moving across Minnesota Avenue. The news anchor was talking his head off, screaming, 'Is this going to be a fight or flight?'

Just then, the Guards with a bullhorn ordered the patriots to stand down and drop their weapons. One man raised his rifle, and a shot rang out as a bullet hit his rifle, knocking it out of his hands. The bullhorn had a new message: 'We love shooting at you but aren't allowed to unless you raise a weapon. You could just disappoint us by dropping yours to the ground. Or we shoot your hands off.'

Four men raised one hand in the air, the other releasing their visible weapons. The TV anchorman exclaimed, 'Look behind the patriots. Guards are approaching. Now what?'

The rear guards had soft rubber shoes that made their steps almost silent. They came up behind the patriots and lifted their hand-guns from the warriors' belts, snapping handcuffs on them before they could react. Twenty guards marched five warriors off to the waiting choppers to take them into custody. The TV anchorman waxed lyrical about the efficiency the guards had displayed.

*   *   *

Shortly after, Terry Copperfield sees the news item and calls his deputies back into a conference. When all five are present, he starts with a replay of the recorded Fox news item.

'Looks like they tried to make a point. Small point. We lost. What is your takeaway from that?' he asked.

Tim Davis quivers like a hunting dog who has spied the hare, and he starts:

'Two things. One is that we need numbers the guards can't match. In terms of personnel and transport. And weapons. The other is that we show those Patriots they need to join us instead. They have over 100,000 members. I want half of that number to come our way and eventually mop up all other organizations. And bingo, we are Kings.'

*   *   *

The White House Pandemic team had also seen the Fox News story of protestors being arrested. They met in their conference room, and Gretchen Whitmer from Michigan got the ball rolling.

'That was a starter to see what we would do. We saw five warriors on the street and sent twenty Guards to arrest and take them away. They did that on purpose, thinking that we would be stonkered when they arrive with 20,000 protestors. How do you even start to handle that?'

Mike DeWine, from Pittsburgh, had experienced protests of 10,000. He did not have a solution, but he thought of something that would stop this nonsense once and for all. He had been a teacher taking a class of fifty on an overnight excursion that had gone out of control. He offered this advice:

'They will keep brawling until you get rougher with them than they had ever expected. If you get really rough, then it's over forever, and if you don't, it's on forever. The same happens in war. This is war, and the best way to fight them without us getting hurt is to call in the Army. Bring them in with troop carrier helicopters with loudhailers setting the conditions, the first being that we shoot anyone raising a rifle. Some idiot will fire at a helicopter, and a sniper in one next to it returns fire. Gets his head blown off. If it's not all over, then it is with the next shot, all captured on TV and broadcast. You'd have to be nuts to try after that.'

'Let's call in the Army right now and set up the earliest possible meeting. They will have shitloads to do if they have to arrest say 5,000 and cart them away.'

Two hours later, the Chief of Army had called in officers with sufficient rank to get stuff done.

February 2

Lt. Col. Freebody of the Army Civil Deployment Brigade called his people into his conference room.

He explained the reason for the meeting. 'Gentlemen, we are here to plan a response to planned mass protests. That includes 2,000 soldiers, airborne transport to the protests, deploy and confront, loudhailer warnings, crowd control, and arrest protesters. We will need transport to take them away, short distance, then long-distance, then a holding pen to keep them off the streets. Thousands of them. Far too many possible infections to have them in the city. To get us started, Captain Braidwood, please outline a proposal.'

Captain Braidwood looked up from his notepad. He was not happy to be put on the spot like that, but by Jeeves, he would show them why he was a Captain and hoped he would deliver, with his boss there and all. This was not a harmless presentation, like one at the golf club. He started:

'Hear this. My plan of attack is that we prepare for three scenarios: Small, medium, and large. To get ready for a mass demonstration, staffed and trained teams will take us, say two days, for a small demonstration of 1,000 protestors, four days for a 10,000 strong mob, and say six days for a bigger crowd of 100,000.'

'We will never be able to arrest all of them. The aim is not to arrest them all, but a sufficient number so that the media can drill home the message: "Don't mess with us". If we arrest five people in a hundred, then we still get mass TV coverage, and if they double down, then we do too. For the larger protests we need to create tent bedding for the prisoners, It needs to hold five thousand people for two weeks.'

Staff Sergeant Thomas enters the conversation: 'Soldiers do not like shooting at civilians, even if the police don't seem to mind. But if confronted by someone who raises a rifle at him, then I think retaliation is dished out with glee. All responders need to be volunteers for this mission, though. We will need loudhailers warning people not to even RAISE rifles or guns at us, or we will mow them down.'

Sergeant Bloodwood has his say, too: 'Soldiers are trained to shoot at people who level a gun at them. They are also trained not to shoot at unarmed people. We will need training sheets with everything the soldiers need to know, including when to shoot. All must have a bodycam in working order, and we must have a written order allowing return or first fire when the men sign up for the mission.'

Lt. Col. Freebody decided that he could issue orders now, and he spoke. 'Most of you know me, but for any newbies, I had been seconded to two Arab countries to train in crowd control. In Syria, the Presidential Guards were killing civilians and laughing. The Egyptian army guys sat on their vehicles, smoking and passing the day with the protestors. That is my preferred option.'

'Today, we need a corps of twenty to pick up an expected test of a small number of protestors so they can see what we do. Staff Sargent, please take charge of that one now. Tomorrow we will get ready for a small protest of 1,000 by February 4, so Captain, please form a team for that and advise by morning.'

'Tomorrow morning, we meet here at 0800 hours, and Captain Braidwood presents his plan, including names of officers to help. Then you, Captain Braidwood, will start this second job. Prepare for a protest of 100,000, ready to deploy by February 6. When done, I will bring in another company for advice on crowd control in case we expect a million protestors. Just one thing to keep in mind. Today we respond to five or ten protestors. By the 4th for 1,000 protestors, by the 6th for 100,000, and by the 8th for 1 million. We do not respond till our plans are in place and manned.

The meeting ended. Plans were in place or being prepared. What would tomorrow bring?

CHAPTER 13

February 3

Argus had returned from a trip to Delhi conferring with his Indian supervisors and took the time to visit his old University professor as well. They discussed the new strain that gave people a blue neck on day two, before death the next day.

His Indian supervisors asked him, 'Argus, tell us about this new phenomenon please.'

'I don't know much about it yet, but since it kills people in three days, no one should be allowed into India or its territories from overseas until further notice. When I get back to Port Blair I will contact a virologist who knows best.'

He caught a flight back that day and started to look at his AI to see what was happening. One search command that included the term 'Blue Neck virus' and the result was all tabulated for him.

The mood in Washington was dreadful. Would there be violence? How infectious would the protestors be? Would they come armed, and if so, would they shoot? The indications were that the protests would happen on February 5. The general population has had pandemic overload, and they don't want to hear about it ever again. They've had a gut-full. But the news about the new deadly strains hasn't sunk into the thick heads of the protestors. They don't care and never would.

* * *

Dorothy Thompson wanted the readers of her bulletin to understand the severity of the new strain. She decided she needed to take people to task. *Make them sit up and listen*, she thinks, and she writes using her nom de plume:

Rebecca Sanders reporting.

It is disturbing that the country is falling into a state of anaesthesia about news regarding the pandemic. There are now new deadly strains. Mothers and fathers, would you allow your five-year-old to run across a busy five-lane highway? Of course not. Then why do you pay no heed to save your children from death within days by going out as if there is nothing to worry about? There is. This new virus kills. You will kill your children if you go about your daily business the way you have been at the moment. Do you understand? You will kill them. You need to wear a mask, preferably one so that it is always clean, to go out anywhere. You should wear gloves that go in the disinfectant after an outing, and, ideally, you do not go out at all for two weeks. Please plan for this.

Some high and mighty supremacists are planning mass protests. Stay away from them. A large number of them will be infected, and if so, by the end of the day, we may have many thousands that will be dead in only a few days from self-inflicted wounds. Hospitals will not admit people coming from the protests. It's just too dangerous. If you need to know more, please call the Pandemic helpline and select the option for 'New Strains.'

* * *

Jason Donovan addressed his team of Braveheart patriots in Washington. They met at his place in V Street, Anacostia, south of Minnesota Avenue. He addressed the assembly:

'OK. Let's go over the objectives and our plan. The objective is to have 10,000 men on a march with banners to show why we are here. The banners will say, "Lockdowns are unconstitutional and illegal". That is why we march. We will carry hidden handguns. Only to be used if anyone points a gun at us, then blaze away. There will be TV crews monitoring all action via drones, so don't show your guns until you have to.'

One of his crew asked, 'Why is it illegal to have lockdowns?'

Jason smoothly sidestepped that one, 'Because we say so. Our Constitution gives us the right to protest, and these lousy Democrats want to take that right away. So it's illegal.' But that crew member wants to know why they organised the lockdown, and Jason sure is ready for that one. 'Because they found a new infectious strain in the UK. In the bloody UK, for God's sake. That's where, and now they want to lock us down because of the UK. The UK is a different country, you know.'

Jason's leadership was restored. Such a clever man.

* * *

Terry Copperfield in Pittsburgh, head of the Forcefield Patriot group, addressed his mob at his home in Shadyside.

'We will march down Bedford Avenue from Upper Hill. We want to field 10,000 protestors. No arms, but plenty of big poles and flags. "Wear your colours" is the theme. Banners to be provided, some with "You can't stop me protesting against this grotesque lockdown" or bring your own. "Let's show them who's boss around here" is the message we want to send. What are they going to do? Arrest 20,000? Not possible.'

There were lengthy debates about no weapons. Matt Davis, Terry's deputy, addressed the crowd:

'They are prohibited from shooting civilians, much as they would want to. It's the law. Let's not give them an excuse. Where would they put 1,000 of us anyway, let alone 10,000? It's just not possible, and the media would show what heroes we are. You'll be famous.'

Matt continued, 'Make sure you don't shave. I want big wild hair. Wear a surf lifesaving cap tied down over the top. It will make your hair stick out. Like *Where the Wild Things Are*. Look ferocious. They don't call us the "Hairy Beasts" for nothing. You guys are upholding our rights. Have big poles and flag poles. Wield them ferociously. People will envy you, and we will attract more members and become more powerful.'

Someone asked, 'Why do they want lockdowns anyway?' The answer he got was not entirely truthful.

'They claim there is a deadly new strain. They found cases in the UK and also in South Africa. Next thing they will tell you they found a case on the moon. Better watch out.'

Ribald laughter removed any remaining traces of concern. They were ready to rock and roll.

*   *   *

The President asked Federico Ponti, his Infectious Disease expert, William Schuster, the Deputy Attorney General and Lt. Col. Freebody to meet.

The President started: 'We discussed this not long ago. Those Anti-Vaxxers plan to protest on the Fifth. First, Dr Ponti, updates on the new strain, please.'

Dr Ponti told him, 'The news is bad. Infections from the old strains are falling, but the new strain cases are rising exponentially, with the new D-xxxx strain outpacing everything else. We need to get people off the streets. Patients with this new strain have visible symptoms, a blue throat. We must prevent those from being admitted to any hospital; we can do nothing for them. If they get into a hospital, we will almost certainly see everyone there dead within two days. We have to keep healthcare workers safe, so we need to issue a warning. The protestors won't listen, but they will pay the price.'

The President asks his Deputy Attorney General, 'Mr Shuster, I will need your advice on how to close hospitals for patients with that D-xxxx strain symptom legally.' Shuster's reply is encouraging.

'You are always allowed to issue instructions that favour the public health. You will need to issue a press release, and that will inform everyone. That is all you need to do.'

'Thanks, William. I will do so straight after this meeting. I now need to confer with the Army Chief of Staff and my civil disorder expert, Lt. Col. Freebody.'

Then Dr Ponti heard the ping of an incoming message, looked at it, and added, 'It says here that a new E848K strain was found in the South African and British strains. That is bad news. Strain in a strain. That makes an already highly infectious strain a lot worse.'

Dr Ponti continued, 'The immunity provided by vaccination is largely due to the antibodies that bind to the Receptor Binding Domain. Mutations in this region allow the virus to escape the antibodies, and mutations like the E848K are called escape mutations for that reason. This could be bad.'

'But the new D-xxxx strain is a real worry; I don't have much information on that one yet, except that infected people get a blue tinge to their neck. At least they are easily identified,' finished Dr Ponti.

They were awed by the bad news. Then the President spoke. 'Dr Ponti, I will need your help with this after the meeting, but let's move on for now.'

When they were ready, the President began, 'First, Lt. Col. Freebody, we talked about crowd control a few days ago. Are you ready now to deal with a large protest of say 100,000 on February 5?'

Lt. Col. Freebody answered. 'We are ready. I conferred with the Army Chief of Staff to add six Companies to make up two Battalions with 900 soldiers each. All armed with sidearms, some with rifles to act as snipers in case we need to take some people out. And, of course, all soldiers are equipped with masks and gloves to allow them to arrest people whilst keeping safe.'

'What about transport?' asked the President.

He was told, 'All taken care of. We use 30 Chinook birds, MH-47G, to carry 30 troops each. We will deploy them to come in from four points close to the main march. There will also be reconnaissance helicopters over the protests, which will drown out the noise of arriving troops. Troops will enter the protest from four points, march with the protestors, then move in behind a row, take their guns, handcuff them and march them out to a side street where they will be shackled to a waiting army truck before the rest notice.'

'How many do you intend to arrest?' asked the President.

Freebody answered, 'We will have forty trucks to hold 25 prisoners each. After we have arrested 100 protestors, the overhead helos will use bull-horns asking people to disperse. After we have arrested 300, we announce that 300 will be taken to a desert camp and ask, "Anyone else want to come?"'

'Then what?' asks the President, and he is shocked by the answer.

'If just 10 out of that mob have been infected with the new D-xxxx strain, then they die, whether taken to the desert prison or if they are dispersed, they will die in the street or at home, and we will need front-end loaders to pick them up. Too infectious to handle manually. We must warn people today that sick people with the new symptom will not be allowed into the hospital or anywhere else. Some may listen. We also have to advise families that if their father comes home, to not let him inside if he has a blue neck or they will all die.'

'Holy Mother of God. That's a big ask of the women. They will have to tell their husbands before they leave for the protests. Otherwise, there will be a bunfight when they return.'

*   *   *

The President calls in the Army Chief of Staff General Andrew Morgan and asks him to organise everything they need to plan for a military invited coup.

General Morgan is a true and tested veteran of many campaigns, including Iraq and Afghanistan. He is a man of colour who had suffered the indignities of racism all his life, mostly quietly. He understood human nature and the need to hurt those who are different and was adored by the men he led. But also feared, as he did not suffer fools gladly. After dressing down some poor soldier, he usually smiled a dazzling smile, and all was forgiven.

General Morgan asks for a takeover of street surveillance by drones, with helicopters flying over mobs, using loudspeakers to tell them to go home. Warnings. They would spray them with a dye to identify them for later arrests.

February 4

The President's Administration finds that the Republicans unite behind Trump, and that impeachment is unlikely to succeed. They look for new ways to remove his influence; sue him and his lawyer, Rudy Giuliani. Trump's supporters get furious about this, and demonstrations with 200,000 are now planned for February 6. The President advises Lt. Col. Freebody to double the protest response task force.

February 6

Tiny, silent Army drones patrolled the skies in Washington, and by ten in the morning, they had picked up movement on both ends of Minnesota Avenue. Drones from other areas were redirected to cover the Minnesota area and surroundings. The Army surveillance centre was now monitoring arrivals on both ends of the street, north and south. The director for the airborne response was looking up and down Minnesota Avenue to find great spots to land his birds.

'Look here, Joe,' he said, 'take a note of these locations. Great landing place a few hundred yards from the southern end at the Ketcham Elementary school. Then three more schools to the northeast end of Minnesota. Coming back down on the northern side of Minnesota, we have five schools and churches. Beautiful; that covers all our needs. Nine great places, not on the streets. We can sneak in there quietly now, and no one will connect the dots.'

Freebody is satisfied with the landing locations. Initially, he had planned to use thirty choppers for nine hundred troops. He had added another ten helicopters after advice on February 4. He addressed his transport commanders.

'It's a great day for flying today and fly you will. We have forty helicopters and nine landing places. We will fly over the Anacostia River and land most of you on Anacostia Park near Field 3. Nine birds will fly to the nine locations I have marked on your maps. Four birds will approach the landing sites from the south, five from the north. Dispatch the troops, return to Anacostia Park and signal that the site is ready for the next lot of soldiers. You leave now for Anacostia Park and get those soldiers in place out of sight of Minnesota. Remember: don't fly over Minnesota Avenue and only hover the shortest time to dislodge your soldiers. Anyone listening from nearby sees that you hovered and left again, three or four times in a row. Nothing to see, right?'

Then Lt. Col. Freebody addressed the motor transport commanders.

'Gentlemen, you now have 40 trucks parked nearby. When you have 30 protestors inside a truck, shut the rear gates and drive to the Andrews Airforce base about ten miles southeast. The Globemaster planes are on standby: comfort is not essential. Those birds fly to the Holloman Airforce Base in New Mexico, two thousand miles away. There will be trucks to take them to a secure desert camp in the White Sands Missile Range. Not many flowers around there, just a few rattlers.'

'Two weeks later, we pick up anyone left alive and transport them back to Andrews Airforce Base by Globemaster before trucks take them back to Anacostia. They should all have two weeks of parking tickets by then; a great help to the local council revenue.'

An hour later the march down Minnesota Ave. in Anacostia was in progress. About 60,000 marched down from the North-East, 60,000 marching up from the South-West. They looked like a benign mob from a distance, but one had to wonder what would happen when they met. The surveillance team honed in. They noticed that the North-East team marching down had banners proclaiming the Braveheart Patriots. The group marching up from the South-West seemed to be the Forcefields. It almost seemed a pity to spoil their party.

Lt. Col. Freebody addressed the airborne division and asked them to fly over Minnesota Avenue and use loudhailers from a low height to announce: 'Disperse and go home now. You've had your fun. Go home now, or you will be arrested.'

A few protestors broke away and were jeered at.

Jason Donovan's deputy walked backwards from the North-East and addressed his Braveheart Patriots.

'Nothing to worry about. How are they gonna do that? With magic? We'll show them some magic. We march. We are invincible. What are we?'

And the shout went up, 'We are invincible! Can't get us!.'

That was true. Until it wasn't. Suddenly there was a disturbance on the northern side of the Avenue. Ten soldiers walked along with the protestors, sang their song with them, and grinned. Then they moved between two rows and marched with the protestors. Making lots of noise. Then a whistle blew, and the soldiers reached forward to remove handguns from men in front of them whilst snapping handcuffs on the protestors, quickly attached those to a rope, then pulled them out of the march. They told the mob, 'We'll take these blokes out to a bar, bring them back in ten minutes and get anyone else who wants a drink.'

The protestors could not see that this was happening in ten rows on both sides of the march. Two hundred marchers were taken out on the north, and the same in the south. In the space of two minutes. The helicopters used their bull-horns to repeat the message:

'Stand down and go home, or get arrested.'

Tim Highfields was still walking in front of his column when he addressed his men. 'Men, stay true. They are bullshitting you.'

Tim turned and moved forward. He did not see that the soldiers had returned, marched with the protestors, and departed with ten men in tow a second time. Half an hour later, he received a message from Jason Donovan. It read, 'They have arrested twelve hundreds of your men. Aren't you watching? Address them now to stand down and go home, you dick!'

Oh dear! What to do? Then a helicopter flew over, loud hailer blaring a message. 'You great patriots. Just to let you know. We have arrested twelve hundreds of your marchers, and if you don't disperse, we'll arrest another thousand. In half an hour, we will drop blue dye on you to find you to arrest you later. Up to you.'

Tim Highfields turned to face his crowd. 'OK, men, we've done what we came for. Let's be smart and go home.'

A shot rang out. A helicopter started to spew black smoke, spinning and slowly sinking. Then another shot and a man screamed in pain. Tim could see the smoke from a gun in a second helicopter. It looked like a sniper rifle. A loud hailer started again.

'Any more of that, and we retaliate with a machine gun. Go home.'

Tim asked someone to run back and see who had screamed in pain. That man came running back. 'He's dead. A bullet through his neck. What do we do?'

Tim addressed his mob with his loud hailer again. 'Men. We are not beaten, but we will leave now. All men on the northern side of Minnesota peel off to the north; those on the southern side peel off to the south. Now. Move it!'

Matt Davis had received a call from Terry Copperfield, and he addressed his Forcefield men.

'Listen, you good men. Some idiot shot at the helicopter, and it's down. Between us and the other mob. Soldiers are spilling out, with arms drawn. The boss wants you to stand down. Men on the northern side of Minnesota peel off to that side; men on the southern side peel off in that direction. No shooting, Come back in two days. That's it. Go.'

The soldiers moved north to the Bravehearts group. And stopped. Feet firmly planted with hands on their rifles. They ask, 'Who's in charge here?' and Tim Highfields answers. They tell him they will move through the middle to find the man who shot the helicopter.

'We returned fire, and he may be dead. If not, we'll take him to the hospital. We need to check that it was his rifle that had fired. Please lead the way through.'

About ten rows in, they found him on the ground. One soldier took off a glove and felt his pulse. Dead. He lifted the rifle, smelt it.

'This was the one.' Then the soldier addressed the crowd, 'The next time anyone shoots at a helicopter or soldier, we will return fire with a machine gun till we run out of ammo. Say 50 rounds to a belt. Tell your friends.'

*   *   *

The TV crews had captured all the action, and it was showing live. A breaking news subtitle declared, 'Army shoots at a peaceful protest. One man killed,' and the two talking heads were having the time of their lives.

One man said, 'Shooting at civilians? What is this government coming to?'

The other anchor, a lady, put a different slant on it. 'Grant, you fuckwit, they shot at a helicopter full of soldiers, and it went down. What do you expect, wise ass? I'm surprised at the restraint. Only one shot in return. Obviously by a sniper. If I had been in that chopper, I would have retaliated with a machine gun and rocket fire. Somebody needs to teach those idiots you don't mess with the Army.'

The media goes crazy, and protestors plan more protests at the Army shooting at civilians. The protestors don't follow the instructions. The media is full of news of new deadly virus mutations, and all these idiots want to do is march.

*   *   *

Dorothy wondered what Argus E would make of all of his and emailed him, asking how the Indian government felt about what they saw, and his reply came back ten minutes later.

> I have just come back from Chennai where I conferred with my supervisors. I had advised them to stop any entry into Indian territory from overseas. And we don't have the luxury of a

White Sands missile testing range where we can set up an isolation camp, which really should be renamed a morgue.

Personally, I think America needs to arrest all protestors and take them away. You should urge your President to arrange a massive arrest scheme. Just get them off the streets. Our country would probably use a nerve gas to put them to sleep. We cannot take them anywhere. I had suggested to our mob something that induces a four-day coma, then pick up blue neck bodies using a helicopter and a sling into large trucks to be delivered into mass graves. all before the good ones wake up.

Dorothy was quick to reply, writing:

Holy Bejeezus, Argus, do you wat to come and work for us? And do you have any of that nerve gas?

They chatted a bit using a messaging app and signed off.

*   *   *

The President wanted a military takeover in two days; all civil affairs to be controlled by the Army, including print and social media. He grinned at the thought of the rage, but cases are up to 10,000 a day in DC alone. It will worsen in a week because of the protests.

The President called Lt. Col. Freebody into a meeting and started:

'We have intelligence that mass protests of 200,000 are planned for February 9. Given the infection rate, it's highly dangerous and I need to stop it. Or rather, you need to. On the night of the eighth, I want to announce that the military has been invited to stage a takeover should there be any mass protests. The following is what my announcement will say:

> Tomorrow at eleven am, the Army will be invited to stage a military takeover of all civil matters if mass protests are planned or have started anywhere in the United States. By noon, they will move in and arrest protesters and spray the remainder with a yellow dye to pick up at a later date. We are not doing this for fun. The pandemic infections are out of control, and hospitals are closed. If you march, you will be dealt with.'

Lt. Col. Freebody responded, 'I like a Commander in Chief who is a commander. Yes, Sir, we will be ready. Ready in Washington and Baltimore. Ready in Houston and Dallas. But I had better get your intelligence on other cities.'

The President said, 'We will start with those cities and see what else pops up, and keep them for another day. The media coverage should disabuse any idea of further demonstrations. I want live TV coverage of those detained in White Sands, entering vast and desolate camps. That will do the trick, and if not, we do it again. You will need the extra time to get tents for new arrivals anyway.'

'Do you wish to know any details? Like how we plan to arrest them?' asks Lt. Col. Freebody. 'I would like to put the planned actions before you. They are:

- We fly over by helicopter and advise them to disperse now.
- Half an hour later, we fly over and spray them with yellow dye.
- Half an hour after that, we fly over with a harmless nerve agent that will put them to sleep. We do this for one

section of the road, from the back of the march. Those ahead of them won't see what is happening.

- Ten minutes later, we move large trucks into place and pick up fifty at a time just as they wake up. They will be groggy and will be prodded by bayonets. No permanent damage but effective.

- We will fill twenty trucks as fast as we can using a hundred soldiers for each of two trucks at a time and off to the Andrews Airforce Base for delivery to the New Mexico White Sands rocket testing site.'

'Mr President, do we have your OK to use nerve gas?' and the President passes the buck.

'Colonel, you are charged with getting them off the street. How you do it is up to you. But remember, the coup may last for three to six months, or even longer, so you need to be able to live with the consequences of your actions. If thousands die at White Sands, it's their own fault. If a thousand die during an arrest, that is your problem.'

Then the President adds a note of concern. 'Tomorrow morning, we will initiate lawsuits against Donald Trump and his lawyer Rudy Giuliani for defamation and spreading vicious lies about election fraud. The Republicans, bless their hearts, will not vote to impeach Trump, and if we do nothing, people will think they can get away with it any time they want.'

'Appeasement stopped when the Republicans united behind Donald Trump to deny an impeachment. This move will drive the protestors crazy with blood lust. The demonstrations on the ninth may turn ugly. You are invited to deal with it with force. Proportionate force. But I need to put an end to all this crap once and for all.'

The President continued, 'There are two more large operations for you. On the thirteenth, I want you to take over the Senate and supervise it until I have spoken to at least ten Republican Senators. I can't get the relief packages through, and it's time to put a stop to Republican obstructionism. They will be spoken to privately and come out smiling and cooperating.'

'I will need you to have a confidential never-to-be-released conversation with some people in Justice to assist me with those discussions. I have a bone to pick with some Supreme Court justices as well. They passed a Bill to suspend a law requiring reduced numbers for religious services. Some of those are mega-churches, seating over 45,000 worshippers, but the churches want their weekly donations. It is all about money. And those Republican judges hide behind the words of the Constitution to allow that, rather than applying the intent.'

'I want you to enter the Supreme Court on the seventeenth and have some very private diplomatic discussions with two or three Republican judges. To diplomatically change their interpretations of many of the contested legal issues, and likewise, I need you to assist me with those persuasions. Legally, of course, but in private.'

'The next big job is on the nineteenth. I want you to announce a new Federal process for Presidential elections. We'll give you our ideas, but it's your blueprint that needs to go out. When you are ready to start on that one, I have news of an Australian who had claimed to have a tamper-proof electronic voting system.'

'It is ridiculous that the states be allowed to control the election process in their states. It's a federal issue. We can build and test this voting system, and when ready, offer a lot of money for anyone who can break in, and when they can't, we have a referendum to see if people want to vote from home or stand in a queue for up to eight hours, maybe in rain or in a snowstorm.

I hope you see the advantage this will eventually bring to this nation. Good luck.'

The Attorney General looked quite stunned. Then he grinned, and said, 'Leave it to me, Mr President.'

CHAPTER 14

February 8

The Andamanese scientist Argus E was monitoring the mood of the nation. That was his job, to observe. Today the mood in Washington depended on who you were. A press release from the President had gone out. It shocked most people. It was intended to. It read:

> Tomorrow morning at eleven, the Army will be invited to stage a military takeover if mass protests have started -anywhere in the United States. By noon they will move in and arrest a large number of protesters and spray the remainder with a yellow dye to arrest at a later date. This is not for fun. The pandemic infections are out of control, and hospitals are closed. If you march, you will be dealt with.

The reaction to the bulletin from Jason Donovan's Bravehearts was the same as that from Terry Copperfield's Forcefield. Outrage. White-hot anger. Somebody had better teach these ass-holes who was boss in this town.

Jason Donovan met with his deputies. 'You see that shit? If there are mass protests, they want to arrest us all. What do you say to that?'

Tim Highfields, his deputy, offered his view: 'I'd like to see them try. Two days ago, they snuck in pretending to be goodies and then whipped handcuffs on unsuspecting patriots. I'd like to see them try that this time. I think we should come armed to the teeth. Bullet belts across our shoulders, rifles in hand. Looking fierce. They lift a rifle to us, and we mow them down.'

Jason quietened him down, 'Tim, I'm proud of you. Willing to donate your body to science after it has been riddled with army bullets. But I won't allow you to sacrifice yourself this way. You are too valuable to me. If you shoot at Army guys, they will mow down a hundred of you in seconds. That's not what we are after.'

'This is what I think we should do,' says Jason. 'We have weapons, yes, but at ease, not threatening. The Constitution allows it. They will fly a chopper overhead and tell us to stand down. Then we spoil their fun and turn and run back to our transport. All wasted effort on the Army's part. The other deputies loved that one, yes Sirree.'

February 9

The Bravehearts got their orders to drive to their parking destinations. They were pretty excited. Play hide and seek with the Army, spoil their day, and get off scot-free.

Tim Highfields assembled his men in tidy lines. He had to work at it and announced on his bull horn, 'Patriots, listen now. We will be on TV, defying the government and the Army. Do you want to look good or like deadbeats?'

The shouts came back: 'We look good!'

Tim Highfields addressed them again: 'In that case, you straggly lot, you need to be in smart straight lines, lines of say 25, and all lines a yard apart. Look like Washington's soldiers. To get their respect. Now!'

They did a good job. From a distant drone, you could not tell; they were just a heaving mass of men. But when the drones flew over? Gloriously disciplined. The TV networks commented on it. Two minutes later, Tim Highfields received a call from Jason.

'Great job. TV news outlets just commented that your lot looked better than an Army parade. Keep it up.'

*   *   *

Noon, February 9

The Army Commander Lt. Col. Freebody thought the demonstrators looked peaceful, and they were expecting a half an hour warning to disperse. *Tough luck, boys,* he thought. *We told you yesterday that you will be arrested if you were seen on the streets. You will love this next announcement.*

He issued the flyover announcement that was delivered by helicopters with loud hailers:

> Leave now. We will arrest as many as we can
> put our hands on as you go back to your cars.
> Anyone not in their vehicles in two minutes will
> face arrest. Do not point guns at us. We are armed
> too but trained. You are not. Get going.

Tim Highfields grabbed his bull-horn and issued one command: 'Run to your cars now!' Then he was seen fleeing the scene. He had played American Football and had been a sprinter.

One of his men laughed as Tim thundered past and said, 'He believes this shit. That's why he is only the Deputy Commander. Ha,' as he leisurely walked back to his car, where he was one of the thousands surrounded by Army soldiers who said:

'You are coming with us. A two-week holiday in the desert.'

Later on, all media and social media networks reported the events. Two thousand arrested and taken to White Sands. Those with blue necks were left in a smaller camp to die. In the main camp, if anyone turns blue, they were kicked out to the 'dying' camp.

At 2 pm, Facebook displayed a warning:

> For an extended period, Facebook and all other social media platforms are now controlled by the Army. The concept of group shares, or even worse, public shares, is blocked and disabled to stop the planning of mass protests. The Army is now in charge of almost everything relating to civil liberties. For a reason. The general population is ignoring government directives, which endangers public health and the nation's safety, so - for a while, you are being told what you can do, whether you like it or not. We have organised a desert camp that we can expand to hold two million prisoners if need be. People wandering around, on foot or by car, will be taken to that desert camp during lockdowns unless you have an exemption. You get to choose, of course. It's a democracy, after all.

> You can still use it to contact one person at a time. Abuse that, and we take that function away as well.

2.10 p.m., February 9

All Free to Air and Cable TV showed a message:

> For an extended period, all TV, Free to Air and
> Cable, will be controlled by the Army. All content
> will be censored, including advertisements. The
> bad news is that you will not be shown in protest
> marches. There is a reason for our actions. Groups
> and individuals think it's their Constitutional right
> to do as they please. This country is in a crisis,
> and if we don't stop anyone from exercising their
> perceived rights, then we have a civil war. That
> is far worse than these temporary restrictions.
> Thank you for reading this message.

2.40 p.m., February 9

On the Senate floor Republican Senate leader, Senator Chuck M. Morris, called for attention:

'Ladies and Gentlemen. You have all seen the announcement. I will now call for submissions from the floor. With fifty of us, I want to limit speeches to five minutes apiece. Say four hours. So if you were going to pontificate, you can forget about it. If you were going to say the same as someone else, please just state whom you agreed with, and then just sit. Quietly, of course.'

'There are obvious routes to defeat them; one is a vote in the Senate which we can lose, obviously, so let's keep that one short, please. The other main avenue is a Supreme Court ruling. That's using the law. So I would like to hear suggestions about how to approach a Supreme Court case. Please discuss with someone now for a few minutes, and let's see if there's any other major topic.'

General chatter went on, but some serious conversations were in process in one corner of the room. Someone had come up with something new, and it was evident to the Senate leader, who gave them thirty seconds, then called the room to order, calling for new ideas.

'Senator Morris,' said one of the Texas senators, 'We have an idea worth discussing. We think we should invite the Chief of Army into a joint sitting of the Houses of Parliament or the Senate and first see what they are up to, then grill them. We might put pressure on them to reduce their interference. They need to be shown how things work in this country.'

Discussions were hard and hopeful. They would show the Army. After an hour of talks, they sent the following invite to the Army Chief of Staff:

> The Honourable General A. Morgan, Army Chief of Staff, White House Offices.
>
> We invite you to present your ideas on the takeover to the joint Senate sitting, preferably tomorrow. We have many concerns and wish to question you. We certainly would like to be ensured that this is a short-term situation, very short term, as you are usurping the civil rights of the people of the United States.
>
> Respectfully,
>
> Senator Chuck M. Morris

General Morgan had returned to his office, and he found the hand-delivered letter from Senator Morris. There was a sardonic smile on his face as he read the letter a second time. He had two choices: One was to decline. The other was to take the fight to the enemy. Those stupid people. They had not served in the military, obviously. He laughed out loud. He read again, '*You are usurping the civil rights of the people of the United States.*'

They were about to be taught a lesson. He issued a curt reply:

'I shall see you in the Senate at 9.00 am sharp', and he wondered if they were happy or petrified. They should be petrified.

February 10

General Morgan entered the Senate Chamber. He was welcomed by Senator Morris, who explained why they had called the General before the Senate. General Morgan smiled to himself. Let them think they would now get concessions. He waited five minutes, and still, Senator Morris droned on until General Morgan stood up and walked out. When he was asked where he was going, he turned and spoke. It was like acid dripping from his mouth:

'Senator, I think you have passed your use-by date. I have a country to save because of the stupidity of people like you. I'm a busy man, and after honouring your stupid request that I justify myself to you, you have the temerity to stand there and lecture me with your nonsense. You have no idea how insignificant you are. Goodbye.'

*   *   *

The President met with the Attorney General, Dr Ferrari, and he greeted him with, 'Thanks for coming at this short notice.' He stated the reason for the meeting.

'Dr Ferrari. I have called you to tell you about my plans for an extended Army takeover. I consulted with your deputy, William Schuster, but this needs all top guns to the fore. What do you think the Senate will do during this takeover? The Republicans, I mean.'

'Easy, they will sabotage every one of your moves, and then they will take their complaints to the Supreme Court, which they still dominate. They will use that court's interpretation of the Constitution to rule that what you and the Army are doing is illegal, and force changes under the plea: "It's unconstitutional", and delay everything you need to do,' says Dr Ferrari.

This was just what the President wanted to hear, and he asked: 'So what would you advise we do?'

And he loved the answer he got from the Attorney General: 'First you need to sack the Republican Senators - or turn them; a polite way of saying you blackmail them. If they take it to the Supreme Court, you need to sack or turn the Republican-leaning judges. You want social distancing, and those idiots change a law to allow churches to have unlimited congregation numbers. I would like to see those judges arrested, stripped of their lifetime jobs, and sent to the White Sands desert camps, where with a bit of luck, they get infected. They need to experience the outcome of their decisions. Sorry, but I'm irate about that.'

The President was delighted. 'Now I will tell you why I had asked you for this meeting. I have been working with Lt. Col. Freebody on the military takeover, obviously with the approval of General Morgan, whom you know.'

'I want a clean sweep of everything in the way of saving this country from a pandemic death and also from civil war. These are the main events:

1. An invited Military takeover of all civil unrest issues, including media and social media. Many thousands will be arrested and shipped off to the White Sands desert camp if they march in protest. Many will die there.

2. We cannot afford to have them roaming in the streets and infecting millions. Those shipped to the desert may live or die; depending on how lucky they get in that camp.

3. William Schuster has helped me outline other actions. Almost the same as you suggested. Dismiss or turn the Republican Senators, dismiss or turn the Republican Supreme Court Justices. The next one is a doozy.

4. Change the Constitution and the Federal Presidential Voting System. This is the reason why I need you.

5. I want your legal, constitutional experts to go over every inch of that document and ensure that judges cannot use incorrect interpretations to suit their tastes. For instance, the judges had ruled that the Constitution allows freedom of religious expression; therefore, it's illegal to suppress attendance. I want every item marked that needs to carry exemptions in the case of national disasters or war. It's your job to make those changes. Dr Ferrari, you might have just one new paragraph stating that all affected instances are marked with an asterisk, but it's your job. Then I want to ensure changes to the Constitution after your update requires a referendum with a 70 per cent agreement.

6. The next item will remove all that privilege the Republicans have enjoyed by having individual state electoral voting systems and counting mechanisms. Lt. Col. Freebody told me he had seen an unsolicited design of a foolproof electronic voting system. A student was working in Cyber Security studies for a Master's degree in Australia. I am sick to death of this idiotic system we have. Bangladesh[52] and India[53] are more advanced than we are, for God's sake. India has a population of over 1.3

---

[52] Bangladesh Uses EVMs For First Time in General Election

[53] Electronic voting in India

billion, and they use one electronic voting machine and results are tabulated that day. What we want is one safe electronic system that gives us the outcome on the same day. No court appeals, no mail voting. We can issue a mobile to anyone who claims not to have a device.'

Attorney General Dr Ferrari was delighted. 'What a stroke of genius. This is a plan for an end to litigation. We've already planned to end starvation. Lawyers, get a real job. We will need to delete the states' right to their own federal election processes. The new law will mean there is only one voting system, and if they want their state to vote, ours is the only one they can use. We will put that into the Constitution.'

After the protests, many families were distressed. Those not arrested had returned home. The Army had warned families and wives not to let the men touch them or the children for three days. After that, if their necks turned blue, they could infect the rest of the family. Wives had to tell husbands to take some money, wear gloves and masks and drive away.

*   *   *

Blew Ohrtman had been arrested for attempted murder when he was caught in Springfield, Ohio. His wife Petal had alerted the FBI, who found him just after a failed attempt. He was locked up, then Petal managed to get him out on bail.

Blew turned up at home, but only after participating in the latest protest marches. He swore with great profanity when Petal told him not to touch her or the kids, Fred and Summer, who were out at the time.

'For how long?' screamed Blew. Petal told him.

'You should have seen the notice. If you've been on that march, you may already be infected. If your neck turns blue, you will be dead one day later, and so will anyone you infect now. I'm serious. Take some money and the car, go for a drive into the country, sleep in the car. Don't mix with other people. If you are still alive in four days and without a blue neck, come home if you are willing to live by my rules, which mean no protests and marches with the mob. I am dead serious.'

*　　*　　*

Terry Balzarini was with his wife Lorraine, son Jason, 14, and daughter Keeta, 12, in the Rachel Carson Conservation Park near Sunshine in Maryland. The kids got on well, but after weeks without new friends, they got pretty restless. This morning they went walking east, and they were chasing a few butterflies and a chipmunk.

It was enough to make them laugh out loud. Those chipmunks! Stand still, swivel head to one side, stay still. Swivel to the other side and stay still. Then race up a tree, and remain still. Completely still, then race back down and across the grass and remain dead still. Dead still or flat out. Jason tried to imitate those movements, which had Keeta in fits. They collapsed into the grass laughing and lay still. And quiet. Then they heard a child crying.

Keeta got up to investigate, Jason followed. Then they saw her, a dear little girl, about five years old. She was sobbing her heart out. She was alone. Keeta got close enough to check that she did not have a blue neck, and spoke to her:

'Hello, little girl. My name is Keeta, and this is Jason. Can you tell us why you are crying?' The child drew her arm across her face to wipe away the snot from so much crying, took a big breath, held her breath, then let it out slowly. Then she was ready to say something.

'I'm crying because my little brother over there has a blue neck. It's just too sad, and I must cry some more.' Which she did, for a minute, and sobbed. 'I feel better now. Please don't go away. I need to tell someone why I'm so sad, or I will be sad till I die.'

The girl sobbed some more, and Keeta asked her what her name was. She had to stop crying to talk, and she told them:

'My name is Natalie, and I'm five. My little brother Henry is over there in a bush, and he's three and a bit. His neck has gone blue, and I know what that means. It means I cannot hug him, even though he wants a hug. He is my only family left. I'm so sad I can't help him. I have always loved him so much, like playing with dolls. With boy dolls, of course. But now I feel as if my heart wants to break in two, and I want to give him one half so he can live.' She stopped, sobbed a bit and then smiled at Keeta.

'Do you want to play with me now? I promise not to touch you because my mum told me about touching, and I need to wait three days before I know it's safe to touch you.'

Jason is impressed.

'Natalie, I'm so impressed by what you know and that you love your little brother so much. You are amazing and so clever. Do you want to be a doctor when you grow up? You already know so much. I want to be a doctor. Shall we look at your brother and see how he is?' asks Jason.

They find Henry, and his neck is not blue. Henry is chewing on a stick; he is hungry; he looks up at Jason and asks, 'Did you bring food? I need some now.'

Jason, Keeta and Natalie laugh. 'We were all worried about you, and all you can say is food. Now, did you know your sister was crying because she thought you had a blue neck? Do you know what that means?' He came back with a child's immutable logic.

'Blue neck I die; not blue I get hungry.' Jason decided for all of them. 'Let's go home to my place, and we get some food.'

When they got there and explained the story to Terry and Lorraine, Terry told them to wait. He had a fast test kit. Five minutes later, the two children were declared free of any virus. Henry wanted food, and Natalie wanted a hug first. Then Henry wanted to sleep, and Natalie wanted a teddy bear.

*   *   *

The Thompson and Anderson families had escaped to a wilderness too. To Woodstream, Maryland, near the big Chester River Sanctuaries.

They had a solar panel and a battery to produce a small amount of electricity for a fridge and light at night, a wood stove and plenty of wood to burn. They caught fish every day. They had built a chicken run, and five birds produced four or five eggs a day. The families had camped together for many years. Despite the children's ages ranging from thirteen to nineteen, they all played well together.

This morning the Thompson kids, Richard and Karen, had wandered north to a creek running into the Corsica River, and they came across a children's holiday camp. Five kids were crying, and one woman was moaning on the ground. She was telling the kids to stay away from her. The kids seemed to be aged three to eight.

The woman told Richard and Karen, 'Darlings, please. Do not come near me. Go to the shed and find my phone. You can google blue neck, and it will show you what is wrong with me. If you touch me, you will die. Do not drink from my bottles. I had gone to town yesterday to shop, and some idiot woman came and shook hands with me.'

Karen was seventeen and had heard about the blue neck. She spoke to the children.

'You must do exactly as I say now, and then you may be OK. Is that your mum?' There was just nodding and sobbing. Then she continued:

'Show me where your things are but leave them there. Do not touch each other for two days. Hopefully, your mum has not infected you. I will take you to our camp, where our mum and dad will wrap each of you in a blanket, so you never touch anyone. Do you understand how important this is?' The kids nodded, and Karen continued. 'We will feed you, keep you warm, and give you each a teddy bear to cuddle. If you are not blue in the neck like your mum, then you are all clear, and we can give you lots and lots of cuddles and take you to a shop and buy things you want.'

Karen asked her brother, 'Richard, can you find your way home and bring our dads back here? Quickly?' Of course he could. He was a scout. Karen told him, 'Bring the biggies and explain what we found, and to bring anything they can think of that would help their mum, and stuff that keeps the kids wrapped up.'

Karen addressed their moaning mother. 'Our parents all work in public health. They know what to do and will bring you something to make it easier for you. But we can promise that we will take care of the kids and hope that you have not infected any of them. My dad will probably bring some whiskey and laudanum, a pain killer, and give you an intense laudanum-induced dream, so you go to sleep. Can you think of anything else you need?'

'Yes. In the shed, there is my bag. When the adults come back, they need to take that. It contains all our identifications and family connections. I need to know my children are well, and if you can help me die quickly and without too much pain, that would be great. Maybe a lolly to suck on.'

Karen covered the woman with a blanket from the shed. She still had her gloves on and hoped that would be enough protection. Then she heard shouting. Her parents were on the way. Running towards her were her father, Michael Thompson, their mother and also Michelle Anderson. All had face masks and gloves on.

Michelle had a bottle, and she asked the sick mother if she understood her and what her name was. 'I'm Betty Simpson, and the kids are all mine. Please look after them till you can get some help. You are a mother, and I see you know what is going through my mind.'

'Hello, Betty dear, My name is Michele Anderson, I wish I had met you under better circumstances. I'm a lecturer in public health and understand this virus. We will take care of all your children, and in two days when it's safe, we will hug them silly for you, don't you worry about that. I brought you a bottle of laudanum. Do you know about it?' Betty didn't.

'It's bitter. You will get to be very sleepy and have weird dreams, and if you are lucky, you will go to sleep and look down on all those children from up there. Are you ready to try it now?'

She was, and she nearly spat it all out and laughed as she said, 'Well, you weren't kidding about that being bitter, so I trust you meant it that you'd look after my kids. But for God's sake, do you have a whiskey to wash that taste away?'

James Anderson bent down to give her the bottle of whiskey but had a good swig first himself.

'All yours, Betty. Knock yourself out.' he said, then grinned sheepishly. 'Well, maybe that isn't such a bad idea. Betty tried one last laugh.

'I think you should be spanked for that, saying such a thing to a dying lady,' and Michelle offered to do that later. With all the nine kids watching. Betty choked with laughter, then sighed and went to sleep. Permanently.

*   *   *

Later, February 10

The President is at the White House Offices when he authorised a White Sands press release. It detailed the number dead, the number sick, and the number of those in good health, separately, for the marching groups they had arrested:

> A new warning is issued to not let anyone with blue necks within arms-length of you. The statistics from the White Sands desert camp are a shocker. A third of the prisoners dead, a third are sick, expected to die, and a third are OK, expected to live. You need to understand this. They marched, and when transported there, did not have blue necks, and five days later, from two thousand, fourteen hundred are dead or will be by the end of the day.
>
> We have taken people to those camps because they attended mass protests and are now infected with this new strain. None had blue necks when

we took them there, and now seventy per cent are dead.

The reason for the deaths and expected deaths is because people did not follow instructions. We have improved the conditions at the camp slightly. A bit easier for those who are sick and dying. It's the best we could do.

We also have news on a new strain. The Brazilian variant[54] has the spike protein mutations, resulting in another new highly infectious strain. Whilst not as deadly as the blue neck strain, which is officially named D=xxxx. The Brazilian variant has caused reinfections in the largest city in Amazonas, previously thought to have reached 'herd immunity' in October last year. This new virus is a monster, and you need to keep off the streets, or you will end up in White Sands and die there.

And for those of you who have relatives in White Sands, the camp has two sections that do not mix. The blue section has dead people and those presenting with the blue neck symptom. Inmates kick out anyone developing a blue neck to the blue section to keep themselves alive. After five days, we will send someone in a hazmat suit into the blue section to bring out anyone left alive. After this, the blue section is burned to the ground to eradicate the virus.

---

[54] UK, South African, Brazilian- a virologist explains each COVID variant and what they mean for the pandemic

Don't be a fool and get arrested; the Army is in charge. To protect you.

The following press release dealt with instructions in case of blue neck infection, and it read:

Urgent. Please circulate this to all your family. If one of you should show the symptoms of the blue neck D-xxxx infection, you must follow these instructions to save your family.

- Warn all family members that you are infected and must not be touched, or they die.
- Put on a mask and rubber gloves immediately to stop any further spread from your hands, and ask the family to clean the house with disinfectant, wiping over every surface.
- Ensure you have a will or make one, sign it, take a photo of it and email it to your spouse or partner.
- Say goodbye to your family without touching, and tell them that you will get some medication to stop any pain but that you will die.
- Family can drive to a drive-through chemist and purchase the allowed morphine overdose for you to die with less discomfort. They will dispense this to anyone with a blue neck.
- Drive somewhere peaceful, take your morphine and just go to sleep. Do not get out of the car.
- The chemist will have given you a blue flag to identify your condition, to attach to your car aerial.
- Your car will be burnt in a safe place and towed away, so don't take your most expensive vehicle.

The following press release dealt with hospital closures and read:

The blue neck infections are not treatable, and you will be dead in a day. Do not go to a hospital if you have a blue neck, as armed guards will stop you from getting out of your car. We need to protect the health workers and other patients from you. Please follow the instructions for blue neck infections. We are sorry that we cannot help you.

Just so that you are clear, we will shoot you if you have blue neck symptoms and step out of the car. Our soldiers are trained to make it a headshot, and you will be dead before you feel pain. It's the best we can do for you.

*   *   *

February 11

It was wakey time at a school camp, and a teacher used a wooden spoon to bang on a saucepan, doing a good imitation of a lousy wakeup song. There were giggles. Some kids just turned over and ignored all the noise. Thirty school kids, all in sleeping bags in the big scout hall, having a great time. They had a schedule to follow:

    6:00 Toilet break
    6:05 Health inspection
    6:30 Dressed and breakfast

All the kids know the procedure. Do not touch anyone else till after inspection tomorrow. They had arrived a day ago and had not been quarantined for three days yet, and it was still possible that one or more of them could get a blue neck. All children were told not to touch anyone until tomorrow, and if done by mistake, to call a teacher immediately who would come with a strong disinfectant and wash the touched child.

At inspection time, girls had to lift their hair so that necks could be better seen.

One boy had a blue neck. He had not touched anyone. The teacher took him aside, wrapped him in a blanket and called his parents to come and get him.

It was a sad farewell as he was driven away. One of the kids gave him his lolly bag to cheer him up. It did not work.

CHAPTER 15

Mood, February 13

It was a good time for Argus E to have another look at what was happening. The mood in Washington DC depends on which side of politics you are on, with anger by the Republicans and glee by the Democrats. Those not interested in politics were terrified of the new D-xxxx strain, commonly referred to as the 'Blue Neck' strain. Most people were worried that blue symptoms did not show until after day two but are infectious on day one.

With only essential workers allowed to work, there was far less traffic, and people mostly avoid public transport, using their cars. Less likely to get infected that way. Some stores refused entry to people not wearing masks, but some enterprising kids sold them outside and made a buck. Fights broke out when some rednecks refused to get a mask, demanding their constitutional right to shop. The Army turned up and took them away. The redneck swore until he was blue in the face, but thankfully not in the neck.

$$* \quad * \quad *$$

The morning looked glorious to anyone looking out beyond concrete canyons of housing estates. Crisp and clear, those walking

246

the streets left condensation puffs as they strolled along, also highlighting the fact that your breath escaped despite the mask. There were not many people, and vapour trails were blowing out the sides of their masks. Could that air infect others? The government had issued new money to those affected by work shutdowns that were supposed to last only two weeks. That would be enough to bring the pandemic under control if everyone played by the rules. Which would not happen.

A fight broke out outside a Walmart store. The store had a guard ensuring that no one entered without a mask. A tough-looking bearded man refused to buy a mask from the kid outside, and when someone gave him one for free, he threw it away. He was a redneck and ass, and a few seconds later, an Army soldier handcuffed him and took him away.

'Where are you taking me?!' he yelled. The bystanders heard the answer.

'To the desert camp in New Mexico. We'll bring you back in two weeks if you are still alive.' The redneck swore till he was blue in the face, not to be confused with a blue in the neck.

A TV crew had turned up and filmed the event. The anchorman was commenting on the problem.

'Trying to get some folks to follow the rules is like herding a hundred cats. People and their inflated view of their Constitutional rights are such a pain in the ass. But so much fun to report on.'

8:30 a.m., February 13

The Army had authorised the following news bulletin:

> Yesterday's new daily infections were up 70 per cent on the previous day, which was up 40 per cent on the day before that. The testing teams are

struggling to identify the most prevalent strains. They are run off their feet. The Army is trying to recruit another fifty-five thousand qualified staff or train new ones, roughly a thousand per state.

As soon as a Bill is passed in the Senate, we will issue lockdown instructions for all hotspot places and provide financial support for those who cannot go to work. Please, all, follow instructions when they are issued.

We have no details of how these strains are transmitted, but we have one bit of good news. And that is that the time from first noticing the blue tinge to when you first become incapable of most physical activity is two hours. That means you have only been infected for two days and could only have infected others for two days. Unfortunately, blue necks are dead the next day, stopping us from doing contact tracing. They cannot tell you where they had been. They are dead.

There will be armed guards at hospitals to prevent anyone with a blue neck from entering, and they will issue a pamphlet explaining what you must do if you have one. Failure to do so will result in prosecution for anyone taking a blue neck to a hospital.

That also means that anyone driving longer distances needs to check in the mirror for signs of blue around their neck, and within two hours of that, you need to get off the road - or you can kill others in a head-on crash, as happened last night. If you are stopped by a highway patrol and display blue neck symptoms, you will be ordered out of your car and taken to a morgue.

Later

Congress has passed fifty Bills to go before the Senate. The Democrats had hoped to pass five of these the next day. They were stumped by the Republicans, who used every trick under the sun to delay the vote. The Republican mantra was: 'Debate and delay as long as you can.' After four days with not one Bill voted on, the Democrats pulled the plug and called for a vote. The Republicans left the Chamber, knowing that there were insufficient senators for a quorum if they did, and the vote could not go ahead. This happened five times, after which their defence expired, and a vote could be taken. Eventually, after six hours of disruptive behaviour, the bill was passed with the swinging vote from the Vice President.

The following Bill to be debated was for urgent financial support for people put out of work because of lockdown orders. After a presentation of the Bills, the Republicans asked for five days to study them. The Republican Deputy leader in the Senate, Senator Jackson, had the floor.

'Ladies and gentlemen, if I have interpreted this Bill correctly, you are asking for about half a trillion dollars in support for nine months for people to live on if they are too lazy to find work. That will come out of our taxes, to be paid for by me, my children, and later my grandchildren. That is not the American way. It is totally irresponsible. And for what? People need to look after their own survival; it's not the government's job. You guys are living in fantasy land.'

The Democrat leader response by Senator Nolene Packard was instant:

'Dear Senator Jackson. If you were to lose your job and had no other savings and no income for three months, a starving family to support, and half the country shut down, who would give you a job? No-one. What would you do? Apply for help from the government, or would you kill to feed your family? I think you need to come off your high horse. This pandemic is brought about because of the Republicans and their mismanagement. You are responsible for this mess because you did not instruct your President to act in the country's interest, you insufferable twit. And whilst I'm at it, I will laugh like a hoon if you get infected and can't come to work.'

The debates went on. And on. Accusations from both sides. No middle ground anywhere. Senator Packard brought the discussion to an end with a barb:

'Senator Jackson, I really believe that you need to experience the disaster your party has visited on this country. If I were to see you sitting on the street with a begging bowl, I might look you in the eye, ask what happened, and walk away.'

*   *   *

The morning dragged on; it was a slog. There was no cooperation. Senator Packard wished these sessions were live on free-to-air TV so the country would see what was happening. *There needs to be a reckoning*, she thought.

The aftermath of the recent demonstrations was visible in the streets. The noon TV shows had the talking heads out in force.

'Did you see all those bodies lying in the street? Where did they come from?' asks one of the anchors.

Somebody suggests, 'I think they drove their cars, felt unwell, stepped out and collapsed. Look there to the west; it's happening as we speak. They are probably infected with the blue strain. I wonder how they will pick them up?'

A bit later, one of them exclaims, 'Well, bugger me stupid! There is one of those trucks that empty garbage bins. It looks as if they modified the arms that grab the bins to pick up the bodies. Here it goes. Lifted and into the truck. Neat if a bit dehumanised.'

The reply was, 'Quite. But how did they get sick? From protest marches? If so, serves them right!'

*   *   *

The President is in the White House Office, furious with the republicans, and called his Army Chief of Staff, General Morgan, for a one-on-one meeting. He had a gutful and spat the dummy about the Senate tactics.[55] Then General Morgan entered.

'General, I take it you are up to speed on the Senate obstructionism and delaying tactics, yes? I want an Army supervision of the Senate in two days. I would love to get rid of Republican senators altogether, lock them up, just charge them on any trumped-up charge you can think of. Fudge some records to show they sent money to Iran. Anything that takes many months to sort out. Please consult with Attorney General Dr Ferrari. We will give them two days to hang themselves. Not a word to anyone else, and I would love to sack the bastards for life.'

'I know they will use the Supreme Court to overturn that, and if the Court does, they will get the same treatment. Arrested on some charge until they demonstrate that we can trust them. Lock

---

[55]   The Confirmation Process for Presidential Appointees Presidential Appointees

them up on a charge that will take nine months to be resolved. Let them self-destruct.'

General Morgan grins from ear to ear.

'Life is good, but what is your plan B?'

The President had this one worked out much earlier, and he told his Army Chief of Staff, 'I already know that. I have another solution. One that won't split the country any further. I just wanted you to hear how committed I am to getting change done.'

Of course the General wanted to know what he could do, and the President invited him to be in the Senate Chambers on the day.

'I will take six senators out for a private chat, and when they come back out, they will all smile and do what I need them to do. It's diplomacy. Which is private.'

*　　*　　*

Almost all TV News channels showed a video of a man turned away from the Washington University Hospital by an armed guard. The man's wife was in the car with him, and she was driving. One guard on the passenger side had looked inside at the man, shook his head and gestured to the other guard on the driver's side to move the car along at gunpoint.

The TV talking heads could not hear what was said but could see the sign.

'No admittance to anyone with a blue neck. Take the instructions handed to you and follow them to avoid prosecution.'

The anchors had all seen the White House Press Release in the morning. Seeing this in practice honed their survival instincts.

One man uttered, 'Holy shit, seeing this in practice is a lot more brutal than reading about it in a news bulletin. They did say the blue strain kills you in a day as well as anyone you get in close contact with, but I do wish they had been a bit more graphic earlier on so that people could prepare themselves for this. This is brutal.'

*   *   *

The senators took their lunch recess and watched the news in their dining room. It raised many voices about the brutal nature of seeing someone turned away from hospitals when they were dying. Everyone had an opinion, and that was okay. It was informal. They returned to the Senate Chambers, where Republican leader Senator Jackson took the floor. He invited senators to propose actions to overturn the rule preventing people infected with the blue neck strain from entering a hospital.

Senator Nolene Packard interrupted.

'Senator Jackson, I think you need to stand down till you've had a health check. I mean an intelligence test. You are so marvellously stupid that you should resign. What is your reason for wanting to kill all the health staff in those hospitals?'

Senator Jackson resumed, first asking Senator Packard to observe the standards in the house and refrain from insulting members, then that she was assuming too much, and continued:

'Ladies and gentlemen, turn to the person next to you and come up with an idea to debate. Two minutes per speaker. Raise your hand to be heard.'

Lots of noise; then one hand was up and invited to speak. It was Senator Marjorie Tumble, Republican, from Texas. She was known to be ambitious and was always working on her re-election prospects. Like so many insecure people, she was known to have a sharp tongue. Someone had described her as smiling at superiors and snarling at lower echelons, and the Democrats wondered if she would get herself into trouble.

'Senator Jackson, my name is Senator Marjorie Tumble, Republican, Texas. I suggest we send a bipartisan delegation of five senators to the Washington University Hospital to see if we can get them to agree with you that this inhumane treatment of sick people needs to be reversed.'

A lot of wasted time, but that was the only suitable proposal made.

*   *   *

February 14

The delegation of senators entered the Washington University Hospital and advised the receptionist that they had sent a hand-delivered message to be received by their Chief Medical Officer. The receptionist asked to see the reply he would have sent. They had not received one.

'When could we see him, please? It is rather urgent.'

They were astounded to hear he would not be available.

'This is not good enough. Why not?' was the aggressive question from one of the senators, and the receptionist pressed an emergency button. A soldier arrived, gun in hand.

'Who are you, and why do you wish to see the CMO?' the soldier asked.

'I am Senator Marjorie Tumble, Republican, from Texas. We had a letter delivered here yesterday requesting a meeting with the CMO this morning. Why is he not here?'

The soldier burst out laughing.

'One, he does not answer to you, two, he is home sick, and three, he will not be back.'

Senator Tumble smirked and wanted to know why not.

The soldier replied, 'Madam, I don't answer to you either, but I will inform you. The CMO has a blue neck, and he will be dead tomorrow; he will not be able to see you.'

'Whom can we see then?' she asked, infuriated.

He said, 'Lady, just go home. We are all busy saving lives here, so please just go, or I will need to escort you out at gunpoint. Which is it?'

Senator Tumble answered him, 'That is so sad. We will leave now, but before we go, whom could we book a meeting with, please? We want to see if the doctors are willing to allow sick, dying people into a hospital for treatment. It is so sad to see them turned away.'

The soldier replied, 'I understand your concern, and it is commendable. We all feel the same, sad, that is. But we already had a vote. If anyone, politician or bureaucrat, allows them in, there will be mass resignations. Not one medical staff member would be left after five minutes. State-wide. You need to get this, Madam. Blue necks got sick because they ignored instructions not to demonstrate, and our much-loved CMO will be dead as a result in the morning. Theirs is a self-inflicted wound. But we want to live. Don't bother coming back. There will be instant mass resignations if you want to force them to allow people showing a blue neck in here. Goodbye.'

*   *   *

The five senators returned to the Chamber. The Democrat Senate leader Nolene Packard had the floor, and she asked the outcome of their meeting. She already knew, of course. She had received a call from Staff Sergeant McAllister at the hospital, but presented a curious face.

'Senator Tumble, you have the floor. Please advise us of the outcome of your meeting with the Chief Medical Officer.'

'Ma'am', she stated, 'We were given no courtesies at all. There was no one there to meet us, and when I politely inquired, I was told that the CMO was absent. When I pressed for details, she told me he was home and was not expected to return. When I enquired further who else could hear our petition, the receptionist called security, and a Staff Sergeant arrived, gun drawn. I told him that the purpose of meeting with the CMO was to allow people showing the D-xxxx strain, meaning they have the blue neck, to be treated in hospital. That rude man told me, "if politicians or bureaucrats ordered hospitals to admit patients with the blue neck, then the medical staff, state-wide, would resign instantly."'

Senator Packard smiled sweetly and asked, 'Did the Staff Sergeant explain why the CMO was home, by any chance?'

'Oh yes,' replied Senator Tumble, 'He was home sick.'

'And what was wrong with him, please?' she asked.

'Oh yes, he had a blue neck and was expected to die that day.'

The Chamber burst into spontaneous laughter. They could not stop. The Democrats were in heaven, nearly choking with laughter.

Senator Tumble tried to recover poise by saying, 'And we were marched out at gunpoint.'

More laughter and they heard someone saying, 'Should have used that gun.'

*   *   *

February 15

General Morgan walked into the Chamber. Republican leader Senator Jackson has the floor and does not welcome him. Instead, he says:

'General. There are rules in this house. You can't just walk in here and disrupt important business. You need to apply to be admitted.'

General Morgan blew a whistle, and six of his soldiers marched in, guns raised, Republican targets identified. A hush descended, and the soldiers invited the identified senators to meet with the President in a private room. They included Senators Jackson and Tumble, and they were marched out. Complaints were heard but not listened to.

General Morgan simply said, 'This was a coup to re-align the senators to the President's wishes, and they will return shortly, unharmed. And Good morning, senators. Seeing your leader did not introduce me, I shall do that now. I am General Morgan, the Chief of Staff, US Army. The President has authorised me to speak to those senators in private.' And they were marched out of the Chamber.

There was silence. Then the Democrat leader spoke.

'Senators, let's get shit done, and get three Bills debated briefly and passed so that they can be signed into law today.'

'Not so fast, senators. We need the other six to return first,' came from the new acting Republican Leader.

The senators return, smiling. At the very next opportunity for delay, one of the returned senators spoke up.

'The American people want this Bill dealt with, and we work for those people. So, shall we get a move on then instead of all this delay, please?' The acting Republican leader asks pointedly:

'Have you lost your mind? You work for the Republican party, or have you forgotten?' The senators smiled, quite disarmingly, and one said:

'I used to work for the Republican party, but the President has made me see that it is imperative to work for the American people during this pandemic. I urge you to do the same, Sir.'

The acting leader splutters, chokes with rage, and threatens expulsion from the party, and the smiling senator's response was:

'Of course you may, senator. You can urge expulsion at the next Senate election. Until then, you will just have to put up with me.'

Later that day, one Republican Senator said to another:

'We have been so intimidated by the old guard. I've wanted to knock their heads together so many times but would have been shot down in flames. They don't really need us here at all, so my goal is to work for the country, so I can go home proud instead of ashamed.'

The evening news was full of one thing only; the 'turning' of two Republican senators.

The Republicans convened to elect a new Republican leader of the Senate. Their choice was Senator Hillary Johnson from Dallas, Texas. It was a fresh start. The new leader took the floor.

'Senators, I know you chose me to be your leader because you hope that I can salvage this disaster. I hope to do that. I will ask you all to submit suitable actions when you have discussed them with the person next to you. Just raise your hand when you are ready. I will call you.'

Lots of urgent murmurs, then a hand went up, and Senator Johnson responded.

'Yes, Senator Mulberry, what is your proposal?'

Senator Mulberry did not get many opportunities to shine, and by God, she would now.

'Senator Johnson, I vote we send a legal team to the Supreme Court first thing in the morning. I suggest we call them now if it is not too late, but we must ask for an urgent hearing. Even if we cannot get them now, they should expect us. The Senate changes will be on the news, so of course, they will expect us. Can I suggest I organise a legal team to be ready in the morning? We already have legal experts on standby since we conscripted them on a retainer a week ago.'

Senator Mulberry was thanked for her proposal and especially for the forethought to conscript a legal team to be ready. She could feel the worry about her future drain away. This move would make her.

* * *

7 p.m., February 15

The TV channels were curious. The President had 'turned' six Senators, but there was no announcement from the President. The talking heads were having a great time. Then there was a breaking news flash: 'Stand by for the President of the United States.'

The President came on the air. He looked stern but at ease.

'Fellow Americans. This is not the news I was hoping to bring you even four days ago. You are already aware that the Army was invited to control all civil issues, including media and social media, to stop the mass protests spreading the new COVID-19 strains at an alarming rate. We now have a new strain, D-xxxx, that turns your neck blue and kills you the next day. We will need to order total hotspot lockdowns, and some of you have already been without unemployment benefits for six weeks.'

'We tried to pass Bills authorising payments and were so horribly delayed by the Republican senators that I had a friendly word with six of them in private. When they returned, one of those senators addressed the Chamber and asked all to work for the country, to pass the Bills without delay.'

'I hope there will not be any more problems, but I assure you that I will act again if there are. Please follow orders as they are issued. Good night and God bless America.'

There was a moment's silence. One thing was sure, though. A new broom had arrived.

*   *   *

The Thompson and Anderson families discussed the news in their wilderness hideout.

They had seen the news on their satellite devices, and were oscillating between dumbfounded and gleeful. All at the same time. But mainly glee. Of course Dorothy had personally spoken with the President beforehand. She knew what he had planned, but even so, she was astounded. Those slimy Republicans and Trumpists had promoted the idea of an asleep President, and he was not asleep.

Eat your hearts out. Then she concentrated on his last statement. The one that said, 'I hope there will not be any more problems, but I assure you I will act if there are.'

'What do you think will happen next?' she asked Michael.

'Easy,' replied her husband. 'I was watching Senator Mulberry. I know her. She is one self-serving woman. She wants glory, and she will try to persuade the Supreme Court of America to overturn the Senators "Turning".'

'Then what?' asks Dorothy again, and Michael's answer put a smile on their faces. How many times had they wished for it? Michael's words stunned her.

'The President will have a private chat with three judges who previously ruled in favour of the maximum church attendances. When they come back out, they will have seen the errors of their ways and do what he wants them to do. Something quite legal. I can think of any number of measures or arm twisting, but it can't be made public. Ha ha. Celebration time.'

Chapter 16

Mood

Argus noted that the mood in Washington was a kaleidoscope of opinions. One thing that could be said is that there was something great for many and something awful for a similar number. Even though people watched TV, they did so with half an ear, because they listened to other people in the room. Why? Because you can argue with other people and were often compelled to. TV was a poor second but provided more ammunition occasionally. From a mental health point of view, it was wonderful; people engaged with talking to each other instead of being couch potatoes staring at the TV anchors repeating news they had heard at least five times that day.

February 16, 2021

The day had come that the republican leaning Supreme Court justices had been waiting for. There had been three days of arguments from the lawyers who brought the anti-abortion case, three days from those opposed, and now the Chief Justice summed up the argument before the vote:

'Ladies and gentlemen, you have heard the arguments, some of them pretty emotional. Our job is to rule according to the Constitution. That is the definition of your job descriptions. The Constitution does not have specific rules relating to abortion, but it specifically shows it is illegal to murder children. And the Constitution calls for punishment of anyone committing murder. It does not ask you to consider if the man killing someone was provoked. You also know that nineteen states ban abortion after 20 weeks.'

'And you are all aware of the US supreme court case Roe v Wade. That bill ruled that interference by the government in a woman's right to privacy was unconstitutional, and the anti-abortion lobby has been trying for 47 years to overturn that decision.'

'This debate could reverberate for weeks on end. I will mark this case as requiring new amendments to be considered in a year's time; after we have dealt with the pandemic. I rule that we have a ten-minute break then start with the next urgent item please.'

*   *   *

Dorothy trolled through the daily news items. Blah, blah, and more blah. Then one item caught her eye. She called Michael to sit with her.

'Read this and then tell me what you would like to do about this one. A thirteen-year-old coloured girl is raped by a famous football star, and is acquitted by three white judges on the grounds the footballer is so famous he would never have to resort to rape. What should we do to those judges?'

Michal does not have to think for long. He thinks of the worst thing to happen to three narcissistic men.

263

'Easy.' he grins, 'We need to go to bed and cuddle so you stop trying to fix all the evils in this world. You have three priorities: me and you, then the same again and only then the judges,' finished Michael. Dorothy wanted to have the last word. She wasn't going to worry about the judges at all, and wanted, 'me and you, then you and me, and if I have any time left over it's the Pandemic.'

*   *   *

It had been an exciting week for General Morgan, Army Chief of Staff. The Military had been invited to supervise the senate after republican skulduggery. The Senate was fixed for now, and more trouble was expected in the Supreme Court. Nothing he couldn't handle, though.

Then he sees the news item on the rape case. He was acquitted because he was so famous that he did not need to rape anyone? And the case was heard by a three-man panel of white judges?

How often did this happen? he wondered. His granddaughter Sally Elisabeth was the same age. Slowly his rage built. He was good at managing his rages to put them to use. He recorded the names of those three judges. He would single them out for his 'Judge re-education' when that was needed.

General Morgan wished the late Ruth Bader Ginsberg was available for advice. He realised that 'turning' of the Supreme Court judges because of the abortion vote would not be possible. It would cause such an emotional response it would split the country. He would find another way to cook that goose. He grinned at the thought that those judges would be spoken to by himself this time. He had learned from the President. He called his go-to man in the justice department to visit him in his office on a private matter.

The General started by saying, 'This matter is absolutely confidential and must never be disclosed outside this office. Does that work for you?' It did.

'I propose to have a friendly talk to two white Supreme Court judges who acquitted a white football star of rape because he was so famous that he would never have to resort to rape. I would like you to discover something that they would never want to be published. I will not mention the circumstances, just a name involved, and ask them to become aligned to my way of thinking. Any attempt by them to say it's blackmail is immediately countered; did I threaten them? No. Did I invite them to use a better interpretation in future? Yes. So all I want from you is a name that will see their jaws drop and face go white, lips quivering. After that, they all walk out smiling. I have saved their asses.'

'So, please have a list of names for me. Do you have the resources to get me that by this time tomorrow?' The President did.

*   *   *

February 17

The President had also written to Dorothy Thompson.

Dear Ms Thompson, I congratulate you on reporting your distress on the famous footballer's rape case where the 'Rape Charge' was thrown out by three judges. She may need an abortion and unfortunately the Supreme Court ruled totally against abortion on the same day. I could not sleep last night, and have this morning submitted a request to have that ruling declared void. Your article was a timely reminder that we need to do this. But please, keep my name out of this if you can.

After reading Dorothy Thompson's article on abortion, the President decided to call her to discuss the issue. After the pleasantries were over, he outlined his idea for change.

'I would like make women's health clinics readily available after counselling to ladies less than fifteen weeks pregnant. I'm sure you're aware that for clinics providing abortions, abortions only make up a very small fraction of their services And instead of having to run the gauntlet outside those clinics, I suggest it's a public health initiative, one that can be performed in hospitals. We don't need a poor little thirteen-year-old girl threatened by white men outside a clinic shouting murder. And it's men who make them pregnant. How would that work for you?' he asked.

After a flippant 'I'm not pregnant,' Dorothy told him she would write an article on the idea and have a voting app to allow readers nationwide to vote on the proposal.

'Piece of cake. Happy with that?' she asked, and he was. Problem solved. For now, anyway. All he needed was to get that Supreme Court decision overturned.

*   *   *

Later, February 17

The Texas megachurches had brought a case against COVID restrictions for their religious services to the state court. It had been rejected, as expected, and the goal had always been an appeal in the Federal Supreme Court to get a national ruling.

The Court had started to debate the issue. The Chief Justice addressed his justices.

'Ladies and gentlemen. I'm sure you are aware of your duties. I must remind you that this Court can only rule on a matter of constitutional interpretation. The Constitution gives people the right to unhindered worship. The government has issued a rule that prevents that for health reasons. You have the challenging job to make a ruling on this.'

The arguments were many and vicious. The churches wanted their attendance undiminished. They were accused of doing so for their collections. The parties provided no way forward to resolve the issue.

Unfortunately, one of the church backers asked, 'What can be so dangerous about attending church', and a tired court decided to allow unrestricted church access.

The following case to be heard was brought by Republican Senators who wanted to overturn the Army supervision of the Senate. The Chief Justice reminded justices that the issue to decide was whether the army supervision of the Senate was constitutional.

The debates were acrimonious. The Republican-appointed judges were furious, the Democrat appointed judges were delighted, but they did not have the numbers.

An hour later, with no end in sight, the Chief Justice addressed them.

'It can't be that hard. If you take the supervision case first, you need to remember that President requested it when public disobedience destroys public health. You can use this to see if that move was constitutional. Then when you consider whether the President needed to persuade some senators to get urgently need bills passed at a time of crisis, you may also find the current Army supervision of the Senate is constitutional at a time of national disaster.'

The Democrat judges were surprised. They had regarded the Chief Justice as their primary obstacle, and he was helping them.

But then a new reality set in. The Chief Justice was in that role because he worked for the good of the country. And they needed to use that knowledge in the future.

The case was deferred.

February 18

The case before the court concerned a request to allow sick people sporting a blue neck into hospitals. The blue neck strain was deadly in three days and it infected everyone close by. The case had been brought on behalf of the now arrested Senator Tumble.

The Chief Justice addressed the justices.

'Ladies and gentlemen, please raise your hand if you think this is a constitutional matter.'

One female Republican justice was given leave to speak.

'I think doctors swear an oath to do the best they can for those in need. They swear that on the Bible. That is tantamount to swearing it on the Constitution as far as I'm concerned.'

The Chief Justice looked at her sternly and suggested she go back to refresher classes. Then common sense prevailed. This should not be a constitutional issue, and the case was dismissed.

General Morgan entered the Supreme Court. He just stood there until there was silence. Deathly, in fact. Then General Morgan asked to address the full bench. He was very polite and was granted leave.

'Good morning, ladies and gentlemen. I bring good news and bad news.'

'The bad news is that I have come to speak privately to two judges. And all of you must function in the country's interest from now on. Most of these cases should not be decided by politics. Fortunately, the Chief Justice has demonstrated that will only just recently, and he is your guide.'

'The country is in crisis, mainly because Republicans failed to compel President Trump to address the pandemic seriously. Until just recently, before the new strains, the United States performed far worse than any developed country and worse than most undeveloped ones as well. Now it's even worse than that. The takeovers are temporary. Those whose names I will read out will accompany me to a private room to be re-educated by me.'

General Morgan beckoned two judges to follow him to a private room, and locked the doors, then spoke, 'Gentlemen, I have an urgent need for you to work for the better of the country instead of following political leanings. Can I have your agreement to that, please?'

One of the judges protested.

'How dare you suggest that we are not impartial? That is a federal offence.'

The General smiled sweetly and replied, 'So was Jennifer Woodstock.' The judge blew a gasket.

'That is blackmail!' Of course, that statement admitted his guilt, but the General smiled and asked:

'Did I threaten you?'

The second judge said, 'General, you do not need to mention any names regarding me. I agree totally that we should act in the interest of the country, and I thank you for handling this distasteful episode in strict privacy.'

The General stood and assured them that he would never disclose the content of their friendly discussion, and the judges returned to their chambers, smiling.

Breaking News

Nobody knew just how many TV channels there were, but all of them carried the same story:

Army General Morgan takes two judges out of Court in private, after which they no longer oppose the government's wishes.

The talking heads were split into two main groups. Those whose job was to stir the pot and make people furious, and those who had a serious following. But if you walked into a bar, you would see five TVs with all of them blaring hatred and revolt. The common theme was, 'They can't just turn Supreme Court Judges. What will they do next?'

And one lone voice told them, 'They will do what they need to do to pull this country from the brink of disaster.'

*   *   *

February 20

Worshippers arrived at the Lakewood Church and the other five megachurches in the 'Bible Belt' of Houston, all within a short distance of the Southwest Freeway.

The churches had all been advised that they should be reducing capacity to 25 per cent, but a last-minute Supreme Court decision had cancelled that limit. People were streaming in. It was their Sunday outing. It was also their community. Most importantly, it was their constitutional right. An Army truck was parked outside with a big sign, which read:

Health notice to worshippers

We want to limit the congregation to 25 per cent, in this case, 12,600, regardless of your beliefs and the Supreme Court decision. If the full capacity enters, you may be stopped from leaving if we notice any parishioners showing symptoms of the blue neck strain. We advise wearing masks during the service to stop the spread of the virus. We will take anyone with a blue neck to a blue truck. If we detect blue necks exiting, we will close the doors and prevent everyone from leaving for four days.

General Morgan, Army Chief of Staff

The notice caused a stir, and the predominant reactions were: 'They can't do that', 'Jesus will protect us', and 'I forgot my mask', but in they went.

'No matter what, how would they lock in 50,000 people? We need to go home for lunch. That's what.' another parishioner said.

Three hours later, and after many knee bendings, hallelujahs, and hymns sung at full voice, they were exhausted and ready to leave. There were many exits, some to street level, some to underground parking. Four soldiers monitored each exit. They all had colourimeters. Within three minutes, ten blue necked worshippers had exited. They were told to go to the blue truck. Staff Sergeant Thomas called Lt. Col. Morgan Freebody on his radio.

'Ten held, blue as that famous fly. Permission to lock up the place?' Permission was granted and SSG Thomas called all stationed soldiers.

'Lock-in permission received from Lt. Col. Morgan Freebody. Please surround all exits and stop anyone exiting. We found ten blue cases so far in three minutes. Dangerous to let them out into the community. Bring one hazmat dressed soldier to each door and enter on my command, then move to the pulpit and make the following announcement:

- 'Ladies and gentlemen. You are effectively under house arrest and cannot leave. Please stay in your seats, and if not too late, don your masks. We found ten excited worshipers admiring their blue necks. They will be dead tomorrow, the third day of the infection. Please come to the front now if you have been near anyone with a blue neck. Use your left aisle, my right one, without touching anyone. To make room, others please move to the back of the hall using your right aisle, my left one.

- Please stay seated as much as possible. Do not shout. Do not breathe on anyone.

- Because it will take up to two days for anyone newly infected to show the blue infections, you need to stay here that long. During the day, every few hours, soldiers in hazmat suits will enter and check that any new blue infections get moved to the front. Anyone starting a fight with the soldiers will be looking at a rifle, so please be sensible.

- Food and water trolleys will come to the door and make their way down the aisle from now on, so there is plenty to eat and drink. Of course, the food may not be what you would have had at home, but feeding 50,000 people three times a day is challenging. Sorry for the inconvenience.'

*   *   *

'OUTRAGE' is the breaking news headline, subtitled 'Army locks people into church for at least two days to stop infected churchgoers returning home.'

The talking heads all started with the announcement made by soldiers in hazmat suits inside the Lakewood Church in Houston. The consensus was that the Army had lost the plot. The Supreme Court had given the church the right to full attendance. All the megachurches on the Bible Beltway had full complement congregations, and Lakewood had been singled out by the Army and had locked up 50,000 people for three days. Gross. Mind you; the others are not complaining.

'How does the Army expect to get away with this? It must be illegal.' One news anchor said.

The beauty of the talking heads is that everyone says the same thing. Group Think, maybe? The beauty is not having to choose which one to listen to. There is just one drawback from all these syndicated blogs: the truth gets lost. Washington Post to the rescue.

Rebecca Sanders Reporting

Dear Readers,

Sorry to be late with my news item, and I hope you are still with me. It takes time to get the truth out there. Plugging for my channel now, the others are all syndicated, all the same, and they see one item and out it goes under ten new network expert names.

I don't consider myself an expert. Why? Because no one much agrees with me anyway. But I do think the President does.

This is the truth; you wonderful and opinionated people. There is a disaster happening, and if we don't stop this strain completely this week, more than half the country may well be dead and bodies left to rot in the street. I have reported from battlefields, and the stink is just too atrocious to describe here. That is what I am afraid of.

But it looks as if the churches have decided Jesus will save them. That is not his job description, by the way. His job is to forgive you for your sins so you can go to heaven.

And the biggest sin you can commit now is to disregard the health and safety instructions. You need to keep your views for your memoirs... If you live that long.

*   *   *

The President had received a meeting request to meet in the White House Office from Lt. Col. Morgan Freebody for an urgent meeting regarding the Lakewood Church in Houston. When seated, Lt. Col. Freebody started:

'Mr President, we have come across some small water cannon machines used in crowded cities, and we can convert those by tomorrow to act as disinfectant sprays. Their wheelbases allow them to move into the Lakewood Church and drench all parishioners not showing the blue neck symptom with this highly effective disinfectant spray. The Chinese used them in cities to spray whole streets and people. I can have two of them ready for use by midnight and another four by 8 AM. Do you want to go ahead?'

'Colonel, I will call the church leaders and ask what time we should come in, with their permission. If we came in from the top, you could move any blue-necked worshippers to the infected mob at the front. How saturated do you want them to be?'

'Mr President, the air needs to be full of disinfectant mist for people to breathe into their lungs. That will also coat their seat arms and anything else they are likely to touch, including their hands and clothes and those of people near them.'

Lt. Col. Freebody continued, 'Then we should get ten machines ready to send to the White Sands camp in New Mexico and see if we can keep more people alive than those stupid idiots deserve.'

It was decided, and the go-ahead was given. The first two machines went in at midnight, with another four sent in later. In the morning, a TV camera recording the event was sent to a TV station ten minutes later.

February 21, 2021

The talking heads from the 'Breaking News' channels started on the wrong foot when one over-anxious anchor man blasted off with the news that 'the Army is spraying poison onto 50,000 people in the Lakewood Church in Houston.' He was taken off the air two minutes later and replaced, and the following announcement went out:

'The previous report is incorrect. The anchor had a medical episode and did not hear correctly. The correct news is that Army, bless them, had cobbled together some small street cleaning tankers and filled them with COVID-killing disinfectants used in a fine mist spray form for people to inhale. The disinfectant is also alcoholic, and many people went to sleep. Alcohol is not allowed in the church, and I'm sure this will blow up in their faces.'

This press release was also corrected. They must have had another anchor with a medical episode, or he was drunk at work.

The TV networks were in an uproar. Army completely controlled and temporary staged an effective takeover of the Supreme Court by converting two judges to the government's perspective. This is was the Army's news announcement:

Army Supervision Notice

Bad news, ladies and gentlemen. And lawyers, and those who use them to gain an unfair advantage. Lawyers will be out of jobs for a long time. This is why.

The Army will supervise the Supreme court for federal constitutional matters indefinitely. By supervising, we mean they will be talked to, quite kindly, to align their interpretations towards the government's views. We will open a voting platform in an hour, and you can vote whether you agree or disagree and want to protest. There will be one other (rhetorical) question whether you want to sack the Army. Republicans, go for it if you want to save the country from dictatorship.

That was just too much, and Dorothy Thompson reported under her own name.

Dorothy Thompson reporting.

The politicisation of the Supreme Court. The last avenue for redress. It has been so politicised that good decisions are few and far between for the country, massively favouring political leanings. That is not supposed to be its job description.

I can just imagine China's Xi Jinping having a good laugh. US commitment to democracy on display; their catchphrase.

Let's leave out the anti-abortion vote for now. It's a worldwide debate anyway. Republican delaying tactics prompted the first reason for the Senate supervision to allow necessary relief to those without unemployment benefits. They had been without support for eight weeks at the time. Then Senator Mulberry tries to overturn a vital bill the Army proposed to keep hospitals safe. She wanted people who were dying that day or the next to be admitted to a hospital and kill everyone there. It was so infectious. All she wanted was re-election brownie points. Mark my words: there will be other obstructions to the army ruling, and they will all go to the Supreme Court, but they no longer have the votes to play silly buggers.

*   *   *

February 23

The Army sent fifty inspectors to the Lakewood Church wearing hazmat suits with face masks to deal with the stink and see who was left alive. They were pleasantly surprised by several facts: first that all the blue-necked cases were in the bottom front rows, all dead, and the others had all moved up to the top, at least ten rows up from the dead bodies. The second piece of good news was that almost all those in the better sections seemed to be OK. Even if they ponged, but not from death. The third piece of good news was that the dead, estimated at 11,000 people, far less than their initial modelling had suggested. That number had been 18,000, derived before the Army had come in and sprayed people with the demister spray. That move had saved 7,000 lives. The last bit of good news was that the congregation had not been the full capacity of 52,000 but only 41,000, and that explained that there were many spare rows between the dead and the alive people. The spray at midnight had worked much better as a result of those empty rows.

TV news bulletin

Good news from the Lakewood Church, very good news. Only 11,000 people dead, 30,000 saved by Army intervention when they arrived at midnight with a killer spray to protect those not already infected by the blue neck virus. The wrong choice of words maybe, but the spray killed the virus.

Now comes the hard part: the clean-up and the disinfecting of the church. The Army has offered two alternatives to the church:

Their preferred option is to cremate all bodies in their seats using flame throwers to kill the COVID virus. They can follow behind a minute later with handheld extinguishers to stop the flames from spreading. They can come in safely the next day and carry people out, taking between five to seven days. They may have to destroy seating to get heavy lifting cranes into rows to remove people over 250 pounds, most of them by the looks of things. The families cannot view the bodies. They will be taken away by the blue trucks used to remove dead bodies from the street and taken to mass graves where they are covered in lime to protect the groundwater from the virus spreading.'

'The other option is to close the church for five months and then remove the dead. Neighbouring properties may complain about the stinks, but that should go away in a month.'

*   *   *

The President had invited Lt. Col. Freebody and Dorothy Thompson to a late breakfast meeting in the White House Offices and made introductions, but they knew each other already.

The President spoke.

'First, congratulations to you, Colonel, for such expert handling of the Lakewood Church disaster, and second to you, Ms Thompson, for doing my White House press for me, even without authorisation. Excellent job.'

'Second, we are now heading for the next big hurdle. Ms Thompson, this is not for release till I advise you. The Constitution will be amended. Colonel, have you kept in touch about this with Attorney General Ferrari? Can we have this ready in two days, do you think?'

'It is almost ready now, Mr President. When would you like to announce it? And where? I do not think the Supreme court needs to be involved at this stage.' replied Lt. Col. Freebody. He continued, 'Because we will engineer cases that will go to court, and we will turn some judges to have a better interpretation than in the past. Everyone will be happy, even the judges.'

CHAPTER 17

Mood

Argus E was still following all events and noted that an attempt would be made to alter the Constitution, that almost sacred document. *I wonder how they will go with that,* he thought, intrigued by how they would do that and expect to get away with it. He remembered the efforts to change the constitution in his country where the large number of political parties made any such change impossible.

The Constitution

The Constitution contains 4,543 words, including the signatures, and has four sheets 28¾ inches by 23⅝ inches each. It contains 7,591 words, including the 27 Amendments. It has been a very stable document, remaining almost unchanged since it was written, 234 years ago.

The Constitution is organised into three parts. The first part, the Preamble, describes the purpose of the document and the Federal Government. The second part, the Seven Articles, establishes how the Government is structured and how the Constitution can be changed. The third part, the Amendments, lists changes to the Constitution; the first ten are called the Bill of Rights. The Founding Fathers established three main principles on which our Government is based:

- Inherent rights, the rights that anyone living in America has
- Self-government, or Government by the people
- Separation of powers, or branches of Government with separate powers

Article II, Section 2, Clause 3, Recess Appointments Power [56]

Article II, S2, C3 is of Interest to the President, especially in regards to Supreme court appointment.

The President shall have the power to fill up all Vacancies that may happen during the Recess of the Senate by granting Commissions which shall expire at the End of their next Session.

Amendment II

The second amendment has been used to allow every man and his minder to carry arms without stipulating the type of arms his means. Surely the fathers of the constitution had not envisages automatic weapons used today with a magazine holding fifty bullets, unlike the muzzle loaders of the 1780s that took a minute to reload. Here is the culprit

---

[56] Browse the Constitution Annotated > Article II > Section 2 > Clause 3 > ArtII. S2.C3.1.1 Recess Appointments Power: Overview

A well-regulated Militia, being necessary to the security of a free State, the right of the people to keep and bear Arms, shall not be infringed.

*　　*　　*

February 23

Not much wrong with the Constitution, thought Attorney General Dr Ferrari, and fortunately, would require no re-write. A re-write would have been totally unacceptable to most people anyway. But they would need a new interpretation of that sacred document and a bit of arm twisting of several Supreme Court justices. The President and Dr Ferrari discussed this. Both men had a good look at the Constitution before the meeting, and the President expressed his utter admiration for the document.

The President began, 'That is amazing. They designed it as a set of principles and guidelines so that it can always be applied. I had a look at it some years ago, but now that we want some change, I am chagrined at my ignorance. It should never be touched except for small amendments.'

They debated the 2nd Amendment to bring it in line with today's proper military rather than the militias of the 1860s. The President started.

'Half the country would love to get rid of guns—the big ones. Whilst we have manoeuvred the Senate and Supreme Court out of revolting for the moment, I intend to get rid of them, the guns. The 2nd Amendment was written when the Government wanted men to carry arms as the militias were the Army. We don't need militias anymore, and in fact, they are quasi-illegal anyway. We have an Army now. That Amendment is antiquated, and I want it changed. How would you go about it legally?'

Dr Ferrari scratches his head. He hums and haws. Then even more. This indicated he was fast at work, but results had not yet appeared on the horizon. After a minute of this, he was ready.

'Mr President. That would split the country. The Army and police will love it. They are the ones always at risk from shooters. I think we need to decide on two issues: The first is, "What guns are they not allowed to carry?" and the second is, "What do we do with the guns they can no longer carry?" A spinoff is "What do we do about all the stores that sell those guns?" Those decisions are yours, Mr President,' said the AG, grinning at the President's dilemma.

It is now the President's turn to squirm. But not for long.

'These are the choices,' said the President. 'I intend to allow them to carry handguns for protection and sporting rifles for hunting and protection in the wilderness. Nothing automatic. None of this fifty rounds a second stuff. There can be exemptions for single-shot rifles: locked and stored at shooting ranges, and farmers for pest control, locked and stored in gun safes attached to their trucks. No automatic weapons. They can be rapid-fire, but none of this "zzzzz" or "brrrr", and fifty rounds are gone. That is for the military at war. All automatic rifles and guns to be handed in at a military depot. Anyone walking in public, or carrying one in their car without exemptions, gets locked up. Finito. Long time. What's your view, Dr Ferrari?'

'Make sure you don't get shot first,' commented the Attorney General. 'This will be one great big bunfight.'

The President replies, 'Yes, but we have the numbers, and the Court can be managed. I can persuade those standing in the way that they will just love to see it my way during the pandemic. Then, in four years, they can vote me out; if I'm still alive. They can change the Constitution to say we can all carry flamethrowers if they can get a two-thirds majority in a referendum for that. It's a democracy. Right now, my democracy says you can't go around and shoot people with military weapons. Or with high powered bows and arrows. They can hate me. Many will love me. Let's talk about compensation for weapons handed in then.'

Dr Ferrari liked this subject. 'Most of the high powered and automatic weapons can be used by the military, or we can sell them to other armies. Take the ArmaLite. We get them at a good price and offer holders of such weapons two-thirds of what we pay; we need to sort them out, check them and repackage them for Army use. I would estimate that there are one hundred and twenty million such weapons in use, average buy price $1000, so to buy them at say $800, I guess you pay about seventy billion dollars. Got money for that?' he asked.

'We need to find a way to reduce that cost,' offered the President. 'If we find someone with an unauthorised rifle, we fine them say $3000. Let's say, back of the envelope, that one quarter does not hand them in, then we can collect ninety billion dollars from thirty million rifles. Come out on top over time.' He grinned, a well-earned smirk of satisfaction.

Then the President decides to discuss his intention for no Constitutional change, but an interpretation that the Supreme Court can support.

'I have a way of persuading the judges to see interpretations my way,' he said. 'I will call the Michigan Governor and encourage her to promote a bill to outlaw all automatic weapons. She had suffered terror previously when armed mobs stormed her Capitol. She will love it, she has the numbers, and it becomes law. That same day the Republicans will attempt to have that thrown out in the State Supreme Court, which will refuse the request. Off to the Federal Supreme Court, they will march, with a glint in their eyes, but I will have a bigger and better glint. I have two judges in mind.'

'I will persuade them to see that automatic rifles are not mentioned in the Constitution. Easy. One of the selected judges had a nephew killed in a mass shooting. I will find a sore point for the other one. Then to soften the blow, I will offer the buy-back I mentioned and make a buck out of it if some are stupid enough to keep their rifles.'

Dr Ferrari laughs his head off, 'Who said you were "Sleepy"?' He wants to move on to the next topic.

The next item was to restrict the number of Supreme Court judges a President can elect in his term and how many in their last nine months of office. Consider campaign donation restrictions for companies doing business with the USA. Consider an entry in the Preamble about the modern USA and its aims to guide all decisions.

The President starts: 'I aim to remove the Gerrymander of state distributions. 'Gerrymandering' was named for Elbridge Gerry, one of the signers of the Declaration of Independence. As Governor of Massachusetts, Gerry approved a redistricting plan for the State Senate that gave the political advantage to Republicans.'

'Then I want to stop the same illegal application of laws that allows a President to allocate an unlimited number of judges to the Supreme Court. And the laws that allow states to have their own rules for the running of Federal elections. And laws that allow large defence companies to make billion-dollar donations to secure defence contracts, not on merit but through bribery. To achieve that, I have an idea for a Federal electronic voting system that I have worked on for years. We will discuss this at the end of all the other work.'

'A good thing you don't want much, Mr President,' said the AG.

'No, Dr Ferrari, I'm not asking for it; the country is. I'm just the messenger,' replied the President.

Dr Ferrari felt silenced. *Is this a new world we live in, or what happened here just now?*' he wondered.

'Mr President, those are all different issues. Let's take them one at a time. Which one first?' The President wanted to deal with Supreme Court appointments.

'Section II of the Constitution states: "The President shall have the power to fill up all Vacancies that may happen during the Recess of the Senate, by granting Commissions which shall expire at the End of their next Session." Notice the expiry after the next session. Donald Trump filled vacancies whether needed or not, lifetime appointments no less, and appointed three judges, the last one a month before the election. That was Amy Coney Barrett.'

'Two things spring to mind. One is that Amy Coney Barrett's appointment was almost certainly made with the view of having the Supreme Court overturn the election result should he lose. Guess who controls the appointments? The Senate. Then I'm looking at having an Amendment that limits new Supreme Court appointments to be made with only six months of the Presidency still to run. But what the Senate has done is appoint judges for life. With the President behind in the polls and the election just around the corner. That needs to be changed. Your job, Dr Ferrari.'

'The last thing that springs to mind comes from the same Section II paragraph again, this time for the appointment of heads of departments. Under President Obama's nominees, there were numerous departments without a permanent head for a very long time. For two years, in fact.[57] Because of a hostile Senate, I want that changed. The Senate's job should be to establish the proper credentials and criminal history, lack thereof, I mean. Appointments need to be approved during the transition period. Can you handle that?' asked the President.

Dr Ferrari's only comment was, 'Here comes my ulcer.'

'Anything else I can do for you, Mr President?' he asks and then wishes he had not.

'Yes, please, Dr Ferrari, I want to drain the swamp. Remember that phrase? I want donations to the Federal party coffers capped for any companies likely to have dealings with the Government. I don't want any more of those defence disasters where we gave contracts to companies with billion-dollar donations that failed to deliver. I have this quote from Forbes.[58]'

> The US Navy spent a decade in the early 2000s building warships that either don't work, cost too much to build in large numbers or whose designs are fundamentally flawed on a conceptual level. Or all three.
>
> These floating lemons include the speedy, inshore Littoral Combat Ship and the huge, under-equipped DDG-1000 'stealth' destroyers.'

'It looks to me as if contracts are given based on donation preferences. I want you to add a section to the Constitution that eliminates badly designed and badly tested proposals. This is bullshit. We can send a man to the moon and can't build satisfactory Navy ships. Please confer with the Chief of Navy and bring me

---

[57] Chances for Obama nominees to be confirmed are falling, even with over two years to go.

[58] The US Navy Wasted A Whole Decade Building Bad Ships

a list of circumstances that led to this disaster, Dr Ferrari.' said the President. As the meeting ended, the President remembered the electoral voting system and started with a question he knew the answer to.

'Dr Ferrari, how easy would it be to change the Constitution to make the running of the Federal elections a federal issue instead of a State one?'

'Not possible. You would get murdered before the Republicans would allow that.'

'I know,' said the President, 'that is why I will do the following. Then you tell me if it will work. I will send you my proposal.'

Dr Ferrari received the proposed election system details from the President

> I received a copy of a design proposal for a secure electronic voting system. It had been sent to our military by an Australian working in Cyber Security for a Master's degree. It is so secure that I can build a test system, run election tests every day for two weeks, invite people to vote from different states each day. Then I offer hackers, and hacker state operators, one million dollars if they can break in for the first week and ten million after that. My security chief has had his team look at it, and they agree the system cannot be busted. It is based on some of the Sun Tzu strategies, the ancient Chinese Strategist and warrior, in particular: know your enemy, deceive your enemy, show your enemy what you want him to see. Stuff like that. This system is brilliant and relatively inexpensive and will drive foreign intelligence agencies nuts trying to get in.

Then we use that system to run a Referendum, and anyone who does not want to stand in a queue in rain or snow in future when they want to be at work will vote for it. The only people who will oppose it are Republican lawmakers, and they are then outnumbered. Bye-bye.

'How do you know it's so safe?' asked the AG when he called the President, who told him, 'If you can't get in, you can't get in. And after the test elections, we will announce how it works and offer another twenty million if they can break it, and when they can't break in, we have the credibility for the referendum.'

'Is it possible?'

'Yes, it is.'

*   *   *

The President invited Dorothy Thompson to a private and somewhat clandestine meeting. He sent a car for her, which picked her up by a shopping mall near the Post to throw off any stickybeaks. After the required courtesies, he started:

'Today, you will be just Dorothy. I need a friend. I need to shoot the breeze and see your reactions. That will tell me what I'm battling with, far better than the learned consultants will give me. This is the point.'

After a moment's pause, he said, 'I want to make changes to the Constitution to serve our country better.'

'Oh my God, I hope you live through this. It's a sacred document. What's so wrong with it then?' she asked.

The President told her, 'It has been used for centuries to subvert the will of the people and give power to political interests. Aside from that, nothing much.'

'And you want me to help you decide what to do, or just listen to the proposals, so you get the population reaction?'

'The latter is exactly what I want. You are close to the pulse of the nation. I will outline my proposal. Interrupt any time.' He continued, 'This is the proposal:'

- Change the Second Amendment – do not allow automatic rifles to be carried unless an exemption is possessed.
- Limit the President's appointments to the Supreme Court and none in the last six months of a presidency.
- Change the appointment of department heads so that a Senate will complete appointments during the transition period.
- Cap the donations for federal or state elections for companies doing business with the Government or hoping to. Drain the swamp.
- Establish a Navy shipbuilding centre of excellence to supervise new constructions. The last ten years have been a total waste of money and resources.'

Dorothy looked gobsmacked. 'Mr President, I need a drink, anything in that cupboard of yours?' she asked, and helped herself. Then she joked and asked, 'You haven't been drinking yourself, have you, Mr President?'

The President was pleased. 'A bit dramatic, is it?' he asked, and she responded.

'It's totally gripping; I will go to Heaven if you can just pull off the first item, guns,' she replies. 'But how will you get this past the Senate or Supreme Court?'

The President grinned. 'Easy. Neutered them both. Till the next election.'

Dorothy spluttered and had another sip of her drink. She asked that critical question. 'What will you do with the guns they can't use?'

The President outlined the repurchase at $800 apiece by the Army, expected cost seventy billion for ninety million weapons. He expected a quarter to not surrender, fined three thousand apiece, raising ninety billion in the process over time.

'So, Dorothy, what I need from you now is the public reaction to all this. First the guns.'

Dorothy had another drink, looked into her glass - looking for wisdom - and found it. 'The nation is equally divided with pro and anti-gun people. The pro-gun people may take matters into their own hands. Shoot people. The National Rifle Association will blow a gasket - but bugger them. The nasties, the militias, need to be outlawed anyway, and you need to have a reason and a big stick to fight them. I suggest you use the Army.'

The President shocked her. 'Protestors walking with rifles need to know they can be shot and killed. Shoot one, and the fight is over, especially if you show very graphic TV coverage. With sound effects.' Dorothy is gobsmacked at all the audacious proposals.

'I have advised the governor of Michigan to call you when she debates a gun law in the State House and Senate to outlaw all automatic guns and rifles, and she has the numbers to get that passed. Then the Republicans will take that to the State Supreme Court and get it blocked. That gives the Republicans the right to lodge a case in the Federal Supreme Court.'

Dorothy is with him now, 'And you will use your diplomacy to help some judges see what is better for the country?'

'Yep. Do you like it?' He asked.

Her answer was, 'Nope. Love it. You didn't want a sounding board. Did you want a fan club or real feedback?'

He replied, 'Your reaction has already given me all the feedback I need, thank you, Dorothy.'

*　　*　　*

After his meeting with Dorothy the President had invited the Secretary of the Navy to discuss Navy shipbuilding disasters, and after a warm welcome, he started:

'Mr Secretary, I called you in to get advice on better shipbuilding contracts. I sent you the Forbes report of the last ten years to be familiar with what I want to change. As CEO of the Department of the Navy, you would be very familiar with the process of offering contracts for new ships. Or even for maintenance, wouldn't you? Please outline the process for starting a new type of ship.'

'Mr President, the process is complicated, as there is always the need for new ships and weapons that have not been built before, whilst there is only knowledge of the ones we have made in the past. New is always a risk. New ships are conceived from an agreement of the required or desired military capabilities. Those capabilities have been changing rapidly in the last decade, with the rapid increase in naval shipbuilding in China.'

He continued, 'The second problem is that we have not been conducting sufficient proof of concept exercises because of haste, and then the budget runs over, and the Defence department cuts back on what we build.'

The President responded. 'Mr Secretary, I can see that the weapons programs could easily change rapidly, but the actual shipbuilding is still the same as ever. The weapons are all developed by contractors. Today, I aim to tell you that I will allocate extra funds for the Navy to have centres of excellence that are better equipped, with estimating future needs and their costs. I would like you to come back to me in a month to tell me how that would work.'

'Mr Secretary, I would like you also to research how many contracts are awarded to defence companies based on political donations. I intend to cap Federal and State political donations from companies dealing with, or hoping to gain defence contracts,' finished the President.

'I must admit, Mr President, that has been a concern for decades. Lovely idea.'

*   *   *

After his meeting with the Navy Secretary he was back to his main job, especially as it was his election promise; to get rid of the pandemic. He was considering the daily cases. Until a week ago, the daily cases and deaths had dropped dramatically from a recent high on January 8, of over 300,000 new cases and 4,000 daily deaths. Now there were 90,000 daily cases and 3,000 new deaths. But the last week had seen a rapid increase in cases and death, because of the new strain, 'D-xxxx.'

The President called in Dr Federico Ponti to discuss the new strain and sudden increase in cases and deaths again. He started with:

'Dr Ponti, I hope you can help me by providing estimated projections of cases and deaths for the next month. Tell me what I need to do to stamp out the D-xxxx strain.'

Dr Ponti answers. 'Mr President, I missed the advance notice for this meeting; hence I will need to ad hoc it. The first problem is that this strain is so deadly that we cannot ask infected patients where they have been. They are already dead. Sometimes the families know, and from that, a picture is emerging. It looks like the new strain spreads easily ten yards through the air of a breathing infected man or woman, so any infections in a tightly packed protest group will probably infect most of the group. If I see a protest of ten thousand, I'm off to Greenland.'

The President asks if he is dramatic.

'Mr President. If you don't order complete lockdowns in areas where this strain is found, we wipe out the whole continental United States in a week. I'm not kidding. You need to do that today. I will need to see a press release announcing this, or I'm on the next flight out with my family. Mass gatherings must include churches not following COVID-safe rules. Those rules need to be changed to four yards distance between anyone else. Today. You need to outlaw church gatherings completely in areas where the blue neck strain has been found within a mile.'

'My word, Dr Ponti. Fortunately, I know you are not threatening me when you say you will leave on the next plane. But please help me get this announcement right, and I need to quote you for this to work with the public.'

The two men worked rapidly to cobble together an effective announcement. It said:

Urgent note to all people residing in the USA.

After advice from Dr Ponti, I am ordering the following changes to public meetings:

- A complete four-day lockdown is ordered in any metro suburb with the D-xxxx strain (blue neck) reported in the last two days. This will be policed by the Army, who will also deliver food.

- A complete ban on all mass gatherings, including churches, is in place for five days for any other areas.
- Public social distancing must be increased to five yards for five days, and masks are mandatory. The Army will police this.
- The lockdown period may be extended or cancelled, depending on the cases detected. Your life depends on this, so please just follow instructions but feel free to complain on social media.

By order of The President of the United States of America.

'OK, Dr Ponti, will that help you stay put?' asked the President.

There was the expected grudging reply: 'Yes, for now.'

*   *   *

Argus E noticed a new group of people exerting an influence: the *Bravehearts* and the *Forcefields*. There was trouble brewing and he would keep an eye out on them. They could disrupt the path to getting rid of the pandemic.

*   *   *

Jason Donovan from the *Bravehearts* lives in Anacostia, Washington, DC. When there were new restrictions that warranted a demonstration, he had to lead, persuade, and occasionally kick ass.

Tim Highfields is his Second in Command, 2IC, and Tim loves his job. He had grown up being bullied, and now he was powerful;.

Terry Copperfield leads 'Forcefield' the group; lives in Shadyside, Pittsburgh. Terry is a smart operator. He knows he has to keep his deputies happy so that they don't gun for his job.

He gives them the freedom to make suggestions and often backs them.

Mat Davis, Terry's deputy, thought: *The worst thing that can happen to the Government is if the protest marches get out of control and the guards shoot a civilian. TV will be live, and if they capture that, all hell will break loose.*

Jason had seen the announcement, and he was boiling, or his blood was. He was ready to blow a gasket, and he had called a meeting of his deputies. Tim Highfields wanted to start:

'They can piss in the wind if they want to, but I'm not following those rules. It did not say effective immediately so that we can get away with a demonstration. Demonstrations happen against lockdowns in most European countries. We must be seen as leaders of the demonstrations, or we lose members. Free board and lodgings if they arrest us.'

Jason Donovan asked just one question, 'How soon can we start?'

CHAPTER 18

February 23

The President wanted to enact one part of the Constitutional changes, effective immediately. He released the following statement to the press, copied to the Supreme Court:

> The President is making emergency changes to an Amendment of the Constitution. When the emergency has passed, there can be a Referendum to alter or remove this change. In total, there will be five changes, and all will be discussed and ratified by the Attorney General and the Supreme Court. One change is announced now and is effective immediately by executive order.
>
> The Second Amendment in the 1780s gave the right to carry arms as the militias were needed to defend the country. Those rifles required time to load and plug, and there was no official Army as we have today.
>
> That Amendment never envisaged that protestors and terrorists could carry automatic rifles shooting between fifty and one hundred rounds per second.

All automatic rifles are now banned from public use. Only the Police and Army may use such weapons. There will be announcements tomorrow morning about an Army weapons buyback. If you are caught with automatic weapons, you will be arrested from midnight tonight onwards. Until midnight tonight, they will be confiscated without arrest.

As previously stated, you will have the opportunity to remove these restrictions subject to a Referendum after the emergency has passed.

Later, the President met with Lt. Col. Freebody. They discussed the latest list of COVID-19 hotspots: counties in South Carolina, Georgia, and Pennsylvania. They are all in the range of 55 to 75 daily infections per 100,000 population. It is difficult to see which of those counties has the highest rate of the new deadly strain.

'Well, I was hoping to identify the hotspots of the D-xxxx strain. It kills young and old. How can we identify them?' asked the President.

Lt. Col. Freebody suggested they contact Dr Ponti. By phone, in case he had advice handy.

They called him, and when he came on the line, the President spoke, 'Dr Ponti, I hope you're in the mood to solve my problems.'

Dr Ponti was no slouch and came back with, 'Sure, if you promise to solve mine.' That was probably the only fun the President had all day, but he needed some answers.

'Dr Ponti, how many D-xxxx infections would qualify a postcode to require a lockdown to wipe out the strain, and how many of those are there?'

'What is the purpose of your enquiry, Mr President?' asked the good doctor, and the President told him that he wanted to order lockdowns for those counties. Utterly locked down for five days.

'I think there are about twenty postcodes with more than one case of D-xxxx. It works best if I email you the list, and you can publish that list. My preference would be to review the list every day so that any county with one single D-xxxx case gets a three-day lockdown. When you've nailed that one, we can go to lockdowns on counties with the less deadly but still highly infectious UK and South African strains,' finished Dr Ponti.

Ten minutes later, the email with the postcode list arrived, and the President and Lt. Col. Freebody went to work. Then a press release went out:

LOCKDOWNS.

The President has ordered the Army to enforce immediate lockdowns for the twenty-one postcodes listed with this announcement. If you live in one of those postcodes and are not at home when you see or hear this announcement, please go home immediately. This applies to workers and ordinary citizens. Your postcode has had at least two cases of the deadly blue neck strain virus, and anyone showing symptoms of a blue neck must call this number to be collected - or you will kill your family. For others, don't even think of hugging anyone goodbye, or they may get infected. Then you will be dead tomorrow. Wear a mask, go home, do not under any circumstances touch anyone. If you develop a blue neck at home, please call the number in your COVID-safe app to be collected. Thank you for your compliance.

The Army will enforce the curfew.

Then followed a list of immediate hotspot lockdowns.

*   *   *

Jason Donovan, leader of the Bravehearts, had seen the announcements, as had Tim Highfields, his 2IC, and they called in their leadership group. Eight people filed into the office, all pretty excited. Shit was going to happen for sure. Jason addressed the assembly:

'Did you see the list of postcodes in lockdown? And did you see that Mitchellville is on that list? Fourteen miles as the crow flies, and they want to shut the place down completely. They need our support, the poor bastards. So we do what?'

Tim Highfields is in protest heaven. 'That means we show our support. That means we protest. Did you see that announcement about weapons? He can't do that without a Referendum. It's bullshit.'

Jason Donovan steps in. 'Listen here, you mob, we want to protest, not get shot. We need to protest today about the complete lockdown because of one or two discoveries of this blue neck virus. Not one or two out of a total of five. No. Out of about fifteen thousand in that area. It's insane, and we protest to let people see how stupid the Government is.'

*   *   *

February 24

The Orthallo and Sanderson families had camped in the Bothe-Napa Valley State Park. They went to Calistoga nearby for small supplies. Today, it was a twenty-mile big shopping trip to Santa Rosa for the two combined families. Off they went,

300

after cleaning the car so they would not be conspicuous. They did not want to be seen as people hiding in the wilderness and be followed. Their minivan had a full load with four adults and the four kids, Peter and Lindsey Orthallo, and Johan and Emily Sanderson, ages 5, 7, 9 and 12. The kids were one team, the parents the other. Shopping was a team effort.

The kids' team went to a milk bar in Santa Rosa. Emily was twelve, the leader. She had told the parents that they needed to load up on calcium by having milkshakes till the cows came home, meaning the parents had two hours to do business whilst the kids bought and browsed magazines and newspapers lying around.

Peter was five and did not read, but he looked at pictures and got the older kids to explain what it was all about. He was fascinated by images of the patriots protesting in the street. They looked wild and scary. When the other kids did not want to answer any more questions, they told him to look up at the TV, at the red line on the bottom - BREAKING NEWS, meaning it was happening now.

There were thousands of protestors. Peter loved the ones dressed as American Indians with their feather headgear and the ones dressed as Vikings. Even though he did not know that, they had helmets with horns sticking out near the top. He wanted a set of those uniforms for when he and Johan were playing cowboys and Indians. The girls could watch and cheer.

The picture changed. There were three helicopters, and they headed for the protest march. They flew low, massive helicopters with rotors at both ends. Peter called the older ones to help explain what was happening. Emily explained the second line on the bottom, which read, 'Stop and go home now, or you will be arrested.'

Emily wondered out aloud. 'How will they arrest thousands?' and she soon found out. Just then, their parents came in and watched it too. John Orthallo told Peter about the announcements they had heard.

'All protests were banned last night. I saw it on the news channel. Those idiots are asking for it.'

The helicopters flew over and suddenly sprayed a red liquid onto all those who were marching. The second byline on TV said:

> The Army has announced that it is spraying dye on protesters so they can be identified later on. The dye is mixed with a surface disinfectant to kill the virus on people's skin and stop infecting those close by.

The TV reporter thought that was a great move: those idiots don't wear masks.

The helicopters went away and came back, this time spraying another liquid. All of a sudden, the protestors were writhing in pain, trying to rub the liquid out of their eyes. They seemed to be blind now.

The TV byline said, 'Army used pepper spray to subdue the mob.' Within half a minute, hundreds of soldiers moved in with handcuffs and marched them off to waiting Army trucks, where the soldiers prodded the protestors along and into the vehicles.

Peter asked his father, 'Dad, why didn't they just run away?' John told him.

'They sprayed them with pepper spray. Stings like hell. Then they were so busy rubbing their eyes, which makes it worse, so they were stuffed, and Army soldiers handcuffed them and attached fifty or so to a rope. That was so smooth. Their eyes will sting for days, but they will get water, later on, to make it a bit better.'

Peter wants to know, 'Are they allowed to do that?'

John counters, 'Were they allowed to protest?'

Peter asks, 'What will they do with them now?' John could see that Peter was barracking for the protestors and called all the kids in to explain.

'People are banned from meeting in big groups; even Church attendance is banned. The reason is that there is a new deadly strain of the virus that kills you in three days. You won't know you have it for the first two days, but you can infect hundreds from one person breathing in their air. On the second day, your neck turns blue, and you know you will die the next day. There is no cure and no vaccine, and it spreads like wildfire. If we don't stop people mixing, then all of America will be dead in a week, and even though we won't be, we can't buy stuff because everybody will be dead,' finished John.

Peter wants to know more things; bless him. 'Dad, what will they do with those protestors? They might be infected already.'

This time Max Sanderson answers. 'First, those guys are lucky they got sprayed with disinfectant, so if they were clean at that point, they are unlikely to get it from someone in their truck now. Those with blue necks are taken to a mass grave and told to lie down. The others are taken to Joint Base Andrews, that's an Air Force place, ten miles south-east, in Maryland.'

'They have some big planes, C-17 Globemasters. They can take over five hundred passengers comfortably, and they fly them to a desert camp in New Mexico. Those infected with the bad strain will be dead the next day. Any that never got infected will live and be returned to Anacostia.'

'What will it be like when they die?' asks Peter, and they all listen. Max answers:

'The reason we took off to our camp is to avoid idiots infecting us. To avoid armed people desperate to get whatever we have. They would shoot us without thinking about it. Bang. Dead.'

Peter replied, 'But Dad, how will they die? What will it be like?'

John answers him, 'They won't be able to breathe, and that kills them.'

Peter wants to know, 'So why did they protest then if staying at home was for their own good?' John has a good laugh and decides on one answer that will stop all further questions.

'Peter, you have nailed it. There are about ten million people who protest. Not at the same time or place, of course. You, Peter, at five years old, understand better than tens of millions of protestors and tens of million people who want to go to churches and spray their viruses on those next to them.'

Peter was impressed. he has no more questions. *I'm smarter than at least twenty million people.* He wanted one last milkshake. Only fair. The others feel too bloated for anything else, happy to go home.

They find a boy about four and a girl a bit older on the way home, walking on the road. Crying.

Max stops the car and gets out, asking them, 'what is wrong, honey?'

'Our Mum has a blue neck, and she told us not to touch her or we die,' sobbed the girl, who looked to be seven.

The boy sobbed and could not talk. All they got from him was, 'I want my Mum.'

Max called the ladies to come and help and to bring some blankets and face masks. Sue Anne was first out of the car and attached her face mask. She had the right mother touch, said soothing things to the boy, and wrapped him in a blanket without touching him. She put a baby face mask on him. Dominique was out by now, too, and doing the same for the girl. Sue Anne then told them:

'First, we will find your Mum; then she can tell us what's wrong and what she wants us to do. But no matter what, we will look after you for three days until we know you are safe, but we can give you a big hug now whilst you are wrapped up, OK?'

They drove in the direction the girl pointed to and found a blue station wagon at the side of the road, the mother inside waving gently. The two ladies got out and did the urgent things.

'Let me see your neck, please,' said Dominique, then, 'Oh dear. The children told us that they were not allowed to touch you. That is so brave of you, and my heart goes out to you. We will take them with us and look after them. We have four kiddies between us. We know what to do. Do you have any special instructions for us?' asked Dominique, and she was told to take her phone as it had all the family contacts and to call for the blue truck that was supposed to take her away.

Then the woman added:

'The boy is four; his name is Max or Maxi. My girl is Emma or Emmy. My husband had been stupid enough to help a man who had fallen during a protest march, and he did not tell me till after he hugged me. Fortunately, the kids were out with neighbours and came home later. I told the children what had happened and that they must not touch either of us. I told them we were going for a drive. To get toys and clothes and put them in a bag and tie the bag shut, and shortly after, the men from the blue truck came and took my husband away.' Then she sobbed.

'It only takes one idiot, and we die, despite all the care we had taken. It's not fair. Maybe you could come back in a day or so, wear protective stuff, and take the bags, give them a spray with disinfectant, take them home and wash them again - but what is inside is safe. They are so little, and they need their toys to feel safe,' she sobbed. She gave them her phone to contact the family.

On the road driving to their camp, the family played games such as, 'I spy with my little eye,' until they arrive home. The parents took them to their base, ran a hot bath, rubbed the new kids with disinfectant, and wrapped them in a new blanket. They were going to sleep in the Orthallo children's room whilst the Orthallo kids would sleep with their parents.

The younger children played a game pretending to be a mouse; the older ones were cats. They sang the Mickey Mouse song, and the two rescued kids fell asleep.

Two days later, there were no blue neck symptoms. Dominique congratulates them but sees sad faces and tears.

'I want my mum; when is she coming back?' was the question.

Dominique tells them, 'I'm so sorry, but your Mum can't come back. She's in heaven by now. It's a great place for her. It's the best place for her to be now. She's probably looking down on you to make sure you stay happy. But I have good news for you. For this week you have two mums, and one of you can sleep with me, and the other with Sue Anne. Is that a good idea?'

They nod their head. Then Sue Anne arrives, and they decide who goes with which mother. They have trouble deciding. The mothers think it's time to lighten everyone up a bit.

Dominique says, 'Shall we do a funny dance so you can decide?' The mums do a great impersonation of a rap dance, and the two new kids burst into giggles. Problem solved. Clever mums.

At morning tea the next day, Sue Anne tackles the problem of relatives. There was plenty of cake for everyone, so no tears. She knows they cannot just take kids. There are laws. So she asks them, 'Who is your favourite, your grandmother, or do you have two, or is it an aunt or uncle?'

Maxi asks her, 'What is a grandmother? We have an aunt and uncle, but we don't like them; they are always drunk.'

Emmy adds her two bits, 'If you take us to those people, we will run away. My uncle tried to touch me on the bum, and Maxi came and hit him. Good brother. Please let us stay. We can wash the dishes.'

Dominique told them that her husband Max had driven to their Mum's car last night and retrieved plastic bags of toys and clothes to get past that bit of bad news.

'Where are they?' asked Maxi. 'I want my teddy.'

Maxi got on well with Peter and Emmy with Emily.

*   *   *

February 2-5

There was an article from the Washington Daily DC News. Dorothy does enjoy reding her opposition's articles.

The National Healthline has released the following news:

One of the hotspot lockdown counties that had initially reported two cases of 'blue neck' virus strain had reported sixty new infections, and fifty deaths, all in their locked houses. The new cases will be dead tomorrow. Thankfully, these cases did not leave their homes due to the lockdown orders. New cases can be avoided by following the issued instructions: 'wear masks, don't touch one another, separate rooms if possible, certainly separate beds, sanitise hands and toilets.'

The other four hotspots have cooled. All initially had one or two blue neck cases taken away, and no new cases have arisen. If there are no new cases in two days, those counties can lift their lockdown restrictions.

*   *   *

Dorothy Thompson saw the news on her device at their camp with the Andersons in Woodstream, north of Centreville, Maryland. They all discussed the utter stupidity of so many people. Her husband Michael said he would write a press release. Michael was a lecturer in Public Health, and this was his domain. He grinned when he handed his piece to Dorothy.

Dorothy read and grinned too but said: 'My editor would remove the twenty words that we're not allowed to print, but great stuff.' What she sent off to the press was:

Rebecca Sanders reporting.

It is wonderful to see that our great country is so diverse. The number of those 'f**king' idiots has not diminished during the pandemic but actually increased, and a significant number of them have honoured us with their demise. Am I sarcastic? No. Good riddance. But we were lucky that a lockdown had been in order, and that they were unable to infect anyone else in the county except their families. The instructions were simple, printed, and handed out by the Army.

Get this, people, in one county, several families did not follow instructions to avoid touching anyone, and we now have fifty dead and sixty new cases, and those will be dead tomorrow, maybe a few more. Get this folks, all from just two cases to start with.

You need to get this too. Many of the dead were children. They did not deserve to die because of you 'Fu..ing' idiots.

Can everyone please, PLEASE, for the next month just follow all instructions, those issued by the President or Army, not your own or your neighbours?

February 27

The President and Lt. Col. Freebody met in the White House Office and discussed the need to shut down churches. The number of cases with the deadly strain was still rising, and the best option was to ban protests, mass gatherings, including mass gatherings in churches. How to word that?

Lt. Col. Freebody knew that singling out churches is a PR disaster, so he suggested:

'Mr President, we should only allow one person per ten square yards of space and insist on mask-wearing at all public places. That is roughly ten per cent of normal capacity. This should apply to pubs, weddings, funerals, and yes, churches.'

The President wanted to add another restriction. He did not trust churchgoers; they might all sit together. He issued the following press release:

Please circulate these instructions immediately.

The current deadly blue neck strain outbreak has not abated, and further restrictions will be effective immediately.

All public indoor gatherings are limited to one person per 10 square yards, including restaurants, bars, funerals, weddings, sporting stadiums and churches.

For events lasting more than an hour, such as sporting events and church, any event exceeding crowds of one thousand will be required to have a blue neck inspection after one hour, and if any are found, those infected are asked to move to one corner, and the others as far away as they can. The building will then be locked down for four days to prevent infections spreading to the community. So, if you don't want to be locked into a dance hall or church, stay home this week. If you were with a group who showed blue neck symptoms, you need to remain in isolation for four days. We apologise for the inconvenience. This is a national emergency.

*   *   *

February 28

The Army had soldiers stationed outside the Lakewood Church, near all the other mega-churches in Houston. They had erected signs with the instructions. The limit for the Lakewood church was now 5,000 and they turned others away to go home. None with a blue neck were allowed in; they sent them to the blue truck to be taken away. Those who entered were given a pamphlet. It told them to keep the ten square yard spacing, and that if there were any blue necks after an hour, they needed to go to an unoccupied corner and not touch anyone. For others, the Army would escort them to their home where they must stay isolated for four days.

Lt. Col. Freebody smothers a laugh and says, 'They have a choice.'

'Overreacting' was the usual comment as churchgoers entered. An hour later, an inspection by soldiers in hazmat suits found ten blue necks, most in the allocated blue corner; one woman was still amongst her friends refusing to move. The Army called soldiers to take her to the blue truck. They took her near neighbours to the blue zone, and handcuffed them to their seats as they had not followed earlier orders.

Some hours later, an inspection by soldiers in hazmat suits found fifty blue necks in the blue zone, and these were taken away to the blue trucks. Ten blue neck worshippers had not moved, and the stupid idiots were surrounded by friends not observing the ten square yards rule. They were all handcuffed to their seats to give the Army time to sort out what to do with them.

The Army captain called his troops in for a discussion.

'How long shall we leave them locked up this time?' He asked. They were tired. Tired of looking after twits.

One sergeant suggested, 'I think this needs a discussion. I think we meet at the hotel down the corner and have a beer and a steak sandwich to help us make a good suggestion.'

'The healthy ones need to be escorted home, and that is a big job. Fifty of us and five thousand of them. My suggestion is to let the good ones travel home in their own cars, and we get their landline phone numbers and call those an hour later to make sure they are home. We could warn them that the fine of not returning home or going out again is five thousand dollars. Stay home for four days.'

The captain applauded the initiative, and they returned to the church and announced their plan. One worshipper wanted to know what the Army would do with the five thousand dollar fine. The captain's response?

'It will pay for the overtime we need to pay our soldiers.'

CHAPTER 19

Mood

The people are anxious. Every day a new 'blue neck' case is discovered, requiring a new lockdown, with never-ending despair. People have stopped worrying about the normal strain. And they want the Government to fix this new menace, especially those infected with it. Protestors mainly. *Well*, thought Argus, *good luck with that.*

Argus E monitored the mood and the protestors indifference to the new strain. A blue neck and you're dead the next day. He wondered how long it would take the nation to have a more appealing name for that. Something like 'The Blue Wave' or 'Blue Death.' He liked 'The Blue Wave.'

February 27

The President met with Lt. Col. Freebody and Dr Federico Ponti to discuss the blue neck strain, D-xxxx. The President began:

'Dr Ponti, have you discovered any methods to kill the virus?'

'There are no methods we can use now to make people better; they die. They have techniques that kill the virus, all strains, in the lab, but they are dangerous to human health. UVC is used in China to kill the virus on buses[59].'

Dr Ponti continued, 'They go into a UV drive-through workshop. But that was before these new strains appeared. We can use that to stop infecting others but not to cure those who have it. I found this in an article about it:

> Scientists have recently discovered a promising new type of UVC less dangerous for human handling, but lethal to viruses and bacteria. Far-UVC has a shorter wavelength than regular UVC, and so far, experiments with human skin cells in the lab have shown that it does not damage their DNA.
>
> UVC-emitting robots have been cleaning floors in hospitals. Banks have even been using ultraviolet light to disinfect their money.
>
> A company in Denmark has accelerated production. It now takes less than a day to make ten robots at their facility in Odense, Denmark's third-largest city and home to a growing robotics hub.
>
> Glowing like light sabres, eight bulbs emit concentrated UVC light. This destroys bacteria, viruses, and other harmful microbes by damaging their DNA and RNA, so they can't multiply.

'How can we use this now?' asked the President.

Dr Ponti replied, 'Those showing blue neck symptoms will die anyway. We need to find a way to treat only the other people infected with the earlier strain. We can't use whole counties for

---

[59]   Bus disinfection through UV lamps in China

lockdowns. Take Los Angeles, a county with over eight million. We need to confine lockdown areas to around five thousand, near the area where the highly infectious D-xxxx strain was found. The Army can use postcodes instead of counties. Then we test every person in that area using many mobile test stations and mobile test labs for super-fast testing.'

'Anyone with the blue strain gets taken away, and they test their family and close contacts. They go into the UVC tunnel, the families get tested daily, and we stop the spread in a day. Most are then detected before they turn blue,' added Dr Ponti.

'What happens to the ones that turn blue?' asked the President.

Dr Ponti answered, 'They die. What the UVC will do is kill the virus on their skin. That stops them from infecting others, as long as they wear a mask to stop the airborne transmission. We don't know who is infected until they are tested. What the tests allow us to do is to pull infected people out early. They will be dead in a day or two but won't infect anyone else then.'

The President turned to Lt. Col. Freebody and asked how the logistics might work.

'I expect that the big city counties will continue to have infections for a while. In the ten big cities, we will need travel restrictions and lockdowns in areas of, say, five to ten thousand. The smaller counties may get one infection. I think we need ten teams for each of the big centres; Los Angeles, San Fran, Chicago, Pittsburgh, New York, Houston, Dallas, and Jacksonville in Florida, two teams for other states. For starters, that's over one-hundred-and-sixty units for testing and test results, plus the UVC tunnels or tents.'

'Fortunately, the Office of the Secretary of the Army is right here in Washington. I can visit General Morgan. We need to set up about a hundred and fifty "Killer" squads of ten soldiers each - to test, monitor, and analyse results. That needs a regiment of two battalions, fifteen hundred soldiers in total, maybe more later - or less. All the stuff they need is readily available, but we need to train the testing and analysis people. They need a training manual and a video.'

'Our soldiers like it when they can identify with a new squad. "Killer" is a great name. Let's call them that; Virus Killer. We should also look at getting those UV robots to keep hospitals clean. Those things come from Denmark. We will be on a waitlist rather than off the shelf. We should order two per squad - say 300 total. We should be able to have that ready in nine days.'

'The order to form that battalion goes out, with some ready the next day, but it's a nightmare to get units to every infected county,' finished Lt. Col. Freebody. He transposed all hotspots onto a map of the USA, and the picture became clearer. It was as though someone had taken a paintbrush and circled it around the outside of the map. All the great city-states. They had the staffing to deal with it.

February 28

A Braveheart member in Anacostia is infected. Well, they called themselves soldiers. He drank Dettol and died the next day. Other soldiers turned blue. They got sent to the blue buses but stupidly shook hands for goodbye on the way out. The Bravehearts planed a new protest because the Government had not provided protection. The Army was monitoring all know Braveheart member phones, and a tap on Jason Donovan's phone had alerted the Army, who arrested all those known to them and sent them to White Sands.

*   *   *

John Orthallo was staying in the Napa-County Regional Park, and he called the family members of the rescued kids. They arranged to meet in Santa Rosa at the Best Western lounge at ten the next day. The families all lived in the San Francisco area, some south like Santa Rosa, some near Napa Valley, others from the Bay area.

John and Max Sanderson arrive on time and order a second breakfast. No one had come by 10:30, so he called the aunt. The call goes to voicemail, and he reminds them they were meeting at the Best Western. He calls the next one and gets a live response from the uncle:

'Looky here, buddy; we won't be takin' any kids. No room and no money. Booze costing too much, youse better off sortin' it with the grannies. Hope they can help youse.'

The next call they received was from one of the grandmothers. It sounded ominous.

'Hold your horses, buddy, where we live, on time means the same day, so pipe down. We are about an hour away, see you then,' and she hung up.

John's response was, 'Manners. One shitfaced bitch.'

Then the phone rang, and the aunt had called back. 'Sorry guys, I won't be coming. I have four children and a bastard of a husband; he threatened to leave if there were any more kids. Ours aren't even allowed to bring kids home, and he threatened to leave if this new lot turns up. I'm stuffed, Don't have a job, and flat out looking after three under-school-age lovely kids. I'm really, truly sorry, and I love the kids. I hope you understand.'

John told her, 'Bless you, lady, you returned my call even when in trouble. People could learn from you.' She sobbed and hung up.

Two hours later, the grandmother turned up and said: 'Told ya we'd be here. I'm Priscilla Walden. That Donna was always a stupid bitch. Can't see what my son Buster saw in her, now she's killed him, and she wants me to look after the kids so she can run around and find a man? So where are those snotty-nosed kids then?'

John was the man to deal with this monster, with his best building-site manners.

'Ma'am, first, my condolences. It must be awful losing a child. From what Donna told us, your son contracted the blue neck because he was kind enough to help a man who had fallen after those Patriot Warriors pushed him aside. Unfortunately, he did not think of safety as he kissed his wife when he got home, poor man. When your son told her the story, she told him to go to a spare bedroom, lock himself up for two days, and not to touch his children - in case he was infected. Long story short, two days later, when he had a blue neck, she called the blue neck disposal team, and they took him away. But you know all that, don't you?' asked John, and she replied:

'Nobody never told me nothing. There was a message from the Army that said my son was in blue detention, and could I please call this number. Stupid morons, my son wasn't even in the Army.'

John decided she needed loving advice. 'Mrs Walden, I can see so much pain in your face. I hope you have good friends at home who can support you and that your husband is kind to you. I'm sorry that you did not think highly of Donna; that would have made it difficult too. You may feel better about her when I tell you that she is dead now, and even when she knew that she was dying because she had the blue neck, all she could think of was to save the children. She would not let them touch her, or they would die. She sent them to walk on the road to find help for them. Not for her, just for the kids. That is when we found them. She had listened to the advice about blue necks and asked us to call the disposal team that picks them up. We were so impressed with her. She had the children pack their toys and clothes into plastic bags that we recovered, so Maxi and Emmy have those things. We gave her a half bottle of whiskey to ease her death. What do you want us to do with her things?'

'That bitch always was a drunk slut, good riddance,' was the answer from her batshit ugly face, and John decided he did not need his smooth manners.

'Lady, you are the coldest bitch I have ever seen, the most intolerant, with the ugliest thoughts of beautiful people. Is it possible that you are so unbelievably obnoxious because they are beautiful?'

She was outraged and replied, 'You can keep her ugly stuff. I want nothing to do with them,' as she stormed off.

'Well, we can sell the car. It would fetch about twenty-five thousand. We can support the kids on that for ages if we get guardianship. Then we sell their house, a couple of hundred thou', and put the money in a trust fund for the kids,' said Max. Then he got out his phone and played back the whole conversation.

'Might come in handy with Child Protection.' he uttered.

March 1

John Orthallo received a call from the Child Protection Agency, Lucy Esposito. The conversation started quite friendly, but John sensed the bully in her when she wanted to visit them, and he told her he did not want anyone to know where exactly he lived. They arranged to meet again at the Best Western; the next day.

The following day at the hotel, Lucy Esposito flounced in and dropped her tent-sized handbag on the table. John and Max introduce themselves, and John starts the conversation. Shortly after, Lucy interrupts them.

'I haven't come to talk. Hand over the kids, and your problems are solved. We will send them to the family, and if none takes them, then foster parents. That's it, go get them.'

John used his silky touch first. 'Well, Lucy, as you work in child protection, you would know how devastating it is for young kids to lose their parents. Our wives have settled them down. They want their mummy, and we have two kids and two mummies, and a child sleeps with one each. We had met their mother on the road; she had a blue neck, and she implored us to take care of them. We found family phone contacts and spoke to them, but no one is willing to take the children.'

Lucy interrupted him, puffed out her chest in anger, and said, 'You must have been very rude for them to be so nasty.'

Max held up a hand and just said, 'You need to listen to this. We recorded the conversation.'

Lucy looked crestfallen. 'Now I need to find foster parents. You can't have them,' she says, John advises her.

'Madam, you seem far more interested in doing your job correctly and by the letter than the welfare of those children. One of our best friends has access to the President, and you can expect a message from his office within days or a broadcast Bulletin for people caring for children who lost parents to the blue neck strain. In the meantime, we will not allow you near those traumatised kids. Am I clear?'

Lucy Esposito got the message, stood, and left with the threat, 'You will hear from me,' as she storms out.

Max grins and holds out his phone. 'All recorded.'

Then John and Max decided to call Dorothy immediately, and she came on the line. They passed quick pleasantries, and John got to the point.

'We found some kids looking for help. Their mum had sent them. She was in her car, blue neck. Her husband had come home infected and stupidly kissed her hello. Kids were out and therefore safe, and when they came back, she told them that they must not under any circumstances touch her or the father, and she left two days later when he turned blue and was taken away. She was now dying and wanted someone to take care of the kids. That's the background. Now comes the rub. The family is a piece of shit. Max recorded our conversations. We'll send you the file. Child Protection came to Santa Rosa. She was worse, all recorded, and the file is on its way to you as well. With more people with blue necks dying, there will be a new big need to care for children. Please call the President and ask him to issue a news release saying that children found wandering may be cared for by a temporary guardian until this emergency is over. Do you think you can get access to him?'

Dorothy said, 'I hope to make a phone call explaining the reason and will tell him the recordings are on the way. All right? If those recordings are shockers, he will act. Speak to you soon.'

Two days later, a News Bulletin went out from the President:

Due to the high death rate from the D-xxxx strain, including parents, now children found alone may be cared for by people willing to take them in. Serious attempts to find family must be made, and if unsuccessful, the people who took them in may act as temporary guardians and apply for foster care benefits. This rule will stay in place until the pandemic is over.

The President of the United States of America. There will be a further announcement when details have been worked out.

March 2, 9:30 a.m.

After Staff Sergeant Jim Bloodwood arrived at the White Sands containment camp, he got dressed in his Hazmat suit to go in and inspect it, and he asked his squad of ten soldiers to do the same. They all had colourimeters to check on blue-neck detainees and used counting devices. First, they went through the white section, counting all whites, and found no blues. The earlier spraying had obviously been successful, and the inmates' self-protection had also been successful, as they had moved any new blue-necked people to the blue section. There were now seven hundred instead of a thousand in the safe section.

The report sent back to Lt. Col. Freebody advised:

> Of the 2005 people arrested last week, 1295 are dead and will be buried here. Of the 710 to be returned home, 15 have symptoms, are already separated from the safe group. They will be isolated from the others. Please send two Globemasters and advise the President.

*   *   *

The President had received a call from Dorothy and voice recordings from the aunt and child protection officer. He shook his head, muttering to himself something like 'I'll fix you lot, and for good measure have departments vet their staff.'

He prepared to meet the Attorney General to discuss the issue Dorothy Thompson had raised with him. He told the AG about his conversation with Dorothy, and he played the two recordings she had sent.

The AG's comment was, 'Not my favourite people. Bitches from hell. What do you want to do?'

'I want to issue a Bulletin. Because of the number of deaths, there are many children left without parents. Those finding them are granted temporary guardianship status until permanent arrangements can be made. Can we do that?' asks the President.

'I agree, nothing we can't sort out in two or three weeks,' replies the AG.

'I hope that the lockdowns will stop the spread of the blue death strain in a week or two,' says the President, concluding the meeting. A Bulletin regarding this is sent out.

The President's next meeting was with Dr Ponti to discuss the new West Coast CAL.2 variant. CAL.2 was much more infectious than the old strain; but not yet more virulent than the D-xxxx variant, but it could merge with a super-spreader any time.

Dr Ponti gave his assessment. 'Even if we get rid of the blue death strain in a week or so, we may need new hotspot lockdowns to kill this new CAL.2 monster, and kill it before it mutates further. Unlike the blue monster, there are no visible symptoms. I project that without lockdowns, you will see a weekly increase of 100 per cent of cases and related deaths. So from say, 90,000 today, you get 180,000, then 360,000, then 720,000 in three weeks. There is no way to treat them, and the hospitals are full anyway. You need to be ruthless about this.'

The President sent out a Bulletin to warn people:

A new highly infectious strain, CAL2, is making the rounds in California to see infections double every week. To prevent this, we will immediately start testing in that state and any other where the strain was found. For a short period of two weeks initially, all travel to or from California by road, sea, train, or plane is suspended. During this time, there will be lockdowns in areas of high infection. Those lockdowns will be eased soon because we will conduct mass testing of every person in the affected areas. The testing and isolation are expected to wipe the strain out completely.

Later that day

Another militia organisation, the 'Western Hoods' from Los Angeles, saw the Bulletin. Their leader was Mitch Waller, and his deputy was Dirk Partenheimer, who saw this and decided to meet. Mitch was a planner. He ensured that any activity, be it protest or violence, had a purpose, was likely to succeed, would generate publicity, and have little likelihood of arresting his members. He was the 'what to do' man. Dirk was their hype man.

Their office was near the LA County Crematorium Cemetery. Dirk had business in Downtown LA, one of the precincts listed as wholly locked down. Dirk just knew he had to protest that lockdown. He addressed the others in the meeting.

'You all know what would look good? We march. We have banners that say, "These stupid lockdowns would not have happened under Trump," and loudhailers singing our song. "I Did it My Way". If the Army comes, we scatter like rats, and they look stupid trying to chase us. Won't be caught, won't be arrested. Who's in?'

The Army had a tap on Dirk Partenheimer's phone, heard the message go out, 'We scatter like rabbits,' and they decided to have their bit of fun. Two weeks ago, there had been a Bulletin banning all protest marches, and yet they kept coming. A Lieutenant would be in charge of a platoon of fifty soldiers if the planned protest is small or a company of 250 soldiers for a larger demonstration.

'We'll have a drone to see where they are and which direction they came from, have three trucks ready to hold fifty each, and round up say a hundred and fifty. Off to Bootcamp with them, where they get drenched in ice-cold sanitiser. You wear good protection. Assign two soldiers to each man, and handcuff him to the truck, all facing in one direction to stop them breathing on each other. Let the lucky ones escape; they will spread the news.'

The evening news had this press release from the Army.

> The Western Hood militias staged a protest. It failed; the Army arrested most of the protesters. There have been daily Bulletins prohibiting mass meetings and rallies, and despite that, some three hundred or so idiots marched. They sent them to a decontamination Bootcamp. We know how to make those people really miserable. The punishments handed out are appropriate for their stupidity, in other words, brutal.

> We have selected some tough Sergeants to run a harder Bootcamp to deter future protests, so we look forward to more stupidity. Next time all those marching will be arrested. Your stupidity will be rewarded with a new experience for you. We don't have time to muck around with you idiots. Come and make our day.

March 5, 9:30 a.m.

The President received the hotspot reports for counties locked down three days ago. The lockdowns and mass testing had been for the highly infectious California CAL.2 strain, and the news was not good.

Mass testing was underway for CAL.2 in California. In downtown Los Angeles the initial CAL.2 strain count had been ten on March 2. They had sent into total isolation. Mass testing of all other residents had brought a new figure; one hundred. If people had followed instructions - no one, even inside a family unit - would have touched another person, and today's total in that small community would remain at ten. But that had not happened. They had a hundred.

Eight other Los Angeles communities, the size of two blocks, had similar results. The President decided to wait until all results were in before he would issue new instructions.

March 6

The results from the forty new hotspot counties had arrived. The President discussed this with Lt. Col. Freebody. He was pleased.

'It worked, and the Army notice of protestors going to a brutal Bootcamp seems to have worked. No new protests.'

National Health reported that forty county areas had reported CAL.2 infections. The two men hammered out a plan to tackle this the same way as the first ten, hoping to shut it down. Dr Ponti was called to the meeting, as the President wanted some new facts.

He asked: 'Dr Ponti, how wide is the spread of this CAL.2 now, and can we contain it?'

'Of the forty counties with this infection, thirty-nine are in the Los Angeles area, and one in Sacramento. To shut it down, we need to enforce travel bans in and out of those county areas until there are no more infections. That is essential. Also, we need the population to follow the rules. Masks, sanitisation, and no physical contact with anyone else in those areas. Hard when kids want to touch their mum. Everybody in those areas needs to be tested. If they get tested the first day, they need another test four days later, and if there are no new cases, the area can be considered safe, and we can lift restrictions.'

The President asked Lt. Col. Freebody if he had the staffing to implement this immediately. He did and agreed to do so after the meeting. The President thanked Dr Ponti but asked Lt. Col. Freebody to stay. When alone, he mentioned his fear of a massive protest, including militias bombing the Houses of Congress, and asked for his advice.

CHAPTER 20

Mood

Nobody liked lockdowns. Even though there were increasing infections, most people did not personally know any families with infections, and to them, it was just so much hoopla. Trying to control movements was like herding cats. There were lockdowns and protests, and Argus was waiting to witness the collision between two powerful opponents: protesters and the Army.

7 March, 8:30 a.m.

The President and his go-to man, Lt. Col. Freebody, discussed the news of the upcoming demonstration. Lt. Col. Freebody had new information and was going to deal with protesters big time.

'Mr President, as there are two demonstrations planned now for Washington, both heading down to the Capitol, I have organised to have forty aerial tankers instead of thirty on standby here at Joint Base Andrews. As discussed, we will have a helicopter with a bull horn fly over them ordering them to go home. And when they don't, they get a bucket of water dumped on them. A million litres of water. I aim to ensure this is the last mass demonstration ever during the pandemic.'

He continued, 'Mr President. I would love to come down on mass protests or marches with machine guns. Not allowed, but I've been thinking of a solution for weeks. This one would nail it. I watched an old British movie in India trying to move protesting ladies who sat on a railway track stopping an Army train from leaving. For a week. A Lieutenant organised a large container of sewerage from the lower castes to be dumped on them. They ran off in disgust. Worked like a charm, did not cause a war even if it did not endear the British to the Indian people.

'Here is my idea. If we have, say, a hundred thousand marchers and we fly fire-fighting water bombers over them - say five litres per protestor - we would need five hundred thousand litres, that is five hundred tons. And the DC10 Air Tankers carry, say, fifty tons of water. And then, wait for this.'

'We mix a dye into the water to identify anyone who got away. If they don't disperse immediately, we repeat it, this time with a stink agent added, half a ton of hydrogen sulphide per air tanker; worse than the smell of rotten eggs. They will be running home for a shower faster than you can say Big Banana.'

'But we cannot afford for that mob to return home. We need to keep them on the ground there for three days. Most of them will be dead or they would infect maybe another 400,000 on the way home. To keep them there, I will deploy five Army Brigades of about 25,000 armed soldiers to enforce their stay.'

He had one last bit of advice.

'A press release goes out: "March, and we will deal with you." But we don't tell them the surprise, eh?' finished Lt. Col. Freebody.

'Ah, Colonel, how to make friends and influence people. Get those Air Tankers to be on standby. They are not needed for fires in March, and their crews will love dumping shit on those pests,' grinned the President.

An Army Demonstrations bulletin:

> All demonstrations are now illegal. We are trying to stop the spread of the virus for the safety of our country. You will be dealt with quite severely if you do not follow orders.

> Lt. Col. Morgan Freebody, Civil Order Division, US Army.

Both men grinned from ear to ear. The President thought a warning to surrounding populations, shops, bars and hotels is needed.

'If you were one of those idiots, wet and stinking, and possibly infected by now, what would you want to do?' he asked.

Lt. Col. Freebody thinks, then says, 'Go anywhere I can have a shower and get new clothes.'

Yes, thought the President, and he wanted to outline a precaution. 'I want to protect the general public from being confronted by these irate and stinking protestors. Let's talk about that.'

Lt. Col. Freebody agreed and suggested, 'Issue a bulletin to clear the surrounding area. Then we start with three brigades to keep the protestors from leaving, 15,000 soldiers. We start with one supervising brigade, and the other two to rotate them, for 24 hours for three days. Then one brigade will be needed to organise and dispose of 20,000 portaloos, and another one to control moving around 50,000 cars to a field for torching. After 3 days there may be 20,000 who are not infected can leave.'

The President wanted to know how he would stop any protestors leaving before three days had passed. Freebody had the answer:

'My soldiers are armed and they surround the returning soldiers and tell them to enter their cars and wait to be allowed to leave.'

'When all are nicely packed in their cars, my soldiers use bull horns to announce they must stay for 3 days, and that porta loos and drinks will arrive shortly, but all must stay in the area. We also warn them that if anyone tries to drive away their tyres will be shot out. Three days later most will be dead and we give car towing companies a job to tow all cars with dead bodies to a big field and torch the cars.'

The two men worked to prepare a bulletin, and a bit later, it went out.

Warning of Mass Demonstrations

The President advises all people in the Washington Area north of the Capitol to note this announcement. We believe a mass demonstration may gather near Le Droit Park to walk south to the Capitol. We do not have specific warnings, but experience suggests they may get very rowdy or violent. We strongly advise you to leave the area, and if you live there, stay indoors, lock the doors. Restaurants, bars and hotels should also close and be shuttered. There will be no public transport between 2 p.m. and 12 a.m. the following day.

*　　*　　*

8 March, 8:30 a.m.

Terry Balzarini was in the Rachel Carson Conservation Park in Maryland. The virologist had seen the news bulletin put out by the President. Terry had an app that allowed him to play 'what if' scenarios with COVID infections for the anticipated mass gatherings. He and his wife Lorraine liked to predict the result of the protests, a bit of an ego trip if they could get very close.

Lorraine asked him, 'Darling, where do you think the protestors will come from?'

They discuss this, and she says, 'Let's see where the worst infected visitors would come from. Why not pick equal numbers from five areas and see what infection projections we can get?'

Terry was in calculation mode. 'OK, let's start with Los Angeles and assume we get 50,000 from there. We'll assume that one in five hundred marchers are infected, not knowing it, that gives you a hundred infections walking around.'

'That strain doubles every day, so we get 200, 400, 800, then 1,600 infections in four days. Say the same for the other 150,000, and you get close to 5,000 infections running around somewhere. After eight days, that will be 10,000, 20,000, 40,000 and 80,000 cases with a highly infectious strain. It's a disaster. By comparison, at present, there are maybe ten infections in county postcode areas. Terry, that's just too scary for words. I need a whiskey. Then I need to prepare a video to show this on TV.'

Terry and Lorraine worked together to make a whiteboard display of the COVID projections and a voice recording of Terry explaining the potential spread. It told the story. He sent it to Dorothy with a request to show it to the President:

> The proposed protests and marches may doom
> the USA to an early grave. I urge the President to

disable the protest movement, preferably painfully and permanently. That mob's utter selfishness and stupidity should attract punishment so severe they will never protest again.

My experts have used projection software to estimate the number of highly infectious cases resulting from the protests. For starters, those men do not wear masks and do not practice social distancing. So out of 200,000, we expect 5,000 to be infected before they leave home. Then the trouble starts. As soon as they arrive near the planned march route they will embrace every likeminded protestor and within an hour 40,000 are infected and an hour later, between 160,000 and 200,000. Let's call it 200,000. The worst thing is to allow them to return home. Let's say they have a wife and a buddy at home, so suddenly you have 600,000 infections, and a day later over a million and only then do they turn blue. They must be stopped where they march.

Doesn't the Second Amendment allow us to bear arms to protect ourselves and shoot them?

Lorraine said, 'A bit rough, but it's the truth', and Terry suggested they send it.

'Let them sanitise it, but the President needs moral support to be totally ruthless with those Neanderthals. He can use Dr Ponti to work the words for public use.'

*   *   *

The president had received Terry Balzarini's report from Dorothy, and he called Lt. Col. Freebody to an immediate meeting.

Once they settled in, he passed the Balzarini report to Freebody, waited for him to read it, and then started:

'Let's set out our strategy for the next few weeks. Our bulletins need to bite. They need to strike fear into their blessed hearts. And we need to follow through on any threats we make. We do this once or twice and all this trouble will stop. Let's start.'

They worked on it and then some. The hardest thing was to avoid too extreme a response. The aim was to educate the rest of the nation, even if they could not educate the protestors, so that the nation would support the measures. After many attempts the first draft was ready.

> From the President of The United States of America
>
> I am ordering new measures to deal with protestors.
>
> First, I will explain. From modelling provided, a mass gathering of 200,000 protestors is estimated to start with 5,000 newly acquired blue neck infections that are undiagnosed. Does 5,000 sound bad? Yes, but that number is peanuts compared to what will happen when you line up to march. Those 5,000 infections will grow exponentially during the joyous reunion with your buddies, an all 200,000 of you will be infected to return home and wreak havoc there.
>
> We cannot let that happen. We will ensure you do not return home, for the safety of your families and the country. We cannot afford for mindless, preventable deaths to continue happening.

*　　*　　*

10 March, 10:30 a.m.

Dorothy worked in Woodstream, Maryland, and watched the Balzarini video in their home hideout. She showed it to her Public Health lecturer husband, Michael, who commented:

'I have my own projection tool, and I will put the numbers through it. Four nasty infection strains floating around. In California, it's the CAL.2, and in most other places, it's the UK, South African or Brazilian strain; those are all so infectious that the number of infections doubles almost daily.'

'It hasn't hit the headlines until now because a large number of regular infections masked them. My biggest worry is where those protestors would have come from. I have just used the Los Angeles strain for 200,000 marchers, with all protestors coming from there, and I get a similar number of infections after three weeks compared to Dr Balzarini's projections.'

'Dr Ponti needs to see this. I'll make a voice recording, and we can send it with the Terry Balzarini video. God help us all if the Army does not immobilise that stupid mob.'

Shortly after, Dorothy sent the video and voice files to the President and released the following bulletin using her pen name:

Rebecca Sanders reporting.

This is urgent. You must stop what you are doing and tell your whole family and neighbours. You must follow these instructions.

The protest marches planned for tomorrow have the possibility of spreading the COVID infectious virus so fast that it will infect the whole of the US within less than a month, and no hospitals will be able to take you.

You can help lessen the impact by absolutely refusing to let any protestors return to your home, touch you, or touch your children. If the man who is your husband has been in a protest march and has a key to the house, leave before he returns. I would like to advocate you shoot him. That is allowed, but I'm not allowed to suggest it. However, if you kill him because you are afraid he will kill you or the children because of his infections, you act in self-defence.

'Well, all done. Time for some fun; let's get the kids and make a play about these protests,' suggested Dorothy. They call Richard, 13 and Karen, 17.

'We're going to make a play, and you kids can be the stars. Is that good?' It was, and Dorothy wanted to know who would be the protestors, and who the Army. The kids wanted the Anderson kids, Mark and Deborah, to join in too, as well as their parents, Michelle and James Anderson.

The kids had many ideas on what they wanted to do with the protestors, give them the power and all the problems would be solved. They included: 'we could arrest them all', and 'no, there's too many', and 'hmm, what if we set up barricades on all the surrounding streets?' as well as 'that could work, but what about people who live and work on the street who aren't part of the protest?'

Dorothy explained that the protestors were planning a massive march, and the Army had to stop them.

'All Army people to the kitchen, all protestors stay here,' she said, then added, 'You cannot shoot protestors, and the protestors cannot shoot at the Army people. Just one thing: you hurt someone and we hurt you back. Go to your rooms and decide what you would do. You have ten minutes each side, then come back and we act it out,' finished Dorothy.

The Army vs protestors division was decided on family lines, and Dorothy, as she had planned this show, told them that the Thompsons were Army. They advised them that the protestors were 100,000 strong, and the Army, 5,000.

They went to their respective rooms. Much squealing laughter and many complaints were heard. Mainly that they could not shoot the opposition.

The Anderson family decided they needed to play this outside in the grass, and as they were 100,000, they should be able to wrestle the Army to the ground.

The Thompson family had a similar problem. 'How can we beat a bigger side if we can't shoot them?' asked Karen, and her younger brother suggests they throw buckets of cold water on them.

Squeals of delight until Michael asked, 'What if the protestors take the buckets away from us and drench us instead? It's freezing out there.'

Soon both rooms were quiet, and everyone returned to the lounge.

'Who won?' asked Dorothy. The only answer was a grunt.

'All so quiet? Any ideas how the Army could win?' asked Dorothy. No one spoke. Then her son Richard spoke up, excited.

'We can't do it here but the Army can. They could fly over with helicopters and dump sewerage on them.' And he squealed in delight.

Dorothy brings the 'war' to an end. 'You thought that the Army could not win, and so did the protestors. The play was a total success because it has shown us all what a dreadful problem this is. Maybe I need to call the President and tell him about Richard's idea. But the President already said the protestors would be dealt a severe blow. Let's wait till we see what happens today. But you all did so well; you came up with the only answer.'

*   *   *

11 March, 11:30 a.m.

Mobs assembled north of the Capitol as Lt. Col. Morgan Freebody received news of the planned protest movement from Rhode Island Avenue to Sixth Street NW. Beauty. He could act now. He ordered 5,000 soldiers to prepare to surround Sixth Avenue, approximately a hundred yards away from the marchers.

He was ready to deploy at about 2 p.m., when the flyover by DC10 Air Tankers was going to happen, and to wait until 2:30 p.m. to arrest as many as he could, all drenched in blue dye and that stink agent, hydrogen sulphide. Their Army truck would need a clean after carrying away protestors. The Colonel received news that they were ready.

The TV crews also had helicopters in the air, and live feeds showed those marvellously outfitted demonstrators having a great time, shouting, poles, flags, and banners held across the whole street proclaiming, 'Can't Arrest Us, We Are Too Many!'

The TV commentators were having a great time too. They were excited. Something would happen, as surely as the sun rose every morning, and TV needed excitement and action. The anchors discussed the likely Army response. They were like spectators in the colosseum waiting for the kill in the Gladiator Games. They were like kids instead of responsible entities warning people that this would end badly, but they were the press.

11 March, 2:00 p.m.

An Army Chinook flew over the Sixth Avenue demonstration from the south. It kept repeating the order to go home or face the consequences. The TV channels reported this, and a talking head said, 'And guess what? Follow the instructions? No, those braves are marching. What can the Army do with hundreds of thousands in the street? They would need the Chinese Communist Party Army to mop them up.'

Tim Highfields of the Washington Bravehearts leads his section. It was a glorious victory for them and him personally; he turned and addressed his followers:

'Bravehearts. You are brave. The Army is neutered; it's outnumbered. We show the world who is boss in his town.' He turned and lead them to victory.

Then five big planes flew over. Really low, and Tim can make out they are DC10s because of the engine in the tail. He yelled to his followers, 'See, they are celebrating our bravery.'

Two minutes later, they came over again. And then water pours from them as though they were firefighters. Marchers drenched, and more and more planes flew over, and the whole of Sixth Avenue was saturated. Tim Highfields turned and addressed his followers.

'The bastards. They wet us, but we need a drink anyway. How can they defend the country if that is the best they can do? We march and we show the world.'

The TV channels praise the protestors, 'Wet but proud, and they march.'

Then nothing happened, and the talking heads of the TV networks worked up a storm of speculation. The theme was, 'Is that the best the Army has to offer? God help our country if we were to be attacked.' Others wanted the Army to employ the protestors to arrest protestors in future; maybe they just needed a job.

The Army units deployed around Sixth Avenue begin ordering people from the neighbourhood to go away or go home. The instructions were to close bars, restaurants, hotels and remove public transport. They were told the Army was about to upset the protesters, who would be very angry and possibly violent. People heard the message. They got it, the danger to them, and they moved away, and businesses closed, shuttered where possible. No one stayed open.

11 March, 2:30 p.m.

The protestors were still marching down Sixth Avenue, and they were defiant. 'It's only water.'

Then the planes came back half an hour after their first pass, as expected, water pouring out, also as expected, but blue, not expected.

The TV channels commented on this. Then they noticed the protestors were writhing in disgust. They received a message from the Army that said:

> The water has dye so we can find and arrest these idiots at leisure later on. We also added a potent hydrogen sulphide smell to it. They will stink for days and no businesses will let them in, they need to shower and change clothes before anyone will let then in. We will prevent them from leaving; they are too infectious to return home, They can stay in their cars. We hope that they have been taught a lesson and will not march again.

Suddenly the TV talking heads and anchors were excited. 'The Army will save this country after all.' was the cry used in subsequent news bulletins.

*   *   *

11 March, 5:30 p.m.

The President was on air and delivered this message.

Americans. With the help of the Army, the Government is protecting you from protestors and the spread of the killer virus. Today we tried water bombing, but they kept marching. Half an hour later, we ratcheted up the incentive to follow orders and go home by adding a blue dye so we could find them later and a stink compound, one that is so bad they will want to vomit.

We have stopped all public transport from the area for a day, as well as taxi pickups, so no one should be able leave. And lastly, for the protection of the public, the Army has surrounded the area where protestors had parked their cars. For those who had returned to their cars, the Army will stop those men from leaving, in their cars or on foot. Toilets and water are provided. With a bit of luck, 20,000 of the total 200,000 are still alive. We have just saved 200,000 or more deaths resulting from the protestors returning home and infecting their families.

We hope this is the last ever demonstration during the pandemic. Rest assured, we have a much nastier response planned if another demonstration takes place, so bad you will wish you were dead.

*   *   *

Argus noted that attention had shifted from Washington to California. There was a new strain there running amok. He was fascinated to see what would happen.

State borders had been locked in California to prevent the spread of the new CAL 2.0 strain. The only exceptions were interstate food deliveries if the drivers had a vaccination certificate; also goods trains with certified drivers.

The Army put out a bulletin about border crossings:

California Border Crossing Restrictions

The Army will be monitoring roadblocks, restricting everything except medical emergencies on all state borders. Ambulances or cars with a police escort that carry emergency patients will be allowed through.

Other cars found from interstate will need to prove they live in the state of entry, or the driver and all passengers will be fined on the spot. The second attempt will see cars impounded. The third attempt will see the car sold to pay for Army efforts to maintain this quarantine.

The Army used helicopters to monitor borders and advised units when cars had crossed a State Border and get a visit. Payment or arrest for a previous offender.

It's pretty boring work monitoring border crossings when nothing happens, so when an Army unit gets notice of a car crossing, they use a few Army cars to give more soldiers a bit of excitement.

*　　*　　*

In Georgia, near Fort Oglethorpe, the army received a call that a car had crossed from Tennessee, and four Army units decided to help. A bit of fun for them, chasing bad guys. It was the meaning of life for them. The call stated that a bottle-green Chevvy dual cab was the culprit. The helicopter kept it in view, just west of Fort Oglethorpe, where it had stopped. It was about a ten-minute drive away, and the Army stepped on it and got there in seven. A gent came out of the store and headed to his truck. Eight grim-looking soldiers suddenly surrounded him. One of them spoke:

'We need to ask you why you crossed from Tennessee to Georgia.'

'Why do you need to know that?' he asked and was told:

'A law was announced yesterday nationally that all borders are closed except for medical emergencies. What is your emergency?'

It was a packet of smokes.

'I didn't know about that law.'

'Oh yes, we can arrest you. You are fined two hundred dollars, and if you don't have that on you, we will take you to barracks for two days to clean and sanitise cars all day long. But tell me, do you listen to the radio in your car, or watch TV at home?'

'Ah, well, the TV at home is in for repairs, and the car radio doesn't work,' he says, and a soldier looks him in the eye and tells him punishment for lies means a two-day Bootcamp. He does not change his statement. One of the sergeants asks for his car keys, turns on the ignition, and music blares from the radio.

'OK fellas, Bootcamp it is for this old sock. He will never lie to the Army again because all his muscles will scream in pain. First fifty push-ups. With a twenty-pound bag on his back. And if he can't make it, he has to do it again with a heavier bag. And after that, a five-mile run carrying a backpack with twenty pounds in it. At a rate of a mile every six minutes. If he has a heart attack, he dies.' And they grin.

'You can't do that to me! I'm an old man, and even you can't do that. Give me a better deal or I'm outa here.' he says. They confer and make him a better offer.

'We make a TV recording where you talk of the punishments you were given, and if you're convincing you can go.'

Well, no prizes for guessing whether he cooperated. They filmed him, and this is what he said:

> I thought I'd be a clever dick and get across the state borders. I got caught. Suppose you're thinking of doing the same, DON'T. The penalty is massive. If you get caught without a valid medical emergency, you go to Bootcamp, and a sergeant makes you wish you were never born. When they told me what I had to do, I fainted, so he halved the punishment. But I will never, ever ignore army orders again. Be smart. Follow orders.

'Good enough?' he asked them after the filming

The soldier replied, 'No, this is the Army. You need to do this a hundred times till you speak it in your dreams every night.' But then he grinned and said, 'Off you go.'

*   *   *

13 March, 8:30 a.m.

Dr Ponti reported on lockdown counties in California.

'Mr President, the number of county areas in lockdown yesterday was forty, and today it's seventy. It could have been worse, but twenty of the original locations are now clean and can stop lockdown. The good news is that lockdown areas seem to prevent the spread quickly. The other good news is that people inside homes follow the orders of no one touching another, wearing masks whenever possible, and not increasing the cases inside their homes.'

'The bad news is that new areas are infected, and unfortunately, we can't test all places to find new cases but need to wait until someone gets sick. We need to send a bulletin warning people in all areas unless they have already been cleared to avoid touching anyone else. Mothers must be protected as they will need to handle children.'

The next day, infections had grown. This was expected, but the rate of increase had slowed.

*   *   *

13 March, 9:30 a.m.

Argus's attention was drawn back to Washington, were the news channels were watching mass burials.

The Washington TV reporters had moved to the Northern Fauquier Community Park about eighty miles west of Washington, where bulldozers were digging ten-foot-deep trenches, hundreds of yards long.

The reporters went live with footage showing blue trucks emptying loads into the trenches, and their voices went live now:

Eastern Star reporting.

You can see those trenches. They had started digging them yesterday. Ten feet deep, with lime dropped in and spread, and the blue trucks picked up the dead bodies. Washington DC and its surroundings had about a thousand bodies each day, now increased to two thousand. It was lucky they did not need to bury those 180,000 dead protestors. They had all been locked in their cars by the Army, and died there, and their cars had been towed to a large field to be incinerated there, out of sight of the public.

The bodies here are highly infectious, so they spread lime on the bodies, dropping more on top, but they stop at four feet from the top of the trench. No loving handling of the dead here, they are just too infectious. Then the graves are covered again with a layer of lime and then earth. The lime stops and kills seepage.

The locations were chosen away from public view to not be too distressing for the public. And sites were selected away from nearby waterways to stop any groundwater and water body pollutions. We are bringing you this gruesome report to ensure you isolate, and then isolate even more. Verbal descriptions of statistics do not show the true cost of this pandemic.

People around the country were mostly shocked. This had brought the disaster home.

CHAPTER 21

Mood

How much worse can it get? That was the question people asked themselves. Lockdowns hurt. Food delivered by the Army was not the same as home-cooked. In lockdown areas, kids went crazy, as they were not allowed outside. Then, a rule is issued so that families living in the street are allowed out for one hour; time staggered depending on the street number. The general mood is pessimism. This lockdown won't end any time soon, and new infections will soon affect them. How bad will that be?

March 14, 8:30 am

The White House had announced lockdowns between all States, except for freight trains and food trucks with driver vaccination certificates.

The President met with Dr Ponti to see how bad the infections were. Dr Ponti reported:

'It seems that we get interstate transmissions of the infectious strains, sometimes into areas where there were none before. Let's keep clean states clean, if we can, by having border crossing lockdowns. Can we see if the Army can enforce that?'

The President called in Lt. Col. Freebody and explained the situation. The Colonel thought for a while, dialled up a map of infectious hotspot states, and he saw that the Western seaboard, across the Gulf states, the north-eastern seaboard, and across the great lakes, all had high infections. All around the outside, with their bigger cities. The inside cities were blessed with significantly lower infection rates.

They discussed lockdowns, and eventually, the press release all three men agreed to was as follows:

From the President of the United States

All traffic in and out of all outside states is prohibited. States excluded from this order are New Mexico, North Dakota, and Montana. The prohibited states have unacceptably high infection rates. We expect to control this outbreak and lift those restrictions in two weeks if the lockdown orders are obeyed. This means any travel by air, sea, train, or car across those borders is prohibited.

Road crossings will have roadblocks monitored by the Army. We will stop people travelling in or out of the state at seaports and airports. Back road attempts to cross will be monitored by drones. There will be a list of exemptions attached, e.g. for some essential workers. Others who try to cross borders will be prosecuted. You may be sent to an Army boot camp where trainee soldiers will ensure you will not do so again. More details will be issued as we firm up our responses.

After Dr Ponti left, the President continued with Lt. Col. Freebody. They discussed how to implement the blockades.

Lt. Col. Freebody spoke first.

'Back roads are not a problem. We have small units along those borders, and with, say, ten drones on any state border, we can detect movement and zero in on it. Then it's Gotcha. Revenue for the Army. Passenger trains will need to be stopped at state borders.'

The President wants to know, 'We need to specify a date and time when this becomes effective. What time did you have in mind, Colonel?'

'We need to work on an announcement that allows trips to be cancelled and flights in the air to be accepted with some quarantine constraints. For airport arrivals, we may have trouble and will need about a hundred soldiers at major airports, men with a mean look in their eyes to prevent trouble. The look that says, 'Don't mess with me.'

9:30 a.m.

The team worked on the lockdown details until a press release was ready.

From the President of the United States:

Traffic into and out of all states identified in the attachment is affected as follows; penalties apply for breaches:

- Air traffic to interstate ports is stopped immediately.
- Air traffic from interstate is stopped at departure immediately. Arrivals from flights in transit before 10 a.m. will need to go into quarantine hotels or self-isolation for four days.
- Passenger trains out of those states to interstate locations will be cancelled immediately.

- Passenger trains will be turned around if arriving at state borders after 6 p.m.
- Road crossing into and out of affected state borders will be stopped immediately or when the Army can arrive to monitor checkpoints. Food and essential goods trucks are excepted.

11:30 a.m.

Oilman Mitch Upton, has his business and wealth dependent on monitoring the vast operations and networks of oil and gas fields, mainly in Houston. There is trouble with drilling in New Mexico and Oklahoma and across the border in Mexico. Mitch had talked to his wife Dannielle after hearing the lockdown news, and he was screaming abuse at the world that was not listening to him. Dannielle patted him on the shoulder with a finger to her lips.

There was silence, then she said, 'You should take that executive jet. They did not say private planes are blocked from leaving.' What a clever wife.

'But won't they still have blocks at the small airports?' he asked.

She told him, 'File a flight plan in the direction you need to go, somewhere near the border, and then just keep going.'

He pursed his lips, then whistled and kissed her. 'Come here, sexy oil girl, and kiss me for good luck.'

All went well. He flew to the place just north of Albuquerque in New Mexico; breach one. He did what he needed to do, went to Oklahoma, allowed, landed at Norman, south of Oklahoma City, did his job, and crossed the border again into Texas, breach two. He then flew on to San Antonio and had an overnight stop. He filed a new flight plan to Crystal City the following day but flew past that and into Mexico to land at San Andres, west of Chihuahua, breach three. He called his wife that night.

'You beauty. Three border crossings and not a lockdown in sight.' After they chatted, he went back to work.

The next day he headed home and crossed near Piedras Negras west of Crystal City in the US, breach four, when he suddenly had company. A fighter jet contacted him on the civilian air frequency.

'I'm escorting you to Crystal City, where we will talk.'

'Oh shit,' was uttered, and more expletives were said when he landed.

The Flight Lt. addressed him. 'Sir, the border is closed, and because you violated the instructions, you are under arrest. You will need to be in quarantine at a quarantined hotel for fourteen days. They have WiFi, so you will be able to conduct your business from there. You will need to pay for the hotel, of course, and a fine of one thousand dollars, cheap for a man with a private jet. A second offence is six months in the locker.'

1:30 p.m.

Dr Ponti had organised a representative, Dr Abrahams, to visit and report on cases at a hospital in San Antonio, selecting that state as Texas is a high infection state. The hospital was an arbitrary choice, one of eight in the area.

Dr Abrahams reported by phone: 'Dr Ponti, I have finished my visit here. It was devastating. The horror of so many children's bodies, so many in ICU unable to breathe, and not being able to help is the worst. You must stop this pandemic any way you can, even if you weld doors shut to ensure people stay inside as they did in China. The report is on its way.'

The report did not pull any punches. It read:

The greater San Antonio area has a population of two and a half million, and Texas has twenty-nine million. So it's a small sample, but near nine per cent of the total population, a good sample. Texas had four thousand deaths yesterday, we had four hundred, with sixty children dead in this hospital. That's statistics. The reality is a bit more emotional. Another hundred and eighty in ICU, and they probably won't make it. That is about three hundred wailing parents who are begging us to do something.

One woman approached me. 'Doctor, you're a doctor, aren't you? I can offer you thousands of dollars for something special for my son. He is our only son. My other son died a week ago, and all we have left is one daughter. You must help,' she sobbed with gasping breaths. 'Anything. I can pay. Please help.' But there is nothing special we can give them except an overdose. The staff is very distraught, watching kids gasp for air, looking at their pleading faces, but unable to help.

Some parents offered five thousand dollars if I could help their child. One couple said to me: 'We have two other children who are still OK, but one is in this hospital near death, and another is already dead. There must be something you can do for us.' It was so devastating to see their crestfallen faces when we could offer no hope other than isolation.

All I could tell the parents was that the President would almost certainly order the strictest lockdowns ever to nip this killer in the bud. And, of course, I did not take their money. They will need it for funerals.

And lastly, the morgue is full. Children's bodies are stored in the City Abattoirs freezers, a ghastly solution but necessary. The people here will happily undertake any lockdowns if it is explained adequately.

That was it, and Dr Ponti sent the report on to the President.

The report upset the President especially the effect on parents and nurses. They discussed the approach needed for the typical COVID infection versus the deadly ones, and the normal ones include all the highly transmissible ones, of course. Dr Ponti offered his view:

'The deadly strain cases do not enter hospitals, but people may turn blue, then die within a day. From a hospital point of view, they are only a disposal problem, nasty as that sounds, but nobody can do anything about it. Other than wiping it out within the next few days. We need an announcement about distancing to go out today.'

'The other strains all clog up hospitals and upset doctors and nurses as well as parents wanting to see their families. We don't have enough nurses. Doctors can only do a little, like administer end-of-life medicine if needed. The nurses are reaching breaking point, and we need to ask for volunteer nurses, who may be employed later if they can hack it.'

The two men decided on two separate press releases so that each had a single important focus, and after a bit of messing about with the text, this is what went out:

From the President of the United States of America

Notice One:

We have nearly but not entirely eradicated the blue neck strain of COVID, COVID-xxxx, thanks to people following distancing and non-touching instructions. You must continue this excellent process for four more days, and it will be all over. The other highly infectious strains are not as deadly, but they cause overflowing in hospitals, and the distancing and non-touching instruction remains in force. When the number of daily infections comes down, we will try contact tracing to eradicate these cases, but how long it all takes is in your hands.

Notice Two:

Dr Ponti, our medical adviser, has advised that we need volunteer nurses to help in hospitals. Patients are desperate for human contact, as many face the end of their lives. Hospitals are so overcrowded there may be one nurse to fifty patients, and the patients need you. If you can do the work, you will be offered a job if you want it.

The two men pondered on the likely effectiveness of getting more nurses. And without protest marches, they could slow the daily cases.

*   *   *

Petal Ohrtman, 53, is a lovely confident woman with a Spanish look. She had a smile to entrance most people. She was an extrovert and easily engaged with other people, a great advantage when working as a nurse.

Her daughter Summer took after her father. She was sweet but less extroverted. She smiled so quickly when she saw children and animals that she was perceived to be warm and engaging. She had worked in a children's hospital ward as a nurse, but both mother and daughter were not working now. Hospitals had cancelled all elective surgery due to the pandemic.

Petal and her daughter had seen the bulletin calling for nurses and were discussing it. What was happening? Summer wondered why they did not have more nurses now. Petal thought that the early nurse protection gear had been inadequate and that many had caught the virus or left. Now they have top-notch equipment but no nurses.

'What do you think, Babs, shall we make a ward team?' asked Petal, and Summer smiled at the thought. They agreed to apply and looked for a hospital close to them. They called the Ohio Health Doctors Hospital. After a few checks on qualifications, they were welcomed with open arms to start tomorrow morning at eight. They were professionals and collected all their certificates and credentials into a zip-lock bag each to hand over to the hospital admin so that they could get straight to work.

The Chief Nurse was impressed with the preparations and told them to go straight to a children's ward with Sister Ruth. On the way, Sister Ruth introduced herself and asked what they were expecting.

Petal replied, 'We saw the President's request for help for patients desperate for human touch, so we came.'

Sister Ruth told Summer, 'There is a little darling five-year-old girl who wants a mummy. She's pretty sick and may give up on living - and she needs to have her desire to live kickstarted. Are you OK to help with that?'

Summer was pretty OK with that. When she saw the poor little girl, her heart went out to her. She managed to make a magic smile and got a response.

The girl asked her, 'Have you come to see me?'

Summer smiled even more and asked, 'Only if you want me to, but can I lie next to you and give you a hug?'

The girl burst into tears but pulled her back and said, 'I have not had a hug forever. If you hug me and smile at me, I promise I will get better, I really promise.' A good start.

Sister Ruth and Petal watched this union in awe. Going, going, gone.

'She'll live now,' said Sister Ruth and turned to Petal. 'Are you OK with helping a man, about thirty, to discover he wants to live?' Off they went down the ward and stopped in front of a moaning man. A lonely moaning man. He looked just like Petal's husband twenty years earlier, and it was so easy for her to like him; and she approached his bed, also with a killer smile.

'Would you like me to sit with you and hold your hand whilst you tell me how you are? And tell me your name too, please?'

The man gulped. That was too much of a good thing, and he was cautious about hoping for too much, asking, 'And why would a pretty lady want to talk to me then?' Petal was no slouch either.

'Because I can.' She just sat down on his bed, and she held his hand.

'Do you know how long it's been since I held a woman's hand?' he asked, and she smiled.

'Why don't you tell me then?' and they got to know each other a bit.

Summer and Petal worked from when they started at eight till eleven to have a break, which they took in a cafeteria. Petal was worried about how her daughter was feeling, and they chatted.

'Mum, I'm exhausted. It's so emotional. But I don't think I've ever had such a privilege of helping young patients. I will sleep like a log tonight,' offered Summer, and she asked her Mum, 'What about you? Feeling OK?'

Her Mum told her that it was similar. 'What really got me is that they had so little hope and yet hung on. Holding a man's hand when he thinks no one cares puts a smile on a tired face that is beyond marvellous, and it wakes me up to what a difference I can make. This COVID shit will be the making of so many people; you mark my words.'

After the break, it was back to work, afternoon tea, another shift, and then time to leave. Sister Ruth came to see them off. 'Fifteen patients each, great work, and out of thirty - only five died.'

Petal said to Summer when outside, 'It's not about statistics. It's about how we made patients feel, and even if they all died but were happier in their final hours, then we did a good job.'

When they got home, Petal suggested they have a hot cup of tea before turning to alcohol. 'If we start on booze we won't stop, but this tea will revive us much faster.' After that, Petal had a cold white wine, Summer a beer, and they discussed the day's events.

'I nearly bawled so many times today. That very first little girl pushed my love button like nothing ever had before. I have seen gratitude from postop kids before. But nothing prepared me for this. It was like a pile driver had hit me and wouldn't stop,' said Summer.

Petal added to that sentiment, 'The first young man I saw was so much like your father when we were all happy and we could not get enough of each other. That beautiful young man held my hand and cried. I think he was overwhelmed that a "beautiful woman" stranger would care, and he wanted to live. I think he found out what is out there for him if only he can keep fighting and live. I think we need to get an appointment diary to see all these lovely people in three weeks-time.'

Summer added, 'I think we should tell Dad; he can't fight about that.' They called him and told him what had happened and got emotional in the process. They were astounded he did not belittle them, then were gobsmacked when he asked Petal if she would please ask Matron if they could use men to kick start life for some ladies.

After that, discussions turned to the drenching of the protestors. It was Petal who had the answer.

'Hon, what do I get if I have the answer" and she was offered a thorough loving after Summer had gone to sleep.

'Why after?' asked Summer.

'I would be embarrassed if you heard us and commented on it in the morning,' replied Blew.

'But that doesn't come free you know,' said Blew, who insisted on the answer.

'When I was at University studying nursing we had many Indian friends and we often talked about the influence of the British. They were delighted to switch the conversation to their own country and they knew their history. One of them had seen the movie based on John Master's book about the train that was blocked from leaving by having high caste ladies sit on the track. Touch them and there would have been war. I kept a copy of that movie all these years and instead of telling you, we play it now, but fast forward it a bit and watch what happened.'

Petal did not know where this would happen, and all got a bit impatient, but suddenly there it was, ladies on the track, then the soldiers with buckets who tipped brown stuff over them.

Petal shuddered, as did Summer. Blew was less sensitive and roared with laughter and said, 'I bet you I know who thought of that. It was that Army guy, Freebody, and he would have seen that during his training.'

When they all calmed down, Summer commented to her mother as they went to bed, 'That's the best family time we've had together for a long time. It's nice. And I now see what it must have been like when you two met,' as they retired for the night.

*　　*　　*

March 15, 8:30 a.m.

The Army State border roadblocks and checkpoints were in place and working. The common excuse for trying to get across was, 'You didn't give us enough warning.' The typical response was, 'Does your car have a radio and do you know how to switch it on?' Some wanted to be shown, and they were shown the way and turned back. There were smart people and smart-arses, and they were the ones at checkpoints trying to get in.

All interstate flights were cancelled. Airlines wanted compensation. The President pressured airlines to offer transfers or refunds to travellers and offered an assistance package. That's all policy, but at airports, it becomes personal. So many people had been afraid of lockdowns and had decided to go now before it was too late. Houston had thousands waiting at the check-in queue when the announcement went out.

Border controls for Houston Airport

Attention, please. All flights in and out of Houston are cancelled. Inbound flights in the air will be allowed to land, but those people need to undergo isolation and testing. This is by order of the President, who is pressuring airlines to give refunds. The blockade is expected to last ten days if everyone commits to social distancing and masks, much longer if you don't. We apologise for the inconvenience.

Fights broke out between would-be passengers and airline staff. Soldiers move in and stand firm. 'You said what?' was their unasked question but expressed in their face, and the fights broke up; business as usual by the look of things.

March 15, 9:30 a.m.

Dr Ponti was with the President, reporting on daily cases and deaths. He received a new report every eight hours, faster than he can act on them, but one thing is sure: the numbers were going up and up and never down. No end in sight yet, and they needed some hard-hitting acts to put an end to this dreadful state of affairs.

Dr Ponti called Army psychologist James Anderson, who had escaped the pandemic to Woodstream in Maryland with his family. The pandemic was their central discussion theme every day. They were disgusted by the behaviour of the people who spread the virus. James took the call from Dr Ponti, whom he and Michelle had gotten to know well during the pandemic.

'James, I need some help from you,' said Dr Ponti.

'What's on your mind then, Doc?' asked James, and he was given a problem to solve; how to get people to isolate and distance from others. James told him he'd work on the psychology and put together something they could use. 'I'll be back with it in two hours, that OK?' They agreed to that.

James called Michelle to join him. They made a coffee and settled down while he explained the problem of getting people to isolate and distance.

James asked Michelle, 'Why do you think they refuse to do what is needed?' Michelle had also tackled this question in class in her lecture, and in a class with 220 students, returning a wide range of opinions.

'It boiled down to three factors: "Not My President", ego, and ignorance. Let's take the first one. Many students whom I asked this question said they had talked to protestors who said:

> 'Why should I follow a President's order if I didn't vote for him? My father is one of those, but my mother hates the idea, and they have lots of fights about it.'

> 'You have to make people see that ex-President Trump is always isolating, first in the White House, now at his golf course. *"Be as smart as the man you voted for"* might be the ticket. Eighty per cent of students put this as the main reason for non-compliance.'

'What about the ego?' asked James. This one needed a bit of knocking about, but they decided that there was one ego that said, 'It can't happen to me.' The other 'Don't tell me what to do,' and variations of that, which is not ego but defiance, and defiance feeds their ego.'

James continued, 'We need to find something that pleases them better than defiance. For ignorance, we need to show shock videos of people dead in the street and people dying while gasping for air. It could be a child actor imitating an asthma attack. They worked through the issues and finally produced a new compliance incentive. We'll write it as if it came from the President.'

An Announcement from the President

This notice lets you know what happens when you don't follow the lockdown orders. You will be arrested and sent to the White Sands infection detention centre in New Mexico because we cannot afford for you to infect others here.

We must stop the spread of the four highly infectious strains of COVID. We are approaching 40,000 deaths a day. This is unacceptable, and if not constrained, everyone in America will be dead. There will be lockdown orders, and you need to follow them. Your reasons for defiance may be that you voted for Donald Trump and not me. That's OK. You can vote for him again in four years if you follow my orders. If you don't, you will almost certainly be dead.

To make sure you all take this seriously, we will be showing shock videos every hour, every day, every channel. They will show the Army with disposal trucks picking up dead bodies in the street and dumping them into mass graves a mile long. Then there will be a shocking video showing a five-year-old child dying, crying out because they can't breathe.

James sent it to Dr Ponti. The President issued the report as a press release, almost unaltered.

Families struggled, often with one or two deaths in the designated bedroom. Some apartments were old buildings, four floors up, and no lifts. The Army had arranged tripods over the stairwells to use pulleys to lower dead bodies down on stretchers. Videos showed soldiers in full-body hazmat suits entering an apartment, coming out with a body on a stretcher, lowered down the stairwells and taken to the street to be picked up by a garbage truck, too infectious to be handled by soldiers. The truck removed another five dead bodies lying in the street. Some neighbours were standing by, weeping.

11:30 a.m.

A new mob of protestors made itself known; they would march and protest about lockdowns. They did not have the following of the patriots or that other mob, and needed to protest to grow their numbers from the current size of 2,000. They were big men, hairy as a wildebeest, rowdy as hell. They only lacked one skill. They did not read the news, and did not see the TV coverage of mass protestors getting sprayed by putrid water. They might have seen the show but had not read the news item lines. They were ready to march and they were not happy. It would be their show alone. Just what the doctor ordered.

People were angry with the extreme right-wing demonstrators; some viewers of the protest threw paint and flour bags onto them from a safe height. After all the announcements, people want to evade this super spreader, and these arseholes were damaging the frail victories.

But they need not have worried. Like a cavalry charge, the Army came to the rescue. People stopped throwing flour bombs and cheered instead. A helicopter flew over, giving them five minutes to disperse. Nothing happened. Then a single DC10 Air Tanker flew over and dropped water. Blue dye could be seen. Something else was not. But the reaction to it was. Marchers retching, trying to tear their clothes off.

They looked like they had a load of ants in their pants. The viewers could hear complaints:

'They were supposed to come over and only drop water on us half an hour later!'

Bystanders inside their homes or offices were laughing at the demonstrators who were trying to get undressed.

An older man on a fourth-floor balcony was reporting. He was eighty, and it was his birthday. His family had come to celebrate, but he knew it was those dreaded demonstrators when he heard the noise in the street. He told his daughter:

'Mary-Lou, when I was fourteen, I was a cub reporter. I had a tape recorder the size of a tissue box. I was interviewing some dead people,' when Mary-Lou interrupted, 'Really? How unusual.'

He corrected himself. 'There were TV reporters with cameras trying to interview a resident from an apartment block where they had found a dead body a week old. The resident did not want to talk on TV. When he walked towards me, I stood in his way. "A moment of your time, please, sir. This is important. It's my first day on the job." So what happened? And guess what, he talked and talked, and eventually the TV cameras came over and started to record me interviewing a man they couldn't get to speak to them. I was on national TV. Now I have this mobile phone with video and a plugin microphone, and I can talk as I film. No worries. I'm gonna have a vantage point of view on the fourth floor. Channel nine is on the line, and I'm gonna be fourteen again. Sorry guys, I'm busy. On national TV.' He stepped out to the balcony again.

He hated the protestors with a passion; for spreading the virus, and he wanted to see what punishment was coming to them. He was sure the President would have ordered something quite spectacular.

He was vulnerable; he could not run fast enough to get away if he had been there. But he was live by phone with video to a TV station, and he was reporting. For the first time in his life, and he quivered with excitement. He had been advised not to swear so he could be live on air. He said:

> Those slack-jawed, big-bellied, drooling faces, with faeces hanging out of their pockets, haha, they got just what they deserved. They make our lives miserable, and now the Army does it back to them. Now the Army is coming in, taking them to a truck. By the looks, they're all smelly and hating their neighbours. They move more trucks close to where the idiots are, lift them into trucks again, and in a minute, all two thousand are taken off the street by truck. All gone. The Army has just excelled itself. This Government doesn't muck around. It does what it says it will do. Bye for now, a pleasure to be a reporter on my eightieth birthday.

He was one happy old man. Those pests were on their way to a desert camp for infected people in New Mexico. He later found out that the Army had added hydrogen sulphide to the water, which stinks worse than a seven-day-old dead body.

*   *   *

The President wanted to know how the story about using hydrogen sulphide originated.

Lt. Col. Freebody answered.

'I told you before; but you seem to be intrigued by the details. Happy to help out.'

He continued, 'Shooting protestors is not a good look, so I'd been thinking of a solution for weeks. This one would nail it, I thought. I watched a movie about the British in India trying to move protesting ladies who sat on a railway line stopping the train. A lieutenant organised a large container of sewerage to be dumped on them from the lower castes. It worked like a charm but did not endear the British to the Indian people.'

'But we would not want to use latrines. Don't have them anymore, but just too messy to clean the streets afterwards. So I needed to find something in liquid form. It would also be easier to clean the tanks in the planes.'

'If we have, say, a hundred thousand marchers and we fly fire-fighting water bombers over them - say five litres per protestor - we would need five hundred thousand litres, that is five hundred tons. And the DC10 Air Tankers carry forty-five tons of water.

*   *   *

The Orthallo and Sanderson families hid from the virus in the Napa-County Regional Park, California, but communicated their ideas to Dorothy who working from her own wilderness getaway in Woodstream, Maryland. They discussed the events they saw.

Sue Anne Orthallo started, 'Dorothy, have you noticed the Army has stopped taking sick people from homes, and they need to stay with families now. What's going on?'

Dorothy told her, 'They used to pick up blue neck patients that would die in a day but were too infectious to stay with families. The blue neck cases were all gone now. Of the highly infectious strain, cases there had been too many to test and take them out. They get better, or they die. Pretty tough on families. But with approaching 40,000 deaths a day, the new infections must be in the multiple hundred thousand a day, but we don't know as we can't monitor in lockdown.'

Sue Anne countered, 'But if we are in lockdown, there should be no new cases. Ah, yes, and no testing. What is the solution?'

Dorothy replied, 'Have a scotch. Wait for the next Presidential announcement.'

Dorothy got hold of Lt. Col. Freebody and asked him what is happening to sick people in homes. He replied:

'Nothing yet. We've been too busy dealing with deadly blue neck infections until now. We are thinking of asking really sick people to be driven to car parks anywhere, and the Army will set up field hospitals and provide them with some bedding, comforting medications, alcohol, and food. For terminal patients, we will offer them life-terminating drugs if they want them. We aim to get them out of family homes, and we will need to send in clean-up teams to sanitise whole apartment blocks at a time.'

'How many do you think there are, all together in all states then?' asked Dorothy.

The sobering answer was, 'In the multiple millions. Hopefully less than ten. Then there will still be infected people in homes who are not too sick and will get better. Hopefully, less than fifteen million. A mammoth task. We will need to employ Reservists and anyone able to help and follow orders,' offered the Colonel.

Then came a bit more. 'We've had Army soldiers break down from such traumatising tasks, and they need counselling before they can continue.'

The Colonel had a report from one of his sergeants who had been retching and vomiting in the street, and he asked him what was wrong. He got an unexpected answer:

"That man was like my father dying. I was with my father when he died. He could not breathe; he was drowning from fluid in his lungs, and he wanted me to help. It was like watching a puppy I had to drown when I was younger, and you look at their eyes, and you feel as guilty as hell. My puppy had been run over by a car, and half his body was squashed. It was the fastest way to stop his pain. No good explaining; you have to experience it."

'What had upset most of them was watching people close to dying. The counsellors had to bring the soldiers to a state of mind where they did not feel responsible for people's stupid behaviour, not practising Covid-safe distancing. It was just something that was. Those people were like their parents, and their parents were just as stupid about isolation, working on the principle of "I'm not infected, and it can't happen to me."'

'They put us at risk, and our parents are just as stupid. But I can tell you this. The soldiers will shoot to kill anyone disobeying orders. They are at breaking point, and we will not prosecute them if they do shoot someone.'

A weird silence remained, so Dorothy thanked him and hung up. Then she called Sue Anne Orthallo to report back. Sue Anne was excited at the call-back, but Dorothy just sobbed and told her she is too upset to talk, instead telling her to watch the news.

A News Bulletin from the President.

My right-hand man, Lt. Col. Freebody, has just reported to me. What he conveys is so distressing. There is one bit of good news. The blue neck strain seems to have been eradicated. Gone. The task of removing blue neck infections had stretched the Army to maximum capacity and left no time for removing sick people from homes. We have no idea how many people are now sick, as contact tracing stopped with lockdowns.

We have developed an app with three buttons for people to report with immediately. The first is, 'I have COVID', and the second is, 'I'm really sick with COVID.' The last one is, 'We have a dead body.' You will find them in your app stores on mobiles. Enter a name and address, and someone will come soon for really sick or dead people. The other helps us know what is happening. I urge everyone to download these apps today and enter the numbers.

Together we will beat the beast and hope to be back to normal in two months if there is a normal. Good day, and God bless America.

March 16, 11:30 a.m.

The President met with Lt. Col. Freebody and Dr Ponti. Their first order of business was to see if any reports from the apps had arrived. Dr Ponti reported over 39,000 reported deaths, all from homes. Hospitals had not yet reported. The President was overwhelmed.

'How do they cope with all that pain?' he wanted to know, but was not looking for an answer. The good news is that people had listened for once and replied with their apps.

'The dead people are not a problem,' says the Colonel. 'We pick them up, and the problem is solved. The problem is the half a million 'really sick' people. We need to pick them up to give them a chance – and to give the families a bit of relief. That would need a lot of soldiers. If one team of four can pick up and deliver sick people to the temporary field hospitals in an hour, say four hours a day, then we need half a million soldiers to clear that backlog in a day. We have less than that number on active duty. I hope it's fewer sick people the next day. We will need to do this for a week. Then we need to look at another two million people with mild symptoms. We will need to leave that for another day.'

'Alright, let's put out a Bulletin to show people what is happening,' said the President.

Presidential Bulletin

People have been fantastic and followed orders. You have entered the dead, the sick, and the mild cases per household, and now we know how much work we have to do. Tomorrow all dead people will be picked up, and tomorrow and the next day, we can pick up all sick people and take them to temporary field hospitals. Over the next week or two, we can attend to the remaining two million with mild symptoms. Have a thought for our soldiers; not one of the three hundred thousand who worked these shifts has contracted the virus so far. A remarkable demonstration of how well **they** have followed orders.

You have demonstrated your willingness to help with the apps, and so now we can help you. Together we will win. Soon.

March 16, Noon

Dorothy had called the President and was lucky to get through.

'Mr President, what can you tell me that is important that you did not put in the Bulletin?' she asked.

'That is such a sneaky way to get close to the unmentionable things. But be careful how or whether you want to write about it. This is a shocker. Do you really want to hear it?' he asked, and Dorothy being Dorothy, of course, wanted to know. What could be so bad?

And he tells her, 'OK. Did you wonder why the soldiers only work four hours a day? It is horrifying work, and they vomit and need time to recover. They are confronted with heavier than usual Americans, those weighing well over three hundred pounds, who need to be transported downstairs. Over half the patients were that size. It's not a one in a hundred but sixty in a hundred,' and he continued:

'I'm so angry with a system that lets them get to this stage. Sugary drinks, ten bottles a day, and you have four-hundred-pound men in bed unable to go to the toilet, and they drink that shit as if their lives depend on it. "But it tastes so good" is their cry. I would like to see a system where they need to present a certificate to buy sugary drinks. Or add a tax, make them cost fifty bucks a can. We needed food stamps during the depression. Now we need food stamps to buy only what we ought to eat, not what they want. My uncle is the same, and everyone runs around to satisfy his needs because they don't like dealing with complaints. We should train people to *love* complaints, or they will never help.'

'They don't walk. They have to be carried. Most of them have soiled their pants as they can't get out of bed. Some are so sick and heavy; soldiers offer them an anaesthetic because they may be dropped. Downstairs. This obesity is a bigger problem than COVID for us. The soldiers have fathers who are the same size, and they feel for those men but wish they'd have helped themselves to a better lifestyle earlier. What truly upsets them is if they drop someone who is not anesthetised who screams abuse at the soldiers.'

Dorothy was silent. This was not a statistic. This is the story of such good men in the Army doing their best for people who should have been sent to weight loss boot camps decades ago. The President asks her if she would like to accompany a troop tomorrow. She needed to do that, horrified though she is. She had reported from battlefronts with soldiers getting their arms shot off. This could not be worse.

But it was. War is war, and people put their lives on the line for the country. Almost something honourable. Carrying those overweight people is doing shit work for people who had not been responsible in the past. She issued a release.

Dorothy Thompson reporting.

The President told me about the brave soldiers doing the mop-up work to carry sick COVID patients to street-level temporary field hospitals. Those soldiers are confronted with horrible scenes and vomit many times a day. It is a dangerous and disgusting job, not because the patients are sick. But because they did not need to be infected,

They had ignored instructions, putting the lives of young men at risk.

You are at risk when you try to carry men weighing over four hundred pounds down four flights of stairs in apartments, and when they trip, a ton of weight falls on you, and all go down together. There are unsanitary aspects I won't go into. But I ask you. If you let yourself become so gross, how on earth do you expect young people to put their lives at risk for you?

After COVID, this issue needs to be addressed. It's a national disaster. Being so big is not what was meant by 'Make America Great Again.' No longer can we have lawsuits from passengers who feel insulted when the airlines want you to buy two or even three seats. The nation must address this. Don't make your responsibility someone else's.

Dorothy wondered how this would go down. She had decided to risk persecution by writing this under her real name. But a stand would need to be taken, which would enable the President to make the national action a bit easier if the truth is out there.

She received a call from the man.

'Dorothy, don't give me more work than I can handle right now, please,' laughed the President. 'But I have wanted to handle this for thirty years. This is why there is such opposition to Obamacare health insurance, which starts with the objection to ensuring people with previously known conditions. This problem is the next big issue for America.'

Dorothy wanted to know if he approved of her Bulletin.

'So you want a bit of praise now, Miss Reporter, do you?' asks the President.

She replies, 'No, Mr President, I just need to know that I haven't lost access to you.'

His reply was, 'Dorothy, you know pretty well. You haven't.'

CHAPTER 22

Mood

Argus E was monitoring the protestors. The mood in Washington was triggered by 40,000 daily deaths and the upcoming protests. Protesters had promised an assault on the Capitol. They were the gung-ho men who wanted to be heroes. They planned to make the January 6th Capitol raids look like child's play, but their leaders were now more cautious. Someone in their midst had leaked the plans, and they did not think the National Guard would hesitate to shoot the lot of them. It was illegal and a PR disaster for the President, but they could lose many men and credibility.

Viewers had seen the shocking videos of people dying in the streets. They were now willing to follow orders to isolate, anything to wipe out this mess, irrespective of personal opinion.

They were sick of it and dobbed in people not obeying orders. The greater good had become more important than personal views. Most did not realise it had been a PR win for the President.

* * *

March 18, 8:30 a.m.

News of the planned armed assault on the Capitol had reached the President, who had a gutful. Who was the boss in this country? Those thugs were about to find out. He released the following Bulletin:

> From the President of The United States of America
>
> The President advises that a curfew has been put in place to prevent mass gatherings because they spread the deadly virus. I have issued new orders to allow Army and Airforce to shoot and kill protestors. This is permissible under emergency laws.
>
> We will meet with force any protest marches or attacks on the Capitol. If anyone gathers within the vicinity of the Capitol in large numbers, the Airforce is instructed to fly over in fighter jets. After two minutes, they have been authorised to kill up to around 200,000 without further warning. Machine guns will do that in seconds.
>
> Elsewhere, unauthorised protestors will have a three-minute warning to run away. After that, they will be dead. We don't need them. God bless America.

That Bulletin had predictable reactions. 'They can't do that! Or can they?' For the first time, the protestors were afraid. But they did not want to appear scared, and they looked to their leaders.

March 18, 9:30 a.m.

The President discussed the days' actions with Dr Ponti and Lt. Col. Freebody. They were fighting a different battle now. The President spoke:

'I had already released a press statement about the planned protests. We have to do something to stop the virus from spreading. The daily death count is now near forty thousand. These strains are racing through the US, and if anyone interferes with the plan with big protest marches, I have signed orders for the Airforce to use machine guns. They will understand that message.'

'Holy shit', muttered Lt. Col. Freebody. 'Our own Tiananmen Square? Are you ready for that?' and the President replied:

'Yes, and remember, police can fire at people who run away from arrest, and during riots they can shoot looters. These guys are killing us, and they get a one-minute warning. Once the machine guns are heard they would be stupid if they did not scatter like rabbits. The main aim is to shorten the time they are gathering, and hopefully in four minutes their infections have not increased too much. But my guess is that when they will see this notice, they will not march again. It's too dangerous for them. But if they want to test me, we may shoot 10 or so before they have all run off the road. Protests will be over forever.'

Then he moved to the next item.

'The highly infectious strains are infecting some family members. Those infected have to stay home, as hospitals are full. There are about 40,000 seriously ill cases nationally and half a million less serious cases. The immediate task is removing those serious cases so that they do not infect other family members, whom we need to give a chance to survive.'

Dr Ponti suggested some priorities.

'First, we must urge people to use the app to report seriously ill family members, and we must remove them the same day to our temporary field hospitals. We should complete that in two days, so please order the Army to prepare for that.'

'Then we must test all those homes where infections had been reported, testing the whole family. A team moves in, street by street, with a test van for fast results. Then we can move infected family members to a lower risk field hospital.'

Dr Ponti concluded, 'The fourth priority is to send in contract cleaners to sanitise every household. We don't need the Army to do that, just to supervise the process.'

He was interrupted as the TV news screamed: 'Peak daily cases are at half a million! And massive lockdowns!'

'Bulletins tell people that no one can touch anyone else, and you must wear masks. Even inside.'

'Wives can shoot returning protest-marching husbands who try to touch them or their kids on return home. Call the Army to remove the body. The Second Amendment allows you to protect yourself, and the pandemic has gone critical, and you are entitled to protect yourself.'

The meeting concluded as the President thought *'One more done, thousands to go.'*

*   *   *

The Orthallo and Sanderson families were staying in the Bothe-Napa Valley State Park, California, and had seen the case details bulletin. They thanked their lucky stars that they were not in the city. But their four children were sick and tired of being cooped up.

The two kids they had found earlier, Maxi and Emmy, had become de facto family and were grizzling too. Sue Anne discussed the problem with Dominique. Sue Anne was a teacher, and she was used to turning grizzlies into smiles.

'Dom, I think they don't really get this pandemic shit. They hear radio statistics. I wonder what they would think if they saw a street with garbage trucks picking up dead bodies, as they do with garbage wheelie bins, to toss them in. It's gross. They would really understand if they saw streets full of army trucks ferrying sick moaning people to field hospitals, where many will probably die.'

Dominique knew the impact that image would have: nightmares. 'I think we need the men to help decide this one. Too scary for me,' said Dom,. They went man hunting, found them, and explained the dilemma.

John thought that a trip into San Francisco would be a great excursion; his kids had never been over the Golden Gate Bridge. Luckily, they had brought their minibus; it could take twelve people. Once over, they were likely to see the garbage collectors picking up bodies and also see people in cars with red flags. They were the ones dying or very sick, waiting for a pickup. But it would be a new vista for everyone. It was agreed, and they told the kids. They made a stop in Santa Rosa to pick up some spare hazmat suits for kids in case one of them had to step outside. They already had their four adult hazmat suits with them.

One man before him was being served, then John asked for six children's suits.

The pharmacist asked if he was joking, but no; 'I have six kids in the car, and we want to go to San Fran to give the kids a view of the Golden Gate,' said Max.

The reply was: 'When I found out about the lockdown, I knew the big stores like Walmart would be closed, so I bought ten six-packs for adults-sized and the same for kids.'

'How many do you think I have left?'

Max tried to be funny, 'One?'

The pharmacist smirked and told him, 'You'd be screwed in that case, but you're in luck.' The storekeeper tapped the side of his nose, 'I bought in volume and I'm laughing as most people wanted a single suit.'

Max was happy that he wasn't screwing the man; he paid him for two kids packs of six; one smaller, the other for the older kids. When he got back into the car, Dominique asked, 'Are you starting a shop?'

His laconic reply was, 'Might as well.' They headed north to the bridge.

The kids were excited. They were told, 'Halfway there, you mob.' Then the bridge claimed their complete attention, and they were over, past a Walt Disney Museum, and headed for Fishermen's Wharf. They did not get there. There was a roadblock, with a sign: 'Do Not Enter. Army removing dead bodies.' They were in Lombard Street. The little ghouls wanted to see the bodies.

Max headed south to Bay Street then back to Lombard, where they stopped. Across the street, left and right, there were garbage trucks. They were picking up stuff. Then the kids all realised that the Army was picking up bodies with the garbage truck and then cried out in horror as one man slipped through the arms of the bin grabber and fell back on the sidewalk.

Johan shouted, 'Dad, they dropped a man, and he's moving! He's not dead. We need to help.'

Max had been in the Army and had served in the war. He told them, 'Sometimes a dead body will move. I have seen it happen, but we can't help him. He's definitely dead.'

Then the man moved and waved his arms like a cry for help. Johan was about to get out of the car, and Max locked all doors and turned around.

'An Army guy will attend to it. The man they had dropped will be dead shortly but may need a painkiller injection. Look! That is just what is happening.' They seemed to give him an injection, and they left him there.

Johan was upset. 'Dad, they just leave him there. Why don't they help and lift him up?' Max points out that moving an injured man would hurt him, and they could not move him anyway.

'Why not?' asked Emily.

Her dad tells her, 'He's too heavy.' She sees that he is huge. Max tells all the kids to listen up.

'The Army has had to carry sick people out of apartments, often old apartments with four stories and no lifts. They have had to carry sick people out every day now for weeks. The soldiers weigh one hundred and thirty-five pounds on average, and an obese American they have to carry down four flights of stairs could weigh over four hundred.'

'Those soldiers have been doing a marvellous job for people who had not looked after themselves. Now they are exhausted.' Four kids were sobbing now, and they wanted to go home. This was not fun. Max swapped driving duties with John Orthallo, and over the Golden Gate and back south they went.

After the outskirts of Marin City, a young girl, about four, was furiously waving her arms. John stopped the car, and Max wound down the window to talk to her. It was hard work understanding her. She was hysterical and sobbing her heart out.

'My Dad just died, and my Mum is dying too. She told me to catch a ride to my Granny's in Siva Island. Max looked puzzled, and the kid said, 'Don't just stand there. It's just down the road. I will show you.'

Well, she was one determined kid. Max told her he was stepping out of the car, he was going to put on a safety suit, and he was going to help her put on a small one for herself. Because she might be infected, and he had to keep everyone in the car safe, and she sobbed some more. 'Just do it but hurry.'

He dressed her, and she smiled when she saw him in his hazmat suit. 'Do I look as funny in this as you do?' she wanted to know.

Max told her, 'Funnier', and she grinned.

When the car was moving, she told John, 'The second street left after we cross the water, then its right, left, right and stop at number 56.

Dominique asked, 'Have you been there before?'

This kid said, 'Why do you ask?'

Four adults responded with laughter, and the kid wanted to know what was so funny, which brought more laughter, but Max relented and said, 'We will tell you later. After you've told us your name, your Granny's name, and if you have a dog, and what is their name.'

Her name was Holly, Holly Whistler, her Granny's name was Roberta, and she had a dog. His name was Fetch, she told them, 'With a capital Eff. And I don't like it if people make fun of me.'

Max decided to do the daddy bit, 'And which one of us looks like your Mum and which one is like your dad?'

She comes out with, 'The ladies don't look like my Mum. My Mum was always cross. My dad looked like that beardy bloke over there. What's his name?' Introductions were made.

'Stop!' yelled Holly. 'This is the street.'

John said, 'Yes, then right, left and right to number 56,' and believe it or not, the kid had the last word.

'Memory like an elephant. John, can you come in with me? You won't scare Granny because you look like my dad.'

Granny tried not to be upset. 'Holly, I do like your spacesuit; is it to keep you safe?' After a bit of chatter, the doorbell rang. An Army soldier came in, excused himself and asked Granny if she could walk to the ambulance by herself.

Granny told Holly, 'It's a good thing you have a spacesuit to keep safe. I'm sick with the virus, and you must not touch me.' Then she turned to John.

'Well, she probably told you that you look like her dad. Could you be her dad for a while, please, until you've contacted family members? Just grab this Rolodex, please? It has all the names you will need to find family members.' Then she was led out by the soldier.

Holly's farewell was, 'Get well, Granny, the world needs you.' She turned to John. 'Got here just in time. That was quick. Now what?'

John had her measure by now. 'Now I play Daddy. You may have to teach me how.

She had the last word. 'You're doing OK. Just be yourself. That's what my dad always told me.'

John quietly told Sue Anne why she did not look like Holly's Mum when heading home. The other kids all told Holly they had seen a garbage truck pick up a dead man and accidentally drop him, but then he woke up.

'He was supposed to be dead.'

* * *

March 19, 8:30 a.m.

Dr Ponti met with the President, who called him to discuss the fastest way to shut down the new infections. Dr Ponti was adamant that the quickest way was a four-day complete lockdown, where nobody could leave home.

He added, 'I would issue these orders:

> 'Stay home, wear masks even at home, and don't touch anyone except mothers touching children. Sanitise the bathroom after anyone sick has used it. Do not visit sick people in their rooms; just poke your head in to say Hello. The Army can deliver food, and if you have used the 'I'm Sick' app, a soldier in a hazmat suit will come and deliver food to the sick ones.'

'Pretty drastic,' said the President. 'Can they do it?'

Dr Ponti replied, 'We show more videos of people dying, a ten-second clip on TV every twenty minutes, 24 hours a day, solid for a week. Scare the pants off them, a different video each time, and they will follow orders.'

The two men worked on getting a Bulletin out, and then they need the Army input.

'Colonel, we want to put out a bulletin about a four-day complete lockdown, you need to help.' The President said. 'This is our proposed bulletin. Can you see if it needs amendments, please?'

A report from the President.

Ladies and gentlemen, I have good news and some that is not so good. The good news is that the new daily infections are coming down. The bad news is that we will enforce a four-day complete lockdown.

This process has proved to be very effective in Australia and New Zealand. The lockdowns may seem forever, but it will seem short and worthwhile when looking back.

We had 40,000 daily deaths two days ago and can only estimate the daily cases as there are too many to test, and it's too hard to do when we don't want anyone walking in the streets.

But from previous statistics, we know it was a hundred times the number of deaths, so that would be four million daily cases. A truly shocking number.

We have evidence that we will have that down to one-fifth of cases and half the deaths if orders are followed. Then we can change the lockdowns and give far less intrusive orders, and hopefully, in four weeks, it's all over. Keep that in mind.

Dorothy Thompson decided the bulletin would benefit from added content from her. She could see that when people got sick at home, the Government would not know what was happening unless people continued using the 'I'm Sick' app.

It was time to take sick people out as quickly as possible. People needed to report, and she prepared this bulletin:

Dorothy Thompson reporting.

The President's bulletin is good news and a reminder of the work to be done. I encourage you to continue using the 'I'm Sick' app. If you indicate if someone has mild, medium or severe symptoms, then the Army can prioritise the work to take very sick people out to a field hospital, where they may receive medical attention.

Of the million infections, there are roughly forty thousand critical cases and another forty thousand who can be helped and will recover. This will only happen if you don't swamp the system with mild symptoms reporting to us as critical.

I recently visited one of those temporary field hospitals looking after seriously ill patients, and its hell in there with nurses run off their feet. It's not a place for malingerers.

Don't claim to be very sick to get to a hospital when you're not. The hospitals and doctors there won't be kind to you if you try that, so please, don't.

March 20, 8:30 a.m.

The President spoke to Lt. Col. Freebody. Deaths were down, and testing in homes had resumed. The Colonel commented on cases, saying that it was impossible to tell if they were old or new.

'Mr President, would you like to go on a holiday if I fix all the COVID cases?' There was only a chuckle at the attempted humour, and the President wanted a report.

'The big city blocks are easy. In high rises, we send in a team that tests one floor, takes the test samples down to the mobile lab, back to that floor and take out infected people. Mild cases may stay with the family. We can be less restrictive now.'

'Are you testing everyone or only those with symptoms?' asked the President.

The Colonel replied, 'Everyone in homes that had reported a case. It takes time to show symptoms. We come back later if anyone reports new symptoms.'

Dorothy was up to a bit of mischief, so she decided to write using her alias.

Rebecca Sanders reporting.

All sick people, ill with COVID symptoms, are now in field hospitals, like honoured guests at a private hotel.

Half may die, and they get special treatment to make their last days a bit easier. They cannot be taken to real hospitals because those are still full. Patients are offered drug choices, including marijuana, poppers, whiskey or bourbon, and for those in a hurry to depart, heroin. Excluded are methamphetamines and other derivatives. As there is no smoking in the field hospitals, the marijuana option is not in great demand.

Despite their illness, there are no complaints about the service.

*   *   *

Nurse Klimmer, 46, spoke to her neighbour Dannielle Upton. Dannielle started talking after pouring tea.

'I had a good bitch with Mitch today,' she laughed as she told Julianne about the earlier fight with Mitch.

'So it's 'Mitch the Bitch' now?' asked Julianne, and the girls made a few alliterations of the words and a few derivatives like, 'Once a bitch and never again,' and they howled with laughter. Then Dannielle wanted to know about the cases in the hospital.

'The intensive care units are a mess. Wards are designed to hold sixteen beds and are packed with twenty-four. It means patients are so close together no one gets to sleep because the person next to you has rattling breathing keeping you awake, often gasping for air. It scares those next to them. Like: *'Will it be like that for me?'* The nurses are run off their feet and are often crying.'

'They witness the horror of someone unable to breathe, crying for help, and there is none. This may sound horrible, but at least the blue neck patients have all died. They did it the hardest, and we gave them morphine, knowing it would ease their breathing and probably kill them, but at least peacefully.'

'But it has left us all at risk. We had threats from some families who want to sue us for giving their old Mum an overdose. I wanted to rub a paper towel with the virus on their faces and kill them. You have no idea how stressful it is to smile with shitfaced people trying it on. They would lose the case and have to pay costs, but we would need to be stood down during the case, and we need all able-bodied nurses. Utter motherfuckers like that.'

Dannielle hugged Julianne and soothed her with a nice cup of coffee and cake.

*   *   *

March 21

Amid all this drama, Iranian Militias had launched rocket attacks on Israel and US Army bases in Iraq. The President had already found that a strong stand and a fearless message achieved more than worrying about opinion polls. He called his Army Chief of Staff, General Morgan, to meet for an urgent meeting.

Once seated, the General offered, 'I think I know why I'm here. Iranian Militias?'

'Too right,' said the President. 'They think we are too weak during a pandemic to retaliate. If we don't retaliate strongly, it will be open slather to bomb US assets, and we are lost. I want an immediate response so graphic that the whole world gets the message. What is the biggest, most dramatic response you can think of?' he asked.

'We have stealth bombers that can evade radar. We have a bomb that is very, very large and has a massive blast radius. It is designed to flatten everything within a three-hundred-foot radius, including concrete structures. What is the picture you want the world to see?'

'I do not want to firebomb anyone. That is gross and unnecessary. I want a graphic result. Daytime if possible. If you have accurate position coordinates of the militia camps, I want something that looks like utter devastation, scorched earth, demonstrating our power. What is the biggest thing you could deliver with that stealth bomber?' asked the President.

'The B-2 bomber has a range of six thousand miles, so we can take off from Germany. That allows us to use the SMOAB,' replied General Morgan.

'SMOAB?' asked the President, with the question framed in his face, and the General explained.

'The MOAB is a bomb with eleven tons of TNT equivalent blast. It's a blast bomb to obliterate everything within a three-hundred-foot radius, but it's too long for the B-2 weapons bay. The shorter version has the same punch. Go for it, Mr President,' urged General Morgan.

'All I want is for TV cameras having trouble focusing on the damage because it is too large,' suggested the President.

'That'll do, General, let's do it,' was the order.

March 22

TV footage showed massive damage in Syria at the site of the Iranian Militia camp. The expected Iranian response was swift. Later that day, Iran released footage of an Iranian frigate towing a hijacked oil tanker. Time for more action, thought the President, as he called General Morgan back for a meeting.

He asked him straight out, 'Can you sink that frigate without getting our planes shot down? Or the missile shot down?'

'I have just the thing, Mr President. I take it you want to teach them a lesson and show the world a bit of fear about American power?' asked the General, and with that mission statement, the General proceeded to outline their new secret weapon.

'Conventional missiles get intercepted and shot down these days. We have a new missile, secret till now, that defeats that. It's code-named *Screwed*, and it travels in a corkscrew path that can't be tracked. It kills the ship before they can report back. Sunk and still secret. Your order, Sir?'

There were only two words. 'Sink it.'

The jet that had delivered the missile had a video of the attack and showed only the last seconds and the explosion that sunk the frigate. It was released to the world.

They showed that short video sinking the frigate on TV and social media worldwide. The message? Don't mess with us.

*   *   *

March 22, evening

Argus E had switched his attention to the west coast, where two new protest groups have become active. Martin Hunter of the 'Right Beasts' and John Penny of the 'Stormtroopers' militias. Their angst was that the President would start lockdowns on their patch. He checked them out. Same but different to the eastern seaboard militias.

Martin Hunter, head of the Right Beasts militia that had planned a protest march, saw the videos. He was now in two minds about marching on the Capitol. He was worried about defying the President's orders. Easy. He called John Penny, head of the Stormtroopers militia. They argued around the issue: to march or not to march?

Eventually, Martin asked John, 'Do you think the President will follow through on his promise to machine gun 200,000 of our soldiers?'

A lot of speculation went on, neither wanting to appear weak.

Then John got realistic. 'This President, love him or hate him, does what he says he's going to do. We have lost the PR battle, and we should stop this. Now. Do it before the soldiers realise what they would let themselves in for. We must not be seen by them as if we are sending them to their death. We need to retain their respect to keep our leadership intact.'

The message went out. 'No marches. None. This President means what he says, and we need to save your lives. He has won the PR war with his sinking of the Iranian frigate. Stand down immediately. That is our order.'

At least they still looked like leaders, by the skin of their teeth.

*　　*　　*

Back on the East Coast, the news channels were full of reports on the conflict with Iran, and the US response that had wiped out the militia camp that had fired rockets at Iraq and Israel. When that blow had been shown, the Iranians had responded by hijacking an oil tanker, and that frigate was now history, delivered to the bottom of the sea.

Dorothy was not sad. She really wanted to sock it to those Iranians but decided to be careful, so she published using her safe name, Rebecca.

Rebecca Sanders reporting.

The President of The United States has sent a message to all countries.

Despite the pandemic, we are strong. Or because of it. It has made us strong to deal with this mess. Mess with us, and you will regret it.

Iran has found out. At a low cost of one warship, but at the cost of public support. Is China watching or ramping up nuclear-armed flights in the Taiwan strait? This is new territory for the world. The US seems to do what it says it will. It's a new reality.

The President called Dorothy Thompson. After a chuckle, he said, 'So much better coming from you, where it is seen as a question. From me, it would be a declaration of war. But they will be cautious for a while, which is good. I'm busy with the pandemic, but thanks for the help.'

The line went dead. *He must be busy*, she thought.

CHAPTER 23

April 4

Tens of thousands daily deaths defined the mood. After hitting a national top of 40,000 daily deaths, almost all cities were still in total lockdown. Deaths had reduced to 20,000. People were itching to see an easing of restrictions. Because they could not leave home, the Army delivered food people had ordered through their Covid-safe apps. The same applied to medications and painkillers for dental problems.

In LA, the lockdowns were not succeeding so well. It was like herding cats. People were arrested and sent to detainee camps. Some tried to get through State borders by back roads and got arrested; their cars were towed to lock-up.

Dr Ponti was reporting. Cases and deaths were down, and it was possible to start contact tracing, America's weakness. The contact tracing started to be effective, and cases came down rapidly.

Hospitals were still nearly full, but some ICU units had almost emptied of COVID patients. The doctor addressed the President:

'Mr President, something weird is happening in Columbus, Ohio. All eight Columbus hospitals have cleared out over ninety-five per cent of ICU patients. It seemed as though they had found a cure, but it was a nurse who had gone to a ward where her seriously ill bother had almost given up the ghost.'

'She sang and danced the chicken song, the beat by J. Geco. It was hilarious. She sang and danced it a dozen times, and the whole ward got into the act. She went through all ten wards and came back every day. Ten days later, they all walked home. Then she went to the other hospitals and did the same there.'

'Dr Ponti, I want you to organise a trip for her to visit all New York City hospitals. Offer whatever she needs. Take a crew for a video, and we can send it all around the country. That result is the first good news for seriously ill people, and it can give them all hope.'

Dr Ponti travelled to Columbus. He contacted his go-to man and asked where the chicken song nurse was. He was told she was back at the Children's Hospital, so he went to find her.

The Chief Nurse brought her to him in a private room, and he introduced himself.

'You haven't come to tell me off, I hope,' Summer joked.

'No. I have come to ask you for help,' said Dr Ponti. 'What do we have to do to get you to go to New York for a week and do what you've been doing here?'

She asked, 'What do you mean, as in what do you have to do?'

He said, 'Obviously, we would pay expenses. But how much money would you need us to pay you?'

'Silly man, I don't do this for money, but you could pay me my nurse's wages for a week. I'm a nurse, and it would be so much fun to empty your hospitals. I hope they don't complain about lost earnings when ten thousand plus walk home.'

Then Summer floored him when she asked him to do the chicken song with her. 'Stand there, ready to move your neck and arms? Then follow this techno beat: do the chicken shuffle, then the voice-over,

> '*Chippy Chippy Cheeeeeep, Cheepy Cheepy Cheeeeeep* turn your neck, and, *Chippy Chippy Cheeeeeep*, flap both arms, and *Chicka Chicka Cheeeeeep*, turn around and *Cheeka Cheeka Cheeeeeep.*' After a minute, they had to bend over, laughing.

Then she joked, 'Not bad, practise before you tell the President.'

In New York City, nurse Summer was sent to three hospitals a day, each with ten ICU wards with twenty beds apiece. Thirteen hospitals later, she had seen 2,500 patients crack up and laugh their heads off. Dr Ponti visited her on two occasions bringing a video team, and the YouTube video was sent to all states. It was named 'The Howler.' It went viral.

On his last day, Dr Ponti asked her, 'You've been able to empty ICU beds without killing the patients. Could you do another trick and stop people from getting infected?'

Summer looked at him askance, pondered and said, 'Dr Ponti, I'm no good at that. You need to talk to the man who walked on water for that one.'

*   *   *

Blew Ohrtman saw the video, discussed it with Petal, and asked, 'Why didn't you mention this to me?'

Petal said, 'I had to go to work early and left a note, and when I saw you at night, you said nothing. WHY NOT?' she yelled at him.

'I'm so proud of her, and you ignore her.'

He was silent, then, 'No, I ignored those stupid notes from you and threw them in the bin. I want a wife who talks to me, and I will ring Summer now and tell her how stupid I've been.' He left a voice recording, told her that he is proud of her and got a call back later.

She laughed, 'You proud of me? Are you feeling OK? Never mind, what took you so long?'

He admitted, 'I was an arsehole.'

She said, 'Ten bucks in the swear jar,' and he laughed for the first time since Trump lost the election.

April 6

Dorothy Thomson discussed the pandemic progress with her husband, Michael. She went to James Anderson, who was staying with her in Woodstream. She wanted to work out a psychology article that would get people past all the despair and use their app to ask for tests if anyone was sick. They got to work on it.

James asked: 'What do you think the real issue is here?'

Michelle replied, 'It is the ongoing forever and forever lockdowns without any hope of it getting better. There is no hope.'

James wanted to know, 'Why not?'

Michelle thought statistics are often meaningless and answered: 'We had two thousand deaths a day at Inauguration, and now we have 40,000. Even if it has dropped to 20,000, it's still ten times as bad as a month and a half ago. This is no improvement for them.'

Her daughter Deborah Hernandez, 19, overheard their discussion and puts in her two pennies worth.

'Mum and Dad, before we left for this place and before school was preparing to shut down, we had a project. Just after the

September Trump rallies when there were rapid increases in cases. Everyone was worried about the future. It seemed as if there wasn't one. We called the project, "What do you need to do to find the future?"'

'Well, Angel, how lucky you were eavesdropping on a private conversation,' said James with a sneaky smile that took the sting out. 'Well, don't just sit there; we need you. Desperately.'

'Going over the top with praise won't get you off the hook for that snide remark, but this is what our group came up with. If you don't understand how we got to this point, you won't deduct the solution. It's like bushfires. The whole of California was burning. On August 19, 2020, California Governor Gavin Newsom reported that the State was battling 367 known fires, many sparked by intense thunderstorms on August 16–17. How could we find a future with that going on? First, we had to understand the cause. Someone said thunderstorms. But is that the cause? No. Was it global warming? Partly. Was it scorching weather and strong winds? Partly. We needed to understand how it all hung together, or we would go round in circles, and why was the summer the hottest on record anyway?'

'You tell me,' said James, intrigued by his daughter. She was pretty articulate.

'It started with global warming and ended with Government inaction. Global warming has for years now caused the arctic permafrost to melt, and that is many million square miles, and it houses the world's greatest time bomb. You need to hear this; the world's greatest time bomb.'

She continued, 'Natalia Shakhova, a recognised expert on Methane Releases in the East Siberian Arctic Shelf, estimated in

2008 that not less than 1,400 gigatonnes of carbon[60] is currently locked up as *methane* and *methane* hydrates under the *Arctic* submarine permafrost.

'Dad, amounting to one-point-four trillion tons of methane with about seventy times the warming effect as carbon dioxide. As the air gets warmer, more methane is released, and it gets hotter and more permafrost melts. They have cities in Siberia where roads and houses have sunk and disappeared. More than 800,000 people have been displaced from their homes there. It can no longer be stopped. The tipping point was reached two years ago, and we need an ice age to stop this.'

'The other factors are the wildfires. Last year wildfires released more carbon dioxide than the whole of California's power stations combined, which gets back to the Arctic. The future for all of us in that? All manner of global cooperation between the US and Russia is needed to beat this beast.'

'The wildfires in California are only a fraction of those in Siberia. One big help would be thousands of DC10s converted to air tankers to extinguish fires as soon as they start. COVID has saved us here. There are thousands of abandoned perfect planes stored in our deserts. A bit of conversion, and we can supply the world with a solution.'

James and Michelle are overwhelmed with ideas, and they ask her to go back to their problem. To summarise, or they will go nuts.

Deborah delivers: 'Everyone needs to understand the problem, how we got here, overcome their scepticism and personal beliefs and commit to the science. Easy.'

---

[60] Shakhova et al. (2008) estimated that not less than 1,400 gigatonnes (Gt) of carbon is presently locked up as methane

James and Michelle decided to take the same approach to the pandemic problem but asked Deborah, 'How would you sum up the whole problem then?'

Deborah thought, 'The problem is people doing it their way. They know what to do, and then they do the opposite. They throw a tantrum if they can't protest. Then they spit the dummy when coming home if the wife won't kiss them. They want to look cool and not wear masks. Then they want to kiss the kids who don't want to be kissed because they've been told not to. Wives need to protect themselves; shoot the husbands maybe?'

'Wow. You are wound up,' exclaimed James.

Deborah replied, 'Yes, and because of them, my life is restricted. I want compensation.' Then she giggles. 'Great idea. They can pay for my college fees,' and she goes back to reading her magazine.

James and Michelle tried a few ideas. The solution was to appeal to their good nature rather than making them wrong, maybe to have a cute kid ask questions that hit home.

Like, 'Why did my Granny die?' When the father answers, 'Because Grandpa went out without a mask and when he came back, he had the virus and gave it to her. He got mildly sick, but she died.' The kid wants to know how Grandpa is now, and the father tells him, 'Better not ask him. He is so upset. And so guilty. But that is all too late now.'

The Frank Sinatra song, 'I Did it My Way,' played. James smacked his head.

'There it is. Gotcha, baby,' and he wrote his submission.

Frank Sinatra sang, 'I Did it My Way', and as long as you do it your way, the country will have more sick people than good ones. We don't want you labouring in guilt for years because you killed your loved ones. You would wish you were dead. Not good. But there is a solution. The new song is, 'I Did it Your Way.' Good on you, look forward to the good life you used to have.

Michelle loved it and called her daughter Deborah. They read it to her, and Deborah cracked up laughing.

'Good one, Dad. You should become a scriptwriter.'

The parents knew they had a message that would be a hit. It would be repeated like folklore, and they sent it off to Dorothy Thompson. Dorothy called back ten minutes later. She told them it would go out as a bulletin under James' name.

'You will be quoted and quoted, and shall I include your bio or photo?' James liked the background more than the razzamatazz foreground.

'Neither, please,' was the reply.

*   *   *

April 8

The President is in a good mood and jokes when he says, 'Dr Ponti, you may be out of a job soon. The cases are down.'

Dr Ponti smirks and says, 'Can't wait. Never wanted this job in the first place,' but then he asks if the President had seen the bulletin Dorothy Thompson had put out, crediting James Anderson.

He had and said, 'I laughed my head off when I read that. Can we see if he is willing to step in here and have a chat?' James had met the President before and was tickled pink.

Two days later, James was invited into the office and made to feel welcome, then the President came to the point.

'James, I saw your bulletin and cracked up. Then I wondered how you arrived at that. Did you just wake up one morning, and there it was?'

James told him, 'I wish that were the case, but then it would not be repeatable. We had a call from Dorothy to work out something that would entice people to follow your orders, and we consulted with our daughter Deborah, who's 19. She's an amazing girl.'

'She had done a school project on beating the Californian bushfires, and if you want help on that, you need to talk to her yourself. But it boiled down to the fact that people had to understand the whole problem, not just parts of it, and give up their beliefs and follow the science. From that, Michelle and I knocked up a spiel about kids asking why grandpa had to die, but that did not work. Then the radio played 'I Did it My Way', and there it was.'

The President had something to show him, turned on a monitor and played the Chicken Song.

James hooted with laughter, and the President told him, 'Now comes the hard part. Stand up. We are going to do the Chicken Song.'

James looked puzzled as the President said, 'Stand there, ready to move your neck and arms. Then follow this techno beat: do the chicken shuffle, then the voice-over,

> 'Chippy Chippy Cheeeeeep, Cheepy Cheepy Cheeeeeep turn your neck, and, Chippy Chippy Cheeeeeep, flap both arms, and Chicka Chicka Cheeeeeep, turn around and Cheeka Cheeka Cheeeeeep.' After a minute, they had to bend over, laughing.

James said, 'You must meet my daughter. She has a handle on the wildfires, and she would love to do the Chicken Song with you.'

Later that day, the President asked Dorothy to send out the Frank Sinatra message again. She did, but added a personal note from the President:

> From the President (with thanks to James Anderson, Washington).
>
> Please sing the new Frankie song, 'I Did it *Your* Way,' until the pandemic is over.
>
> Frank Sinatra sang, 'I Did it My Way', and as long as you do it your way, the country will have more sick people than healthy ones. We don't want you labouring in guilt for years because you were responsible for the death of your loved ones. You would wish you were dead in their place. Not good. But there is a solution. The new song is, 'I Did it Your Way.' Good on you, look forward to the good life you used to have by doing it our way: by following instructions.

*　　*　　*

April 10

Dr Ponti was pleased. He can be sacked shortly or quit, and that sounded better. Why was he so happy?

He spoke, 'I've seen your endorsement of the Frank Sinatra song, the one that says, 'I Did it Your Way.' New daily cases are down from twenty thousand to now ten thousand. I would have loved to meet that James Anderson.'

The President told him to stay around and meet his daughter Deborah Hernandez. 'She's been invited to teach me how to fight the Californian bushfires. She will be here in fifteen minutes. Then she will do the chicken dance with me.'

'Oh God,' said Ponti, 'I did that with Summer Ohrtman in New York. I can't wait. I'll record a video, and you can send it to her.'

The President welcomed Deborah, and at first, she was a bit nervous. The President noticed and asked her if she ever swore at home. She looked dubious about answering that one.

'Don't you like swearing?'

Her reply was, 'Not if I get into trouble.'

He said, 'I'd be in real trouble if people could hear me swear. So I do it late at night but not in front of my wife.'

Deborah burst out laughing, 'I don't believe you unless you show me now.

So he did. '@#$%&! and Fuck, I forgot the rest.'

She howled with laughter. 'You want to be my uncle?' she asked, and he agreed.

'Honorary, OK?'

Then she set out to work the problem. She finished with, 'It was our class that did the work, but it boiled down to avoid the simplistic solution that addresses only a small part. They need to extract the methane out of the air in the tundra and burn it to produce electricity. That produces almost no global warming and removes this most deadly methane greenhouse gas. In the meantime, you must fight wildfires when they first start, not when they are mega-fires.'

The President was pleased, and he told her, 'We were going to purchase several thousand planes stored in the desert because of the collapse of air travel and convert them into air tankers. The DC-10 can carry 80 tons of cargo.' Then he told her that he wanted another thousand to send overseas. To Russia for Siberian fires, then France and Spain and Greece.

Deborah added, 'If a greenie gets in the way, take him along for a rise in an Airtanker.'

Then he told her to stand. 'I have a treat for you, Deborah. Stand there, ready to move your neck and arms? Then follow this techno beat: do the chicken shuffle, then the voice-over of these chicken noises,

> '*Chippy Chippy Cheeeeeep, Cheepy Cheepy Cheeeeeep* turn your neck, and, *Chippy Chippy Cheeeeeep*, flap both arms, and *Chicka Chicka Cheeeeeep*, turn around and *Cheeka Cheeka Cheeeeeep*.' then they stopped when they had to bend over laughing.

Dr Ponti told her he had recorded a video. She was very excited when she saw it and asked if she could have a copy.

'Yes,' said the President, 'And you can show it to your class and tell them it was a thank you for helping with bushfires.'

'You're not too bad for a young bloke, Mr President,' she laughed. It had been a good morning.

*   *   *

April 12

The Army had set up temporary field orphanages in most cities. Traumatised children were crying for Mummy and Daddy, but many were easily distracted. There were children to play with, and the Army had sent soldiers to be childcare teachers. The motto was, 'Good training for later on in life.' But the kids badly needed dolls and teddy bears.

Lt. Col. Freebody discussed this with the President, and he suggested, 'Mr President. We have thirty thousand plus kiddies, and we need that number of bears and dolls. I think most kids would love a dog, even though some would be scared. Why don't we advertise for them? Fifteen thousand dolls, the same number of teddies, and be dressed in Army uniforms.'

He continued, 'All those old biddies would have a field day making lady doll Captain's dresses and boy teddy Sergeants. Great PR exercise, good for mental health as well. Each State does its bit. People will love it.'

It was agreed, and the orders went out.

*　　*　　*

April 14

Near Washington Avenue Elementary School, the Army took the toddlers to the orphanages from wherever they had found them. One soldier, a Private, had been assigned ten kids. He knew nothing about kids. But he knew he'd have to make them smile. He asked them, 'What is my name?'

One kid knew. 'It's Sir.'

The Private was impressed. 'Yes. My parents could not think of a name, so they called me "Sir". A great name in the Army. When somebody says, "Who are you?" I reply, "Yes, Sir," and they want to know what the question was. I say, "Who are you?" and I get locked up for insubordination. Do you know what that is?'

One kid said, 'Yes, it means you're in the poo.' That did the trick.

Then he asked them who needed a doll or teddy bear. One of the boys wanted a doll, and some girls wanted a teddy.

'I've got good news for you guys,' said Private Sir. 'We had made thousands of dolls and bears, and none of the soldiers wanted a doll, and none wanted a teddy bear either. So I have a box outside. Full of them. Who wants to help me carry it in?' They all did. There was a bit of commotion when the box was opened.

All the dolls were in Army uniform. Lovely little dolls like a Barbie in uniform, with stylish Kepi hats and tight skirts. The bears were all little fat bears, wearing blue Army trousers as they had in the Cavalry a hundred years ago, with red braces and black boots. All the boys loved them. The girls wanted to undo the skirts on the dolls. Why? To see what was on underneath. Nice undies?

An officer stepped into the room.

'How's it going?' he asked.

The Private reported, 'No tears insight, Sir.'

The Officer left. The kids liked that Private Sir. He played Cowboys and Indians with them.

'Who wants to be the Indians?'

The boys wanted to be the US Army Cavalry, and Indians had to look different, so the girls were the Indians. Whether they liked it or not. But Indian squaws were so pretty, so they liked it a lot.

*   *   *

Deborah Hernandez was at Woodstream in her wilderness hideout at much the same time. When she had come home from the White House, she didn't exactly hold back on telling the family about the President and the Chicken Song. Her mum

Michelle wanted to know about that, and James, her dad, told them all, for the first time, that he had done the Chicken Song dance with the President.

'Oh, so you chicken danced with the President and never told anyone? How come?'

James told them he knew that Deborah was going to the White House, and he didn't want to spoil her surprise.

'OK, everyone. In a line. We do this now.' She made sure they would do the chicken dance with her. 'Stand there, ready to move your neck and arms? Then follow this techno beat: do the chicken shuffle, then the voice-over,

> 'Chippy Chippy Cheeeeeep, Cheepy Cheepy Cheeeeeep turn your neck, and, Chippy Chippy Cheeeeeep, flap both arms, and Chicka Chicka Cheeeeeep, turn around and Cheeka Cheeka Cheeeeeep.' then they sceeched with laughter

Deborah told them that the President had shown her a video of a nurse singing and dancing the Chicken Song in a hospital in Columbus. How her nearly dying brother recovered, and how she went through all the wards and everyone got better. James, being James and a psychologist, suggested that the laughter may have triggered an immune system response. The Medical Association of America had distributed the video through all hospitals and emptied the ICU units of patients. They walked home after ten days. Unheard of.

Deborah decided to drive home and get a few things, including her iPad that she had left behind. The car radio was on, and it told of a field orphanage that was just near where she was right now. She had an idea, stopped, and asked who was in charge.

Who was in charge was a gangly soldier with a Kepi cap playing Cowboys and Indians with a wild mob of kids. He had wound those kids up and didn't know how to wind them down. He grinned and said, 'Help.'

Deborah decided she could. She put two fingers in her mouth and let out a piercing whistle. It was like a movie playing havoc, and suddenly the movie stopped. They looked at her, and little Johnnie said, 'Miss, we're having fun. So hurry up.'

She made sure they would do the Chicken Song with her. 'Stand there, ready to move your neck and arms? Ready? Then follow this techno beat: do the chicken shuffle, then the voice-over,

> 'Chippy Chippy Cheeeeeep, Cheepy Cheepy Cheeeeeep turn your neck, and, Chippy Chippy Cheeeeeep, flap both arms, and Chicka Chicka Cheeeeeep, turn around and Cheeka Cheeka Cheeeeeep.' and keep going till you have to bend over, laughing.

She whistled again. Silence. She addressed them.

'I have to go home now, but shall I come back before I'm heading back to Maryland?'

There was a chorus of approval, but they wanted her to teach Sir first. That was even funnier. He wasn't a dancer. He was stiff, and the kids howled at his discomfort.

Then she took him in her arms and said, 'I won't hurt you,' but he blushed. A girl was holding him. That did it, and he went from shy to an extrovert in a second. He was doing great when his Officer walked back in.

*   *   *

April 16

Mary Rose Tehan was in their hideout at Beech Fork State Park in West Virginia when she decided to take the kids to Charleston. Even though the wilderness was attractive, they were a long way from home in Tennessee and had come here to be with friends; Jason and Lilly Pennewell from Pittsburgh.

The men had both been Trump supporters, and Gus Tehran's son Buster, 16, wanted to be like Trump too. The rest were all Democrat-leaning, but Gus had moral support from his son Buster and Jason Pennewell.

The women were a perfect friendship match – humour, ideas, and, as a teacher Lilly was good at empathy, as well as running a daily two-hour class in their cabins. Sometimes Jason attended. He was always impressed with her way of dealing with things.

This morning she discussed the pandemic, how bad it had gotten and how the daily cases were almost down to nothing. Jason interrupted her shortly after she started to rattle off the case numbers. And he complained:

'We are just back to where we were when Trump was still in the White House, and you make it seem like a miracle that we are back to those numbers.'

Eliza Tehan, 19, a university student, was keen to exert her influence and asked, 'What do you get when you compare apples and oranges?'

Jason was content to think you got a bullshit answer, and Eliza elaborated what she had learned.

'First, we had a virus you could catch from man a yard away, and many people managed to stay healthy. That was during the Trump era - if they practised social distancing and wore masks. Then the virus mutated, and now much more infectious strains appeared: the UK, South African, Brazilian, and after the blue neck strain that killed in three days, the recent West Coast strain. Get within four yards away from an infected person, and you get it too.'

'So why did we get those mutations only after Trump?' asked Jason, gleeful to put her on the spot.

'They were first discovered early December and went rampant from there. Trump was still in the White House, by the way. Or he was playing golf. Nobody was testing for the new strain until doctors realised what was happening, and no contact tracing was in place to stop it. Now almost all infections are these new virulent strains.'

Then she added a Trump teaser, 'And the reason we were unable to trace the new strains was that there were so many of the Trump era cases, that we were run off our feet and could not catch up with testing. The danger of mutation increased daily as more infected people were in close contact.'

'So how did that stop then, oh smart one?' asked Jason, and Eliza was ready for him.

'The President did what any President would do. He locked the places down, first some postcodes, then cities, then everything. If you want to, compare that with Trump. There would have been no lockdowns. Do you like that? We would all be dead by now. Place stinking with dead bodies.'

'You don't believe that, do you?' asked Jason, and Eliza told him.

'Next week, when I have time, I will do the maths and get the case projections software and prove it to you. What do I get if I'm right?' she asked.

'Why not now?' Jason wanted to know.

'Because the panic about the pandemic is over, and the lockdowns are gone. Can you believe it? I'm going to town to have my hair done, then my nails, then a pedicure, and then a pizza. Mum, too.'

CHAPTER 24

Mood

'If the cases are down, why do we still need lockdowns?' was the question on most people's minds a month later in May. The pandemic was almost over. New cases were down to 1,000 per day, and contact tracing and social distancing continued. Local lockdowns were only ordered when there was a new outbreak. Miraculously, people did not complain; but quite a few ignored the instructions.

Lockdowns were now more challenging than before, as there were now many small areas in lockdown instead of just the whole state. It was just for two or three days to get on top of new outbreaks. Pandemic fatigue was growing, and James Anderson had sent a message with his 'I Did it Your Way' campaign. People had related to that one instantly.

Argus had woken early and watched a new dawn, and after some quick research, found that America was facing a new dawn too. He wondered if there would be any speed humps on the way to zero daily cases. There were bound to be, but even so, it would be all over in a week or two. He wondered how that Holly Whistler kid was going, and he sent a quick email to John Orthallo.

Dear Mr Orthallo

My name is Argus E from the Andaman Islands in the Bay of Bengal. I have been advising the Indian government on how the US handles the pandemic, as our islanders would be very susceptible to any virus outbreak here.

Dorothy Thompson gave me your email when I asked her after sharing the news you had picked up Holly. We were both so intrigued that she wanted a new daddy rather than a mummy. I would love to see that spunky kid and would love to hear back from you. A picture or even a video would be handled with utter discretion. Please let me know if I can email you again.

Dr Eashan Acharya, a.k.a Argus E

MSc., Port Blair, Andaman Islands, India

*   *   *

May 17

The President and Dr Ponti faced a new battle. The daily cases had been down to one thousand. This morning showed that yesterday's total was closer to two thousand. Some people were not following instructions. The President wanted action, and it was Dr Ponti's job to formulate it.

The aim was to propel people into action to follow orders. How? Scare the pants off them? How? The big bad wolf, the fourth wave, was being caused by a few and will affect the whole country, and if **you** are responsible, people will gang up on you. Not good.

With that, Dr Ponti crafted his bulletin. That was the only weapon available to him, and it was going to get used right now.

From the President's Health Advisor

There is good news and bad news. First off, the good news. You already know the daily case numbers had come down to a thousand. A miracle. It was created by YOU, by following instructions.

Now, the bad news. Yesterday's case numbers are up again, double. How will this affect you? It could be a fourth wave, more extensive than anything we've seen. If your neighbours have noticed that YOU had not followed instructions and another lockdown is implemented, they may well come after you. They will be after blood. Anyone ignoring orders will be arrested and jailed for three months. That's a long time in jail.

Dr Federico Ponti, Health Adviser to the President

Dr Ponti asked the President if that was too tough, he replied, 'Dr Ponti, I love it when your name is on that, as it's pretty tough, and I won't get a bad name.'

The bulletin went out. Then they discussed the Medical Association of America (MAA) bulletin.

The MMA had distributed the YouTube clip of the Chicken Song impersonation and dance by Summer Ohrtman to all hospitals. By this time, over 40,000 COVID ICU patients had seen it played over and over, until they walked home ten days later.

The President asked Dr Ponti to recall his experience with Summer Ohrtman and said: 'I think we should sponsor a Civic Function for her in Columbus. Nothing too over the top.'

'She is not shy, but she does not seek the limelight. She is the most un-affected and decent young lady I have ever met, so we should not embarrass her with pomp and ceremony,' advised Dr Ponti. The President had an idea:

'I know what I will do. Summer will love this. I will send my granddaughter, Nancy. They are of a similar age, and they will hit it off, I'm sure.'

*   *   *

TV channels had shown people doing fun and crazy things in the streets to amuse people isolated in lockdown. Even though not paid work, artists stepped up and generated a whole new medium and following, many becoming famous when their YouTube videos went viral. That was good for future employment. Rappers had a field day. The Techno beat of the Chicken Song suited them. They added words like:

> 'Chippy Chippy Cheeeeeep, Cheepy Cheepy Cheeeeeep turn the neck, and, Chippy Chippy Cheeeeeep, flap both arms, and Chicka Chicka Cheeeeeep, turn around and Cheeka Cheeka Cheeeeeep.'

Whilst the Summer Ohrtman video was distributed to all hospitals, the new wave became the dominant entertainment.

The kids in the orphanages started with the Chicken Song in the morning. Not one child felt alone. They were all in this together.

*   *   *

May 18

New outbreaks threatened this fragile success. Case numbers were suddenly rising again. The President issued a new order:

> New Lockdown orders.
>
> Lockdowns will apply immediately in hotspots. The Army is chasing contact details like a ferret after a rabbit. Their new motto is 'Off the street with you.'
>
> The aim is to have close contacts of new infections identified in ten minutes and tested minutes later. We urge all to continue checking in using your QR codes if you go to any public venue so that this testing is feasible.
>
> Most people used their QR-Code tracing app, so it was quick work to identify contact trails. Some were not, and they need a nudge.

May 19

The Orthallo and Sanderson families were in the Bothe-Napa Valley State Park. They listened to the daily news bulletins, John rounded up all seven kids, and asked, 'What do you want to hear first? Good news or bad news?'

They all wanted the good news first and no bad news.

John told them, 'The good news is that we're all going home tomorrow.'

Peter, one of the kids, broke rank and wanted to know the bad news. 'Just whisper in my ear; the others don't want to hear.'

John whispered, 'The bad news is we're all going home.' Peter burst out laughing, a lovely gleeful sound, and the others wanted to know what it was.

'Can't tell you; you didn't want to know.' replied Peter.

They were a typical family, but John took pity on them. 'The bad news is that we're going home tomorrow. That means we need to clean up this campsite. Let's make it fit for a mummy bear with three cubs.' That did the trick. They couldn't have cute baby bears getting hurt from the mess lying around. Needed to protect them, and mummy bear too.

The Orthallo family returned to Portland, Oregon, with their kids, plus Holly Whistler from Marin City just south of San Fran. They had found her more than a month ago, walking the road waving frantically to get help. She liked John, bearded as her Dad had been. She had what was known as lip, and John described her as four going on ten. She had been an only child and was used to adult language, which sounded so cute on a four-year-old.

When asked which of the two-family parents looked like hers, she had picked 'the bearded one.' He had to be her interim Dad, whether he liked it or not. As far as Holly was concerned, 'Looks like my Dad, is my Dad,' after she had heard her Dad often say, 'Looks like a duck and quacks like a duck, it is a duck.' So there.

Peter, 5, and Lindsey Orthallo 7, adored her. Lindsey had always wanted a sister, and this one was perfect. She was like a toy, but you didn't have to wind her up. 'She winds herself up, Mum,' she was heard saying one day.

Sue Anne Orthallo was a teacher, and after another of Holly's adult quips that had them in stitches, her mum said, 'I'm gonna have to teach that ten-year-old to become a four-year-old again.'

The good news in Portland was, the schools were open again. Even better, plenty of kids to play with.

Sue Anne occasionally picked up Holly to hug her, but Holly soon wriggled out of Sue Anne's arms. *Something is going on here*, she thought. *I must find out without pressuring her*, and asked 'Holly, did you like hugging your mum?' The answer floored her.

'I never hugged my mum. I just hugged my Dad.'

Something is going on here, thought Sue Anne, determined to go slow on this one. Holly would need to talk about something, obviously, but she did not seem to want to. *I wonder what it is? It must be pretty potent. It's as though she never loved her mum.*

*   *   *

Max and Dominique Sanderson had taken the orphaned Walden kids they had picked up two months earlier; Maxi, 4, and Emmy, 7. The Sanderson kids, Johan and Emily, now had a toy brother and toy sister to play with. Emily loved playing dollhouse games with Emmy. Emily was the mummy teaching her daughter Emmy. Johan was a cheerful dreamer and liked playing with his toy animals. He had a toy spider the same size as his toy elephant. He loved telling Maxi how big elephants were and how tiny spiders were. They discussed which was the more dangerous.

*   *   *

May 25

Argus E wanted to see what the republicans were up to. Just to get a balanced view and he monitored Mitch Upton, who had proved to be a pretty responsible man, even if he did break rules when it suited him.

Mitch Upton complained about a three-day lockdown because of three new infections in Houston. His wife Dannielle chatted with her neighbour, nurse Julianne Klimmer. Julianne had seen the Summer Ohrtman Chicken Song, and she explained what had happened. Then they do the chicken dance, just as Mitch walks in.

'Is that the way you behave when I'm not around?' he hooted with laughter.

Then they get onto the QR codes, which Mitch hated.

*   *   *

May 26

It was time for the President to attend to other issues that had figured prominently in his election promises, namely Global Warming and how to tackle it.

The President had invited six oil executives to a meeting. This meeting was about politics, and to get something, he would give them something first. An incentive and he started the discussion:

'Gentlemen. First I want to thank you for coming. You may be thinking "what does he want to take away from us?" So, hands up all those of you who had that worry?' Six hands went up.

'But I have good news too. I need you to start a new multi-trillion-dollar industry before I can afford to tackle the oil and coal issues. Because I know you are all busy executives, anyone not interested in hearing about this new industry is free to leave. We will start straight after I return from the bathroom.' The President left, had a glass of water, waited two minutes and returned. No one had left.

'Before I start, you need to know this. I have a plan to beat wildfires, not only in California but also in all major fire risk places around the world. Could anyone please tell me of the other biggest fires last year?'

Suggestions included Alaska, Spain, Greece.

'Any others?'

Mitch Upton volunteered Siberia.

'Good, someone does know his fires. Now to the opportunities. I will tell you what I know, and you will get a handout when you leave. These are the actions I have taken so far.'

'We have brought over three thousand planes from desert storage. Those DC10s, 747s and some MD-11s. The 747s can carry 100 to 110 tons of cargo, depending on the model. The DC-10 Series 30 can take 80, and the MD-11 can carry 89 tons. They will all be converted to air tankers to bombard wildfires, with infra-red heat seekers to help locate fire fronts accurately in smoke. I have bought engineering maintenance and pilots from airlines, and Airforce pilots will be training the new pilots in low-level water bombing.'

The President allowed that to sink in, then continued:

'We are keeping one thousand for the US, including Alaska. Drones will monitor from a height - looking for fires, and within ten minutes, birds will take off with eighty or more tons of water to put the fires out there and then. No more mega-fires.'

'A thousand will be sold to Russia for Siberian fires, at cost plus, and the same for southern Europe.'

'Now comes the why. The real why. The scary reason is that the carbon dioxide released by fires last year in California exceeded the total greenhouse emissions from power generators. Why is that bad? Because the warming had started a significant melt of arctic permafrost. Bad why? Because it has released millions of tons of methane, which has seventy times the global warming effect of carbon dioxide. Bad why? The total methane holdings in arctic permafrost were estimated to be one point four *trillion* tons of methane - and artic summer temperatures are? Any offers?'

Mitch Upton had a go, 'Minus fifty in winter, so maybe a maximum of plus ten in summer?'

The President answered, 'Last year the maximum Siberian temperature reached 42 degrees Celsius, and it has been rising by three degrees a year. You could say global warming has passed a tipping point and cannot be corrected. Did you know that methane spurts out of the ground there and just ignites?

'I have started an international program to extract methane from Siberia's air, to feed power stations generating electricity at low emissions, and take the harmful methane gas out of the atmosphere. If we don't achieve that, how hot do you think the maximum temperature in California will be, say fifty miles inland?'

There was silence, and the President filled it. 'Last year, we had 54 degrees Celsius in Death Valley. If we get the same increases as Siberia, that could be 54 degrees in Los Angeles in three years. Millions would die.'

The President changed direction.

'When you leave, there will be a handout. You can do the maths later, but we need to get to carbon neutral ASAP. And here is a present for you.'

They looked puzzled. The executives are suddenly afraid, a world where oil spells death, what can save them?

'Gentlemen, I need your skills to develop two or three infrastructures. The first is to assist the new development of hydrogen-powered heavy-duty combustion engines in replacing diesel, from trucks to trains and ships. The technology exists. It needs to be scaled up. It's a new capability, and you can make a motza if you support it.'

'The second is coal power plants. If you think there is a long-term future in them, then good luck. We need electricity storage, such as batteries for short-term support, or hydro or pumped hydro for longer-term support. There is also the experiment in nuclear fusion, nearing operational capability. It does not generate deadly nuclear by-products or those suitable for warheads. The electric car is already a going concern but needs decent grid charging infrastructure.'

'And lastly, we need people working with oil and gas to work on methane extraction to generate electricity. It keys in with your industries. It's a half a trillion-dollar industry waiting for you to pick up. I can smooth all the hurdles. Let me know what you need from me. Other than the money, I mean, but the days of three to four-year approval processes are gone, believe me.'

The six oil and gas executives left, quite excited. One was heard saying, 'And here I was expecting to have my balls chopped off, and instead I get a Christmas present come early.'

*   *   *

A fourth wave had started. There were now 4,200 new cases. In April, there were 2,000 and trending down. The President called for a council of war meeting. This was a war, and he needed to win it in a week, then he needed a month of no infections to allow Independence Day celebrations to go ahead. The President met with his go-to men; Dr Ponti, Lt. Col. Freebody, his Army Chief of Staff, and his Attorney General. He outlined the purpose of the meeting, even though it was included in the invitation. When he started to speak, they noticed immediately the difference between the steel of his words and the kind written invitations; worlds apart. He had started:

'I have one goal today: to put in place enforceable actions to ensure that there are no new cases by this time next week. I mean none. That means some tough measures for penalties for non-compliance that we will announce today. It also means new measures that must ensure the outcome. I want to announce that if we retain zero cases for thirty days from June 4, then we can have normal Independence Day celebrations. With masks, of course. If we get just one case, it's off; no holiday, no fun. No future. So starting with you, Dr Ponti, how do we achieve that?'

Dr Ponti had heard the steel in the President's voice. This was not a friendly picnic. This was total war on people not following instructions, the toughest ever. He suggested:

'If you want to kill the outbreak with the resources we have, then we need a three-day lockdown on any area that had two or more cases, and test all family members in their home, with a test van out in the street for instant feedback. When we find infections, we need to follow them and trace all contacts. Therefore, as of today, we police people entering any large shopping area. They have to scan the shop QR codes before entry. A soldier will need to be on sentry.'

He continued, 'We should offer devices to all testing officers to immediately email search centres to identify close contact identification and testing. Infected cases must be immediately taken to a field hospital to get them out of the community. Families of infected people should be tested and again in two and four days. We need to make changes to get absolute adherence to orders, so we had better work on those.'

The President asked Lt. Col Freebody to work on the details to achieve that. Freebody knew that he had to deliver, no matter how hard it would be, as the story starts with people doing the right thing. He was the civil disorder control expert for the Army; it was his job to manage that. He outlined his proposed bulletin.

> By Order of the President.

> Anyone in a lockdown area must stay home for three days, effective immediately. When not in lockdown or at home, masks must be worn, social distancing maintained, and QR codes scanned on entry to any venue. This fourth wave must be contained and eliminated in a hurry, which can only be achieved by following these orders. Anyone not following orders will be detained in jail, not to be released until two months after zero cases have been achieved.

When the President approved the orders, Lt. Col. Freebody sent the testing and monitoring instructions to his headquarters, who would distribute it to all states.

*　　*　　*

May 27

There were now 4,900 new cases. Yesterday there were 4,200, so the numbers were still trending up. The President asked:

'What happened; who stuffed up, how many were arrested, how many tests were conducted, how many places had three or more infections? How many contracts were found via the QR codes? How many people failed to log into QR codes at all places they had visited?'

Dr Ponti answered. 'I knew you would want to know all that. I had set up a dashboard yesterday for all those questions, and the dashboard can display totals by state, city zip code, or lockdown area. I can show you on my tablet later. One case had been discovered, but the contacts they had made in the last 48 hours covered tens of miles.'

He continued, 'So, if someone now infected had been at a Walmart ten miles away, we know who else was at Walmart, in contact with a teller or two, but that does not mean he was in contact with all other visitors. We found out what he, or she, had purchased and tested all tellers involved. Then we posted a radio and TV bulletin to ask anyone who visited the store between the advertised times to return for a fast test.'

'The vast majority of new cases came from people who had been in contact with the first discovered cases the day before. As most recent infections were highly infectious, we can expect new numbers to go upwards for a few days that it takes for the new infections to be detectable.'

'We had twenty arrests for not wearing masks, a hundred for not social distancing, and a thousand leaving home when their area was in lockdown.'

The President was impressed by the amount of work done but wanted the Colonel to issue a new bulletin with the number of arrests, who were now jailed for at least three months.

The President received the next daily update. There were now 6,200 new cases, 750 arrests, and a new warning was issued:

From the President

It is totally unacceptable that some people are not following orders. They will be jailed. It is highly suggested that these people look up the statistics of what happens to people in jail before they do something stupid. The cost is too high. The Covid-safe app on your cell phone will show the lockdown areas for your current location. Remember, although your home address may not be in lockdown, you must not enter any lockdown location. Those arrested yesterday and the day before who inadvertently wandered into a lockdown area will be released from detainment today, as they may not have known about this rule. This has been the one warning and will not be repeated.

The next daily update was presented to the President. There were now 7,100 new cases, ten arrests. It almost looked as if the cases had peaked.

May 29

Again, the President received the daily update. There were now 4,200 new cases, no arrests. Dr Ponti wanted to bet with the President on tomorrow's figures. The offer was not accepted, but the President offered Dr Ponti a one-week holiday at any place of his choosing if they could clear the cases by June 4.

'You too, Colonel,' added the President, 'But not together,' he chuckled.

On the last day of May, there were now 1,200 new cases, and things were looking good.

June 1

There were now 200 new cases, and the President remarked:

'Mopping up the last ones seems to take forever. Almost like good behaviour fatigue. We must put out a bulletin. When we allow Independence Day celebrations, we need to maintain this vigilance for a whole month. Shall we use the stick or the carrot, Colonel?'

Lt. Col. Freebody thought he would like to use the stick, a massive one, but his experience won out over his frustrations. The following is what he sent out:

> The American people have made an amazing discovery. Earth-shattering. They discovered that they could follow orders, and the result will be that we will almost certainly be able to announce Independence Day celebrations. That would be so marvellous.
>
> The nation has waited for this for a year or more. If just one person ignores health orders and starts a fifth wave, their name and photo will be in all newspapers. Not a great way to be famous. Is this a celebration? Yes. Is it also a risk? Definitely.
>
> Lt. Col. Freebody, US Army Washington.

The next day there were just two new cases. One day to go.

June 3

At last, a week after the President's Independence Day campaign starting, the outbreak was under control. The President issued a bulletin:

> From the Presidents
>
> The nation has pulled together.
>
> We need to maintain this outstanding cooperation for a month to get the reward. Every day we need to do this for each other. Because Americans are so good at it by now, they will need to do this for two more months after that.
>
> Then we need to help other countries wipe this foul Pandemic off the face of the earth. At least

America can show them how it's done. The vaccines will help but not for all strains, not until new vaccines are developed. That is why your achievement is so magnificent. Your cooperation did it, not the vaccines.

When other countries are virus-free, airlines and tourist operations worldwide can recover. It's all waiting for your country.

CHAPTER 25

Mood

The joy was so visible; people smiled just because they could. They had their country back and their jobs were coming back, or on the way. They were the Americans they used to be: optimistic.

Argus had been monitoring the mood across the country. Yes, it was like V Day in 1945; well, not quite, as people were only now noticing that the lockdowns had ended. There was no ticker tape, but the anxiety felt by so many had disappeared.

'What's next? It's not Independence Day yet, but surely there would be some celebrations.' He would celebrate anyway.

June 16, Midday

John and Sue Anne Orthallo commented on the recent effort to wipe out a fourth wave.

Sue Anne said, 'I don't know if you noticed this. Three weeks ago, we were down to a thousand cases daily and trending down. Suddenly it raced back up to almost 8,000 daily. I was worried we'd start all over again.'

John had not noticed. He was back on building sites. All he wanted was a beer when he returned home from work and then to play with the kids. Sue Anne explained the statistics and how they got the outbreak under control.

'The President issued a bulletin that had the strictest instructions I have ever seen. In effect, it said that if we catch you ignoring orders, you will be jailed, with no appeal, for a minimum of 90 days, to make sure the country is free of the virus for one month; and to allow for safe Independence Day celebrations. And that people would remain jailed for another two months to ensure we are in the clear. The bulletin said: "We don't trust you if you ignore instructions, and we can't afford to endanger the community". And it said, "You go to jail. It's not a great place to be".

John went to see his daughter Lindsey, who was playing with Holly, his cracker newcomer. John had given up feeling guilty about loving Holly the same as Lindsey.

He told them there was a party coming up. Lindsey suggested 'Independence Party,' and John asked them what they wanted to do.

'Party,' Lindsay answered.

'I have four conditions,' said John. 'One is you have to be good all day.'

Holly interrupted, 'Won't happen.'

John smirked and went on. He had done that on purpose to feed the smart-mouth attitude that Sue Anne was trying to stamp out. 'Two is you have to watch me all day standing on my head.'

This time Holly smirked, like, 'Who are you kidding?'

'We can have a picnic at the Oregon Redwood trail. They have a rope ladder, and if you don't fall off, the sky's the limit. I'll come up with you and help you onto a flying fox. Do you know what that is?' asked John, and Holly thought it was a fox that flies.

'Not quite. Did you want to fly?' John asked and proceeded to explain the Flying Fox.' Do you know why we are going to do that?' he asked.

Holly said, 'Party.'

John asked her, 'But why are we partying?'

Holly offered, 'To celebrate?'

'What are we celebrating?' asked John.

Holly had the answer: 'no more dead people,' and that is how Independence Day became 'End of Dead Day' for her.

'When?' was the only remaining question.

'In three weeks,' and this was a slight disappointment.

The next day there was a buzz in the air. There was going to be a gathering in Portland, and the Orthallos were preparing to attend. John asked all the kids if they had seen any wildfires last year. Lindsey had.

'Dad, it was so scary. People with fire trucks had to drive into the fire. I couldn't have. It's too scary.'

John told them the Government had a new way to fight fires now. A big plane flies over the fire and drops tons and tons of water on them to put them out.

Holly asked, 'Why didn't they do that before?'

John told her, 'The new Government decided to do something about that. They acquired all the planes that could not fly because of the pandemic and turned them into firefighter planes to put out fires before they became monster fires no one could put out. John told them all they would get in the car now and drive to a demonstration.

Someone directed them to a football stadium car park. Thousands had already gathered; there was a buzz of voices. It seemed everyone was excited. A speakerphone announced the planes would come over any minute. The crowd went silent. A noise penetrated the air as a massive plane flew over. It was so close to the ground that the kids ducked their heads. They saw it turn around and come back from the other direction over a ploughed wheat field, and then the skies seemed to open, and more water than a whole swimming pool dropped onto the field. Peter and Lindsey Orthallo had to hold on to Holly, who wanted to play in the wet.

Then a bit closer, they noticed someone had dropped a large load of timber. Crappy stuff, maybe ten semi-trailer loads of it; all in a great big fat line. Someone lit a flare and threw it on the wood, which had obviously been soaked in petrol, and up she went. The plane came back, and blood seemed to pour out from under it. It was a spectacular red liquid. The next thing they knew, there was no fire.

There was an announcement from behind them:

'Please give a warm welcome to Deborah Hernandez, the young lady who went to see the President with this ingenious idea.'

Everyone turned around, and they were facing a raised podium. A young woman entered by the steps from the right, and an older woman, the MC, welcomed her. People clapped and cheered even if they did not know what she had done. The MC introduced herself first. She was the Mayoress of Portland North and continued:

'You have someone here who did what she could to solve our bushfire problems. You have just seen the planes. A big cheer if you think that was awesome.' She waited for the roar to die down and continued.

'Please welcome Deborah Hernandez again, and then she can tell you all.'

Deborah took the microphone:

'Thank you, Mayoress, for that heart-warming introduction. I am an ecology student at Washington State University. We had a project about how to stop the bushfires, and someone said, "Put them out". Yes, and that is what those planes did. But there's more to it. Don't groan. There's always more to it. Bear with me. It only takes one minute.'

'We started to look at global warming being the cause of bushfires. Then, I overheard my parents discussing the big problem of people following the lockdown instructions. It boiled down to looking at the whole problem. The President invited my Dad James Anderson to help with the psychology of people following orders, and the President wanted to know how he arrived at the solution. Dear old Dad, over there on my right, said I had helped and that I also had a solution for the wildfires ravaging huge tracts of forests. I'm here because he could not keep his mouth shut.'

Loud applause for 'dear old dad' was heard, and she waited until it had died down.

'He is the one who came up with the message to take that Frank Sinatra song and make it into "I Did it Your Way", and it worked.' She stopped and looked at her watch.

'On time. That's all I did. But you know, I do love medals.'

The Mayoress signalled to a young woman waiting in the wings. She then introduced her. 'Ladies and Gentlemen, as a special thank you to this young lady. The President of the United

States has sent an envoy to present an award. Please give a warm welcome to Mairie.'

The applause died down once Mairie stepped onto the stage and announced, 'That's enough, or I will blush.'

A few voices asked for 'More blushes please, Mairie,' and she smiled timidly. Then she spoke:

'For the last three months, the President has had to deal with such a vast number of problems that it made my head spin. He's four times my age. He asked me to thank Deborah because she helped shift the load. Her father, James Anderson, did too. He will be honoured later tonight at City Hall at seven, and you are all invited! Drinks at six. Masks still to be worn, of course. Let's all be safe'

'Back to Deborah now. My grandfather had these specially made for her. They are the only ones in existence,' said Mairie, and at the snap of her fingers, a man was ushered in with a five-foot replica of a DC10 water bomber and a three-foot fire truck. He held one in each hand.

Deborah said, 'I think my Dad needs to carry them for me - but please hold them high so everyone can see them. My brother will go crazy when he sees these.'

Now there was genuine applause, and voices called for 'Dear old Dad.' Dad came to the microphone.

'Now you're in trouble,' he said with a smiling face.

John and Sue Anne Orthallo were close to the front, and she said, 'Look, John, it's James Anderson. And Michele. What a coincidence.' Sue Anne waved. Michelle's face lit up, and she waved back, indicating to stay, and they met up.

James and Michelle had met the two kids before, but now there was a third one. 'Fast work, buddy,' he said, and they mentioned how they had met Holly.

Michelle looked pitifully at Holly and asked her how she felt now.

'My dad had a beard, and he looks just like my new dad, so I told him that my father used to say, "Looks like a duck, walks like a duck, quacks like a duck, is a duck", so I thought, "Looks like my dad, speaks like my dad, smells like my dad, must be my dad." Easy.' She wandered off to look at the microphone.

'Stop her!' yelled Sue Anne. 'You never know what's going to come out of that mouth.' She dragged her away to something more interesting.

The kids had an older sister now, all in safe hands. John wanted to know how the 'I Did it Your Way' song came about.

'The start was Deborah's insistence that we had to look at the whole story to get a solution that worked, so I wrote a fable where a bloke arrived at the Pearly Gates and was sent to an eternity punishment centre because he had not followed instructions. A bit weird, but ten minutes later, I heard the Frank Sinatra song, "I Did it My Way." Bingo. I transposed Frank Sinatra's song to be "I Did it Your Way". So obvious.'

Michelle spoke to Sue Anne about Holly. She wanted to know how this four-year-old was coping without her Mum. She seemed to have replaced her Dad by adopting John.

Sue Anne asked, 'Holly, you never talk about your Mum. Do you miss her?'

There was just a laconic 'No,' which surprised Sue Anne. Holly said, 'Mum wasn't well. In the head. My first Dad used to tell me not to worry if she was always cross with me.' Holly burst into tears and sobbed for the first time since they had picked her up.

'She. Didn't. Love. Me.' Big racking sobs continued. 'Was it too much to ask? She. Didn't. Love. Me. All. My. Life.' One more big sob, then. 'I waited for her to smile at me. Just one smile.' Another sob. 'All I want now is for you to love me. Is that too much to ask?'

Sue Anne was overwhelmed. She had not wanted to force herself on Holly, but Holly had a way of nixing that. Sue Anne picked her up, Holly's head over her shoulder, next to her face, and she hugged her as hard as Holly wanted.

After five minutes, Holly wriggled free. 'Better now. More later, OK? Have to play now.'

Sue Anne was relieved. *So that is what it was,* she thought. *A good thing that one piercing question had unravelled that emotional block.*

Sue Anne settled down to enjoy the rest of the day. She was so proud of how far along the country had come and smiled. It was all going to be OK.

Then Sue Anne caught John. He spoke first, and told her that he had captured the whole episode on his phone, a nice video for later, then said: 'We must go tonight. It's been ages since we've seen the Andersons.' Then he told her that he would send a copy of the video to that man, Argus E, in India, who had expressed interest in seeing what happened to Holly.

Later that evening, people arrived at the Portland North Civic Hall at six. The bar was open and liberally used by the patrons. People huddled in small groups, and most of them had no idea about the coming event. Did it matter? Of course not. It was a beautiful Monday evening, and the stars were almost out, not locked up at home. And free drinks. Who could say no to that?

John and Sue Anne Orthallo were talking with James and Michelle Anderson. They want to know how talking about following the President's orders led to Deborah saving Redwood trees and the Government Bulletins hitting the airwaves with 'I Did it Your Way.' They wanted to meet her again.

Michelle started. 'Poor old James, he was stuck. It was only a simple problem, but he needed my input to sort it out. But he muddled me up, and we got nowhere and argued. He lost,' she grinned. James didn't care; he would get her later when she least expected it.

James took up the conversation. 'I can make it simple and short if you like, or you can get the full three-hour spiel from Michelle.' That earned him a punch on the arm. There was no invitation to the full gory three-hour version, so he continued.

'I had a request to provide a psychological perspective for the problem of people not following Covid-safe rules. I got stuck. Michelle and I had thoughts of our own, and obviously, she just had to muck it all up.' That earned him another punch on the arm.

Sue Anne asked if it hurt.

'No, she's not really hitting me. She just wants to feel my biceps.'

James continued, 'Deborah had the advantage of knowing nothing about our problems.' He got ready for a punch on the arm, this time from Deborah who was standing with him.

'Deb is a student at Washington State University doing ecology and environmental policy. They just had a class exercise to determine what to do about the wildfires in California. Some smart-arse said, "Put them out". With so many greenies in class, it turned to global warming and going round and round in circles. In the end, they needed to solve so many problems for that; only a small but vitally important proportion was extinguishing wildfire for global warming issues, not the destruction of forests. She told us they had learned that you need to understand the *whole* problem and that I should look at it that way for my solution for the President.'

'My first attempt was a fable of a non-conforming citizen dying, arriving at the Pearly Gates and Saint Peter sending him to a punishment room for a few thousand years. He was big on punishment, Saint Peter. Great story for kids, but no public appeal, and five minutes later, I had that Frank Sinatra song in my head.'

'When in the President's office, he started to talk about global warming and the wildfires, so I told him about Deborah. He called her and sent a car to bring her to the White House.'

Just then, Deborah returned from playing with the Orthallo kids.

'That Holly is a cracker. Does she have attitude or what? I want to take her with me for a few days at uni.'

John asked, 'Do you know how old she is?'

'Yes, she said she is eight. A bit small for her age but so cute.'

John told her she was four going on ten, and Sue Anne added, 'She has only just recovered; she lost both parents to COVID, and she wants me to be her Mummy. But next time we come, yes, take her to uni. She'll turn the place upside down with her four-year-old smarts.'

The Mayoress stepped up to the podium and tapped the microphone. The place quietened down, and when she had everyone's attention, she started to speak.

'We love celebrations, whether for a good reason or for no reason at all. We all have something to celebrate this time. Don't think I'm exaggerating when I say the pandemic is under control. For now. Cheers from everyone who loves the idea,' and a big cheer broke out. Someone yelled out "Yes, the bitch is dead".

'Did COVID just pack up and go?' she asked. 'I can't hear you when you shake your head,' and a big gutsy 'NOOO' filled the hall.

'Did we have to do something special to make it go away?' she asked. 'I can't hear you when you nod your head', and a big gutsy 'YEESSS' filled the hall.

'OK then. We are now ready to introduce you to the man who did that special something. Please welcome Dr James Anderson,' and loud applause ensued.

James went to the mike, thanked the Mayoress, and said, 'Do you want to know what I did?' And then, 'I can't hear you when you nod your head.' A big gutsy 'YEESSS' filled the hall.

'First, I asked my wife what I should do. She had no clue.' There was some laughter, and someone said, 'She probably didn't want to outsmart you.' The crowd was audibly cheery.

'Then I thought I'd ask my grandfather.' Silence. 'He's 95, by the way.' Plenty of laughter then. 'But then I thought he probably still thinks that the world is flat.'

That did the trick. He had the crowd's full attention now. 'That wasn't quite true. I asked my daughter.'

A wit on the floor yelled out, 'How old is she?'

He answered, 'I can't tell you. Ladies don't like their age disclosed. Unless they are a hundred.'

It was a happy audience now, and he was ready to deliver. 'I am employed by the Army to make soldiers who feel bad feel better. I am a psychologist. Do you know what we do?'

Someone had the answer. 'Yep, if you're screwed, you see one of those guys, and they unscrew you.'

James was delighted. and asked them, 'So what did I do to the President?' Fifty voices yelled, 'You unscrewed him.'

It took a minute to regain control, but then James spoilt it all by asking, 'Who wants to be a psychologist now?' Hundreds of hands went up.

'No more funnies for the next hour, please. We had a pandemic, and many people died, and over fifty thousand orphan kids ended up on the street. The Army had set up tent orphanages in most cities and got soldiers to play pre-school or kindy teacher. They didn't like kids that cried a lot, which they all did at the beginning. "I want my Mummy", was the common theme. So what did the Army Privates do? They made them laugh.'

'Kids will laugh when adults don't seem to know what they're doing. Then the Privates clowned up even more. It was hilarious until their Commanding Officers came and wanted to know what was going on. That did it for the kids, and they wet their pants laughing, and after a while, they did too.' That brought the house down.

'Not funny. Soldiers were trying to put nappies on toddlers.' More laughter. 'But the important thing was, now the Army has a few thousand soldiers trained to be pre-school teachers instead of being good for soldiering.' Everyone and I mean everyone, was visualising this dilemma and laughing like hyenas.

'That left the Army and the President with a problem. How to find homes for 50,000 kids? You can't sell them.'

More laughter and the inquisitive ones asked, 'Why not?'

'My job was to find a way to 'sell' 50,000 kids that we couldn't sell. How do you get people to adopt 50,000 crying children? You can't. Solution? Make them laugh. Get soldiers to change their nappies, play cops and robbers. Anything, and if they still don't laugh? Tickle them. We filmed them, took photos, like, "How cute is this kid?" Found out later child protection would be after our asses with all those children's photos. And as we weren't allowed to sell them, we auctioned them off.'

That brought the house down again. 'Not quite true, but we needed to find suitable parents who really wanted to have these children. We set up psychology tests, you know all about that now, and set up income tests. We charged prospective parents $1,000 for the tests. That's not selling them.' Chaos erupted again, and James added, 'That's Psychology,' which added to the chaos.

'Easy now, folks, I haven't finished yet,' James asked them whether kids in orphanages with about fifty kids would have made friends. There was loud agreement. 'We asked the kids to find one or two special friends who would like to come with them if a parent selected them. Those kids and the soldiers were the only people they knew, but they could not take the soldiers with them.'

'Then we worked on the parents. It's not quite twisting their arms, but preference was given to desperate parents who would be ecstatic to take two or even three children. We made a rule: parents up to age 25 could take babies and toddlers, parents up to age 35 could take kids from one to four years old, parents up to 45 could take kids to twelve, and parents up to 55 could take kids aged to seventeen. And parents over 55 could put their names down as grandparents.'

'Then we made a video of kids sleeping like angels, eating like little messy ones, kids running around like kamikaze bombers, and posted it on YouTube. All sold in five days, I mean auctioned off, no that wasn't the word, it was "Parent Aligned". On the way out, you will find handouts with the links on there. Go home and have a good laugh. The Army excelled themselves, and the nation is grateful. But I forgot one selection criteria. A limit of one set of parents per kid.'

'The orphanages emptied in two weeks. The soldiers who had played Mummy and Daddy were quite bereft, so much better than war training, and many put their name down to kindy training. Not exactly an Army occupation.'

Each State had a 'Passing Out' ceremony, and the President sent envoys to present a thank you certificate in each State. He would attend one personally in Washington.

*   *   *

June 17

The President was at the Smithsonian National Air and Space Museum. He tapped the microphone; yes, working, and he started:

'Ladies and Gentlemen, when I woke up this morning I was scared. I was scared there'd be no one here when I present three trophies today.' There was a little tittering. 'Not because I need an audience. I'm happy talking to myself.' A little more tittering.

'But how would the recipients of these trophies feel if there was no one here. They all made important contributions the nation is grateful for, and they need you here to feel the honour bestowed on them today. My first recipient is Private Sir, who worked in the temporary field orphanage near Washington Avenue Elementary School. Come up please, Private Sir.' and then he addressed the Private:

'You have been granted an Honorary Certificate in Child Minding. It allows you to work in pre-school teaching should you wish to, but the Army does not need those skills. You'd make a good father as you know how to handle those kids. But if you decide to stay in the Army, I'm here to announce that you are now Sergeant Sir. For our audience, could you please tell us what the first few days were like?'

The now Sergeant Sir took the mic and stood there staring into the crowd. Then he told the audience:

'"Order", I said to the children. Suddenly there was silence, and I asked the kids what my name was. One little six-year-old who had watched TV said, "Sir, your name is Sir." I asked him how he knew that, and he answered, "It says so on your shirt." That bit of fun didn't last long. The general outpouring was, "I miss my Mommy". So I asked them what I had to do to look like a mom. The next one said, "You have to wear a dress and look cross." I asked him why his Mom would be cross, and he said, "I pooed in my pants, and I need you to clean me up." I made a horrible noise pretending to die, and they all got the giggles. After that, it was easy. Say the word poo, and you have them in your hand.'

'If you wonder why someone would call a child Sir, my father was responsible for that. He named me after himself when filling out the birth certificate information, and his name, by chance, was Israel, and he messed it up a bit, and the certificate we got back was Sir.' He then took a deep breath and said, 'I tell a lie, but you believed me.'

'Thank you, Mr President. It was an honour to be a kindy teacher for a while and serve this nation.' He stepped back, indicating he was done.

The President stepped to the mic, waving to an aide. The aide presented Sergeant Sir with a toy. 'In case you stay in the kindy business.'

Next, the President waved to an elderly man standing nearby in military posture. The man came to the microphone, and the President spoke:

> 'Ladies and gentlemen, I am delighted to introduce Captain Rex Alexander, retired. This gentleman was in a fourth-floor apartment celebrating his eightieth birthday. His window had the perfect view of the Army drenching protestors, and in a flash, he was hooked up to a TV station. His reporting was over the top excitement, and the whole nation could watch in glorious detail how the protestors got soaked in water and two minutes later with a stink bomb. Same smell as a week-old dead body. I obtained a voice copy which I will play with my dinner guests. But first, he had been warned not to swear. He didn't need any. It was the first time in my life that I heard continuous swearing for two minutes, without repeating any swear words.'

'A loud round of applause please for Captain Rex Alexander.' They obliged by applauding his arrival on stage, and the President asked the captain to say a few words.

'Thank you, Mr President. When I was fourteen, I had been a cub reporter with one of those tissue box-sized tape recorders, and a TV crew were trying to interview a resident about a dead man. And when the protest marches started, I told my granddaughter that I had tried to interview the dead man back then. Her response? "Oh really? How unusual".' He added, 'My career never recovered from there.'

The captain knew he had to stop after that punchline and indicated he would be able to elaborate later at the bar.

The President asked Rex how many times he had been able to dine out on either of those stories, and he replied, 'Still going, haven't had to cook for a month.'

'The last job for this morning,' said the President. 'I've got such a great job just thanking people all day.' He gestured Dorothy Thompson to come forward and introduce herself, and asked the crowd to get rowdy with applause, then continued:

'Sometimes I'm not allowed to say what I want in my bulletins. Not if I want good results. You know? The carrot and the stick? When I just want to say certain things to certain groups of delinquents for not following orders, I do a mental telepathy trick with Dorothy, and she writes under a pseudonym, getting away with murder. She's not a bad stick. Such a great team, and she's not paid by the taxpayer or me either.' Some gentle applause is heard.

'To thank you, Ms Thompson, I hand over a boarding pass for an Airforce One seat next to mine, but it may be delegated down the aisle if there is an emergency. I'm sure your colleagues at the Post are envious.'

Dorothy stepped up to the President, shook his hand and spoke into the mice, 'There I was, only looking for a one-week holiday in Tahiti, and now I have to work all year round. For many years to come.' The audience loved that one, all captured on TV as well. Dorothy had a last piece for the audience. 'When it comes to mental telepathy, could you be brief, please, Sir? You know, bullet points - so I can go back to sleep?'

The audience loved that one, and left hoping for more civil acknowledgement functions later on.

*   *   *

June 20

In Columbus, Ohio, Summer Ohrtman was being honoured at a Civil function in City Hall. She was going to get the key to the city, and both her parents were there. A young woman came up to the podium, and she only wanted to be known by her first name, Nancy.

She walked to Summer and asked, 'Can I give you a hug from 50,000 patients, please?'

'I'm Nancy, and I've been told to say all sorts of wonderful things about you - but I forgot them. Hang on a minute.' She turned around and yelled, 'Grandpa, you're needed here.'

There was stunned silence as the President came up to the stage. He waved a finger at Nancy and took the mice:

'We would not be here today or in this position if this young woman had not decided to save her brother from COVID death. She loved him and decided to make him better by making him laugh. Then the whole ward, then all wards in that hospital, then all hospitals in Columbus, then all hospitals in New York City. The AMA filmed that, now playing in every hospital in the country. And now they all complain. Why? Their beds are empty as all patients walked home ten days later. When my go-to health expert Dr Ponti asked if she could cure all the other diseases as well, she suggested that he needs to talk to the man who walked on water.'

That did the trick. The crowd was enthusiastic as the President beckoned Summer. 'Let's show them.' They did the chicken dance for thirty seconds, gasping with laughter. The crowds had taken up the chant to a techno beat.

'*Cheepy Cheepy Cheeeeeep*, turn the neck, *Cheepy Cheepy Cheeeeeep*, flap both arms, and *Chika Chika Cheeeeeep*, turn around and *Cheeka Cheeeeeep*, and then start again.'

'I'll leave you in the capable hands of Nancy now,' he said as he walked off stage. His aides whisked him away, and he was gone.

Blew Ohrtman was impressed and puzzled. 'Why did he tear away so quickly? Trump would have milked it for hours.'

His wife Petal said, 'It wasn't about the President. It wasn't even Summer's occasion. It was about the patients who discovered they could laugh, over 50,000 of them. The President knew this. He did well. It's so much more effective, don't you agree?'

The end.

But no. You need to read the epilogue.

Epilogue

A New Era

Argus E was preparing to journey home from Andaman Island to Tarmugli Island. He had submitted his final reports and could now switch off his dispassionate mode and have a bit of fun.

There were so many things he had learned from the Americans that he loved passionately. Love was almost a new experience for him, and he intended to take the good experiences back home.

The experience uppermost in his mind was, of course, that the people had learned to follow instructions to isolate to beat the pandemic. He remembered that phrase from the presentation by the lady mayoress in Portland when she was celebrating that the pandemic was over. She encouraged the citizens to celebrate, ad someone from the audience ramped it up by shouting that "The bitch is dead." That experience featured uppermost in his report to the Indian union – to keep his island safe. Mission accomplished.

Yes, he realised. The people had learned from a leader. But only because they were led. First, the President had added that stink compound, hydrogen sulphide, to the water bombing of the protest marchers and then demonstrated to the world that this President does what he says he will do. When he threatened to use the Air Force to strafe the marchers with machine guns, they got the message and backed down. That fight was over.

He had intercepted communications between John Orthallo and Dorothy Thompson and had learned about the orphaned girl Holly that they had found. He was intrigued and did his Alpha Dynamics trick to get into a deep meditative trance where he could see and hear her. At least he thought he could, and he was thrilled. So he had emailed Sue Anne Orthallo to get a video of John with Holly. He was glad; it was even better than he had imagined.

His felt a new more powerful feeling of love when he watched Holly Whistler, the four-year-old girl described as four going on ten. Argus had a granddaughter with a name he found hard to pronounce, Lolllanfairpwllgwyngyll. His son had travelled before marrying and had given his daughter a Welsh town name. The full name was a bit longer but never used. He would call her Holly from now on, and he was sure that Lolllanfairpwllgwyngyll would love her new name. He was convinced that her Mum would too. As Holly's new Mum had described Holly as four going on ten, he would boost his granddaughter's talk from five to fifteen if he could, even better.

John had sent him a video where he heard her sobbing. Sue Anne had asked, 'Holly, you never talk about your Mum. Do you miss her so much then?' There was just a laconic 'No,' and Holly had burst into tears and sobbed for the first time in a long while. 'She. Didn't. Love. Me.' Big racking sobs had continued. 'I'm FOUR. She. Didn't. Love. Me. All. My. Life.'

Argus got hit with a thunderbolt of painful emotion. It was love and compassion so intense he had trouble breathing.

And he had learned new things. About love, and about fun. About psychologists, in particular James Anderson. They could be funny. No one on his remote islands was funny. They were busy surviving. It must have been stamped out. He decided he would start an inter-island school of humour. The school would have the honorary name "The Anderson School of Pun". He liked pun better than fun. His people didn't do pun, and it would be so much fun to teach them pun, even if he himself was not entirely sure of the difference. But he found out, curtesy of Mr Google

He had never encountered what he now knew as repartee at home, the art form of a quick comeback. He thought of Dorothy Thompson's response to the President's comment that he used mental telepathy to make her write articles he could not get away with. Her immediate response had been that she preferred it if he would use dot points in future so she could get back to sleep.

He loved the way Holly had chosen her new father. She had wanted 'the beardy bloke over there', bloke being a man in Australia but used by Holly. He really liked that John loved Holly equally as much as his 'first' daughter. Fancy loving someone else's kid. He thought of setting up an orphanage. One where all children were loved as much, if not more than those with parents. Maybe so much that kids who were afraid of their parents could go to the orphanage and get a better deal.

And he loved that Summer nurse, the one who cured over 50,000 patients in ICU in hospitals. So he had intuited her as well. He wondered if she could visit him if he got sick but realised it was too far to come to his islands. Bingo, he made a hologram of her, and wait, yes, of all the people he had loved or admired, and took them with him on his journey back home to his island. By canoe. He siphoned the holograms into a memory device, like a genie getting back into the bottle. All ready to go.

Appendix

Friends in America

I had worked in the US twice, once for eight weeks in Houston, Texas, in December 1972 and again for five months in Champagne, Illinois, in 1996. I was there during an election campaign.

I added this section to thank some people. After my return in 1996 I lost my address book and didn't know how to get hold of friends from 24 years ago, and if any of my friends from the US read this book, I hope they will contact me. gartelbooks@gmail.com

The first experience was in Houston in 1972. I had gone into a shopping mall trying to buy things for my family in Australia, and when I came out, it was dark, except for street lights. Above-ground express ways surrounded the mall, and I had no idea how to get to Austin, where I was to meet my offsider two hours later. I asked someone. I put on what I thought was a good Texas accent as in, 'Can you awl show me how to get me old jalopy down to that there Austin Town?' This gent found out I came from a country where they drive on the wrong side of the road, said, 'looks like I'm gonna have to teach you not only Texan but how to drive properly. Hop in your car and follow me.' He stopped twenty-two miles later. I asked, 'Oh, you live over here?' and his laconic response was. 'No, I live where I picked you all up, drive safely now, and have a good day', and he drove off. I never knew his name, but I love that man.

My next experience was in Champagne, Illinois, in 1996.

After 24 hours on a plane and bus, I finally arrived. I had imagined the rolling hills dotted with the French wine region oak trees but had spent two hours going through a pancake flat vista and not a tree in sight, then trying to readjust my mental clock to sleep. Two days later, I met a delightful lady at the bank of Illinois who advanced me money to buy a car. LOVED it. Electric adjustment for seats, all the bells and whistles of a great Buick. Preloved, and on the fourth of July, I needed to find a forest and drove till I found a clump of trees. That would do, I thought, and drove into a driveway.

This was America at its best. A twenty-foot-wide white raked pebble driveway. Nice tyre crunching as I eased forward. Two acres of immaculately mowed fresh lawns on either side and greeted by small American flags on both sides every ten or so yards. Then an elegant curve and to a clump of Oak trees. And I met my first real country Americans. Even though I was trespassing, I was welcomed. My excuse? I needed to see the trees, and after that, we were friends. And this is the pivotal moment that helped make my time in Illinois so special. When I mentioned that I had sung Barbershop in Australia, a delightful lady said, 'Come with me.' She did not want our discussion to disturb the others and gave me a piece of paper with the phone number of the Champagne Urbana Men's Barbershop Chorus contact. Lady, if you read this, I INSIST you email me. I cannot find that barbershop in the list of chapters in Illinois by Google now, so this is the only way to find some of the wonderful people I met.

The barbershop chorus had four gents who took me to the Mississippi. To help you remember, I was the Aussie who swam the river, and you paddled a canoe to keep me safe from passing barges. I was 55 at the time, and many of you were from the University there. I can still picture you but your names are missing. I hope you are still alive and singing, and if you see this, round up that mob and celebrate that you found me; and contact me, please.

Five months later, I had a farewell drinks party in a pub in late November. Most of you were there. One man missing. Oh dear, I wanted to say goodbye, and an hour later, the door burst open. From a snowstorm blizzard in walked this dude in tennis shoes and shorts. Would he accept a drink? No. Why not? 'Sorry, Dieter, I can't. I'm playing in a squash tournament twenty odd miles away, and I need to get back to my next match in thirty minutes.' That man! Love you, man, you were never forgotten. I hope you get to see this and contact me.

The next one's that need to be thanked were all the people I worked with. Without you, it would have been so lonely. I hope you recognise yourself in this. I had worked in downtown Champaign in the old Bank of Illinois building, and the morning ritual was to go next door for a coffee. And after I got to know people, I started to invite some to come with me. What was unusual for the work environment was that the technology was aging. The firm, CSC, had to attract contractors from all over the world, so there were quite a few single men, some from Ireland and Australia. Here it comes. There were men with unrequited love dramas, but more with men trying to get rid of ladies who pestered them. I became the resident Dorothy Dixon adviser. How much better to discuss someone else's dramas than my own. You guys are not forgotten, just your names, and to jog your memory, Simon Pamment says hello. He recognised me in a shop in Adelaide four years ago, and I latched on to his phone number.

There was also a blind man in New York whom I met in Carnegie Hall, and he took me for an after-show supper, telling me to watch for the pothole on my left. Sorry, I lost all contacts, but please buy him dinner if someone knows this man.

PEOPLE IN THE STORY PART II

Main New Administration Characters

Lt. Col. Morgan **Freebody** had been a career officer with no blemishes on his record. He never took shortcuts when it came to morals; in his case, the morals needed to lead soldiers into battle, and he needed to ensure his valuable soldiers did not lose the plot and shoot unarmed people during the demonstrations.

General **Andrew Morgan**, Army Chief of Staff, is a true and tested veteran of many campaigns, including Iraq and Afghanistan. He has coloured roots and had suffered the indignities of racism all his life, mostly quietly. He understood human nature and the need to hurt those who are different, and he was adored by the men he led. But also feared, as he did not suffer fools gladly. After dressing down some poor soldier, he usually smiled a dazzling smile, and all was forgiven.

Dr Federico **Ponti**, is the Infectious Diseases expert.

Dr Alessandro Lorenzo Ferrari, his new Attorney General.

Governor Gretchen Whitmer

Governor Gretchen Whitmer had been the target of a kidnapping plot by a far-right militia group during the election campaign.

DEMONSTRATORS

Patriot Bravehearts

Washington DC HQ. They were Trump supporters who were heavily armed and threaten violence to anyone disagreeing with their pro-Trump view. The patriots are a national loosely woven web of state-based groups.

The Michigan group was responsible for armed and threatening demonstrations against Governor Gretchen Whitmer.

Jason Donovan

Jason is a political operator leading the Washington Bravehearts. Being top dog has many benefits, and others are after his position, so he knows he needs to deliver.

He is not married. Women and armed thugs don't mix well too often. He is tough but mostly leads from his office.

Tim Highfields

Tim loves his job. He had grown up being bullied. He was small and wiry with a bent nose de to too many street fights. That was when he did not have a rifle. He does now and feels powerful.

Pittsburgh Forcefields

The Forcefield group is an unarmed version of the Patriots. Most of its members came from families where the father was feared. If they did not follow orders, they were thrashed when younger but grew big and strong till they could flatten their old man. After years of oppression, they ruled the roost and now belonged to a gang.

Terry Copperfield

Terry had grown up fearing his father, and now he wanted everyone to fear him. That required that he look fearsome, and he had some suitable outfits. He had a Viking uniform with a horned helmet and a belt sporting several swords. Next, he had an American Indian outfit with feather headgear and bow and arrows.

Matt Davis

Matt loved his mother, Terry Copperfield, and no one else. No one outside the Forcefield gang, that is. He had a brain that was used for two main purposes. The first was self-preservation and power. The second was to protest against authority wherever it reared its ugly head.

Minor roles

Martin Hunter, Washington Right Beasts

John Penny, Washington Stormtroopers

Mitch Waller, Los Angeles Western Hoods

Dirk Partenheimer, his 2IC

Prominent Republicans

General Christopher Paul Roberts, retired, gentleman, Dallas

Colonel George Jeffry Edwards, Ohio retired, gentleman

Nathan Luke Walker. Chattanooga, Tennessee, pro-Trump

Capitol Police

Commander Mathew Wade, the man in charge. Coloured. Takes job seriously

Lt. Superintendent Abraham Wilcox, Union Boss, white, supports Trump.

Sgt. Andrew Kenworth, Coloured, goes by the rule book.

Sgt. John McKenzie, White, Unionist but not Trump supporter

Republican Senators

Chuck M. Morris, Republican Leader for a while

Marjorie Tumble, from Texas.

Hillary Johnson, New Republican leader, Dallas

Democrat Senators

Nolene Packard, Senate leader

Administration and Governors

Dr Alessandro Lorenzo Ferrari, Attorney General.

William Schuster, Deputy Attorney General

Dr Federico Ponti, Infectious Diseases expert

Real People Used in References

Jay Inslee, Washington Governor

Gretchen Whitmer, Michigan Governor

Mike DeWine, Ohio Governor

Viruses

Fiction or WHO	Strain	Type, Symptoms
WHO	B.1.351	South African strain.
WHO	B-1.1.7	UK strain that increased the ability of the virus to infect cells.
WHO	C- X666	New mystery strain found in Texas.
WHO	CAL2.0	West Coast CAL 2.0 variant, much deadlier, not yet more infectious, but it could merge with a super spreader any time.
FICTION	Covid-666	1 day to red rash, two to five to die.
WHO	D614G	Variant from SARS Caused Covid-19, showed up in Australia and India.
FICTION	D-xxxx	Blue neck. As yet unnamed by the WHO, five times as infectious.
who	E848K, N501Y, E484K and K417N	The Brazilian variant mutation were found in South African B.1.351 variant and in British B-1.1.7. Scientists worried about mutations in the virus's spike protein, specifically it's receptor-binding domain.

FOOTNOTE REFERENCES

1. Novel Coronavirus (2019-nCoV)
    https://www.who.int/docs/default-source/
    coronaviruse/situation-reports/20200121-sitrep-
    1-2019-ncov.pdf

2. Taiwan Responding Successfully to COVID-19
    https://www.internationalaffairs.org.au/
    australianoutlook/responding-successfully-to-
    covid-19-a-case-study-of-taiwan/

3. Lessons from Italy's Response to Coronavirus
    https://hbr.org/2020/03/lessons-from-italys-
    response-to-coronavirus

4. First-wave COVID-19 transmissibility and severity in
    China
    https://www.thelancet.com/journals/lancet/
    article/PIIS0140-6736(20)30746-7/fulltext

5. Why Singapore's coronavirus response worked
    https://theconversation.com/why-singapores-
    coronavirus-response-worked-and-what-we-can-
    all-learn-134024

6. The U.S.-China Trade War Has Become a Cold War https://carnegieendowment.org/2021/09/16/ u.s.-china-trade-war-has-become-cold-war- pub-85352

7. First Trump-Biden meeting marked by constant interruptions by Trump https://www.washingtonpost.com/elections /2020/09/29/presidential-debate-live-updates/

8. Trump Selects Amy Coney Barrett to Fill Ginsburg's Seat on the Supreme https://www.nytimes.com/2020/09/25/us/ politics/amy-coney-barrett-supreme-court.html

9. How the Congress decision could see Trump Win https://theconversation.com/how-congress- could-decide-the-2020-election-146054

10. Trump Continues Attacks On Election Results At Georgia Senate Runoff Rally https://www.theguardian.com/us-news/ live/2021/jan/04/donald-trump-georgia-votes- joe-biden-brad-raffensperger-senate-covid- coronavirus-us-politics-live

11. US cybersecurity chief fired for contradicting Trump https://www.computerweekly.com/news/ 252492286/US-cyber-security-chief-fired-for- contradicting-Trump

12. Just 27 of 249 Republicans in Congress willing to say Trump lost, survey finds https://www.theguardian.com/us-news/2020/ dec/05/house-republicans-trump-election- defeat-joe-biden

13. President Donald Trump has tweeted that he will be "intervening" in the Presidential election
https://www.independent.co.uk/news/world/americas/us-election-2020/trump-texas-election-legal-challenge-b1768666.html

14. A long-shot lawsuit against Georgia, Michigan, Pennsylvania and Wisconsin is a latest legal effort
https://www.theguardian.com/us-news/2020/dec/08/texas-lawsuit-donald-trump-election-georgia-michigan-pennsylvania-wisconsin

15. Trump demands the names of Congressional Republicans who have acknowledged Biden's election victory
https://thehill.com/homenews/campaign/528899-trump-demands-names-of-the-congressional-republicans-who-said-they

16. 1st reported US case of COVID-19 variant found in Colorado
https://apnews.com/article/public-health-united-kingdom-jared-polis-coronavirus-pandemic-denver-755cd6f5e9189b1890f34f625d6a37f8

17. Here's the full transcript and audio of the call between Trump and Raffensperger
https://www.washingtonpost.com/politics/trump-raffensperger-call-transcript-georgia-vote/2021/01/03/2768e0cc-4ddd-11eb-83e3-322644d82356_story.html

18. Growing number of Trump loyalists in the Senate vow to challenge Biden's victory
https://www.washingtonpost.com/politics/senators-challenge-election/2021/01/02/

81a4e5c4-4c7d-11eb-a9d9-1e3ec4a928b9_story.
html

19. Iran fears Trump preparing attack in final weeks in office
https://www.theguardian.com/world/2020/
dec/31/iran-says-trump-is-trying-to-fabricate-
pretext-for-war

20. Republican efforts to undermine Biden victory expose growing anti-democratic streak
https://edition.cnn.com/2021/01/03/politics/
trump-republicans-electoral-college-new-
congress-democracy/index.html

21. Trump claims to have evidence coronavirus started in Chinese lab but offers no details
https://www.theguardian.com/us-news
/2020/apr/30/donald-trump-coronavirus
-chinese-lab-claim

22. Chinese defector virologist Dr Li-Meng Yan publishes report claiming COVID-19 was made in a lab
https://www.reddit.com/r/worldnews/
comments/it4l7n/chinese_defector_virologist_
dr_limeng_yan/

23. The age in which American economic and military dominance is now past
https://www.lowyinstitute.org/the-interpreter/
debate/coronavirus-pandemic

24. Trump protesters warned not to carry guns as Washington DC calls up National Guard
https://www.theguardian.com/us-news/2021/
jan/05/trump-protesters-warned-not-to-carry-
guns-as-washington-dc-calls-up-national-guard

25. Protesters storm Capitol building, woman shot
    https://securitytoday.com/articles/2021/01/06/
    protestors-storm-capitol-congress-evacuated.
    aspx?m=1

26. With brazen assault on election, Trump prompts critics to
    warn of a coup
    https://twitter.com/washingtonpost/status/
    1346644764586893314

27. US Capitol secure after violent protest, occupation,
    bombs, shots
    https://www.cbc.ca/news/world/washington-
    protesters-capitol-breached-1.5863486

28. Chaos at the Capitol – Washington Post
    https://mail.google.com/mail/u/0/?tab=
    wm&ogbl#inbox/FMfcgxwKkRDpqcxpP
    zHsnnDfFnHFpMhW

29. New COVID Strain Spreading Across U.S. - What We Know
    https://nymag.com/intelligencer/article/what-
    is-the-new-covid-19-strain-that-shut-down-
    england-u-k.html

30. Why the search for the first origin of the coronavirus is a
    global concern
    https://www.washingtonpost.com/world/
    2021/01/07/who-coronavirus-origin-search-
    china/?=

31. Dominion sues pro-Trump lawyer Sidney Powell, seeking
    more than $1.3 billion
    https://www.cnbc.com/2021/01/08/dominion-
    brings-defamation-suit-against-sidney-powell.
    html

32. Donald Trump's parting gift to the world? It may be war with Iran
https://www.theguardian.com/commentisfree/2021/jan/08/donald-trump-war-iran-tehran-daniel-ellsberg

33. Republican Senator Lisa Murkowski calls on Trump to resign
https://www.theguardian.com/us-news/live/2021/jan/08/donald-trump-capitol-impeachment-joe-biden-election-coronavirus-covid-live-updates

34. Dejected Trump supporters leave Washington, create new theories for Capitol violence
https://www.nbcnews.com/news/us-news/dejected-trump-supporters-leave-washington-create-new-theories-capitol-violence-n1253407

35. Man pictured carrying away Pelosi's lectern, two others charged in Capitol riot
https://www.nbcnews.com/news/us-news/man-pictured-carrying-pelosi-s-lectern-during-capitol-riot-arrested-n1253628?icid=recommended

36. US Capitol rioters arrested as senator urges mobile and social media providers to keep data
https://www.abc.net.au/news/2021-01-10/horned-trump-protesters-charged-in-us-capitol-riot/13045518

37. Post-Riot, the Capitol Hill IT Staff Faces a Security Mess
https://www.wired.com/story/capitol-riot-security-congress-trump-mob-clean-up/

38. Trump's rush to execute prisoners proves the death penalty is arbitrary
https://www.latimes.com/opinion/story/2020-12-09/trump-barr-executions-death-penalty-montgomery-brandon-bernard

39. 'Dangerous time' - Tensions rise as nuclear foes Iran, Israel and the US face off
https://www.news.com.au/technology/innovation/military/dangerous-time-tensions-rise-as-nuclear-foes-iran-israel-and-the-us-face-off/news-story/47b6d23a5b74ee2afe984d961c494154

40. Trump's final days put the country at a dangerous crossroad
https://edition.cnn.com/2021/01/10/politics/donald-trump-mike-pence-final-days-25th-amendment/index.html

41. Pence refuses to renew Trump for another season
https://www.smh.com.au/national/pence-refuses-to-renew-trump-for-another-season-20210108-p56sql.html

42. UK coronavirus cases top 3 million as death toll passes 80,000
https://www.bloomberg.com/news/articles/2021-01-09/u-k-total-coronavirus-cases-exceed-3-million-deaths-top-80-000

43. two UK hospitals stagger as new virus variant takes a huge toll
https://money.yahoo.com/england-faces-lockdown-last-least-095158618.html

44. California governor's budget booms despite pandemic problems
https://apnews.com/article/gavin-newsom-california-coronavirus-pandemic-8d01e88ceeb4b0bc6cb1fb0d6a8d72b7

45. California budget proposes $15 billion for economic relief
https://www.abc10.com/article/news/local/california/california-budget-proposal/103-e58563ef-aff2-432d-8445-5ae6cd7e8a7c

46. Pandemic. Recession. Political strife - The Texas Legislature's toughest 2021 challenges
https://www.dallasnews.com/news/politics/2021/01/10/pandemic-recession-political-strife-the-texas-legislatures-toughest-2021-challenges/

47. The Most American COVID-19 Failure Yet
https://www.theatlantic.com/politics/archive/2020/08/contact-tracing-hr-6666-working-us/615637/

48. The need to reckon with Trump's lies
https://www.washingtonpost.com/world/2021/01/11/trump-lies-capitol-mob-analysis/?=

49. Off-duty police were part of the Capitol mob. Now police are turning in their own.
https://www.washingtonpost.com/politics/police-trump-capitol-mob/2021/01/16/160ace1e-567d-11eb-a08b-f1381ef3d207_story.html

50. FBI report warned of 'war' at Capitol prior to riot
https://www.washingtonpost.com/national-security/capitol-riot-fbi-intelligence/2021/01/12/30d12748-546b-11eb-a817-e5e7f8a406d6_story.html

51. That hurricane is coming' - expert warns US to brace for virulent Covid strain
https://www.theguardian.com/us-news/2021/jan/31/us-covid-uk-variant-strain-spread

52. Bangladesh Uses EVMs For First Time in General Election
https://www.news18.com/news/world/bangladesh-uses-evms-for-first-time-in-general-election-1987081.html

53. Electronic voting in India
https://en.wikipedia.org/wiki/Electronic_voting_in_India

54. UK, South African, Brazilian - a virologist explains each COVID variant and what they mean for the pandemic
https://theconversation.com/uk-south-african-brazilian-a-virologist-explains-each-covid-variant-and-what-they-mean-for-the-pandemic-154547

55. The Confirmation Process for Presidential Appointees
Presidential Appointees
https://www.heritage.org/political-process/heritage-explains/the-confirmation-process-presidential-appointees

56. Browse the Constitution Annotated > Article II > Section 2 > Clause 3 > ArtII.S2.C3.1.1 Recess Appointments Power: Overview
https://constitution.congress.gov/browse/essay/artII-S2-C3-1-1/ALDE_00001144/

57. Chances for Obama nominees to be confirmed are falling, even with over two years to go
Ref no longer available

58. The U.S. Navy Wasted A Whole Decade Building Bad Ships
https://www.forbes.com/sites/davidaxe/2021/01/05/the-us-navy-wasted-a-whole-decade-building-bad-ships/?sh=3fe2a0b554e9

59. Bus disinfection through UV lamps in China
https://www.sustainable-bus.com/news/bus-disinfection-through-uv-lights-a-way-to-fight-coronavirus-in-shanghai/

60. Shakhova et al. (2008) estimate that not less than 1,400 gigatonnes (Gt) of carbon is presently locked up as methane
https://en.wikipedia.org/wiki/Arctic_methane_emissions